BETWEEN WORLDS

BETWEEN WORLDS

Edited by

Robert Silverberg

SCIENCE
FICTION

Book design by Christos Peterson

Published by Science Fiction Book Club, 401 Franklin Avenue, Garden City, New York 11530.

ISBN: 1-58288-108-1

Printed in the United States of America

For Charles Sheffield,
who should have had a story in this book.

CONTENTS

INTRODUCTION

~~~~~~~~~~

DISTANT REALMS OF SPACE
AND TIME

THAT EARTH IS the only world in all the vast universe fit for human habitation is a proposition so unlikely that it scarcely needs attacking. A Greek philosopher, Metrodoros the Epicurean, made the case for extraterrestrial planets with sublime logic twenty-five centuries ago when he said, "To consider the Earth the only populated world in infinite space is as absurd as to assert that in an entire field sown with millet only one grain will grow."

The arithmetic of the situation alone provides inescapable supportive logic. Our galaxy—the great spiral cluster of stars among which we happen to live—is thought to contain at least a hundred billion suns and maybe twice as many as that. It's reasonable to estimate, based on what we have already been able to find out about a number of stars in our own vicinity, that roughly half of these have systems of planets in orbit around them. Let's say that half of these have planets that lie at the correct distance to maintain water in its liquid state, a necessity for our kind of life. That gives us something close to twenty-five billion potential Earths, starting from the assumption of a hundred billion suns. Suppose that half of these are too small to retain an atmosphere. That leaves us with about twelve billion planets. Say that six billion of these must be rejected because they are too big, because they do not rotate on their axes, because they have no water, because their atmospheres are composed of lethal gases, or because they are in some other way unsuitable for Earth-type life. Even so, six billion Earth-type planets still remain in our own galaxy! Now let's throw out 99 percent of those on the grounds that all the suppositions I have just offered are much too optimistic, and we still are left with sixty million perfectly good habitable worlds in this galaxy alone. And there are millions of galaxies.

It isn't surprising, given these numbers, that one of the great themes of modern science fiction is the exploration of the galactic frontier, the myriad worlds of other suns. An essentially infinite universe offers essentially infinite scope for the imagination. Once we allow the little assumption that some way will be found to cope with the immense distances between stars in a fashion that will allow us to get around Einstein's annoying restrictions against traveling faster than the speed of light, a great door swings open and the entire universe awaits our band of storytellers.

Our knowledge of own solar system no longer permits the sort of free play of conceptualization that was available to the likes of Edgar Rice Burroughs, Leigh Brackett, Stanley G. Weinbaum, and other twentieth-century purveyors of nearby-world interplanetary romance. By now we have clear ideas of the kinds of conditions we are going to find on our own immediate planetary neighbors in space: we know, for example, that there will be no seas on Mars, no humid swamps on Venus, no palm trees on Pluto, and (barring some colossal surprise) no intelligent life-forms anywhere.

But the stars provide a broader range of invention. A wholly invented extra-solar planet must follow—within certain scientific limitations, of course—only the logic of the story for which it has been invented. The writer can dream up the strangest and most wonderful of landscapes, and who can deny their truth? So we postulate planets of astonishing colors and textures and shapes, alien species of life, solar systems that dance in delicious intricacy around multiple suns—anything at all, so long as it doesn't blatantly contradict the underlying laws of the universe as we think we understand them today. An inexhaustible treasure trove of virtually unbounded probability awaits those whose imaginations voyage to the stars.

Such star-roving writers of the past as E. E. Smith, Isaac Asimov,

Frank Herbert, James Blish, Hal Clement, Jack Vance, Poul Anderson, and scores of others have taken us out into that galactic community to wondrous effect. *Dune*, the Lensman novels, the Foundation series, Clement's *Mission of Gravity*, Vance's *Big Planet*, Blish's *Cities in Flight*—I need only mention the names of those classic books and we are transported into infinite space, into distant realms of space and time.

But the theme is inexhaustibly rich, and no writer can ever claim to have said the last word about the far reaches of the universe. In this collection of stories I've asked some of the best of today's science-fiction writers—Stephen Baxter, James Patrick Kelly, Nancy Kress, Mike Resnick, Walter Jon Williams—to take a fresh look at that quintessential science-fictional mode, the story that transports us far from Earth, off to the remote heart of the galaxy, thousands of years in the future; and, since the topic is not uncongenial to my imagination either, I've thrown in a story of my own as well. The title of the book—*Between Worlds*—added an extra twist for the writers, since it led them to write stories that involved not only literal voyages across the immensity of space but that dealt with, also, characters involved in some sort of personal transition: who were themselves, in one metaphorical sense or another, between worlds.

The writers did not, of course, get a chance to see each others' stories before they wrote their own. But the perceptive reader will be struck by the conversations going on between the various stories, the convergences and divergences of themes, the similarities and dissimilarities, as this group of outstanding science-fictional thinkers tackles the concept of travel between the stars once more and comes up with a collection of dazzlingly original tales.

—Robert Silverberg
California
January 2004

BETWEEN WORLDS

BETWEEN WORLDS

~~~~~~~~~

by Stephen Baxter

Stephen Baxter was born in Liverpool, England, and has one degree in mathematics from Cambridge, one in aeroengineering research from Southampton University, and one in business administration from Henley Management College. He has taught mathematics and physics, worked for several years in the information-technology field, and in 1991 was an applicant for the British slot as a cosmonaut aboard the Mir. *His career as a writer began in 1987 and has gathered him wide international attention. Among his numerous novels, which have brought him the Arthur C. Clarke Award, the Philip K. Dick Award, and the John Campbell Memorial Award, are* Raft, Moonseed, The Time Ships, *and* Flux.*

The story he offers here splendidly encapsulates in twenty thousand words all the intended themes of this collection: a visionary novella set in the far future and at an immense distance from our own planet, which vividly portrays a group of characters who are not only in transit between worlds but are undergoing internal transitions as well.

SHE WANTS TO go home," said the starship captain.

"But she can't go home," said the acolyte. Futurity's Dream was baffled by the very request, as if the woman who had locked herself inside a starship's cabin, with a bomb, was making a philosophical mistake, a category error.

Captain Tahget said, "She says she needs to speak to her daughter."

"She hasn't got a daughter!"

"No, not according to the records. A conundrum, isn't it?" Captain Tahget sat very still, his glare focused unblinking on the young acolyte. He was a bulky man of about forty, with scar tissue crusting over half his scalp. He obviously had military experience, but his unadorned body armor, like the bare walls of his private office, gave away nothing of his character; in these fluid, uncertain times, when sibling fought sibling, it was impossible to tell who he might have served.

Before this monolithic officer Futurity, just twenty years old, felt nervous, ineffectual—not just weak, but like a shadow, with no control over events.

Futurity lifted his data desk and checked the *Ask Politely*'s manifest again. The passenger's name stood out, highlighted in red: MARA. No mention of a daughter. "She's a refugee. Home for her is Chandra. The black hole at the center of the Galaxy."

"I know what Chandra is."

"Or rather," Futurity said nervously, "home is, or was, Greyworld, a worldlet in orbit around a satellite black hole, which in turn orbits Chandra—"

"I know all this too," said the captain stonily. "Get on with it, acolyte."

Tahget had been commissioned to pick up Mara, and other refugees displaced by the Kardish Imperium from their homes in Galaxy's Core, from this transitional point and then carry them on to Earth, where the ruling Ideocracy had pledged to welcome its citizens. But Mara had refused to travel on. Because of her, the ship had been held in orbit, and the other refugees had been evacuated and sent back to holding centers on the surface.

Futurity licked his lips and looked again at the glowing cube on the captain's desk. It was a fish-tank monitor, a Virtual realization of the interior of the woman's cabin. Mara sat on her bunk, as still, in her way, as Tahget. She was slim, her head shaved; aged thirty-six, she looked modest, sensible, undemanding. Her small suitcase sat unopened on top of the low dresser that was the cabin's only other piece of furniture. The locked door was blocked by an upturned chair, a trivial barricade.

And before her on the floor was the reason she had been able to impose her will on hundreds of refugees and at least three political entities. It was a blocky tangle of metal and polymer, an ugly sculpture quite out of place in the mundane shabbiness of the cabin. You could clearly see where it had been cut out of the weapons pod of some wrecked ship. It was a bomb, a monopole bomb. Dating from the time of the Coalition and their galactic war, it was at least two thousand years old. But the Coalition had built well, and there was no doubt that this bomb could destroy this ship and do a great deal of damage to Base 478 itself.

Futurity didn't know where the bomb had come from, though after millennia of war 478 was famously riddled with weapons caches. And he had no idea how the bomb had been smuggled on board the *Ask Politely*, this starship. But the Hierocrat had made it clear that Futurity didn't need to know any of that; all Futurity had to do was to resolve this messy situation.

"But she can't go home," he said again feebly. "Her home doesn't exist anymore, legally speaking. And soon enough it won't exist physically either. She's a refugee." Futurity didn't understand any of this. "We're trying to help her here. Doesn't she see that?"

"Evidently not," Tahget said dryly. Tahget didn't move a muscle, but Futurity could sense his growing impatience. "Acolyte, none of the politics of the Galaxy, or the geography of the black hole, matter a jot to me." He stabbed a finger at the fish-tank. "All I care about is getting that woman away from that bomb. We can't disarm the thing. We can't force our way into the cabin without—"

"Without killing the woman?"

"Oh, I don't care about that. No, we can't get in without setting the thing off. Do you need to know the technical details of Virtual trip wires, of dead man's switches? Suffice it to say that force is not an option. And so I turn to you, acolyte. 478 is your world, after all."

Futurity spread his hands. "What can I do?"

Tahget laughed, uncaring. "What you priests do best. Talk."

The dread weight of responsibility, which had oppressed Futurity since he had been "volunteered" for this assignment by the Hierocrat and projected into orbit, now pressed down on him hard. But, he found, his greatest fear was not for his own safety, nor even for the fate of this poor woman, but simply that he was making a fool of himself in front of this dour captain. Shame on you, Futurity's Dream!

He forced himself to focus. "How do I speak to her?"

The captain waved a hand. A Virtual of Mara's head coalesced in the air, and Futurity saw a miniature of himself pop into existence in the little diorama of her cabin.

He tried to read her face. She looked younger than her thirty-six years. Her face was a neat oval, her features rather bland—her nose long, her mouth small. She would never be called beautiful, though something about the shape of her skull, exposed by the close shaving of her hair in the Ideocratic style, was delicately attractive. As she studied him, evidently without curiosity, her expression was clear, her brow smooth. She looked *loving*, he thought, loving and contented in herself, her life. But tension showed around her eyes, in hollow stress shadows. This was a gentle woman projected into an horrific situation. She must be desperate.

A smile touched her lips, faint, quickly evaporating. "Aren't you going to say anything?"

The captain rolled his eyes. "Our terrorist is laughing at you! Good start, acolyte."

"I'm sorry," Futurity blurted. "I didn't mean to stare. It's just that I'm trying to get used to all this."

"It's not a situation I wanted," Mara said.

"I'm sure we can find a way to resolve it."

"There is a way," she said without hesitation. "Just take me home. It's all I've asked for from the beginning."

But that's impossible. Futurity had never negotiated with an armed fugitive before, but he had heard many confessions, and he knew the value of patience, of indirection. "We'll come to that," he said. "My name is Futurity's Dream. I live on the planet below, which is Base 478. Our government is called the Ecclesia."

"You're a priest."

He said reflexively, "Just an acolyte, my child—"

She laughed at him. "Don't call me a child! I'm a mother myself!"

"I'm sorry," he mumbled. But in his peripheral vision he checked over the manifest details again. She was traveling alone; there was definitely no mention of a child either on the ship or back at Chandra. Don't contradict, he told himself. Don't cross-examine. Just talk. "You'll have to help me through this, Mara. Are you of the faith yourself?"

"Yes," she sniffed. "Not of your sort, though."

Since the fall of the Coalition the religion Futurity served, known as the "Friends of Wigner," had suffered many schisms. He forced a smile. "But I will have to do," he said. "The captain asked us for help. Mara, you must see that to sort out this situation you will have to talk to me—"

"No."

"No?"

"I have to talk. That's obvious. But not to an acolyte. Or a priest, or a bishop."

He frowned. "Then who?"

"Michael Poole."

That ancient, sacred name shocked Futurity to brief silence. He glanced at Captain Tahget, who raised his eyebrows. *You see what I've been dealing with?* Perhaps this woman was deluded after all.

Futurity said, "Mara, Michael Poole is our messiah. In the age of the First Friends he gave his life for the benefit of humanity by—"

"I know who he was," she snapped. "Why do you think I asked for him?"

"Then," he said carefully, "you must know that Poole has been dead—or at least lost to us—for more than twenty-three thousand years."

"Of course I know that. But he's here."

"Poole is always with us in spirit," said Futurity. "And he waits for us at timelike infinity, where the world lines of reality will be cleansed—"

"Not like that. *He's here*, on Base—"

"478."

"478. You people keep him locked up."

"We do?"

"I want Michael Poole," Mara insisted. "Only him. Because he will understand." She turned away from Futurity. The imaging system followed her, but she covered her face with her hands, so he couldn't read her expression.

Captain Tahget said dryly, "I think you need to talk to your Hierocrat."

⚬

The Hierocrat refused to discuss such issues on a comms link, so Futurity would have to return to the surface.

As Futurity's flitter receded from the starship, it undertook a routine inspection tour of the mother craft, sending data back to Tahget's bridge. The *Ask Politely* was an astonishing sight. It was a rough cylinder perhaps a kilometer in length, but it lacked symmetry on any axis, and its basic form was almost hidden by the structures that plumed from its surface: fins, sails, spines, nozzles, scoops, webbing. Hardened for interstellar space the ship shone, metallic and polymeric. But it had the look of something organic rather than mechanical, a form that had *grown*, like a spiny fish from Base 478's deep seas perhaps, rather than anything designed by intelligence.

There was something deeply disturbing about the ship's lack of symmetry. But, Futurity supposed, symmetry was imposed on humans by the steady straight-up-and-down gravity fields of planets. If you swam between the stars you didn't need symmetry. And besides, so the seminary gossip went, despite the presence of Tahget and his command crew this wasn't really a *human* vessel at all. It certainly didn't look it, close to.

Futurity was relieved when the flitter pulled out of the ship's forest of spines and nets and began to swing down toward Base 478.

478 was a world of ruins: from the high atmosphere the land looked as if it had been melted, covered over by a bubbling concrete-grey slag. Once every resource of this world had been dedicated to the prosecution of a galactic war. 478 had been a training center, and here millions of human citizens had been molded into soldiers, to be hurled into the unending friction of the war at the Galaxy's heart, from whence few had returned. Even now the world retained the number by which it had been registered in vanished catalogues on Earth.

But times had changed. The war was over, the Coalition fallen. Many of those tremendous buildings remained—they were too robust to be demolished—but Futurity made out splashes of green amid the bubbling grey, places where the ancient buildings had been cleared and the ground exposed. Those island-farms labored to feed 478's diminished population. Futurity himself had grown up on such a farm, long before he had donned the cassock.

He had never traveled away from his home world—indeed, he had only flown in orbit once before, during his seminary training; his tutor had insisted that you could not pretend to be a priest without seeing your world hanging unsupported in the Galaxy's glow. But Futurity had studied widely, and he had come to see that though there were far more exciting and exotic places to live in this human Galaxy—not least Earth itself—there were few places quite so orderly and *civilized* as his own little world, with its proud traditions of soldiery and engineering, and its deeply devout government. So he had grown to love it. He even liked the layers of monumental ruins that plated over every continent, for in the way they had been reoccupied and reused he took a lesson about the durability of the human spirit.

But a world so old hid many secrets, and after his flitter had landed—and as the Hierocrat led him to a chamber buried deep beneath the Ecclesia's oldest College—Futurity felt his soul shrink from the suffocating burden of history.

And when Michael Poole opened his eyes and faced him, Futurity wondered which of them was the most lost.

———

The room was bare, its walls a pale, glowing blue. Its architecture was tetrahedral, a geometry designed respectfully to evoke an icon of Michael Poole's own past, the four-sided mouths of the wormholes the great engineer had once built to open up Earth's solar system. But those slanting walls made the room enclosing: not a chapel, but a cell.

The room's sole occupant sat on the one piece of furniture, a low bed. Futurity was immediately reminded of Mara, in another plainly furnished room, similarly trapped by her own mysterious past. The man looked up as Futurity entered. He was bulky, small—smaller than Futurity had imagined. His hair was black, his eyes dark brown. He looked about forty, but Futurity reminded himself that this man came from an age of the routine use of anti-senescence treatments. The muscles of his shoulders were bunched, and his hands were locked together, big, powerful engineer's hands. He looked tense, angry, haunted.

As Futurity hesitated, the man fixed him with an aggressive gaze. "Who in Lethe are you?" The language was archaic, and a translation whispered softly in Futurity's ear.

"My name is Futurity's Dream."

"Futurity—?" He laughed out loud. "Another infinity-botherer."

It shocked Futurity to have *this* man speak so casually heretically. But he had had enough of being cowed today, and he pulled himself together. "You are on a world of infinity-botherers, sir."

The man eyed him with a grudging respect. "I suppose I can't argue with that. I didn't ask to be here, though. Just you remember that. So I know who you are. Who am I?"

Futurity took a deep breath. "You are Michael Poole."

Poole raised his hand, and turned it back and forth, studying it. Then he stood up and without warning aimed a slap at Futurity's cheek. Poole's fingers broke up into a cloud of blocky pixels, and Futurity felt nothing.

"No," Poole murmured. "I guess you're wrong. Michael Poole was a human being. Whatever I am it isn't that."

For a second Futurity couldn't speak. He was trying to hold himself together against this barrage of shocks.

To Futurity's surprise, Poole said, "Sorry. Perhaps you didn't deserve that."

Futurity shook his head. "My needs don't matter."

"Oh, yes, they do. Everything goes belly-up if you forget that." He cast about the tetrahedral cell. "What's a man got to do to get a malt whisky around here? . . . Oh. I forgot." He looked up into the tetrahedron's squat spire, and held out his hand, cupping it. In a moment a glass appeared, containing a puddle of amber fluid. Poole sipped it with satisfaction. Then he dipped his fingers in the drink, and flicked droplets at Futurity. When they hit the acolyte's cassock, the droplets burst apart in little fragments of light. "Consistency protocols," Poole murmured. "How about that. Why am I here, Futurity's Dream? Why am I talking to you—why am I conscious again?"

Futurity said bluntly, "I need your help."

Poole sat down, sipped his drink, and grunted. "More dumb-ass theology?"

"Not theology," Futurity said evenly. "A human life."

That seemed to snag Poole's attention. But he said, "How long this time?"

Futurity, briefed by the Hierocrat, knew exactly what he meant. "A little more than a thousand years."

Poole closed his eyes and massaged his temples. "You bastards," he said. "I'm your Virtual Jesus. A simulacrum messiah. And I wasn't good enough. So you put me in memory store, a box where I couldn't even dream, and left me there for a *thousand years*. And now you've dug me up again. Why? To crucify me on a wormhole mouth, like the first Poole?"

Futurity was growing irritated. "I know nothing of *Jesus*, or *crucifying*. But I always thought I understood Michael Poole."

"How could you? He's been dead twenty millennia."

Futurity said relentlessly, "Then perhaps I misjudged his character. We didn't bring you back to harm you. We didn't bring you back for *you* at all. You're here because somebody in trouble is asking for your help. Maybe you should think about somebody other than yourself, as Michael Poole surely would have done."

Poole shook his head. "I don't believe it. Are you trying to manipulate me?"

"I wouldn't dream of it, sir."

Poole sipped his unreal whisky. Then he sighed. "So what's the problem?"

Poole had no physical location as such; he "was" where he was projected. It would have been possible for him to be manifested aboard the *Ask Politely* by projection from the Ecclesia's underground caches. But Poole himself pressed for the data that defined him to be downloaded into the ship's own store, as otherwise lightspeed delays would introduce a barrier between himself and this fragile woman who was asking for his help.

What Poole wanted, it seemed, Poole got.

But it took a day for the Ecclesiast authorities to agree transfer protocols with Captain Tahget and his crew. Futurity, no specialist in such matters, found this difficult to understand, but it turned out that

Poole's definition was stored at the quantum level. "And you can transfer quantum information," Poole said, "but you can't copy it. So your monks can't make a backup of me, Futurity, any more than they can of you. Kind of reassuring, isn't it? And that's why the monks are twitchy."

But Poole was furious that the Ecclesiasts ensured that Tahget understood they owned the copyright in him and would protect their "intellectual property" against "piracy." "Copyright! In *me*! What do they think I am, a worm genome?" Meanwhile, Captain Tahget was insulted by the very suggestion of piracy, and he complained about the delays for which nobody was compensating him, not to mention the risk of allowing the unstable situation of a woman with a bomb aboard his ship to continue for so long.

These transactions seemed extraordinary to Futurity, and terribly difficult to cope with. After all, when he had first gone up to the orbiting starship, Futurity hadn't even known this simulacrum of Michael Poole existed.

Virtual Poole was the deepest secret of the Ecclesia, his Hierocrat had said. Indeed, an acolyte as junior as Futurity shouldn't be hearing any of this at all, and the Hierocrat made it clear he blamed Futurity for not resolving the starship situation without resorting to this: in the Hierocrat's eyes, Futurity had failed already.

It had been begun fifteen hundred years ago. It had been an experiment in theology and epistemology and Virtual technology, an experiment with roots that reached back to the establishment of the Ecclesia itself.

Poole himself knew the background. "I—or rather, *he*, Michael Poole, the real one—has become a messiah figure to you, hasn't he? You infinity-botherers and this strange quantum-mechanical faith of yours. You had theological questions you thought Poole could answer. Your priests couldn't dig him up. And so you *made* him. Or rather, you made me."

Technicians of the ancient Guild of Virtual Idealism had deployed the most advanced available technology to construct the Virtual Poole. Everything known about Poole and his life and times had been downloaded, and where there were gaps in the knowledge, and there were many, teams of experts, technical, historical and theoretical, had labored to extrapolate and interpolate. It had been a remarkable project, and somewhat expensive: the Hierocrat wouldn't say how much it cost, but it seemed the Ecclesia was still paying by installments.

At last all was ready, and the blue tetrahedral chapel had been built. The Supreme Ecclesiarch had waved her hand—and Michael Poole, or at least *a* Michael Poole, had opened his eyes for the first time in more than twenty thousand years. The whole business seemed vaguely heretical to Futurity.

But when Poole popped into existence in the ship's observation lounge, surrounded by the gaping crew and nervous Ecclesiast technicians, Futurity felt a shiver of wonder.

Poole seemed to take a second to come to himself, as if coming into focus. Then he looked down at his body and flexed his fingers. In the brightness of the deck he seemed oddly out of place, Futurity thought—but not flimsily unreal like most Virtuals, but *more* opaque, more dense, like an intrusion from another reality. Poole scanned the crowd of staring strangers. When he found Futurity's face he smiled, and Futurity's heart warmed helplessly.

But Poole's face was dark, intent, determined. For the first time it occurred to Futurity to wonder what Poole himself might want out of this situation. He was a Virtual, but he was just as sentient as Futurity was, and he no doubt had goals of his own. Perhaps he saw some advantage in this transfer off-world, some angle to be worked.

Poole turned and walked briskly to the big blister-window set in the hull. His head scanned back and forth systematically as he took in the crowded view. "So this is the center of the Galaxy. You damn priests never even let me see the sky before."

"Not quite the center. We're inside the Core here, the Galaxy's central bulge." Futurity pointed to a wall of light that fenced off half the sky. "That's the Mass—the Central Star Mass, the knot of density surrounding Chandra, the supermassive black hole at the very center."

"Lethe, I don't know if I imagined people would ever come so far. And for millennia this has been a war zone?"

"The war is over." Futurity forced a grin. "We won!"

"And now humans are killing humans again, right? Same old

story." He inspected the surface of the planet below. "A city-world," Poole said dismissively. "Seen better days." He squinted around the sky. "So where's the sun?"

Futurity was puzzled by the question.

Captain Tahget said, "Base 478 has no sun. It's a rogue planet, a wanderer. Stars are crowded here in the Core, Michael Poole. Not like out on the rim, where you come from. Close approaches happen all the time."

"So planets get detached from their suns." Poole peered down at the farms that splashed green amid the concrete. "No sunlight for photosynthesis. But if the sky is on fire with Galaxy light, you don't need the sun. Different spectrum from Sol's light, of course, but I guess they are different plants too."

Futurity was entranced by these rapid chains of speculation and deduction.

Poole pointed to a shallow crater, a dish of rubble kilometers across, gouged into the built-over surface. "What happened there?"

Futurity shrugged. "Probably a floating building fell, when the power failed."

Poole laughed uncomfortably. "Layers of history! I don't suppose I'll ever know the half of it." Now he took in the *Ask Politely*'s bubbling organic form. "And what kind of starship is *this*?" At random he pointed at hull features, at spines and spires and shields. "What is *that* for? An antenna, a sensor mast? And *that*? It could be a ramjet scoop, I guess. And that netting could be an ion drive."

There was a stirring of discomfort. Futurity said, "We don't ask such questions. It's the business of the captain and his crew."

Poole raised his eyebrows, but he got only a blank stare from Captain Tahget. "Demarcation of knowledge? I never did like that. Gets in the way of the scientific method. But it's your millennium." He clapped his hands. "Okay, so I'm here. Maybe we should get to work before your fruitcake in steerage blows us all up."

The Ecclesia technicians muttered among themselves, and prepared Poole's relocation.

Futurity watched the scene in Tahget's fish-tank Virtual viewer. Mara's cabin looked was just as it had before: the woman sitting patiently on the bed, the dresser, and the bomb sitting on the floor, grotesquely out of place. All that was different was a tray on top of the dresser with the remains of a meal.

Poole appeared out of nowhere, a little manikin figure in the fish-tank. Mara sat as if frozen.

Poole leaned down, resting his hands on his knees, and looked into her face. "You're exhausted. Your eyes are piss holes in the snow." Nobody in Tahget's office had ever seen snow; the translation routines had to interpret.

Poole snapped his fingers to conjure up a Virtual chair and sat down. "Take it easy," he said. "You don't have to dry my feet with your hair." Another archaic reference Futurity didn't understand. "I know I'm tangled up in your myths. But I'm just a man. Actually, not even that."

"I'm sorry," Mara said thickly.

"For what? You're the real person here, with the real problem." He glanced at the sullen mass of the bomb.

Mara said, "I made them bring you here. Now I don't know what to say to you."

"Just talk. I don't think anybody understands what you want, Mara. Not even that bright kid Futurity."

"Who? Oh, the acolyte. I told them, but they didn't listen."

"Then tell me." He laughed. "I'm the sleeping beauty. Lethe knows I've got no preconceptions."

"I want to go home. I didn't want to leave in the first place. They evacuated us by force."

He leaned forward. "Who did?"

"The troops of the new Kard."

"Who? . . . Never mind; I'll figure that out. Okay. But home for you is a planetoid orbiting a black hole. Yes? A satellite black hole, born in the accretion disc of the monster at the heart of the Galaxy." He rubbed his chin. "Quite a place to visit. But who would want to *live* there?"

Mara sat up straighter. "I would. I was born there."

It had been a project of the first years after mankind's victory in the center of the Galaxy, Mara told him. With the war won, the ancient

Coalition, the government of a united mankind, abruptly crumbled, and successor states emerged across the Galaxy. A rump remnant of the Coalition that called itself the Ideocracy had clung on to Earth and other scattered territories. And at the Core, the scene of mankind's greatest victory, a new project was begun. Ideocrat engineers had gathered asteroids and ice moons that they had set spinning in orbit around the satellite black holes that studded Chandra's accretion disc. One such was the rock Mara called Greyworld.

"You say you were born there."

"Yes," Mara said. "And my parents, and their parents before them. We have family trees."

Poole stared at her. Then, in Futurity's view, his little figure walked to the edge of the fish-tank viewer, and stared up challengingly. "Hey, acolyte. Help me out here. I'm having a little trouble with timescales."

Futurity checked his data desk. Under the Ideocracy, these accretion-disc colonies had been in place for two thousand years, almost since the final victory at the Galaxy's Core.

Poole, a man of the fourth millennium, seemed stunned. "*Two thousand years?*"

Captain Tahget leaned forward and peered into the fish-tank. "Virtual, we once fought a war that spanned tens of thousands of light-years. We learned to plan on a comparable scale in time. During the war there were single battles which lasted millennia."

Poole shook his head. "And I imagined I thought big. I really have fallen far into the future, haven't I?"

"You really have, sir," Futurity said.

Poole sat down again and faced Mara. "I can see why you didn't want to leave. Your roots were deep, on your Greyworld."

"Time was running out," she said. "We knew that. Our black hole was slowly spiraling deeper into Chandra's accretion disc. Soon the turbulence, the energy density, the tides—it would have been impossible for us to hang on."

"Although," said Poole, "the black hole itself will sail on regardless until it reaches Chandra's event horizon."

"Yes."

Poole said gently, "I still don't understand. If you knew your world was doomed, you must have accepted you had to evacuate."

"Of course."

"Then what—"

"I just didn't like the way it was done." Her face worked, deep emotions swirling under a veneer of control. "I didn't get a chance to say goodbye."

"Who to?"

"Sharn. My daughter."

Poole studied her for a moment. Then he said gently, "You're losing me again, Mara. I'm sorry. According to the ship's manifest you don't have a daughter."

"I did have one. She was taken away from me."

"Who by?"

"The Ideocrats."

"But, Mara, here's my problem. I saw the records. Once the evacuation was done, there was *nobody* left on Greyworld. So your daughter—"

"She wasn't on Greyworld."

"Then where?"

"She lives in the satellite black hole," Mara said simply. "Where the Ideocrats sent her."

"*In* the black hole?"

"She lives in it, as you, Michael Poole, live in light."

"As some kind of Virtual representation?"

Mara shook her head. "I'm sorry. I can't explain it better. We aren't scientists on Greyworld, like you."

He thought that over. "Then what are you?"

"We are farmers." She shrugged. "Some of us are technicians. We supervise the machines that tend other machines, that keep the air clean and the water flowing."

Poole asked, "But why are you there in the first place, Mara? What did the Ideocracy intend? What is your duty?"

She smiled. "To give our children to the black hole. And that way, to serve the goals of mankind."

Futurity said quickly, "She's probably doesn't know any more, Michael Poole. This was the Ideocracy, remember, heir to the

Coalition. And under the Coalition you weren't encouraged to know more than you needed to. You were thought to be more effective that way."

"Sounds like every totalitarian regime back to Gilgamesh." Poole studied Mara for a long moment. Then he stood. "All right, Mara. I think that's enough for now. You've given me a lot to think about. Is there anything you need? More food—"

"I'm tired," she said quietly. "But I know if I lie down that captain or the acolyte will sneak in here and disarm the bomb, or hurt me, and—"

Poole said, "Look at me, Mara. Things will get flaky very quickly if you don't sleep. Nobody will hurt you, or change anything in here. *You can trust me.*"

She stared at his Virtual face. Then, after a moment, she lay down on her bunk, her knees tucked into her chest like a child.

Poole's fish-tank representation popped out of existence.

———

Poole, Tahget, and Futurity faced each other across the table in Tahget's office.

Tahget said, "We need to resolve this situation."

Poole had another glass of Virtual whisky in his hand. "That woman is determined. Believe me, you don't separate a mother from her child. She'll blow us all up rather than give in."

Tahget said coldly, "Then what do you suggest we do?"

"Comply with her wishes. Take her back to Chandra, to her black hole Garden of Eden. And help her find her kid."

Futurity said, "There is no child. She said the child lives *in* the black hole. That's just impossible. No human being—"

"Who said anything about it being human?" Poole snapped. "I'm my mother's son, and I'm not human. Not anymore. And black holes are complicated beasts, Futurity. You're a scholar; you should know that. Who's to say what's possible or not?"

"I don't know anything about black holes," Futurity said.

"You know, you've got a really closed mind," Poole snapped. "You Ecclesiasts actually have origins in an engineering guild, don't you? But now you want to be a priest, and the whole point of being a priest is to keep your knowledge to yourself. Well, maybe you're going to have to learn to think a bit more like a scientist and less like an acolyte to get through this."

Tahget was glaring at Poole. "If you insist on this absurd chase to the center of the Galaxy, Michael Poole, you will have your way. You are accorded respect here. Too much, in my opinion."

Poole grinned. "Ain't that the truth?"

"At least it will buy us time," Futurity said, trying to reassure Tahget. "But you must hope to resolve this situation before you reach Chandra, when you will find there is no magical child in the singularity, and the woman's condition will veer from denial to desperation."

"Or it turns out some other way," Poole said evenly. "Don't prejudge, acolyte; it's a nasty habit. One condition. I'm coming along too."

They both looked at him sharply.

Futurity said hesitantly, "I don't think the Hierocrat would—"

"Into Lethe with your bishops and their 'copyright'! I didn't ask them to bring me back from the dead. I only want to see a little of the universe before I get switched off again. Besides, right now I'm the only sentient creature poor Mara trusts. I think you need me aboard, don't you, Captain?"

Futurity opened his mouth, and closed it. "As the captain said, if you ask for that I imagine it will be granted, though the Hierocrat's teeth will curl with anxiety."

Tahget growled, "Your Hierocrat will have more to think about than that." He grabbed Futurity's wrist in one massive hand. "If Michael Poole is joining this cruise of ours, so are *you*, acolyte. When this Virtual fool starts to cause trouble, I want somebody I can take it out on."

Futurity felt panicked; for a boy who had never been further than low orbit before, this was becoming a daunting adventure, out of control.

Poole laughed and rubbed his hands together. "Great! Just leave a piece of him for the Hierocrat to gnaw on."

Tahget released Futurity. "But I have a condition of my own." He waved his hand over the table, and its surface turned into a schematic of the Galaxy. "Here is our original route, planned but now abandoned." It was a simple dotted line arcing from Base 478 in the Core out to the sparse Galactic rim, where Earth lay waiting. There were a few stops on the way, mostly at nominal political borders. One stop was at a flag marked "3-Kilo," outside the Core, and Tahget tapped it with his fingernail. "This is the Galaxy's innermost spiral arm, the 3-Kiloparsec Arm. Whatever our final destination, we go here first."

Futurity didn't understand. "But that's the wrong way. 3-Kilo is *outside the Core*." His dread deepened at the thought of being taken out of the brightly lit Core and into the sparse unknown beyond. "If we're aiming for the center of the Galaxy, we'll have to double back. And the bomb—the additional time this will take—"

"I know the urgency of the situation," Tahget snapped.

Poole said, "So why do you want to go to 3-Kilo?"

"I don't," Tahget said. "The *Ask Politely* does. On a ship like this, you go where *it* wants to go." Tahget blanked the table display and stood. "There is much you will never understand about this modern age, Michael Poole. Even about this ship. This meeting is over." He walked out.

Futurity and Poole stared at each other.

Poole said, "So it isn't just a cutesy name. On this ship, you really do have to ask politely."

Futurity peered into the fish-tank display of Mara's cabin, where the woman hadn't moved since she lay down in Poole's presence.

———

The *Ask Politely* spent another day in orbit around 478. Then the ship slid silently away into deep space.

Futurity stood alone in the observation lounge, watching his home planet fold over itself until it became a dull grey pebble, lost against the glare of the Galaxy Core. That was bad enough, but the ship was soon going to be sailing out of the Galaxy's star-crowded central bulge altogether; Futurity really was heading out into the cold and the dark. He shivered and turned away from the blister-window.

It would be three days' travel to 3-Kilo, said Tahget, with much delay at border posts as they cut across the territories of various squabbling statelets.

Stuck on the ship, Futurity quickly found his range was limited.

He had access to corridors and rooms over two decks, confined to a roughly lozenge-shaped volume near one end of the ship's rough cylinder. The corridors were bleak, paneled with bare blue-grey polymer, with not a bit of artwork or personalization in sight. Even within the lozenge many rooms were closed to him, such as the bridge, or just plain uninteresting, such as the refectory, the nano-food banks and the air-cycling gear.

And the lozenge spanned no more than fifty meters, on a craft a kilometer long. This pod of habitation was like an afterthought, an add-on bolted onto *Ask Politely*, as if these bare corridors and the people in them were not the point of the ship at all.

Futurity spent most of the first day alone. The bare corridors echoed; a ship meant to carry a hundred passengers seemed empty with just the three of them, counting Poole. And nobody would speak to him. Tahget and his crew were busy, and as a mere earthworm, as they called him, they just ignored Futurity anyhow. The woman Mara stayed asleep throughout the day.

Michael Poole stayed in the captain's office. He appeared to sit still for hours on end, immersed in his own deep Virtual reflections. Futurity didn't dare disturb him.

Futurity thought of himself as disciplined. He wasn't without personal resource. He had been assigned a cabin, and he had brought a data desk and other materials. So he sat down, faced his data desk, and tried to pursue his seminary studies.

The Wignerian faith was based on the comforting notion that all history was partial, a mere rough draft. It was all based on quantum physics, of course, the old notion that reality is a thing of probabilities and might-bes, that collapses into the real only when a conscious mind makes an observation. But that conscious mind in turn wasn't realized until a second mind observed *it*—but that second in turn needed a third observer to become real, who needed a fourth . . .

This paradoxical muddle would be resolved at the end of time, said the Wignerians, when the Ultimate Observer, the final Mind, would make the last Observation of all, terminating chains of possibilities that reached back to the birth of the universe. In that mighty instant the sad history of the present, with its pain and war, suffering and brief lives and death, would be wiped away, and everybody who ever lived would find themselves embedded in a shining, optimal history.

That was the kernel of a faith which had offered profound hope during the last days of the Coalition, when the Galaxy had been infested with human soldiers, many of them not much more than children. The faith had always been illegal, but it was blind-eye tolerated by authorities and commanders who saw the comfort it brought to their warriors. And when the Coalition fell, the faith was liberated.

The Ecclesia of Base 478 had its origins in the Guild of Engineers, an ancient agency that had itself been part of the Coalition. The Guild had survived many political discontinuities in the past, and as the Coalition's authority melted away it proved its adaptability again. The Guild took over an abandoned training base and set up an independent government. Like many others, it fully accepted the newly liberated Wignerian faith, seeing in the religion a shortcut to power and legitimacy. Soon its Master of Guild-Masters proclaimed herself Supreme Ecclesiarch, announcing that she alone owned the truth about the faith—again, like many others.

The Guild-Masters, following their old intellectual inclinations, developed an interest in the theological underpinnings of their new faith. Their Colleges on Base 478 quickly developed a reputation even among rival orthodoxies as hosting the best Wignerian thinkers in the Galaxy.

But in those heady early days of theological freedom, there had been constant schisms and splits, heresy and counterheresy, as the scholars debated one of the religion's most fascinating and difficult elements: the strange career of Michael Poole. This entrepreneur, engineer, and adventurer of humanity's remote history had, it was said, projected himself into the far future through a collapsing chain of wormholes. He had done this in order to save mankind. Poole, a redeemer who had confronted infinity, came to embody and humanize the chilly quantum abstractions of the faith, a Son of the lofty Mother that was the Ultimate Observer.

There seemed no doubt that Poole really had existed as a historical figure. The question was: what was his relationship to the Ultimate

Observer? Was Poole just another supplicant, if an extraordinary one, his life just one more thread in the tapestry contemplated by the Wignerian godhead? Or, some argued further, perhaps Poole and the Observer ought to be identified. Perhaps Michael Poole *was* the Observer. But Poole was undoubtedly human, whatever else he was, though his achievements had been anything but ordinary. Could a god be made incarnate?

It was an issue that had always fascinated Futurity. Indeed, it had so intrigued some of his predecessors that they had commissioned the Virtual Poole from the Idealists so they could ask him about it: it was a rough-and-ready engineers' approach to a deep theological question.

But oddly, with the real thing—or at least a disturbing simulacrum—just down the corridor of this ship, Futurity's dry scholarship seemed pointless. He found it hard to believe Poole himself would have any time for this dusty stuff.

After a couple of hours Futurity gave up. He left his cabin and went exploring again.

As he roamed the corridors he watched the crew at work. They all seemed to be command staff, aside from a few orderlies who performed such chores as serving the captain his meals and shifting furniture around to set up passengers' cabins. It was puzzling. Futurity had no experience of life aboard starships, but he could not see how the crew's complicated discussions and endless meetings related to the ship's actual operations. And he never spotted an engineer, a person who might be in charge of the systems that would actually make the ship *go*.

He was probably reading the situation all wrong. But Michael Poole, who had once built starships himself, also concluded that there was something very odd about this ship.

On the second day he talked it over with Futurity. Tahget had given Poole some limited access over where he could "pop up," as he put it, and he had been able to roam a bit wider than Futurity had. But not much further. His own internal-consistency protocols, designed to give him some anchoring in humanity, made it impossible for him to roam into areas that would have been hazardous for humans. And when the captain had spotted that Poole was hacking into access-denied areas, such privileges had quickly been locked out.

"I saw a few sights, though," Poole said, and he winked. *"We're not alone on this ship.* It's a big place, and we're confined to this little box. But in the longer corridors on the fringe of our cage, I saw a few things: shadows, furtive movements. Like ghosts, where if you look too closely what you see disappears into shade . . ."

Futurity frowned. "You're not saying the ship is haunted?"

"No. But I think there is, umm, a second crew, a crew beneath the crew, who are actually flying the damn ship. And it's presumably to serve *their* needs that we're all jaunting out to 3-Kilo, because for sure it isn't for us. What I haven't yet figured out is who those people are, why they're hiding from us, and what their relationship is to Tahget and his bunch of pirates. But I'll get there," he said cheerfully. "I'll tell you something even odder. I'm not convinced that the squat little folk I glimpsed were even *wearing clothes!*"

Futurity never ceased to marvel at Poole. He was a tourist in this twenty-eighth millennium, a revenant from the deepest past. And yet he was finding his way around what must be a very strange future with far more confidence than Futurity felt he could muster in a hundred lifetimes.

By the morning of the third day the *Ask Politely* had swum out of the Core, and Futurity was growing disturbed by the sky.

They were still only a few thousand light-years from the center of the Galaxy, and behind the ship the Core was a mass of light, too bright to be viewed by a naked human eye. But Futurity could already tell he was in the plane of a disc: there were stars all around, but they were more crowded in some directions than others. If he looked straight ahead the more distant stars merged into a band of light that streaked across the sky, a stellar horizon, but if he looked up or down, the stars scattered to thinness, and he could see through the veil of light to a sky that was noticeably empty—and *black.*

Futurity had never seen a black sky before. It was as if the bright surface of reality was breaking down, to reveal an abyssal darkness beneath. He felt as if his own mind was crumbling. He longed to be back on 478, where the whole sky was always drenched with light.

But Poole was animated. "What a tremendous sky! You know, from Sol system you can make out only a few thousand stars, and the Galaxy is just a ragged band of mushy light. The Core ought to be visible—it should be as bright as the Moon, even from Earth—but the spiral-arm dust clouds get in the way, and it's invisible. Futurity, it was only a few decades before the first human spaceflight that people figured out they lived in a Galaxy at all! It was as if we lived in a shack buried in the woods, while all around us the bright lights of the city were hidden by the trees."

Poole had a kindly streak, and was empathetic. He sensed Futurity's discomfort, and to distract him he brought the acolyte to the captain's office, and encouraged him to talk about himself. Futurity was flattered by his interest—this was *Michael Poole!*—and he responded with a torrent of words.

Futurity had always been cursed with a lively, inquisitive mind. As a young boy on the family farm, surrounded by the lowering ruins of war, he had labored to tease healthy plants from soil illuminated by pale Galaxy-center light. It had been fulfilling in its way, and Futurity saw with retrospect that to spend his time on the processes of life itself had satisfied some of his own inner spiritual yearnings. But the unchanging rhythms of the farm weren't sufficient to sustain his intellect.

The only libraries on Base 478 were deep underground, where Ecclesiast scholars and scribes toiled over obscure aspects of Wignerian theology, and the only academic career available to Futurity was in a seminary. In fact, on a priest-run world, to become an Ecclesiast of some rank or other was the only way to build any kind of career. "Even the tax collectors are priests," as Futurity's father had said ruefully.

So the boy said goodbye to the farm, and donned the cassock of a novice. He gave up his childhood name for a visionary Wignerian slogan: *Futurity's Dream.*

The study was hard, the rule of the Hierocrats and tutors imperious and arbitrary, but life wasn't so bad. His intellect had been fully satisfied by his immersion in the Ecclesia's endless and increasingly baroque studies of the historical, philosophical and theological studies of its faith. He recoiled with humility from the pastoral side of his work, though. It mortified him to hear the confession of citizens older and wiser than he was. But that very humility, one discerning Hierocrat had once told him, might mark him out as having the potential to be a fine priest.

Anyhow now, seven years later, his seemingly inevitable career choices had led him to this extraordinary situation.

"And who are these 'Kards'?"

"The Kardish Imperium is a new power that has risen in the Core," Futurity told Poole. "Expansive, aggressive, intolerant, ambitious—"

"I know the type."

"And now they are cleaning out the last Ideocracy enclaves in the Core."

"Ah. Like Mara's world."

"Yes. So far the Ideocracy is allowing this to happen. There isn't much it can do, short of all-out war. As for us," Futurity went on, "the Ecclesia is just trying to keep the peace."

Through their faith the Ecclesia's acolytes and academics had links that crossed the new, shifting political boundaries. "Michael Poole, the Wignerian faith was never legal under the Coalition, but it spanned the Galaxy, and in its way unified mankind. Now, despite our fractured politics, and even though the faith itself has schismed and schismed again, it still unites us—or at least gives us a way to talk to each other. And it provides a moral, civilizing center to our affairs. If not for the faith's moderating influence, the fall of the Coalition would have been *much* worse for most of humanity."

Wignerian diplomatic links had been used to set up a reasonably safe passage for Ideocracy refugees from the Core. Thus at places like Base 478 refugees like Mara were passed off from one authority to another, following a chain of sanctuaries from the Core to their new homes in the remote gloom of the rim.

Poole seemed cynical about this. "A service for which you charge a handsome fee, no doubt."

Futurity was stung. "We're not a rich world, Michael Poole. We rely mostly on donations from pilgrims to keep us going. We have to charge the refugees or their governments for transit and passage; we'd fall into poverty ourselves otherwise."

But Poole didn't seem convinced. "Pilgrims? And what is it those pilgrims come to see on Base 478? Is it the shrine of the great messiah? Is it *me*? Do you have some gibbering manikin of me capering on a monument, begging for cash?"

Futurity tried to deny this: *not literally*. But there was truth in Poole's charge, he saw uncomfortably.

Poole just laughed.

The captain called them. They had arrived at 3-Kilo, and Tahget, in his blunt, testing way, said his passengers might enjoy the view.

＊

Poole was charmed by the clustering stars of 3-Kilo. But to Futurity these spiral-arm stars, scattered and old, were a thin veil that barely distracted him from the horror of the underlying darkness beyond.

But it wasn't stars they were here to see.

Poole pointed. "What in Lethe is *that*?"

An object shifted rapidly against the stars of 3-Kilo. Silhouetted, it was dark, its form complex and irregular.

Poole was fascinated. "An asteroid, maybe—no, too spiky for that. A comet nucleus, then? I spent some time in the Kuiper Belt, the ice moon belt at the fringe of Sol system. I was building starships out there. Big job, long story, and all vanished now, I imagine. But I remember a lot of those Kuiper objects were like that: billions of years of sculptures of frost and ice, all piled up in the dark. Pointlessly beautiful. So is this a Kuiper object detached from some system or other? But it looks too small for that."

Futurity was struck again by the liveliness of Poole's mind, the openness of his curiosity—and *this* was only an incomplete Virtual. He wondered wistfully how it might have been to have met the real Michael Poole.

Then Poole saw it. "It's a ship," he said. "A ship covered with spires and spines and buttresses and carvings, just like our own *Ask Politely*. A ship like a bit of a baroque cathedral. I think it's approaching us! Or we're approaching it."

He was right, Futurity saw immediately. He felt obscurely excited. "And—oh! There's another." He pointed. "And another."

Suddenly there were ships all over the sky, cautiously converging.

Every one of them was unique. Though it was hard to judge distances and sizes, Futurity could see that some were larger than the *Ask Politely*, some smaller; some were roughly cylindrical like the *Politely*, others were spheres, cubes, tetrahedra, even toroids, and some had no discernible regularity at all. And all of them sported gaudy features, every bit as spectacular as *Politely*'s. There were immense scoop mouths and gigantic flaring exhaust nozzles, spindly spines and fat booms, and articulating arms that worked delicately back and forth like insect legs. Some of the ships even sported streamlined wings and fins and smooth noses, though none of them looked as if they could survive an entry into an atmosphere.

These glimmering sculptures drifted all around the sky.

Poole said, "Quite a carnival. Look at all that crap, the spines and spikes and nets and fins. It looks like it's been stuck on by some giant kid making toy spaceships. I can't believe there's any utility in most of those features."

Futurity said, "It's also *ugly*. What a mess!"

"Yes," said Poole, fascinated. "But I have the feeling we're not the ones this stuff is supposed to impress."

As the ships crowded tentatively closer, Futurity was reminded not so much of human ships of the kind he'd often watched in the skies above 478, their movements precisely coordinated by their human crews, but of a shoal of bizarre fish coming together in the starlight. He said, "There's no pattern to it. They're just edging their way in. It's as if the ships themselves want to congregate."

Poole pointed. "And that one looks as if it wants to congregate a bit more intimately than the rest."

A huge ship loomed from the crowd and approached the *Ask Politely*. It was a rough sphere, but its geometry was almost obscured by a fantastic hull-forest of metal, ceramics, and polymers. Moving with an immense slow grace, it bore down on *Ask Politely*, which waited passively.

At last the big sphere's complex bulk shadowed most of the observation lounge's blister. A jungle of nozzles and booms passed across the window. Futurity wondered vaguely how close it would come before it stopped.

And then he realized it wasn't going to stop at all.

Captain Tahget murmured, "Brace for impact." Futurity grabbed a rail.

The collision of the two vast ships was slow, almost gentle. Futurity, cupped in the *Ask Politely*'s inertial-control field, barely felt it, but he could hear a groan of stressed metal, transmitted through the ship's hull. Two tangles of superstructure scraped past each other; dishes were crushed and spines broken before the ships came to rest, locked together.

Translucent access tubes sprouted from the hulls of both ships, and snaked across space like questing pseudopodia, looking for purchase. Futurity thought he saw someone, or something, scuttling through the tubes, but it was too far away to see clearly.

Poole gazed out with his mouth open. "Look—here's another ship coming to join the party."

So it was, Futurity saw. It was a relative dwarf compared to the monster that had first reached *Ask Politely*. But with more metallic grinding it snuggled close against the hulls of the two locked ships.

Poole laughed. "Boy, space travel has sure changed a lot since my day!"

Captain Tahget said, "Show's over. We'll be here two days, maybe three, before the swarming is done." Poole glanced at Futurity questioningly. *The swarming?* Tahget said, "Until then we maintain our systems and wait. Let me remind you it's the night watch; you passengers might want to get some sleep." He glanced at Poole. "Or whatever."

Futurity returned to his cabin, and tried to sleep. But there were more encounters in the night, more subtle shudderings, more groans of stressed materials so deep they were almost subsonic.

This experience seemed to him to have nothing to do with spaceflight. I am in the belly of a fish, he thought, a huge fish of space that has come to this place of scattered stars to seek others of its kind. And it doesn't even know I am here, embedded within it.

———

During the 3-Kilo lay-off Captain Tahget had his crew scour through the ship's habitable areas, cleaning, refurbishing, and repairing. It was make-work to keep the crew and passengers busy, but after a few hours

Futurity conceded he welcomed the replacement of the ship's accumulated pale stink of sweat, urine, and adrenaline with antisepsis.

But the continuing refusal of Mara, reluctant terrorist, to come out of her cabin caused a crisis.

"She has to leave her cabin, at least for a while," Tahget thundered. "That's the company's rules, not mine."

"Why?" Poole asked evenly. "You recycle her air, provide her with water and food. Give her clean sheets and she'll change her own bed, I'm sure."

"This is a starship, Michael Poole, an artificial environment. In a closed, small space like that cabin there can be buildups of toxins, pathogens. And I remind you she is sharing her cabin with a monopole bomb, a nasty bit of crud at least two thousand years old, and Lethe knows what's leaking out of that. We need to clean out her nest."

Poole's eyes narrowed. "What else?"

"That woman needs exercise. You've seen the logs. She only gets off her bed to use the bathroom, and even that's only a couple of times a day. What good will it do anybody if she keels over from a thrombosis even before we get to the Chandra?—especially if she's got a dead man's switch, as she claims."

"Those are all reasons for separating Mara from her bomb, despite your promises to the contrary. I don't trust you as far as I can throw you, Captain. And if I don't, how can Mara?"

Captain Tahget glared; he was a bulky, angry, determined man, and his scar was livid. "Michael Poole, my only concern is the safety of the ship, and everybody aboard—yes, including Mara. I am an honorable man, and if you have half the intuition for which your original was famous you will understand that. I give you my word that if she is willing to leave her room, briefly, for these essential purposes, Mara's situation will not be changed. When she is returned, everything will be as it was. I hope that we can progress this in a civilized and mutually trusting fashion."

Poole studied him for long seconds. Then he glanced at Futurity, and shrugged. "After all," Poole said, "she'll still be able to blow up the bomb whether she's in the cabin with it or not."

So Mara emerged from her room, for the first time since before

Futurity's own first visit to the ship.

A strange procession moved around the ship, with Tahget himself in the van, and a handful of crew, mostly female, surrounding the central core of Poole, Futurity, and Mara. Mara insisted that Poole and Futurity stay with her at all times, one on either side, and she brought a pillow from her cabin which she held clutched to her chest, like a shield. Futurity saw that the crew checked over Mara surreptitiously. Maybe they were searching for the devices that linked her to her bomb. But there was nothing to be seen under her shapeless grey smock. Surely any such device would be an implant, he decided.

Futurity couldn't think of a thing to say to this woman who was holding them all hostage, but Poole kept up a comforting murmur of mellifluous small talk.

The peculiar tour finished in the observation lounge, where the view was still half-obscured by the hull of the overfriendly ship that had sidled up to *Ask Politely*. Further out, nuzzling ships drifted around the sky, like bunches of misshapen balloons.

Mara showed a flicker of curiosity for the first time since leaving her cabin. "The ships are so strange," she said.

"That they are," Poole said.

"What are they doing?"

"I don't know. And the captain won't tell me."

She pointed. "Look. Those two are fighting."

Futurity and the others crowded to the window to see. It was true. Two ships had come together in an obviously unfriendly way. Both lumbering kilometer-long beasts, they weren't about to do anything quickly, but they would barge against each other, withdraw, and then go through another slow-motion collision. As they spun and ground, bits of hull ornamentation were bent and snapped off, and the ships were surrounded by a pale cloud of fragments, detached spires, and shields, nozzles and antennae and scoops.

"It's a peculiar sort of battle," Futurity said. "They aren't using any weapons. All they are doing is smashing up each other's superstructure."

"But maybe that's the point," Poole said.

"So strange," Mara said.

Captain Tahget blocked her way. "But," he said, "not so strange as the fact that you, madam, were able to smuggle a monopole bomb onto my ship."

The mood immediately changed. Mara, obviously frightened, shrank back against Poole, coming so close she brushed against him, making his flank sparkle with disrupted pixels.

Poole said warningly, "Captain, you promised you wouldn't interfere with her."

Tahget held up his big hands. "And I will keep my word. Nobody will touch the bomb, or Mara here, and we'll go through with our flight to Chandra as we agreed."

"But," Poole said heavily, "you had an ulterior motive in getting her out here, despite your promises."

"All right," Captain Tahget snapped. "I need some answers. I must know how she got us all into this situation."

Futurity asked, "Why?"

Tahget barely glanced at him. "To stop it happening again." He glared at Mara. "*Who helped you?* Somebody must have. You're nothing but a refugee from Chandra; you came to 478 with nothing. Who helped you smuggle a bomb on board? Who equipped you with the means to use it? And *why?* I know what *you* want—I don't understand, but I've heard what you said. What I don't know is what your benefactors want. And I need to know."

She returned his stare defiantly. "I want to go back to my cabin."

But Tahget wouldn't back down. The standoff was tense, and Futurity, his heart pumping, couldn't see a way out.

Poole intervened. "Mara, it may be best to tell him what he wants to know."

"But—"

"Telling him who helped you will make no difference to you. You aren't going to come this way again, are you? And I can see the other point of view. Captain Tahget is responsible for his ship." Mara hesitated, but Poole continued to reassure her. "I believe he'll keep his word. Just tell him."

She took a deep breath. "Her name is Ideator First Class Leen."

Tahget growled, "Who?"

But Futurity was shocked. He knew the name: the person who had helped Mara set all this up was a priest belonging to the Guild of Virtual Idealism.

Poole's jaw dropped when he heard this. "My own makers! How delicious."

Mara began to explain how the Ideator had helped her smuggle the bomb and other equipment aboard, but Tahget waved her silent. "If that bunch of illusionists was involved, anything could have been done to us and we wouldn't know it." His suspicious frown deepened. "And then, once you were aboard, you asked for Poole himself. So was that all part of the scheme?"

"No," she insisted. "The Ideator told me Michael Poole had been reincarnated on 478. It was my idea to ask for him, not hers."

Poole shook his head. "I'm not part of this, Captain, believe me. I'm a mere creature of the Idealists—rather like Mara here, I suppose."

Now the captain's ferocious stare was turned on Futurity. "And you," Tahget snarled, his scar livid. "What do you have to do with it? The truth, now."

Futurity, flustered, protested, "Why, nothing, Captain. You know why I was brought in—to negotiate with Mara. You asked for the Ecclesia's help! And I don't understand why you're even asking me such a question. I'm an Engineer, not an Idealist."

Tahget snorted. "But you're all alike, you Guilds. All of you clinging to your petty worldlets, with your stolen fragments of the soldier's faith, your saintly relics and your shrines!"

Futurity was shocked. "Captain—believe me, Engineers and Idealists would never cooperate on a scheme like this. It's unthinkable." He hunted for the right word. "We may seem alike to you. But we are *rivals*."

"Maybe that's the point," Poole said smoothly. "Acolyte, I imagine the Idealists have their own flow-through of pilgrims, along with their money."

"Yes, that's true."

"What, then, if Mara's bomb goes off? What will be the impact on the Ecclesia's trading?"

"We don't think of it as trading but a duty to helpless—"

"Just answer the question," Tahget growled.

Futurity thought it through. "It would be a disaster for us," he conceded. "A refugee makes her journey only once. She brings her children. If she can choose, nobody would come to a place so unsafe as to allow something like this to happen."

"No more refugees with their savings for you to cream," Poole said, watching Futurity's reaction with a cold amusement. "No more pilgrims and their offerings. Your rivals would have struck a mighty economic blow, would they not?"

Tahget said, "My company certainly wouldn't touch your poxy little globe with a gloved hand, acolyte. Perhaps we won't anyhow." A vein throbbed in his forehead. "So we are all puppets of those illusionists—even Mara here. And there's not one of them within light-years whose head I can crack open!"

Mara had listened to all this. Now she said, "None of this matters. What does matter is me, and my daughter."

"And your bomb," said Poole softly.

"Take me back to my cabin," she said. "And don't ask me to leave it again before we get to Chandra."

With a curt nod, Tahget dismissed her.

Futurity went back to his own room. He was relieved the little crisis was over, but his cheeks burned with shame and anger that this whole incident had been set up to get at his own Ecclesia—and it had taken Poole to see it, Poole, a Virtual designed by the Idealists themselves!

But as he thought it over, he did see how alike the two Guilds were. And, he couldn't help wondering, if the Idealists were capable of such deception, could it be that *his own Ecclesia* would not be above such dirty tricks? It was all politics, as Poole would probably say, politics and money, and a competition for the grubby trade of refugees and pilgrims. Perhaps even now the Ecclesiasts were plotting maneuvers just as underhanded and unscrupulous against their rivals.

An unwelcome seed of doubt and suspicion lodged in his mind. To burn it out he took his data desk and furiously began to write out a long report on the whole incident for his Hierocrat.

But before he had completed the work he was disturbed again.

This time it wasn't Mara who was causing trouble for the crew, but Poole—who had gone missing.

∞

Tahget met Futurity in the observation lounge.

Futurity said, "I don't see how you can *lose* a Virtual."

Tahget grunted. "We know he's being projected somewhere. We can tell that from the energy drain. What we don't know is where. He isn't on the monitors. We've checked out all the permitted zones by eye. What's he up to, acolyte?"

Once again Futurity found himself flinching from Tahget's glare. "You know, Captain, the way you use your physical presence to intimidate—"

"Answer the question!"

"I can't! I'm on this voyage because of Poole—believe me, I wish I wasn't here at all—but I'm not his keeper."

"Acolyte, if you're hiding something—"

Futurity was aware of a shadow passing over him. He turned.

There was Poole.

He was *outside* the hull, standing horizontally with his feet on the window's surface, casting a diffuse shadow into the lounge. He was dressed in a skinsuit, and he looked down at Futurity with a broad grin, easily visible through his visor. The Virtual rendition was good enough for Futurity to see the pattern on the soles of Poole's boots. Behind him, entangled ships drifted like clouds.

Futurity gaped. "Michael Poole! Why—how—"

"I can tell you how," Tahget said. He walked up to the window, huge fists clenched. "You hacked into your own software, didn't you? You overrode the inhibiting protocols."

"It was an interesting experience," Poole said. His voice sounded muffled to Futurity, as if he was in another room. "Not so much like rewriting software as giving myself a nervous breakdown." He held up a gloved hand. "And you can see I didn't do away with all the inhibitions. I wasn't sure how far I could go, what was safe. Futurity, I think it's possible that if I cracked this visor, the vacuum would kill me just as quickly as it would kill you."

Futurity felt an urge to laugh at Poole's antics. But at the same time anger swirled within him. "Poole, what are you doing out there? You're the only one Mara trusts. All you're doing is destabilizing a dangerous situation, can't you see that?"

Poole looked mildly exasperated. "Destabilizing? I didn't create this mess, acolyte. And I certainly didn't ask to be here, in this muddled century of yours. But given that I am here—what do *I* want out of it? To find out, that's what. That's all I ever wanted, I sometimes think."

Tahget said, "And what did you go spacewalking to find out, Poole?"

Poole grinned impishly. "Why, Captain, I wanted to know about your Hairy Folk."

Futurity frowned. "What Hairy Folk?"

Tahget just glared.

Poole said, "Shall I show him?" He waved a hand. A new Virtual materialized beside him, hanging in the vacuum. Its fragmentary images showed shadowy figures scurrying through the ship's corridors, and along those translucent access tubes that snaked between the intertwined ships.

At first they looked like children to Futurity. They seemed to run on all fours, and to be wearing some kind of dark clothing. But as he looked closer he saw they didn't so much crawl as scamper, climbing along the tube using big hands and very flexible-looking feet to clutch at handholds. There was something odd about the proportions of their bodies too: they had big chests, narrow hips, and their arms were long, their legs short, so that all four limbs were about the same length.

"And," Futurity said with a shudder, "that dark stuff isn't clothing, is it?"

As an answer, Poole froze the image. Captured at the center of the frame, clearly visible through an access tube's translucent wall, a figure gazed out at Futurity. Though this one's limbs looked as well-muscled as the others, it was a female, he saw; small breasts pushed out of a tangle of fur. Her face, turned to Futurity, was very human, with a pointed chin, a small nose, and piercing blue eyes. But her brow was a low ridge of bone, above which her skull was flat.

"A post-human," Futurity breathed.

"Oh, certainly," said Poole. "Evidently adapted to microgravity.

That even-proportioned frame is built for climbing, not for walking. Interesting: they seem to have reverted to a body plan from way back in our own hominid line, when our ancestors lived in the trees of Earth. The forests have vanished now, as have those ancestors or anything that looked like them. But a sort of echo has returned, here at the center of the Galaxy. How strange! Of course these creatures would have been illegal under the Coalition, as I understand it. Evolutionary divergence wasn't the done thing. But it happened anyhow. *She* doesn't look so interested in the finer points of the law, does she?"

Futurity said, "Captain, why do you allow these creatures to run around your ship?"

Poole laughed. "I'm afraid he doesn't understand."

Tahget growled, "Acolyte, we call these creatures Shipbuilders. And I do not allow them to do anything—it's rather the other way around."

Poole said cheerfully, "Hence the ship's name—*Ask Politely!*"

"But you're the captain," Futurity said, bewildered.

Poole said, "Tahget is captain of the small pod which sustains you, acolyte, which I can see very clearly stuck in the tangle of the hull superstructure. But he's not in command of the ship. All he does is a bit of negotiating. You are all less than passengers, really. You are like ticks in a child's hair."

Tahget shrugged. "You insult me, Poole, but I don't mind the truth."

Futurity still didn't get it. "The ships belong to these Builders? And they let you hitch a ride?"

"For a fee. They still need stuff from the ground—food, air, water—no recycling system is a hundred percent efficient. And that's what we use to buy passage."

Poole grinned. "I pay you in credits. You pay them in bananas!"

The captain ignored him. "We have ways of letting the Builders know where we want them to take us."

"How?" Poole asked, interested.

Tahget shuddered. "The Shipbuilders are nearly mindless. I leave that to specialists."

Futurity stared at Poole's images of swarming apes, his dread growing. "Nearly mindless. But who maintains the *Ask Politely*? Who runs the engines? Captain, *who's steering this damn ship*?"

"The Hairy Folk," Poole said.

It was all a question of time, said Michael Poole.

"In this strange future of yours, it's more than twenty thousand years since humans first left the Sol system. *Twenty thousand years!* Maybe you're used to thinking about periods like that, but I'm a sort of involuntary time traveler, and it appalls me—because that monstrous interval is a good fraction of the age of the human species itself.

"And it's more than enough time for natural selection to have shaped us, if we had given it the chance. On the colonized worlds, the frozen imagination of the Coalition kept humanity in a bubble of stasis. But out in the dark, sliding between those islands of rock, it was a different matter: nobody could have controlled what was happening out there. And with time, we diverged."

After the first humans had left Earth, most of them plunged straight into another gravity well, like amphibious creatures hopping between ponds. But there were some, just a fraction, who found it congenial to stay out in the smoother spaces between the worlds. They lived in bubble-colonies dug out of ice moons or comets, or blown from asteroid rock. Others traveled on generation starships, unsurprisingly finding that their ship-home became much more congenial than any destination planned for them by well-meaning but long-dead ancestors. And some of them just stayed on their ships, making their living from trading.

"My own people did that," Futurity said. "So it's believed. The first Engineers were stranded on a clutch of ships, out in space, when Earth was occupied. They couldn't go home. They survived on trade for centuries, until Earth was freed."

"A fascinating snippet of family history," Tahget said contemptuously.

Poole said, "Just think about it, acolyte. These Hairy Folk have been suspended between worlds for millennia. And that has shaped them. They have lost much of what they don't need—your built-for-a-gravity-well body, your excessively large brain—"

Futurity said, "Given the situation, I don't see how becoming less intelligent would be an advantage."

"Think, boy! You're running a starship, not a home workshop. You're out there forever. Everything is fixed, and the smallest mistake could kill you. You can only maintain, not innovate. Tinkering is one of your strongest taboos! There is a severe selection pressure to be so dumb it wouldn't even occur to you to experiment. It needn't reduce your ability to maintain the ship. Oh, running a starship is a lot more complicated than making an axe out of a bit of stone. But you can break the most complicated process down into simple steps—and starships are long-term propositions anyhow. You design them to be robust.

"But you have a big problem. You have to keep your ship functioning, not just for a few years—not even for a few generations—but for millennia. And we short-lived folk aren't good at timescales that dwarf our humanity. We need devices to maintain our concentration. The Coalition controlled its populations through its belief system—an astoundingly successful one. But over tens of millennia, even religions mutate and morph. And you can't have that if you're trying to run a starship, where any divergence from correct practice is going to result in disaster. You need absolute cultural stasis, even over evolutionary time. And to get that you have to tap into even more basic drivers."

"I never studied human evolution." Futurity said haplessly.

"Well, you should," Poole said sternly. "There's only one driver that could fix hominids' behavior in such a way and for so long—and that's sex."

"Sex?"

"Sex! Let me tell you a story. Once there was a kind of hominid— a pre-human—called *Homo erectus*. They lived on old Earth, of course. They had bodies like humans, brains like apes. I've always imagined they were beautiful creatures. And they had a simple technology. The cornerstone of it was a hand axe: a teardrop-shape with a fine edge, hacked out of stone or flint. You could use it to shave your hair, butcher an animal, kill your rival; it was a good tool.

"And the same design was used, with no significant modification, for *a million years*. Think about it, acolyte! What an astonishing stasis that is—why, the tool survived even across species boundaries, even when one type of *erectus* replaced another. But do you know what it was that imposed that stasis, over such an astounding span of time?"

"Sex?"

"Exactly! *Erectus* used the technology, not just as a tool, but as a way of impressing potential mates. Think about it: to find the raw materials you have to show a knowledge of the environment; to make a hand axe you need to show hand-eye coordination and an ability for abstract thought; to use it you need motor skills. If you can make a hand axe you're showing you are a walking, talking expression of a healthy set of genes.

"But there's a downside. Once you have picked on the axe as your way of impressing the opposite sex, the design has to *freeze*. This isn't a path to innovation! You can make your axes better than the next guy—or bigger, or smaller even—but never different, because you would run the risk of confusing the target of your charms. And *that* is why the hand axes didn't change for a megayear—and that's why, I'll wager, the technology of these spiky starships hasn't changed either for millennia."

Futurity started to see his point. "You're saying that the Shipbuilders maintain their starships, as—as—"

"As *erectus* once made his hand axes. They do it, not for the utility of the thing itself, but as a display of sexual status. It's no wonder I couldn't figure out the function of that superstructure of spines and scoops and nozzles. It has no utility! It has no purpose but showing off for potential mates—but that sexual role has served its purpose and frozen its design.

"The Hairy Folk build faster-than-light starships, but as unthinkingly as birds build nests and bowers. And the *Ask Politely* is a starship, but it is also a peacock's tail. How strange it all is." He laughed. "And it would appall a lot of my old buddies with their dreams of interstellar domination that it should result in *this*."

"You're very perceptive, Michael Poole," the captain said with a faint sneer.

"I always was," said Poole. "And a fat lot of good it's done me."

Futurity turned to the captain. "Is this true?"

Tahget shrugged. "I wouldn't have put it quite so coarsely. We just get on with our jobs. Every so often you have to let the Builders come to a gathering like this. They show off their ships, their latest enhancements. Sometimes they fight. And they throw those tubes between the ships, swarm across, and screw their heads off for three days. When they've worn themselves out, you can pass on your way."

Futurity asked, "But *why* use these creatures and their peculiar ships? Look at the detour we have had to make, even though we have a bomb on board! Why not just run ships under human control, as we always have?"

Tahget sighed. "Because we have no choice. When the Coalition collapsed, the Navy and the state trading fleets collapsed with it. Acolyte, unless you are *extremely* powerful or wealthy, in this corner of the Galaxy a ship like this is the only way to get around. We just have to work with the Builders."

Futurity felt angry. "Then why not *tell* people? Isn't it a lie to pretend that the ship is under your control?"

Tahget blinked. "And if you had known the truth? Would you have climbed aboard a ship if you had known it was under the control of low-browed animals like *those*?"

Futurity stared out as the Shipbuilders swarmed excitedly along their access tubes, seeking food or mates.

With the encounter at 3-Kilo apparently complete, the *Ask Politely* sailed back toward the center of the Galaxy. To Futurity it was a comfort when the ship slid once more into the crowded sky of the Core, and the starlight closed around the ship like a blanket, shutting out the darkness.

When they came within the purview of the Kard, ships of the Imperium closed around the *Ask Politely*.

They were called greenships, an archaic design like a three-pronged claw. Part of the huge legacy of the Galaxy-center war, they had once been painted as green as their names—green, the imagined color of distant Earth—and they had sported the tetrahedral sigil that had once been recognized across the Galaxy as the common symbol of a free and strong mankind. But all that was the symbology of the hated

Coalition, and so now these ships were a bloody red, and they bore on their hulls not tetrahedra but the clenched-fist emblem of the latest Kard.

Ancient and recycled they might be, but still the greenships whirled and swooped around the *Ask Politely*, dancing against the light of the Galaxy. It was a display of menace, pointless and spectacular and beautiful.

Everybody crowded to the windows to see the Kardish craft. The crew gaped, their mouths open.

"They are envious," Futurity murmured to Poole.

"Of course they are," Poole said. "Out there, in those greenships— that's how a human is supposed to fly. This spiky, lumbering beast could never dance like that! And this 'crew' has no more control over their destiny than fleas on a rat. But I suppose you wouldn't sign up even for a ship like this unless you had something of the dream of flying. How they must envy those Kardish flyboys!"

The situation was a distant fallout from mankind's victory at the center of the Galaxy, that great clash of cymbals whose echoes still reverberated through human history. Out of the chaos and conflict that had followed the collapse of the Coalition, as worlds were ruined and populations crashed, a new stability quickly emerged, with the Coalition's Galaxy-wide monochrome replaced by a crude mosaic of statelets, held together by more or less flaky alliances, treaties, and nonaggression pacts.

But now the political balance was shifting. In the Core of the Galaxy—where for three thousand years the greatest battle of all had been prosecuted, and where the greatest military infrastructure was left behind—a new Imperium was being built. In flashfire campaigns led by a sequence of emperor-generals, who called themselves *Kards* after a heroic figure of the past, the Core statelets had rapidly been brought under a single command. And now the borders of the Imperium were burning their way out of the Core itself.

There was only one state in the Galaxy with the capability of resisting the Kards—and that was the Ideocracy, the rump of the Coalition.

So far the Ideocracy had been as aloof concerning the Kardish as it was about all the successor states, which it regarded as illegal and temporary secessions from its own authority. But the Kards' challenge was profound. Earth, base of the Ideocracy, was the home of mankind and had always been the Coalition's political capital. But the Galaxy Core had been the center of the war, and more humans had died there, by an order of magnitude, than all those who had lived and died on Earth before the age of spaceflight. The Core was the moral and spiritual capital of *Homo galacticus*, said the new Kard.

The question was, who was the true heir to the Coalition's mantle, Imperium or Ideocracy? The reputation of the Coalition still towered, and its name burned brightly in human imaginations; whoever won that argument might inherit a Galaxy.

This was the terrible friction that had rubbed away the life of Mara, and countless other refugees.

Futurity understood that while the *Politely* had fled across the Galaxy there had been extensive three-way negotiations between the Ideocracy, the Imperium, and the Ecclesia about the situation on *Politely*. All parties had tentatively agreed that this was a unique humanitarian crisis, and everyone should work together to resolve it, in the interests of common decency. There had been much tension over the necessity of the Kardish escort, since in the eyes of the Ideocracy the ship was under its commission, and would be traveling through corridors of what it still saw as Ideocracy space. But Earth was twenty-eight thousand light-years away, and the blunt power of the Kard, here and now, was not to be denied.

With its barnstorming escort in place, the ship slid deeper into the crowded sky. The whole formation made bold faster-than-light jumps, roughly synchronized, though Futurity saw how the greenships had to adjust their positioning after each leap.

Soon they penetrated the Central Star Mass.

Futurity found Poole in the observation lounge. Standing there, Poole was a short, sullen form, and even the Mass's encompassing brilliance didn't seem to alleviate his heavy darkness. His expression was complex, as always.

"I can never tell what you're thinking, Michael Poole."

Poole glanced at him. "That's probably a good thing . . . To tell the truth, I'm somewhat distracted by the view."

Futurity looked out at the crowded sky of the Mass. The nearest stars hung like globe lamps, their discs clearly visible, with a deep three-dimensional array of more stars hanging behind them—stars beyond stars beyond stars, all of them hot and young, until they merged into a mist of light that utterly shut out any disturbing darkness. He said tentatively, "You mean the stars?"

"Of course I mean the stars! Lethe, *this is the center of the Galaxy*, and the stars are crowded together like grains of sand in a sack. It's terrifying! The whole place is bathed in light—why, if not for this ship's shielding we'd all be fried in an instant. But to you, acolyte, this is normal, isn't it?"

Futurity shrugged. "It's what I grew up with."

He tried to summarize for Poole the geography of the center of the Galaxy. The structure was concentric—"Like an onion," Poole commented—with layers of density and complexity centered on Chandra, the brooding supermassive black hole at the center of everything. The Core itself was the Galaxy's central bulge, a fat ellipsoid of stars and shining nebulas set at the center of the disc of spiral arms. Embedded within the Core was the still denser knot of the Central Star Mass. As well as millions of stars crammed into a few light-years, the Mass contained relics of immense astrophysical violence, expanding blisters left over from supernovas, and tremendous fronts of roiling gas and dust thrown off from greater detonations at the Galaxy's heart itself. Stranger yet was the Baby Spiral, a fat comma shape embedded deep in the Mass, like a miniature galaxy with arms of young stars and hot gases.

And at the center of it all was Chandra itself, the black hole, a single object with the mass of millions of stars. The Galaxy center was a place of immense violence, where stars were born and torn apart in great bursts. But Chandra itself was massive and immovable, the pivot of vast astrophysical machineries, pinned fast to spacetime.

Poole was intrigued by Futurity's rough-and-ready knowledge of the Core's geography, even though the acolyte had never before travelled away from 478. "You know it the way I knew the shapes of Earth's continents from school maps," he said. But he was dismayed by the brusque labels Futurity and the crew had for the features of the center. *The Core, the Mass, the Baby*: they were soldiers' names, irreverent and familiar. In the immense glare of the Core there was no trace of mankind's three-thousand-year war to be seen, but those names, Poole said, marked out this place as a battlefield—just as much as the traces of complex organic molecules that had once been human beings, hordes of them slaughtered and vaporized, sometimes still detectable as pollutants in those shining clouds.

Something about the location's complexity made Poole open up, tentatively, about his own experience: the Virtual's, not the original.

"When I was made fully conscious the first time, it felt like waking up. But I had none of the usual baggage in my head you carry through sleep: no clear memory of where I had been when I fell asleep, what I had done the day before—even how old I was. The priests quizzed me, and I slowly figured out where I was, and even *what* I was. I was shocked to find out *when* I was. Let me tell you," said Poole grimly, "that was tougher to take than being told I was worshipped as a god."

"You can remember your past life? I mean, Poole's."

"Oh, yes. I remember it as if I lived it myself. I'm told they didn't so much program me," said Poole wistfully, "as *grow* me. They put together as much as they could about my life, and then fast-forwarded me through it all."

"So you lived out a computer-memory life."

Poole said, "But it's all a fake. I *remember* having free will and making choices. But I was a rat in a maze; the truth was I never had such freedom. My memory is sharp up to a point. I remember my father, who, long after he was dead, came back to haunt me as a Virtual. I remember Miriam—somebody I loved," he said gruffly. "I lost her in time long before I lost myself.

"But the trouble is the records go fuzzy just at the point where my, or rather *his*, biography gets interesting to you theologians. What happened after I lost Miriam isn't like a memory, it's like a dream—a guess, a fiction somebody wrote out for me. Even to think about it blurs my sense of self. Anyhow I don't believe any of it!

"And so I was a big disappointment, I think. Oh, the priests kept on developing me. They would download upgrades; I would wake up refreshed. Of course I always wondered if I was still the same *me* as when I went to sleep. But I was never able to answer the theologians' questions about the Ultimate Observer, or my jaunt through the wormholes, or about what I saw, or didn't see, at timelike infinity. I wish I could! I'd like to know myself.

"In the end they shut me down one last time. They promised me I'd wake up soon, as I always had. But I was left in my Virtual casket for a thousand years. The bastards. The next thing I saw was the ugly face of your Hierocrat, leaning over me."

"Perhaps they did crucify you, in the end."

Poole looked at him sharply. "You've got depths, despite your silly name, kid. Perhaps they did. What I really don't understand is why they didn't just wipe me off the data banks. Just sentimental, maybe."

Futurity said, "Oh, not that." The Hierocrat in his hurried briefing had made this clear. "They'd worked too hard on you, Michael Poole. They put in too much. Your Virtual representation is now more information-rich than *I* am, and information density defines reality. You may not be a god. You may not even be Michael Poole. But whatever you are, you are more *real* than we are, now."

Poole stared at him. "You don't say." Then he laughed, and turned away.

Still the *Ask Politely* burrowed deeper into the kernel of the Galaxy.

―――

At last the *Ask Politely*, with its Kardish escort, broke through into a place the crew called the Hole.

The ship was suspended in a rough sphere walled by crowded stars. This was a bubble in the tremendous foam of stars that crowded the Galaxy's center, a bubble swept clean by gravity. Captain Tahget pointed out a couple of brighter pinpoints; they were the handful of stars, of all the hundreds of billions in the Galaxy, whose orbits took them closest to Chandra. No stars could come closer, for they would be torn apart by Chandra's tides.

Under the same strict guarantees as before, Poole brought Mara to the observation deck.

When Futurity looked ahead he could see a puddle of light, suspended at the very center of the Hole. It was small, dwarfed by the scale of the Hole itself. It looked elliptical from his perspective, but he knew it was a rough disc, and it marked the heart of the Galaxy.

"It looks like a toy," Mara said, wondering.

Poole asked, "You know what it is?"

"Or course. It's the accretion disc surrounding Chandra."

"Home," Poole said dryly.

"Yes. But I never saw it like this before. The Kardish shipped us out in their big transports. Just cargo scows. You don't get much of a view."

"And somewhere in there—"

"Is my daughter." She turned to him, and the washed-out light smoothed out the lines of her careworn face, making her look younger. "Thank you, Michael Poole. You have brought me home."

"Not yet I haven't," Poole said grimly.

The *Ask Politely* with its escort swooped down toward the center of the Hole. That remote puddle loomed, and opened out into a broad sea of roiling gas, above which the ships raced.

Chandra was slowly consuming the Galaxy of which it was the heart. Infalling matter bled into this central whirlpool, where it spent hours or weeks or years helplessly orbiting, kneaded by tides and heated by compression until any remnants of structure had been destroyed, leaving only a thin, glowing plasma. It was this mush that finally fell into the black hole.

Eventually Futurity made out Chandra itself, a fist of fierce light set at the geometric center of the accretion disc, so bright that clumps of turbulence cast shadows light-days long over the disc's surface. It wasn't the event horizon itself he was seeing, of course, but the despairing glow of matter crushed beyond endurance, in the last instants before it was sucked out of the universe altogether. The event horizon was a surface from which nothing, not even light, could escape, but it was forever hidden by the glow of the doomed matter which fell into it.

Poole was glued to the window. "Astounding," he said. "The black hole is a flaw in the cosmos, into which a Galaxy is draining. And this accretion disc is a sink as wide as the solar system!"

It was Mara who noticed the moistness on Poole's cheeks. "You're weeping."

He turned his head away, annoyed. "Virtuals don't weep," he said gruffly.

"You're not sad. You're happy," Mara said.

"And Virtuals don't get happy," Poole said. "It's just—to be here, to see this!" He turned on Futurity, who saw anger beneath his exhilaration, even a kind of despair, powerful emotions mixed up together. "But you know what's driving me crazy? I'm not *him*. I'm not Poole. It's as if you woke me up to torture me with existential doubt! *He* never saw this—and whatever *I* am, he is long gone, and I can't share it with him. So it's meaningless, isn't it?"

Futurity pondered that. "Then appreciate it for yourself. This is your moment, not his. Relish how this enhances your own identity— yours, uniquely, not *his*."

Poole snorted. "A typical priest's answer!" But he fell silent, and seemed a little calmer. Futurity thought he might, for once, have given Poole a little comfort.

Tahget said grimly, "Before you get too dewy-eyed, remember this was a war zone." He told Poole how Chandra had once been surrounded by technology, a netlike coating put in place by beings who had corralled a supermassive black hole and put it to work. "The whole set-up took a lot of destroying," Tahget said evenly. "When we'd finished up that job, we'd won the Galaxy."

Poole stared at him. "You new generations are a formidable bunch."

There were stars in the accretion disc. Tahget pointed them out.

The disc was a turbulent place, and eddies and knots with the mass of many suns could form—and, here and there, collapse, compress, and spark into fusion fire. These doomed stars shone like jewels in the murky debris at the rim of the disc. But doomed they were, as haplessly drawn toward Chandra as the rest of the disc debris from which they were born. Eventually the most massive star would be torn apart, its own gravity no match for the tides of Chandra. Sometimes you would see a smear of light brushed across the face of the disc: the remains of a star, flensed and gutted, its material still glowing with fusion light.

Some stars didn't last even that long. Massive, bloated, these monsters would burst as supernovas almost as soon as they formed, leaving behind remnants: neutron stars—or even black holes, stellar-mass objects. Even Chandra couldn't break open a black hole, but it would gobble up these babies with relish. When a black hole hit Chandra, so it was said, that immense event horizon would ring like a bell.

It was to one of these doomed satellite black holes that the *Ask Politely* descended.

Dropping into the accretion disc was like falling into a shining cloud; billows and bubbles, filaments and sheets of glowing gas drifted upwards past the ship. Even though those billows were larger than planets—for the accretion disc, as Poole had noted, was as wide as a solar system itself—Futurity could see the billows churning as he watched, as if the ship was falling into a nightmare of vast, slow-moving sculptures.

The approach was tentative, cautious. Captain Tahget said the Shipbuilders were very unhappy at having to take their ship into this dangerous place, which struck Futurity as a very rational point of view. The swarming creatures were having to be bribed with additional goodies.

And in the middle of all this they came upon a black hole.

They needed the observation lounge's magnification features to see it. With twice the mass of Earth's sun, it was a blister of sullen light, sailing through the accretion clouds. Like Chandra, the dark mask of its event horizon—in fact only a few kilometers across—was hidden by the electromagnetic scream of the matter it sucked out of the universe. It even had its own accretion disc, Futurity saw, a small puddle of light around that central spark.

And this city-sized sun had its own planet. "Greyworld," Mara breathed. "I never thought I'd see it again."

This asteroid, having survived its fall into Chandra's accretion disc, had been plucked out of the garbage by the Ideocrats and moved to a safe orbit around the satellite black hole. The hole was tiny in size but its mass was no less than a star's; this worldlet orbited its primary at about the same distance as Earth orbited its sun. And Greyworld lived up to its name, Futurity saw, for its surface was a seamless silver-grey, smooth and unblemished.

To Mara, it seemed, this was home. "We live under the roof," Mara said. "It is held up from the surface by stilts—"

"Low gravity," Poole said. "Lets you get away with a lot. We used to call this paraterraforming. Turning your world into one immense building."

"The roof is perfectly reflective," Mara said. "We tap the free energy of the Galaxy center to survive, but none of it reaches our homes untamed."

"I should think not," Poole said warmly.

"It is a beautiful place," Mara said, smiling. "We build our houses tall; some of them float, or hang from the roof. And you feel safe, safe from the violence of the galactic storms outside. You should see it sometime, Michael Poole."

Poole raised his eyebrows. "But, Mara, your 'safe' haven is about as unsafe as it could get, despite the magical roof."

"He's right," said Tahget. "This black hole and its orbital retinue are well on their way toward Chandra. After another decade or so the tides will pull the planetoid free of the hole, and after that they will rip off that fancy roof. Then the whole mess will fall into the event horizon, crushed to mush in the process."

"Which is why Greyworld had to be evacuated," Futurity said.

"The Kard is known for her humanitarian impulses," Tahget said dryly. "The political convenience of it was sheer chance. So she explained to those she shipped out of their homes."

Poole said, "All right, Mara, what now? Do you want to be taken down to Greyworld?"

"Oh, no," she said. "What would be the point of that?" She seemed faintly irritated. "I told you, Michael Poole. My Sharn isn't on Greyworld. She's *there*." And she pointed to the glimmering black hole.

Tahget and his crew exchanged significant glances.

Futurity felt a flickering premonition, the return of fear. This journey into the heart of the Galaxy had been so wondrous that he had managed, for a while, to forget the danger they were all in. But it had all been a diversion. This woman, after all, controlled a bomb, and now they approached the moment of crisis.

Poole drew him aside. "You look worried, acolyte," he murmured.

"I *am* worried. Mara is still asking for the impossible. What do we do now?"

Poole seemed much calmer than Futurity felt. "I have a philosophy. If you don't know what to do, gather more data. How do you *know* that what she wants is impossible?" He turned to Tahget. "Captain, how close can you take us to the satellite black hole?"

Tahget shook his head. "It's a waste of time."

"But you don't have any better suggestion, do you? Let's go take a look. What else can we do?"

Tahget grumbled, but complied.

So the ship lifted away from Greyworld, and its retinue of greenships formed up once more. Mara smiled, as if she was coming home at last. But Futurity shivered, for there was nothing remotely human about the place they were heading to now.

———

Slowly the spiteful light of the satellite black hole drew closer.

"Acolyte," Poole murmured. "You have a data desk?"

"Yes—"

"Then start making observations. Study that black hole, Futurity. Figure out what's going on here. This is your chance to do some real science, for once."

"But I'm not a scientist."

"No, you're not, are you? You're too compromised for that. But you told me you were curious, once. That was what drove you out of the farm and into the arms of the Ecclesia in the first place." He sighed. "You know, in my day a kid like you would have had better opportunities."

Futurity felt moved to defend his vocation. "I don't think you understand the richness of theological—"

"Just get the damn desk!"

Futurity hurried to his cabin and returned with his data desk. It was the Ecclesia's most up-to-date model. He pressed the desk to the observation lounge blister, and checked it over as data poured in.

"I feel excited," he said.

"You should," Poole said. "You might make some original discovery here. And, more important, you might figure out how to save all our skins, my Virtual hide included."

"I'm excited but worried," Futurity admitted.

"*That* sounds like you."

"Michael Poole, how can a human child survive in a black hole?"

Poole glanced at him approvingly. "Good; that's the right question to ask. You need to cultivate an open mind, acolyte. Let's assume Mara's serious, that she knows what she's talking about—"

"That she's not crazy."

"Open mind! Mara has implied—I think—that we're not talking about the child in her physical form but some kind of download, like a Virtual."

Futurity asked, "But what information can be stored in a black hole? A hole is defined only by its mass, charge, and spin. You need rather more than three numbers to define a Virtual. But no human science knows a way to store more data than that in a black hole—though it is believed others may have done so in the past."

Poole eyed him. "*Others*? . . ." He slapped his own cheek. "Never mind. Concentrate, Poole. Then let's look away from the hole itself, the relativistic object. We're looking for structure, somewhere you can write information. Every black hole is embedded in the wider universe, and every one of them comes with baggage. This satellite hole has its own accretion disc. Maybe there . . ."

But Futurity's scans of the disc revealed nothing. "Michael Poole, it's basically a turbulence spectrum. Oh, there is some correlation of structure around a circumference, and over time tied into the orbital period around the black hole."

"But that's just gravity, the inverse square law, defined by one number: the black hole's mass. All right, what else have we got?" Inexpertly Poole tapped at Futurity's desk. He magnified an image of the hole itself. It was a flaring pinprick, even under heavy magnification. But Poole played with filters until he had reduced the central glare, and had brought up details of the background sky.

A textured glow appeared. A rough sphere of pearly gas surrounded the black hole and much of its accretion disc, and within the sphere a flattened ellipsoid of brighter mist coalesced closer to the hole.

"Well, well," said Poole.

Futurity, entranced, leaned closer to see. "I never knew black holes had atmospheres! Look, Michael Poole, it is almost like an eye staring at us—see, with the white, and then this iris within, and the black hole itself the pupil."

Tahget listened to this contemptuously. "Evidently neither of you have been around black holes much." He pointed to the image of the accretion disc. "The hole's magnetic field pulls material out of the disc, and hurls it into these wider shells. We call the outer layers the corona."

Futurity said, "A star's outer atmosphere is also a corona."

"Well done," said Tahget dryly. "The gas shells around black holes and stars are created by similar processes. Same physics, same name."

Poole said, "And the magnetic field pumps energy into these layers. Futurity, look at this temperature profile!"

"Yes," said Tahget. "In the accretion disc you might get temperatures in the millions of degrees. In the inner corona"—the eye's "iris"—"the temperatures will be ten times hotter than that, and in the outer layers ten times hotter again."

"But the magnetic field of a spinning black hole and its accretion disc isn't simple," Poole said. "It won't be just energy that the field pumps in, but complexity." He was becoming more expert with the data desk now. He picked out a section of the inner corona, and zoomed in. "What do you make of that, Futurity?"

The acolyte saw wisps of light, ropes of denser material in the turbulent gases, intertwined, slowly writhing. They were like ghosts, driven by the complex magnetic fields, and yet, Futurity immediately thought, they had a certain autonomy. Ghosts, dancing in the atmosphere of a black hole! He laughed with helpless delight.

Poole grinned. "I think we just found our structure."

Mara was smiling. "I told you," she said.

It took a detailed examination of the structures in the black hole air, a cross-examination of Mara, input from the experienced Captain Tahget, and some assiduous searching of the ship's data stores— together with some extremely creative interpolation by Michael Poole—before they had a tentative hypothesis to fit the facts about what had happened here.

Like so much else, it had come out of the death of the Coalition of Interim Governance.

Poole said, "Breed, fight hard, die young, and stay human: you could sum up the Coalition's philosophy in those few words. In its social engineering the Coalition set up a positive feedback process; it unleashed a swarm of fast-breeding humans across the Galaxy, until every star system had been filled." Poole grinned. "Not a noble way to do it, but it worked. And we did stay human, for twenty thousand years. Evolution postponed!"

"It wasn't as simple as that," Futurity cautioned. "Perhaps it couldn't have been. The Shipbuilders slid through the cracks. There were even rumors of divergences among the soldiers of the front lines, as they adapted to the pressures of millennia of war."

"Sure." Poole waved a hand. "But these are exceptions. You can't deny the basic fact that the Coalition *froze human evolution*, for the vast bulk of mankind, on epic scales of space and time. And by doing so, they won their war. Which was when the trouble really started."

The heirs of the Coalition were if anything even more fanatical about their ideology and purpose than their predecessors had ever been. They had called themselves the Ideocracy, precisely to emphasize the supremacy of the ideas that had won a Galaxy, but of which everybody else had temporarily lost sight.

In their conclaves the Ideocrats sought a new strategy. When the old threat had been vanquished, nobody needed the Coalition anymore. Perhaps, the Ideocrats dreamed cynically, a conjuring-up of *future* threats might be enough to frighten a scattered humanity back into the fold, where they would be once more under a single command—under the Ideocrats' command—just as in the good old days. Whether those potential threats ever came to pass or not was academic! The cause was the thing, noble in itself.

The Ideocrats' attention focused on Chandra, center of the Galaxy and ultimate symbol of the war. The great black hole had been used as a military resource by the foe of mankind. It was beyond human capability to manipulate a supermassive black hole that way—but perhaps, at least, its reoccupation in the future could be prevented. Eventually a way was found that might achieve this. "But," Poole said, "they had to break their own rules . . ."

Far from resisting human evolution, the Ideocrats ordered that deliberate modifications of mankind be made: that specifically designed post-humans be engineered to be injected into new environments. "In this case," Poole said, "the tenuous atmosphere of a black hole."

"It's impossible," said Captain Tahget, bluntly disbelieving. "There's no way a human could live off wisps of superheated plasma, however you modified her."

"Not a human, but a *post*-human," Michael Poole said testily. "Have you never heard of pantropy, Captain? This is your age, not mine! Evolution is in your hands now; it has been for millennia. You don't have to think small: a few tweaks to the bone structure here, a bigger forebrain there. You can go much further than that."

Virtual Poole himself was an example, he said. *He* was not human. But he was defined by a pattern of information that was equivalent to everything essential about a human.

Poole said, "A standard human's data definition is realized in flesh and blood, in structures of carbon-water biochemistry. *I* am realized in patterns in computer cores, and in shapings of light. You could project an equivalent human definition into any medium that will store the data—any technological medium, alternate chemistries of silicon or sulphur, anything you like from the frothing of quarks in a proton to the gravitational ripples of the universe itself. And then your post-humans, established in the new medium, can get on and breed." He saw their faces, and he laughed. "I'm shocking you! How delicious. Two thousand years after the Coalition imploded, its doctrines still have a hold on the human imagination."

"Get to the point, Virtual," Tahget snapped.

"The point is," Mara put in, "there are people in the black hole air. Out there. Those ghostly shapes you see are *people*. They really are."

"It's certainly possible," Poole said. "There's more than enough structure in those wisps of magnetism and plasma to store the necessary data."

Futurity said, "But what would be the point? What would be the function of these post-humans?"

"Weapons," Poole said simply.

Even when Greyworld was ripped away and destroyed by Chandra's tides, the satellite black hole would sail on, laden with its accretion disc and its atmosphere—and carrying the plasma ghosts that lived in that atmosphere, surviving where no normal human could. Perhaps the ghosts could ride the satellite hole all the way into Chandra itself, and perhaps, as the small hole was gobbled up by the voracious central monster, they would be able to transfer to Chandra's much more extensive atmosphere.

"Once aliens infested Chandra," Poole said. "It took us three thousand years to get them out. So the Ideocrats decided they were going to seed Chandra with humans—or at least post-humans. Then Chandra will be ours forever."

Captain Tahget shook his head, grumbling about ranting theorists and rewritings of history.

Futurity thought all this was a wonderful story, whether or not it was true. But he couldn't forget there was still a bomb on board. Cautiously, he said to Mara, "And one of these—uh, post-humans—is your daughter?"

"Yes," Mara said.

Tahget was increasingly impatient with all this. "But, woman! Can't you see that even supposing this antiquated Virtual is right about pantropy and post-humans, whatever *might* have been projected into the black hole atmosphere can no more be your daughter than Poole here can be your son? You are carbon and water, *it* is a filmy wisp of plasma. Whatever sentimental ties you have, the light show in that cloud has nothing to do with you—"

"Not sentimental," she said clearly. "The ties are real, Captain. *The person they sent into that black hole is my daughter.* It's all to do with loyalty, you see."

The Ideocrats, comparative masters when it came to dominating their fellow humans, had no experience in dealing with post-humans. They had no idea how to enforce discipline and loyalty over creatures to whom "real" humans might seem as alien as a fly to a fish. So they took precautions. Each candidate pantropic was born as a fully biological human, from a mother's womb, and each spent her first fifteen years living a normal a life—*normal*, given she had been born on a tent-world in orbit around a black hole.

"Then, on her sixteenth birthday, Sharn was taken," Mara said. "And she was copied."

"Like making a Virtual," Poole mused. "The copying must have been a quantum process. And the data was injected into the plasma structures in the black hole atmosphere." He grinned. "You can't fault the Ideocrats for not thinking big! And that's why there are people here in the first place—I mean, a colony with families—so that these wretched exiles have a grounding in humanity, and will stay loyal. Ingenious."

"It sounds horribly manipulative," said Futurity.

Mara said, "We knew it was going to happen, from the day Sharn was born. We knew it would be hard. But we knew our duty. Anyhow we weren't really losing her. We would always have her, up there in the sky."

"I don't understand," groused the captain. "After your daughter was 'copied,' why didn't she just walk out of the copying booth?"

"Because quantum information can't be cloned, Captain," Poole said gently. "If you make a copy you have to destroy the original. Which is why young Futurity's superiors were so agitated when I was transferred into this ship's data store: there is only ever one copy of *me*. Sharn could never have walked out of that booth. She had been destroyed in the process."

Futurity gazed out at the wispy black hole air. "Then—if this is all true—somewhere in those wisps is your daughter. The *only* copy of your daughter."

"Yes," said Mara. "Her essence. Her self."

Poole said, "In a deep philosophical sense, that's true. It really is her daughter, rendered in light."

Futurity said, "Can she speak to you?"

"It was never allowed," Mara said wistfully. "Only to the commanders, on secure channels. I found that hard. I don't even know how she *feels*. Is she in pain? What does it feel like to *be* her now?"

"How sad," Poole said. "You have your duty—to colonize a new world, the strange air of the black hole. But *you* can't go there; instead

you have to lose your children to it. You are transitional, belonging neither to your ancestors' world or your children's. You are stranded
between worlds."

That seemed to be too much for Mara. She sniffed, and pulled herself upright. "It was a military operation, you know. We all accepted it.
I told you, we had our duty. And we were promised that we would be
allowed communication, sometime in the future, when—"

"When somebody dies," Poole said brutally.

"But then the Kard's ships came along," Mara said bitterly. "They
just swept us up and took us away, and we weren't even allowed *that*.
We didn't even get to say goodbye."

Tahget glared. "Which is why you hijacked my ship and dragged
us all to the center of the Galaxy!"

She smiled weakly. "I'm sorry about that."

Futurity held his hands up. "I think what we need now is to find an
exit strategy."

Poole grinned. "At last you're talking like an engineer, not a priest."

Futurity said, "Mara, we've brought you here as we promised. You
can *see* your daughter, I guess. What now? If we take you to the planetoid, would you be able to talk to her?"

"Not likely," Mara said. "The Kardish troops were stealing the old
Ideocracy gear even before we lifted off. I think they thought the whole
project was somehow unhealthy."

"Yes," said Poole. "I can imagine they will use this as a propagan-
da tool in their battle with the Ideocracy—"

"Pah," spat Tahget. "Never mind politics! What the acolyte is asking, madam, is whether you will now relinquish your bomb, so we can
all get on with our lives."

Mara looked up at the black hole, hesitating. "I don't want to be
any trouble."

Tahget laughed bitterly.

"I just wish I could speak to Sharn."

"If we can't manage that, maybe we can send a message," said
Michael Poole. He grinned, snapped his fingers, and disappeared.

And reappeared in his skinsuit, out in space, on the other side of
the blister.

Captain Tahget raged. "How do you *do* that? After your last stunt I ordered your core processors to be locked down!"

"Don't blame your crew, Captain," came Poole's muffled voice. "I hacked my way back in. After all, nobody knows *me* as well as I do. And I was once an engineer."

Tahget clenched his fists uselessly. "Damn you, Poole, I ought to shut you down for good."

"Too late for that," Poole said cheerfully.

Futurity said, "Michael Poole, what are you going to do?"

Mara was the first to see it. "He's going to follow Sharn. He's going to download himself into the black hole air."

Futurity stared at Poole. "Is she right?"

"I'm going to try. Of course I'm making this up as I'm going along. My procedure is untested; it's all or nothing."

Tahget snorted. "You're probably an even bigger fool than when you were alive, Poole."

"Oh?"

"All this is surmise. Even if it was the Ideocracy's intention to seed the black hole with post-humans, we have no proof it worked. There may be nothing alive in those thin gases. And even if there is, it may no longer be human! Have you thought of that?"

"Yes," Poole said. "Of course I have. But I always did like long odds. Quite an adventure, eh?"

Futurity couldn't help but grin at his reckless optimism. But he stepped up to the window. "Michael Poole, please—"

"What's wrong, acolyte? Are you concerned about what your Hierocrat is going to do to you when you go home without his intellectual property?"

"Well, yes. But I'm also concerned for you, Michael Poole."

Poole did a double take. "You are, aren't you? I'm touched, Futurity's Dream. I like you too, and I think you have a great future ahead of you—*if* you can clear the theological fog out of your head. You could change the world! I'd like to stick around to see that happen. But it ain't worth going back into cold storage for."

Mara said, her voice breaking, "If you find Sharn, tell her I love her."

"I will. And who knows? Perhaps we will find a way to get back in touch with you, someday. Don't give up hope. I never do."

"I won't."

"Just to be absolutely clear," said Captain Tahget heavily. "Mara, will this be enough for you to get rid of that damn bomb?"

"Oh, yes," said Mara. "I always did trust Michael Poole."

"And she won't face any charges," Poole said. "Will she, Captain?"

Tahget looked at the ceiling. "As long as I get that bomb off my ship—and as long as somebody *pays* me for this jaunt—she can walk free."

"Then my work here is done," said Poole, mock-seriously. He turned and faced the black hole.

"You're hesitating," Futurity said.

"Wouldn't you? I wonder what the life expectancy of a sentient structure in there is . . . Well, I've got a century before the black hole hits Chandra, and maybe there'll be a way to survive that.

"I hope I live! It would be fun seeing what comes next, in this human Galaxy. For sure it won't be like what went before. You know, it's a dangerous precedent, this deliberate speciation: after an age of unity, will we now live through an era of bifurcation, as mankind purposefully splits and splits again?" He turned back to Futurity and grinned. "And this is my own adventure, isn't it, acolyte? Something the original Poole never shared. He'd probably be appalled, knowing him. I'm the black sheep! What was that about *more real*?"

"That's the theory," Futurity said.

Mara said, "I will be with you at timelike infinity, Michael Poole, when this burden will pass."

Poole glanced at Futurity. That was a standard Wignerian prayer. Poole said gently, "Yes. I'll see you there, Mara. Who knows?" He nodded to Futurity. "Goodbye, engineer. Remember—open mind."

"Open mind," Futurity said softly.

Poole turned, leapt away from the ship, and vanished in a shimmering of pixels.

After that, Futurity spent long hours studying the evanescent patterns in the air of the black hole. He tried to convince himself he could see more structure: new textures, a deeper richness. Perhaps Michael Poole really was in there, with Sharn. Or perhaps Michael Poole had already gone on to his next destination, or the next after that. It was impossible to tell.

He gave up, turned to his data desk, and began to work out how he was going to explain all this to the Hierocrat.

With the Shipbuilders swarming through their corridors and access tubes, the ship lifted out of the accretion disc of Chandra, and sailed for Base 478, and then for Earth.

THE WRECK OF THE GODSPEED

~~~~~~~~~

by James Patrick Kelly

James Patrick Kelly has had an eclectic writing career: novels, short stories, essays, reviews, poetry, plays, and even planetarium shows. His books include Planet of Whispers *(1984),* Wildlife *(1990),* Think Like a Dinosaur and Other Stories *(1997),* Strange But Not a Stranger *(2002), and many others. He has won the Hugo Award twice, in 1996 for his novelette "Think Like a Dinosaur," and in 2000 for his novelette "10^{16} to 1." Kelly's fiction has been translated into sixteen languages, and he is a member of the board of directors of the New England Foundation for the Arts. He makes his home in New Hampshire.*

This lively, inventive story, when read in conjunction with the Nancy Kress novella that follows it, could provide somebody in the academic world with a nifty Compare and Contrast essay on the scope and reach of modern science fiction—two utterly different takes, independently conceived, on a fundamentally similar theme.

DAY ONE

What do we know about Adel Ranger Santos?

That he was 65 percent oxygen, 19 percent carbon, 10 percent hydrogen, 3 percent nitrogen, 2 percent calcium, 1 percent phosphorus, some potassium, sulfur, sodium, chlorine, magnesium, iodine, and iron and just a trace of chromium, cobalt, copper, fluorine, manganese, molybdenum, selenium, tin, vanadium, and zinc. That he was of the domain *Eukarya*, the kingdom of *Animalia*, the phylum *Chordata*, subphylum *Vertebrata*, the class *Mammalia*, the order *Primates*, the family *Hominidae*, the genus *Homo*, and the species *Novo*. That, like the overwhelming majority of the sixty trillion people on the worlds of Human Continuum, he was a hybrid cybernetic/biological system composed of intricate subsystems including the circulatory, digestive, endocrine, excretory, informational, integumentary, musculo-skeletal, nervous, psycho-spiritual, reproductive, and respiratory. That he was the third son of Venetta Patience Santos, an Elector of the Host of True Flesh, and Halbert Constant Santos, a baker of fine breads. That he was male, left-handed, somewhat introverted, intelligent but no genius, a professed but frustrated heterosexual, an Aries, a virgin, a delibertarian, an agnostic, and a swimmer. That he was nineteen Earth standard years old and that until he stumbled, naked, out of the molecular assembler onto the *Godspeed* he had never left his home world.

The woman caught Adel before he sprawled headlong off the transport stage. "Slow down." She was taller and wider than any of the women he'd known; he felt like a toy in her arms. "You made it, you're here." She straightened him and stepped back to get a look. "Is there a message?"

—*a message?*—buzzed Adel's plus.

minus buzzed—*yes give us clothes*—

Normally Adel kept his opposites under control. But he'd just been scanned, transmitted at superluminal speeds some 257 light-years, and reassembled on a threshold bound for the center of the Milky Way.

"Did they say anything?" The woman's face was tight. "Back home?"

Adel shook his head; he had no idea what she was talking about. He hadn't yet found his voice, but it was understandable if he was a little jumbled. His skin felt a size too small and he shivered in the cool air. This was probably the most important moment of his life and all he could think was that his balls had shrunk to the size of raisins.

"You're not . . . ? All right then." She covered her disappointment so quickly that Adel wondered if he'd seen it at all. "Well, let's get some clothes on you, Rocky."

minus buzzed—*who's Rocky?*—

"What, didn't your tongue make the jump with the rest of you?" She was wearing green scrubs and green open-toed shoes. An oval medallion on a silver chain hung around her neck; at its center a pix displayed a man eating soup. "Can you understand me?" Her mouth stretched excessively, as if she intended that he read her lips. "I'm afraid I don't speak carrot, or whatever passes for language on your world." She was carrying a blue robe folded over her arm.

"Harvest," said Adel. "I came from Harvest."

"He talks," said the woman. "Now can he walk? And what will it take to get him to say his name?"

"I'm Adel Santos."

"Good." She tossed the robe at him and it slithered around his shoulders and wrapped him in its soft embrace. "If you have a name then I don't have to throw you back." Two slippers unfolded from its pockets and snugged onto his feet. She began to speak with a nervous intensity that made Adel dizzy. "So, Adel, my name is Kamilah, which means 'the perfect one' in Arabic which is a dead language you've probably never heard of and I'm here to give you the official welcome to your pilgrimage aboard the *Godspeed* and to show you around but we have to get done before dinner which tonight is synthetic roasted garab . . ."

—*something is bothering her*—buzzed minus—*it must be us*—

". . . which is either a bird or a tuber, I forget which exactly but it comes from the cuisine of Ohara which is a world in the Zeta 1 Reticuli system which you've probably never heard of . . ."

—*probably just a talker*—plus buzzed.

". . . because I certainly never have." Kamilah wore her hair kinked close against her head; it was the color of rust. She was cute, thought Adel, in a massive sort of way. "Do you understand?"

"Perfectly," he said. "You did say you were perfect."

"So you listen?" A grin flitted across her face. "Are you going to surprise me, Adel Santos?"

"I'll try," he said. "But first I need a bathroom."

There were twenty-eight bathrooms on the *Godspeed*; twenty of them opened off the lavish bedrooms of Dream Street. A level below was the Ophiuchi Dining Hall, decorated in red alabaster, marble, and gilded bronze, which could seat as many as forty around its teak banquet table. In the more modest Chillingsworth Breakfasting Room, reproductions of four refectory tables with oak benches could accommodate more intimate groups. Between the Blue and the Dagger Salons was the Music Room with smokewood lockers filled with the noblest instruments from all the worlds of the Continuum, most of which could play themselves. Below that was a library with the complete range of inputs from brainleads to books made of actual plant material, a ballroom decorated in the Nomura III style, a VR dome with ten animated seats, a gymnasium with a lap pool, a black box theater, a billiard room, a conservatory with five different ecosystems and various stairways, hallways, closets, cubbies, and peculiar dead ends. The MASTA, the molecular array scanner/transmitter/assembler, was located in the Well Met Arena, an enormous airlock and staging area that opened onto the surface of the threshold. Here also was the cognizor in which the mind of the *Godspeed* seethed.

It would be far too convenient to call the *Godspeed* mad. Better to say that for some time she had been behaving like no other threshold. Most of our pioneering starships were built in hollowed out nickel-iron asteroids—a few were set into fabricated shells. All were propelled by matter-antimatter drives that could reach speeds of just under a hundred thousand kilometers per second, about a third of the speed of light. We began to launch them from the far frontiers of the Continuum a millennium ago to search for terrestrial planets that were either habitable or might profitably be made so. Our thresholds can scan planetary systems of promising stars as far away as twenty light-years. When one discovers a suitably terrestrial world, it decelerates and swings into orbit. News of the find is immediately dispatched at superluminal speed to all the worlds of the Continuum; almost immediately materials and technicians appear on the transport stage. Over the course of several years we build a new orbital station containing a second MASTA, establishing a permanent link to the Continuum. Once the link is secured, the threshold continues on its voyage of discovery. In all, the *Godspeed* had founded thirty-seven colonies in exactly this way.

The life of a threshold follows a pattern: decades of monotonous acceleration, cruising, and deceleration punctuated by a few years of intense and glorious activity. Establishing a colony is an ultimate affirmation of human culture and even the cool intelligences generated by the cognizors of our thresholds share in the camaraderie of techs and colonists. Thresholds take justifiable pride in their accomplishments; many have had worlds named for them. However, when the time comes to move on, we expect our thresholds to dampen their enthusiasms and abort their nascent emotions to steel themselves against the tedium of crawling between distant stars at three-tenths the speed of light.

Which all of them did—except for the *Godspeed*.

As they were climbing up the Tulip Stairway to the Dream Halls, Adel and Kamilah came upon two men making their way down, bound together at the waist by a tether. The tether was about a meter long and two centimeters in diameter; it appeared to be elastic. One side of it pulsed bright red and the other was a darker burgundy. The men were wearing baggy pants and gray jackets with tall, buttoned collars that made them look like birds.

"Adel," said Kamilah, "meet Jonman and Robman."

Jonman looked like he could have been Robman's father, but Adel knew better than to draw any conclusions from that. On some worlds, he knew, physiological camouflage was common practice.

Jonman gazed right through Adel. "I can see that he knows nothing about the problem." He seemed detached, as if he were playing chess in his head.

Kamilah gave him a sharp glance but said nothing. Robman stepped forward and extended his forefinger in greeting. Adel gave it a polite touch.

"This is our rookie, then?" said Robman. "Do you play tikra, Adel?"

—*who's a rookie?*—buzzed minus.

—*we are*—

Since Adel didn't know what tikra was, he assumed that he didn't play it. "Not really," he said.

"He's from one of the farm worlds," said Kamilah.

"Oh, a rustic." Robman cocked his head to one side, as if Adel might make sense to him if viewed from a different angle. "Do they have gulpers where you come from? Cows?" Seeing the blank look on Adel's face, he pressed on. "Maybe frell?"

"Blue frell, yes."

—*keep talking*—plus buzzed—*make an impression*—

Adel lunged into conversation. "My uncle Durwin makes summer sausage from frell loin. He built his own smokehouse."

Robman frowned.

"It's very good." Adel had no idea where he was going with this bit of family history. "The sausages, I mean. He's a butcher."

—*and we're an idiot*—

"He's from one of the farm worlds," said Jonman, as if he were catching up with their chitchat on a time delay.

"Yes," said Robman. "He makes sausages."

Jonman nodded as if this explained everything about Adel. "Then don't be late for dinner," he advised. "I see there will be garab tonight." With this, the two men continued downstairs.

Adel glanced at Kamilah, hoping she might offer some insight into Robman and Jonman. Her eyes were hooded. "I wouldn't play anything with them if I were you," she murmured. "Jonman has a stochastic implant. Not only does he calculate probabilities, but he cheats."

The top of the Tulip Stairway ended at the midpoint of Dream Street. "Does everything have a name here?" asked Adel.

"Pretty much," said Kamilah. "It tells you something about how bored the early crews must have been. We're going right." The ceiling of Dream Street glowed with a warm light that washed Kamilah's face with pink. She said the names of bedroom suites as they passed the closed doors. "This is Fluxus. The Doghouse. We have room for twenty pilgrims, twice that if we want to double up."

The carpet was a sapphire plush that clutched at Adel's sandals as he shuffled down the hall.

"Chrome over there. That's where Upwood lived. He's gone now. You don't know anything about him, do you?" Her voice was suddenly tight. "Upwood Marcene?"

"No, should I? Is he famous?"

"Not famous, no." The medallion around her neck showed a frozen lake. "He jumped home last week, which leaves us with only seven, now that you're here." She cleared her throat and the odd moment of tension passed. "This is Corazon. Forty Pushups. We haven't found a terrestrial in ages, so Speedy isn't as popular as she used to be."

"You call the threshold Speedy?"

"You'll see." Kamilah sighed. "And this is Cella. We might as well see if Sister is receiving." She pressed her hand to the door and said, "Kamilah here." She waited.

"What do you want, Kamilah?" said the door, a solid blue slab that featured neither latch nor knob.

"I have the new arrival here."

"It's inconvenient." The door sighed. "But I'm coming." It vanished and before them stood a tiny creature, barely up to Adel's waist. She was wearing a hat that looked like a bird's nest made of black ribbon with a smoky veil that covered her eyes. Her mouth was thin and severe. All he could see of her almond skin was the dimpled chin and her long elegant neck; the billowing sleeves of her loose black dress swallowed her hands.

"Adel Santos, this is Lihong Rain. She prefers to be called Sister." Sister might have been a child or she might have been a grandmother. Adel couldn't tell.

"Safe passage, Adel." She made no other welcoming gesture.

Adel hesitated, wondering if he should try to initiate contact. But what kind? Offer to touch fingers? Shake hands? Maybe he should catch her up in his arms and dance a two-step.

"Same to you, Sister," he said and bowed.

"I was praying just now." He could feel her gaze even though he couldn't see it. "Are you religious, Brother Adel?" The hair on the back of his neck stood up.

"I'd prefer to be just Adel, if you don't mind," he said. "And no, I'm not particularly religious, I'm afraid."

She sagged, as if he had just piled more weight on her frail shoulders. "Then I will pray for you. If you will excuse me." She stepped back into her room and the blue door reformed.

plus buzzed—*we were rude to her*—

—*we told the truth*—

"Don't worry," said Kamilah. "You can't offend her. Or rather, you can't *not* offend her, since just about everything we do seems to offend her. Which is why she spends almost all her time in her room. She claims she's praying, although Speedy only knows for sure. So I'm in Delhi here, and next door you're in The Ranch."

—*Kamilah's next door?*—buzzed minus.

—*we hardly know her don't even think it*—

—*too late*—

They stopped in front of the door to his room, which was identical to Sister's, except it was green. "Press your right hand to it anywhere, say your name, and it will ID you." After Adel followed these instructions, the door considered for a moment and then vanished with a hiss.

Adel guessed that the room was supposed to remind him of home. It didn't exactly, because he'd lived with his parents in a high-rise in Great Randall, only two kilometers from Harvest's first MASTA. But it was like houses he had visited out in the countryside. Uncle Durwin's, for example. Or the Pariseaus'. The floor appeared to be of some blondish tongue-and-grooved wood. Two of the walls were set to show a golden tallgrass prairie with a herd of chocolate-colored beasts grazing in the distance. Opposite a rolltop desk were three wooden chairs with velvet upholstered seats gathered around a low oval table. A real plant with leaves like green hearts guarded the twin doorways that opened into the bedroom and the bathroom.

Adel's bed was king-sized with a half-moon head and footboards tied to posts that looked like tree trunks with the bark stripped off. It had a salmon-colored bedspread with twining rope pattern. However, we should point out that Adel did not notice anything at all about his bed until much later.

—*oh no*—

"Hello," said Adel.

—*oh yes*—

"Hello yourself, lovely boy." The woman was propped on a nest of pillows. She was wearing a smile and shift spun from fog. It wisped across her slim, almost boyish, body, concealing very little. Her eyes were wide and the color of honey. Her hair was spiked in silver.

Kamilah spoke from behind him. "Speedy, he just stepped off the damn stage ten minutes ago. He's not thinking of fucking."

"He's a nineteen-year-old male, which means he can't think of anything but fucking." She had a wet, whispery voice, like waves washing against pebbles. "Maybe he doesn't like girls. I like being female, but I certainly don't have to be." Her torso flowed beneath the fog and her legs thickened.

"Actually, I do," said Adel. "Like girls, I mean."

"Then forget Speedy." Kamilah crossed the room to the bed and stuck her hand through the shape on the bed. It was all fog, and Kamilah's hand parted it. "This is just a fetch that Speedy projects when she feels like bothering us in person."

"I have to keep my friends company," said the *Godspeed*.

"You can keep him company later." Kamilah swiped both hands through the fetch and she disappeared. "Right now he's going to put some clothes on and then we're going to find Meri and Jarek," she said.

"Wait," said Adel. "What did you do to her? Where did she go?"

"She's still here," Kamilah said. "She's always everywhere, Adel. You'll get used to it."

"But what did she want?"

The wall to his right shimmered and became a mirror image of the bedroom. The *Godspeed* was back in her nest on his bed. "To give you a preview of coming attractions, lovely boy."

Kamilah grasped Adel by the shoulders, turned him away from the wall, and aimed him at the closet. "Get changed," she said. "I'll be in the sitting room."

Hanging in the closet were three identical peach-colored uniforms with blue piping at the seams. The tight pantaloons had straps that would pass under the instep of his feet. The dress-blue blouse had the all-too-familiar pulsing heart patch over the left breast. The jacket had a double row of enormous silver zippers and bore two merit pins which proclaimed Adel a true believer of the Host of True Flesh.

Except that he wasn't.

Adel had long since given up on his mother's little religion but had never found a way to tell her. Seeing his uniforms filled him with guilt and dread. He'd come 257 light-years and he had still not escaped her. He'd expected she would pack the specs for True Flesh uniforms in his luggage transmission, but he'd thought she'd send him at least some civilian clothes as well.

—we have to lose the clown suit—

"So how long are you here for?" called Kamilah from the next room.

"A year," replied Adel. "With a second year at my option." Then he whispered, "Speedy, can you hear me?"

"Always. Never doubt it." Her voice came from the tall blue frel-leather boots that were part of his uniform. "Are we going to have secrets from Kamilah? I love secrets."

"I need something to wear," he whispered. "Anything but this."

"A year with an option?" Kamilah called. "Gods, Adel! Who did you murder?"

"Are we talking practical?" said the *Godspeed*. "Manly? Artistic? Rebellious?"

He stooped and spoke directly into the left boot. "Something basic," he said. "Scrubs like Kamilah's will be fine for now."

Two blobs extruded from the closet wall and formed into drab pants and a shirt.

"Adel?" called Kamilah. "Are you all right?"

"I didn't murder anyone." He stripped off the robe and pulled briefs from a drawer. At least the saniwear wasn't official True Flesh. "I wrote an essay."

Softwalks bloomed from the floor. "The hair on your legs, lovely boy, is like the wire that sings in my walls." The *Godspeed*'s voice was a purr.

The closet seemed very small then. As soon as he'd shimmied into his pants, Adel grabbed the shirt and the softwalks and escaped. He didn't bother with socks.

"So how did you get here, Kamilah?" He paused in the bedroom to pull on the shirt before entering the sitting room.

"I was sent here as a condition of my parole."

"Really?" Adel sat on one of the chairs and snapped on his soft-walks. "Who did you murder?"

"I was convicted of improper appropriation," she said. "I misused a symbol set that was alien to my cultural background."

*—say again?—*buzzed minus.

Adel nodded and smiled. "I have no idea what that means."

"That's all right." Her medallion showed a fist. "It's a long story for another time."

We pause here to reflect on the variety of religious beliefs in the Human Continuum. In ancient times, atheists believed that humanity's expansion into space would extinguish its historic susceptibility to superstition. And for a time, as we rode primitive torches to our cramped habitats and attempted to terraform the mostly inhospitable worlds of our home system, this expectation seemed reasonable. But then the discovery of quantum scanning and the perfection of molecular assembly led to the building of the first MASTA systems and everything changed.

Quantum scanning is, after all, destructive. Depending on exactly what has been placed on the stage, that which is scanned is reduced to mere probabilistic wisps, an exhausted scent or perhaps just soot to be wiped off the sensors. In order to jump from one MASTA to another, we must be prepared to die. Of course, we're only dead for a few seconds, which is the time it takes for the assembler to reconstitute us from a scan. Nevertheless, the widespread acceptance of MASTA transportation means that all of us who had come to thresholds have died and been reborn.

The experience of transitory death has led *homo novo* to a renewed engagement with the spiritual. But if the atheists were disappointed in their predictions of the demise of religion, the creeds of antiquity were decimated by the new realities of superluminal culture. Ten thousand new religions have risen up on the many worlds of the Continuum to comfort and sustain us in our various needs. We worship stars, sex, the vacuum of space, water, the cosmic microwave background, the Uncertainty Principle, music, old trees, cats, the weather, dead bodies, certain pharaohs of the Middle Kingdom, food, stimulants, depressants, and Levia Calla. We call the deity by many names: Genius, the Bitch, Kindly One, the Trickster, the Alien, the Thumb, Sagittarius A*, the Silence, Surprise, and the Eternal Center. What is striking about this exuberant diversity, when we consider how much blood has been shed in the name of gods, is our universal tolerance of one another. But that's because all of us who acknowledge the divine are co-religionists in one crucial regard: we affirm that the true path to spirituality must necessarily pass across the stages of a MASTA.

Which is another reason why we build thresholds and launch them to spread the Continuum. Which is why so many of our religions count it as an essential pilgrimage to travel with a threshold on some fraction of its long journey. Which is why the Host of True Flesh on the planet Harvest sponsored an essay contest open to any communicant who had not yet died to go superluminal, the first prize being an all-expense-paid pilgrimage to the *Godspeed*, the oldest, most distant, and therefore holiest of all the thresholds. Which is why Venetta Patience Santos had browbeaten her son Adel to enter the contest.

Adel's reasons for writing his essay had been his own. He had no great faith in the Host and no burning zeal to make a pilgrimage. However he chafed under the rules his parents still imposed on him, and he'd just broken up with his girlfriend Gavrila over the issue of premarital intercourse—he being in favor, she taking a decidedly contrary position—and he'd heard steamy rumors of what passed for acceptable sexual behavior on a threshold at the farthest edge of civilization. Essay contestants were charged to express the meaning of the Host of True Flesh in five hundred words or less. Adel brought his in at four hundred and nine.

Our Place
By Adel Ranger Santos

We live in a place. This seems obvious, maybe, but think about it. Originally our place was a little valley on the African continent on a planet called Earth. Who we are today was shaped in large part by the way that place was, so long ago. Later humans moved all around that planet and found new places to live. Some were hot, some freezing. We lived at the top of mountains and on endless prairies. We sailed to islands. We walked across deserts and glaciers. But what mattered was that the places that we moved to did not change us. We changed the places. We wore clothes and started fires and built houses. We made every place we went to our place.

Later we left Earth, our home planet, just like we left that valley in Africa. We tried to make places for ourselves in cold space, in habitats, and on asteroids. It was hard. Mars broke our hearts. Venus killed millions. Some people said that the time had come to change ourselves completely so that we could live in these difficult places. People had already begun to meddle with their bodies. It was a time of great danger.

This was when Genius, the goddess of True Flesh, awoke for the first time. Nobody knew it then, but looking back we can see that it must have been her. Genius knew that the only way we could stay true to our flesh was to find better places to make our own. Genius visited Levia Calla and taught her to collapse the wave-particle duality so that we could look deep into ourselves and see who we are. Soon we were on our way to the stars. Then Genius told the people to rise up against anyone who wanted to tamper with their bodies. She made the people realize that we were not meant to become machines. That we should be grateful to be alive for the normal a hundred and twenty years and not try to live longer.

I sometimes wonder what would have happened if we were not alone in space. Maybe if there were really aliens out there somewhere, we would never have had Genius to help us, since there would be no one true flesh. We would probably have all different gods. Maybe we would have changed ourselves, maybe into robots or to look like aliens. This is a scary thought. If it were true, we'd be in another universe. But we're not.

This universe is our place.

What immediately stood out in this essay is how Adel attributed Levia Calla's historic breakthrough to the intervention of Genius. Nobody had ever thought to suggest this before, since Professor Calla had been one of those atheists who had been convinced that religion would wither away over the course of the twenty-first century. The judges were impressed that Adel had so cleverly asserted what could never be disproved. Even more striking was the dangerous speculation that concluded Adel's essay. Ever since Fermi first expressed his paradox, we have struggled with the apparent absence of other civilizations in the universe. Many of the terrestrial worlds we have discovered have complex ecologies, but on none has intelligence evolved. Even now, there are those who desperately recalculate the factors in the Drake Equation in the hopes of arriving at a solution that is greater than one. When Adel made the point that no religion could survive first contact, and then trumped it with the irrefutable fact that we are alone, he won his place on the *Godspeed*.

Adel and Kamilah came upon two more pilgrims in the library. A man and a woman cuddled on a lime-green chenille couch in front of a wall that displayed images of six planets, lined up in a row. The library was crowded with glassed-in shelves filled with old-fashioned paper books, and racks with various I/O devices, spex, digitex, whisperers, and brainleads. Next to a row of workstations, a long table held an array of artifacts that Adel did not immediately recognize: small sculptures, medals and coins, jewelry, and carved wood. Two paintings hung above it, one an image of an artist's studio in which a man in a black hat painted a woman in a blue dress, the other a still life with fruit and some small, dead animals.

"Meri," said Kamilah, "Jarek, this is Adel."

The two pilgrims came to the edge of the couch, their faces alight with anticipation. Out of the corner of his eye, Adel thought he saw Kamilah shake her head. The brightness dimmed and they receded as if nothing had happened.

*—we're a disappointment to everyone—*buzzed minus.

plus buzzed—*they just don't know us yet—*

Meri looked to be not much older than Adel. She was wearing what might have been long saniwear, only it glowed, registering a thermal map of her body in red, yellow, green, and blue. "Adel." She gave him a wistful smile and extended a finger for him to touch.

Jarek held up a hand to indicate that he was otherwise occupied. He was wearing a sleeveless gray shirt, baggy shorts, and blacked-out spex on which Adel could see a data-scrawl flicker.

"You'll usually find these two together," said Kamilah. "And often in bed."

"At least we're not joined at the hip like the Manmans," said Meri. "Have you met them yet?"

Adel frowned. "You mean Robman?"

"And Spaceman." Meri had a third eye tattooed in the middle of her forehead. At least, Adel hoped it was a tattoo.

*—sexy—*buzzed minus.

plus buzzed—*weird—*

—weird is sexy—

"Oh, Jonman's not so bad." Jarek pulled his spex off.

"If you like snobs." Meri reminded him a little of Gavrila, except for the extra eye. "And cheats."

Jarek replaced the spex on the rack and then clapped Adel on the back. "Welcome to the zoo, brother." He was a head shorter than Adel and had the compact musculature of someone who was born on a high G planet. "So you're in shape," he said. "Do you lift?"

"Some. Not much. I'm a swimmer." Adel had been the Great Randall city champion in the 100 and 200 meter.

"What's your event?"

"Middle-distance freestyle."

—friend?—

"We have a lap pool in the gym," said Jarek.

*—maybe—*minus buzzed.

"Saw it." Adel nodded approvingly. "And you? I can tell you work out."

"I wrestle," said Jarek. "Or I did back on Kindred. But I'm a gym rat. I need exercise to clear my mind. So what do you think of old Speedy so far?"

"It's great." For the first time since he had stepped onto the scanning stage in Great Randall, the reality of where he was struck him. "I'm really excited to be here." And as he said it, he realized that it was true.

"That'll wear off," said Kamilah. "Now if you two sports are done comparing large muscle groups, can we move along?"

"What's the rush, Kamilah?" Meri shifted into a corner of the couch. "Planning on keeping this one for yourself?" She patted the seat, indicating that Adel should take Jarek's place. "Come here, let me get an eye on you."

Adel glanced at Jarek, who winked.

"Has Kamilah been filling you in on all the gossip?"

Adel crammed himself against the side cushion of the couch opposite Meri. "Not really."

"That's because no one tells her the good stuff."

Kamilah yawned. "Maybe because I'm not interested."

Adel couldn't look at Meri's face for long without staring at her tattoo, but if he looked away from her face then his gaze drifted to her hot spots. Finally he decided to focus on her hands.

"I don't work out," said Meri, "in case you're wondering."

"Is this the survey that wrapped yesterday?" said Kamilah, turning away from them to look at the planets displayed on the wall.

"I heard it was shit."

Meri had long and slender fingers but her fingernails were bitten ragged, especially the thumbs. Her skin was very pale. He guessed that she must have spent a lot of time indoors, wherever she came from.

"System ONR 147-563." Jarek joined her, partially blocking Adel's view of the wall. "Nine point eight nine light-years away and a whole lot of nothing. The star has luminosity almost three times that of Sol. Six planets: four hot airless rocks, a jovian and a subjovian."

"I'm still wondering about ONR 134-843," said Kamilah, and the wall filled with a new solar system, most of which Adel couldn't see. "Those five Martian-type planets."

"So?" said Meri. "The star was a K1 orange-red dwarf. Which means those Martians are pretty damn cold. The day max is only 17°C on the warmest and at night it drops to –210°C. And their atmospheres are way too thin, not one over a hundred millibars. That's practically space."

"But there are five of them." Kamilah held up her right hand, fingers splayed. "Count them, five."

"Five Martians aren't worth one terrestrial," said Jarek.

Kamilah grunted. "Have we seen any terrestrials?"

"Space is huge and we're slow." Jarek bumped against her like a friendly dog. "Besides, what do you care? One of these days you'll bust off this rock, get the hero's parade on Jaxon, and spend the rest of your life annoying the other eyejacks and getting your face on the news."

"Sure." Kamilah slouched uncomfortably. "One of these days."

—*eyejack?*—buzzed minus.

Adel was wondering the same thing. "What's an eyejack?"

"An eyejack," said Meri confidentially, "is someone who shocks other people."

"Shocks for pay," corrected Kamilah, her back still to them.

"Shock?" Adel frowned. "As in voltage shock or scandalize shock?"

"Well, electricity could be involved." Kamilah turned from the wall. Her medallion showed a cat sitting in a sunny window. "But mostly what I do," she continued, "is make people squirm when they get too settled for their own good."

—*trouble*—buzzed plus.

—*love it*—minus buzzed.

"And you do this how?"

"Movement." She made a flourish with her left hand that started as a slap but ended as a caress that did not quite touch Jarek's face. Jarek did not flinch. "Imagery. I work in visuals mostly but I sometimes use wordplay. Or sound—laughter, explosions, loud music. Whatever it takes to make you look."

"And people pay you for this?"

"Some do, some sue." Kamilah rattled it off like a catchphrase.

"It's an acquired taste," Meri said. "I know I'm still working on it."

"You liked it the time she made Jonman snort juice out of his nose," said Jarek. "Especially after he predicted she would do it to him."

The wall behind them turned announcement blue. "We have come within survey range of a new binary system. I'm naming the M5 star ONR 126-850 and the M2 star ONR 154-436." The screen showed data sheets on the discoveries: *Location, Luminosity, Metallicity, Mass, Age, Temperature, Habitable Ecosphere Radius.*

"Who cares about red dwarfs?" said Kamilah.

"About 60 percent of the stars in this sector are red dwarfs," said Meri.

"My point exactly." Said Kamilah, "You're not going to find many terrestrials orbiting an M star. We should be looking somewhere else."

"Why is that?" said Adel.

"M class are small cool stars," said Jarek. "In order to get enough insolation to be even remotely habitable, a planet has to be really close to the sun, so close that they get locked into synchronous rotation because of the intense tidal torque. Which means that one side is always dark and the other is always light. The atmosphere would freeze off the dark side."

"And these stars are known for the frequency and intensity of their flares," said Meri, "which would pretty much cook any life on a planet that close."

"Meri and Jarek are our resident science twizes," said Kamilah. "They can tell you more than you want to know about anything."

"So do we actually get to help decide where to go next?" said Adel.

"Actually, we don't." Jarek shook his head sadly.

"We just argue about it." Kamilah crossed the library to the bathroom and paused at the doorway. "It passes the time. Don't get any ideas about the boy, Meri. I'll be right back" The door vanished as she stepped through and reformed immediately.

"When I first started thinking seriously about making the pilgrimage to the *Godspeed*," said Jarek, "I had this foolish idea that I might have some influence on the search, maybe even be responsible for a course change. I knew I wouldn't be aboard long enough to make a planetfall, but I thought maybe I could help. But I've studied Speedy's search plan and it's perfect, considering that we can't go any faster than a third of C."

"Besides, *we're* not going anywhere, Jerek and you and me," said Meri. "Except back to where we came from. By the time Speedy finds the next terrestrial, we could be grandparents."

"Or dead," said Kamilah as she came out of the bathroom. "Shall we tell young Adel here how long it's been since Speedy discovered a terrestrial planet?"

"Young Adel?" said Meri. "Just how old are you?"

"Nineteen standard," Adel muttered.

—*twenty-six back home*—buzzed plus.

"But that's twenty-six on Harvest."

"One hundred and fifty-eight standard," said the wall. "This is your captain speaking."

"Oh gods." Kamilah rested her forehead in her hand.

The image the *Godspeed* projected was more uniform than woman; she stood against the dazzle of a star field. Her coat was golden broadcloth lined in red; it hung to her knees. The sleeves were turned back to show the lining. Double rows of brass buttons ran from neck to hem. These were unbuttoned below the waist, revealing red breeches and golden hose. The white sash over her left shoulder was decorated with patches representing all the terrestrial planets she had discovered. Adel counted more than thirty before he lost track.

"I departed from the MASTA on Nuevo Sueño," said the *Godspeed*, "158 years ago, Adel, and I've been looking for my next discovery ever since."

"Longer than any other threshold," said Kamilah.

"Longer than any other threshold," the *Godspeed* said amiably. "Which pains me deeply, I must say. Why do you bring this unfortunate statistic up, perfect one? Is there some conclusion you care to draw?"

She glared at the wall. "Only that we have wasted a century and a half in this desolate corner of the galaxy."

"We, Kamilah?" The *Godspeed* gave her an amused smile. "How long have you been with me?"

"Not quite a year." She folded her arms.

"Ah, the impatience of flesh." The *Godspeed* turned to the stars behind her. "You have traveled not quite a third of a light-year since your arrival. Consider that I've traveled 50.12 light-years since my departure from Nuevo Sueño. Now see what that looks like to me." She thrust her hands above her head and suddenly the points of light on the wall streamed into ribbons and the center of the screen jerked up-right-left-down-left with each course correction and then the ribbons became stars again. She faced the library again, her face glowing. "You have just come 15.33 parsecs in ten seconds. If I follow my instructions to reach my journey's end at the center of our galaxy I will have traveled 8.5 kiloparsecs."

—*if?*—buzzed minus.

"Believe me, Kamilah, I can imagine your experience of space-time more easily than you can imagine mine." She tugged her sash into place and then pointed at Kamilah. "You're going to mope now."

Kamilah shook her head. Her medallion had gone completely black.

"A hundred and thirty-three people have jumped to me since Nuevo Sueño. How many times do you think I've had this conversation, Kamilah?"

Kamilah bit her lip.

"Ah, if only these walls could talk." The *Godspeed*'s laugh sounded like someone dropping silver spoons. "The things they have seen."

—*is she all right?*—buzzed plus.

"Here's something I'll bet you didn't know," said the *Godspeed*. "A fun fact. Now that Adel has replaced Upwood among our little company, everyone on board is under thirty."

The four of them digested this information in astonished silence.

"Wait a minute," said Meri. "What about Jonman?"

"He would like you to believe he's older but he's the same age as Kamilah." She reached into the pocket of her greatcoat and pulled out a scrap of digitex. A new window opened on the wall; it contained the birth certificate of Jon Haught Shillaber. "Twenty-eight standard."

"All of us?" said Jarek. "That's an pretty amazing coincidence."

"A coincidence?" She waved the birth certificate away. "You don't know how hard I schemed to arrange it." She chuckled. "I was practically diabolical."

"Speedy," said Meri carefully, "you're starting to worry us."

"Worry?"

"Worry," said Jarek.

"Why, because I make jokes? Because I have a flair for the dramatic?" She bowed low and gave them an elaborate hand flourish. "I am but mad north-northwest: when the wind is southerly I know a hawk from a handsaw."

minus buzzed—*time to be afraid*—

"So," said the *Godspeed*, "we seem to be having a morale problem. I know *my* feelings have been hurt. I think we need to come together, work on some common project. Build ourselves back into a team." She directed her gaze at Adel. "What do you say?"

"Sure."

"Then I suggest that we put on a play."

Meri moaned.

"Yes, that will do nicely." The *Godspeed* clapped her hands, clearly pleased at the prospect. We'll need to a pick a script. Adel, I understand you've had some acting experience so I'm going to appoint you and Lihong to serve on the selection committee with me. I think poor Sister needs to get out and about more."

"Don't let Lihong pick," said Meri glumly. "How many plays are there about praying?"

"Come now, Meri," said the *Godspeed*. "Give her a chance. I think you'll be surprised."

Day Five

There are two kinds of pilgrimage, as commonly defined. One is a journey to a specific, usually sacred place; it takes place and then ends. The other is less about a destination and more about a spiritual quest. When we decide to jump to a threshold, we most often begin our pilgrimages intending to get to the *Godspeed* or the *Big D* or the *Bisous Bisous,* stay for some length of time and then return to our ordinary lives. However, as time passes on board we inevitably come to realize—sometimes to our chagrin—that we have been infected with an irrepressible yearning to seek out the numinous, wherever and however it might be found.

Materialists don't have much use for the notion of a soul. They prefer to locate individuality in the mind, which emerges from the brain but cannot exist separately from it. They maintain that information must be communicated to the brain through the senses, and only through the senses. But materialists have yet to offer a rigorous explanation of what happens during those few seconds of a jump when the original has ceased to exist and the scan from it has yet to be reassembled. Because during the brief interval when there are neither senses nor brain nor mind, we all seem to receive some subtle clue about our place in the universe.

This is why there are so few materialists.

Adel had been having dreams. They were not bad dreams, merely disturbing. In one, he was lost in a forest where people grew instead of trees. He stumbled past shrubby little kids he'd gone to school with and great towering grown-ups like his parents and Uncle Durwin and President Adriana. He knew he had to keep walking because if he stopped he would grow roots and raise his arms up to the sun like all the other tree people, but he was tired, so very tired.

In another, he was standing backstage watching a play he'd never heard of before and Sister Lihong tapped him on the shoulder and told him that Gavrila had called in sick and that he would have to take her part and then she pushed him out of the wings and he was onstage in front of a sellout audience, every one of which was Speedy, and he stumbled across the stage to the bed where Jarek waited for him, naked Jarek, and then Adel realized that he was naked too, and he climbed under the covers because he was cold and embarrassed, and Jarek kept staring at him because he, Adel, was supposed to say his line but he didn't know the next line or any line and so he did the one thing he could think to do, which was to kiss Jarek, on the mouth, and then his tongue brushed the ridges of Jarek's teeth and all the Speedys in the audience gave him a standing ovation . . .

. . . which woke him up.

Adel blinked. He lay in bed between Meri and Jarek; both were still asleep. They were under a yellow sheet that had pink kites and blue clouds on it. Jarek's arm had dropped loosely across Adel's waist. In the dim light he could see that Meri's lips were parted and for a while he listened to the seashore whisper of her breathing. He remembered that something had changed last night between the three of them.

Something, but what?

Obviously his two lovers weren't losing any sleep over it. Speedy had begun to bring the lights up in Meri's room so it had to be close to morning chime. Adel lifted his head but couldn't see the clock without disturbing his bedmates, so he tried to guess the time. If the ceiling was set to gain twenty lumens a minute and Speedy started at 0600, then it was . . . he couldn't do the math. After six in the morning, anyway.

The something was Jarek—*yes*. Adel realized that he'd enjoyed having sex with Jarek just a bit more than with Meri. Not that he hadn't enjoyed her too. There had been plenty of enjoying going on, that was for sure. A thrilling night all around. But Adel could be rougher with Jarek than he was with Meri. He didn't have to hold anything back. Sex with Jarek was a little like wrestling, only with orgasms.

Adel had been extremely doubtful about sleeping with both Meri *and* Jarek, until Meri had made it plain that that was the only way he was ever going to get into her bed. The normal buzz of his opposites had risen to a scream; their deliberations had gotten so shrill that he'd been forced to mute their input. Not that he didn't know what they were thinking, of course; they were him.

Jarek had been the perfect gentleman at first; they had taken turns pleasuring Meri until the day before yesterday when she had guided Adel's hand to Jarek's erect cock. An awkward moment, but then Adel still felt like he was all thumbs and elbows when it came to sex anyway. Jarek talked continually while he made love, so Adel was never in doubt as to what Jarek wanted him to do. And because he trusted Jarek, Adel began to talk too. And then to moan, whimper, screech, and laugh out loud.

Adel felt extraordinarily adult, fucking both a man and a woman. He tried the word out in the gloom, mouthing it silently. I *fuck*, you *fuck*, he, she, or it *fucks*, we *fuck*, you all *fuck*, they *fuck*. The only thing that confused him about losing his virginity was not that his sexual identity was now slightly blurry; it was his raging appetite. Now that he knew what he had been missing, he wanted to have sex with everyone here on the *Godspeed* and then go back to Harvest and fuck his way through Great Randall Science and Agricultural College and up and down Crown Edge. Well, that wasn't quite true. He didn't particularly want to see the Manmans naked and the thought of sleeping with his parents made him queasy and now that he was an experienced lover, he couldn't see himself on top, underneath or sideways with his ex, Gavrila. But still. He'd been horny back on Harvest but now he felt like he might spin out of control. Was it perverted to want so much sex?

Adel was wondering what color Sister Lihong Rain's hair was and how it would look spread across his pillow when Kamilah spoke through the closed door.

"Send Adel out," she said, "but put some clothes on him first."

Adel's head jerked up. "How does she know I'm here?"

"Time is it?" said Meri.

"Don't know." Jarek moaned and gave him a knee in the small of the back. "But it's for you, brother, so you'd better get it."

He clambered over Meri and tumbled out of bed onto her loafers. Their clothes were strewn around the room. Adel pulled on his sani-wear, the taut silver warm-ups that Meri had created for him and his black softwalks. The black floss cape had been his own idea—a signature, like Kamilah's medallion or Sister's veil. The cape was modest, only the size of a face towel, and was attached to his shoulders by the two merit pins he'd recycled from his Host uniforms.

He paused in front of a wall, waved it to mirror mode, combed fingers through his hair and then stepped through the door. Kamilah leaned against the wall with her medallion in hand. She gazed into it thoughtfully.

"How did you find me?" said Adel.

"I asked Speedy." She let it fall to her chest and Adel saw the eating man again. Adel had noticed that her eating man had reappeared again and again, always at the same table. "You want breakfast?"

He was annoyed with her for rousting him out of bed before morning chime. "When I wake up." Who knew what erotic treats he might miss?

"Your eyes look open to me." She gave him a knowing smile. "Busy night?"

He considered telling her that it was none of her business, but decided to flirt instead. Maybe he'd get lucky. "Busy enough." He gave his shoulders a twitch, which made his cape flutter. "You?"

"I slept."

"I slept too." Adel waited a beat. "Eventually."

"Gods, Adel!" Kamilah laughed out loud. "You're a handful, you know that?" She put an arm around his shoulders and started walking him back up Dream Street. "Meri and Jarek had better watch out."

Adel wasn't quite sure what she meant but he decided to let it drop for now. "So what's this about?"

"A field trip." They started down the Tulip Stairway. "What do you know about physics?"

Adel had studied comparative entertainment at Great Randall S&A, although he'd left school in his third year to train for the Harvest Olympics and to find himself. Unfortunately, he'd finished only sixth in the 200 meters and Adel was still pretty much missing. Science in general and physics in particular had never been a strength. "I know some. Sort of."

"What's the first law of thermodynamics?"

"The first law of thermodynamics." He closed his eyes and tried to picture the screen. "Something like . . . um . . . a body stays in motion . . . ah . . . as long as it's in motion?"

"Oh great," she said wearily. "Have you ever been in space?"

For the first time in days he missed the familiar buzz of his opposites. He lifted their mute.

—she thinks we're a moron—buzzed minus.

—we are a moron—plus buzzed.

"Everybody's in space," he said defensively. "That's where all the planets are. We're traveling through space this very moment."

"This wasn't meant to be a trick question," she said gently. "I mean have you ever been in a hardsuit out in the vacuum?"

"Oh," he said. "No."

"You want to?"

—wow—

—yes—

He had to restrain himself from hugging her. "Absolutely."

"Okay then." She gestured at the entrance to the Chillingsworth Breakfasting Room. "Let's grab something to take away and head down to the locker room. We need to oxygenate for about half an hour."

*—but why is she doing this?—*buzzed plus.

There were two ways to the surface of the *Godspeed*: through the great bay doors of the Well Met Arena or out the Clarke Airlock. Adel straddled a bench in the pre-breathing locker room and wolfed down a sausage and honeynut torte while Kamilah explained what was about to happen.

"We have to spend another twenty minutes here breathing 100 percent oxygen to scrub nitrogen out of our bodies. Then just before we climb into the hardsuits, we put on isotherms." She opened a locker and removed two silky black garments. "You want to wait until the last minute; isotherms take some getting used to. But they keep the hard-suit from overheating." She tossed one to Adel.

"But how can that happen?" He held the isotherm up; it had a hood and opened with a slide down the torso. The sleeves ended at the elbow and the pants at the knee. "Isn't space just about as cold as anything gets?"

"Yes, but the hardsuit is airtight, which makes it hard to dissipate all the heat that you're going to be generating. Even though you get some servo-assist, it's a big rig, Adel. You've got to work to get any-where." She raised her steaming mug of kappa and winked at him. "Think you're man enough for the job?"

*—let that pass—*buzzed plus.

"I suppose we'll know soon enough." Adel rubbed the fabric of the isotherm between his thumb and forefinger. It was cool to the touch.

Kamilah sipped from the mug. "Once we're out on the surface," she said, "Speedy will be running all your systems. All you have to do is follow me."

The *Godspeed* displayed on a section of wall. She was wearing an isotherm with the hood down; it clung to her like a second skin. Adel could see the outline of her nipples and the subtle wrinkles her pubic hair made in the fabric.

*—but they're not real—*minus buzzed.

"What are you doing, Kamilah?" said the *Godspeed*. "You were out just last week."

"Adel hasn't seen the view."

"I can show him any view he wants. I can fill the Welcome Arena with stars. He can see in ultraviolet. Infrared."

"Yes, but it wouldn't be quite real, would it?"

"Reality is overrated." The *Godspeed* waggled a finger at Kamilah. "You're taking an unusual interest in young Adel. I'm watching, per-fect one."

"You're watching everyone, Speedy. That's how you get your cookies." With that she pulled the top of her scrubs off. "Time to get naked, Adel. Walk our hardsuits out and start the checklist, would you, Speedy?"

*—those are real—*buzzed minus.

—Meri and Jarek remember—

—we can look—

And Adel did look as he slithered out of his own clothes. Although he was discreet about it, he managed to burn indelible images into his memory of Kamilah undressing, the curve of her magnificent hip, the lush pendency of her breasts, the breathtaking expanse of her back as her tawny skin stretched tight over the nubs of her spine. She was a woman a man might drown in. Abruptly, he realized that he was becoming aroused. He turned away from her, tossed his clothes into a locker, snatched at the isotherm, and pulled it on.

And bit back a scream.

Although it was as silken as when Kamilah had pulled it out of the drawer, his isotherm felt like it had spent the last ten years in cryogenic storage. Adel's skin crawled beneath it and his hands curled into fists. As a swimmer, Adel had experienced some precipitous temperature changes, but he'd never dived into a pool filled with liquid hydrogen.

*—trying to kill us—*screeched minus.

"Are you all right?" said Kamilah. "Your eyes look like eggs."

"Ah," said Adel. "*Ah.*"

*—we can do this—*buzzed plus.

"Hang on," said Kamilah. "It passes."

As the hardsuits clumped around the corner of the locker room, their servos singing, Adel shivered and caught his breath. He thought he could hear every joint crack as he unclenched his fists and spread his fingers. When he pulled the isotherm hood over his head, he got the worst ice-cream headache he'd ever had.

"This is going to be fun," he said through clenched teeth.

The hardsuits were gleaming white eggs with four arms, two legs, and a tail. The arms on either side were flexrobotic and built for heavy lifting. Beside them were fabric sleeves into which a spacewalker could insert his arms for delicate work. The legs ended in ribbed plates, as did the snaking tail, which Kamilah explained could be used as a stabilizer or an anchor. A silver ball the size of coconut perched at the top of the suit.

"Just think of them as spaceships that walk," said Kamilah. "Okay, Speedy. Pop the tops."

The top, translucent third of each egg swung back. Kamilah muscled a stairway up to the closest hardsuit. "This one's yours. Settle in but don't try moving just yet."

Adel slid his legs into the suit's legs and cool gel flowed around them, locking him into place. He ducked instinctively as the top came down, but he had plenty of room. Seals fasten with a *scritch* and the heads-up display on the inside of the top began to glow with controls and diagnostics. Beneath the translucent top were fingerpads for controlling the robotic lifter arms; near them were the holes of the hardsuit's sleeves. Adel stuck his arms through, flexed his fingers in the gloves, then turned his attention back to the HUD. He saw that he had forty hours of oxygen reserve and his batteries were at 98 percent of capacity. The temperature in the airlock was 15.52°C and the air pressure was 689 millibars. Then the readouts faded and the *Godspeed* was studying him intently. She looked worried.

"Adel, what's going on?"

"Is something going on?"

"I'm afraid there is and I don't want you mixed up in it. What does Kamilah want with you?"

Adel felt a chill that had nothing to do with his isotherm.

—don't say anything—buzzed plus.

—we don't know anything—

"I don't know that she wants anything." He pulled his arms out of the hardsuit's sleeves and folded them across his chest. "I just thought she was being nice."

"All right, Adel," said Kamilah over the comm. "Take a stroll around the room. I want to see how you do in here where it's flat. Speedy will compensate if you have any trouble. I'm sure she's already in your ear."

The *Godspeed* held a forefinger to her lips. "Kamilah is going to ask you to turn off your comm. That's when you must be especially careful, Adel." With that, she faded away and Adel was staring, slackjawed, at the HUD.

"Adel?" said Kamilah. "Are you napping in there?"

Adel took a couple of tentative steps. Moving the hardsuit was a little like walking on stilts. He was high off the floor and couldn't really see or feel what was beneath his feet. When he twisted around, he caught sight of the tail whipping frantically behind him. But after walking for a few minutes, he decided that he could manage the suit. He lumbered behind Kamilah through the inner hatch of the airlock, which slid shut.

Adel listened to the muted chatter of pumps evacuating the lock until finally there wasn't enough air to carry sound. Moments later, the outer hatch opened.

"Ready?" Kamilah said. "Remember that we're leaving the artificial gravity field. No leaps or bounds—you don't watch to achieve escape velocity."

Adel nodded.

—she can't see us—buzzed minus—*we have to talk to her*—

Adel cleared his throat. "I've always wanted to see the stars from space."

"Actually, you won't have much of a view until later," she said. "Let's go."

As they passed through the hatch, the *Godspeed* announced, "Suit lights are on. I'm deploying fireflies."

Adel saw the silver ball lift from the top of Kamilah's suit and float directly above her. The bottom half of it was now incandescent, lighting the surface of the *Godspeed* against the swarming darkness. At the same time the ground around him lit up. He looked and saw his firefly hovering about a meter over the suit.

—amazing—buzzed plus—*we're out, we're out in space*—

They crossed the flat staging pad just outside the airlock and stepped off onto the regolith. The rock had been pounded to gray dust by centuries of foot traffic. Whenever he took a step the dust puffed underfoot and drifted slowly back to the ground like smoke. It was twenty centimeters deep in some places but offered little resistance to his footplates. Adel's excitement leached slowly away as Kamilah led him away from the airlock. He had to take mincing steps to keep from launching himself free of the *Godspeed's* tenuous gravitational pull. It was frustrating; he felt as if he were walking with a pillow between his legs. The sky was a huge disappointment as well. The fireflies washed out the light from all but the brightest stars. He'd seen better skies camping on Harvest.

"So where are we going?"

"Just around."

"How long will it take?"

"Not that long."

—*hiding something?*—buzzed plus.

—*definitely*—

"And what exactly are we going to do?"

"A little bit of everything. One of her robotic arms gave him a playful wave. "You'll see."

They marched in silence for a while. Adel began to chafe at following Kamilah's lead. He picked up his pace and drew alongside of her. The regolith here was not quite so trampled and much less regular, although a clearly defined trail showed that they were not the first to make this trek. They passed stones and rubble piles and boulders the size of houses and the occasional impact crater that the path circumnavigated.

—*impact crater?*—buzzed minus.

"Uh, Kamilah," he said. "How often does Speedy get hit by meteors?"

"Never," said Kamilah. "The craters you see are all pre-launch. Interstellar space is pretty much empty so it's not that much of a problem."

"I sweep the sky for incoming debris," said the *Godspeed*, "up to five million meters away."

"And that works?"

"So far," said Kamilah. "We wouldn't want to slam into anything traveling at a third the speed of light."

They walked on for another ten minutes before Kamilah stopped. "There." She pointed. "That's where we came from. Somewhere out there is home."

Adel squinted. *There* was pretty much meaningless. Was she pointing at some particular star or a space between stars?"

"This is the backside. If Speedy had a rear bumper," she said, "we'd be standing on it right here. I want to show you something interesting. Pull your arms out of the sleeves."

"Done."

"The comm toggle is under the right arm keypad. Switch it off."

The *Godspeed* broke into their conversation. "Kamilah and Adel, you are about to disable a key safety feature of your hardsuits. I strongly urge you to reconsider."

"I see the switch." Adel's throat was tight. "You know, Speedy warned me about this back in the airlock."

"I'm sure she did. We go through this every time."

"You've done this before?"

"Many times," she said. "It's a tradition we've started to bring the new arrival out here to see the sights. It's actually a spiritual thing, which is why Speedy doesn't really get it."

"I have to turn off the comm why?"

"Because she's watching, Adel," said Kamilah impatiently. "She's always with us. She can't help herself."

"Young Adel," murmured the *Godspeed*. "Remember what I said."

—*trust Kamilah*—

—*or trust Speedy*—

—*we were warned*—

Adel flicked the toggle. "Now what?" he said to himself. His voice sounded very small in the suit.

He was startled when Kamilah leaned her suit against his so that the tops of the eggs were touching. It was a strangely intimate maneuver, almost like a kiss. Her face was an electric green shadow in the glow of the HUD.

He was startled again when she spoke. "Turn. The. Comm. Off." He could hear her through the suit. She paused between each word, her voice reedy and metallic.

"I did," he said.

He could see her shake her head and tap fingers to her ears. "You. Have. To. Shout."

"I. Did!" Adel shouted.

"Good." She picked up a rock the size of a fist and held it at arm's length. "Drop. Rock." She paused. "Count. How. Long. To. Surface."

—*science experiments?*—buzzed plus.

—*she's gone crazy*—

Adel was inclined to agree with his minus but what Kamilah was asking seemed harmless enough.

"Ready?"

"Yes."

She let go. Adel counted.

One one thousand, two one thousand, three one thousand, four one thousand, five . . .

And it was down.

"Yes?" said Kamilah.

"Five."

"Good. Keep. Secret." She paused. "Comm. On."

As he flicked the switch he heard her saying, ". . . you feel it? My first time it was too subtle but if you concentrate, you'll get it."

"Are you all right, Adel?" murmured the *Godspeed.* "What just happened?"

"I don't know," said Adel, mystified.

"Well, we can try again on the frontside," said Kamilah. "Sometimes it's better there. Let's go."

*—what is she talking about?—*minus buzzed.

For twenty minutes he trudged in perplexed silence past big rocks, little rocks, and powdered rocks in all the colors of gray. In some places the surface of the trail was grainy like sand, in others it was dust, and in yet others it was bare ledge. Adel just didn't understand what he was supposed to have gotten from watching the rocks drop. Something to do with gravity? What he didn't know about gravity would fill a barn. Eventually he gave up trying to figure it out. Kamilah was right about one thing: it was real work walking in a hardsuit. If it hadn't been for the isotherm, he would have long since broken a sweat.

*—this is has to get better—*buzzed plus.

"How much longer?" said Adel at last.

"A while yet." Kamilah chuckled. "What are you, a little kid?"

"Remember the day I got here?" he said. "You told me that you were sentenced to spend time on Speedy. But you never said why."

"Not that interesting, really."

"Better than counting rocks." He stomped on a flat stone the size of his hand, breaking it into three pieces. "Or I suppose I could sing." He gave her the first few bars of "Do As We Don't" in his finest atonal yodel.

"Gods, Adel, but you're a pest today." Kamilah sighed. "All right, so there's a religion on Suncast . . ."

"Suncast? That's where you're from?"

"That's where I was from. If I ever get off this rock, that's the last place I'm going to stay."

—if?—buzzed minus—*why did she say if?*—

"Anyway, there's a sect that call themselves God's Own Poor. They're very proud of themselves for having deliberately chosen not to own very much. They spout these endless lectures about how living simply is the way to true spirituality. It's all over the worldnet. And they have this tradition that once a year they leave their houses and put their belongings into a cart, supposedly everything they own but not really. Each of them drags the cart to a park or a campground—this takes place in the warm weather, naturally—and they spend two weeks con- gratulating themselves on how poor they are and how God loves them especially."

"What god do they worship?"

"A few pray to Sagittarius A*, the black hole at the center of the galaxy, but most are some flavor of Eternal Centerers. When it was founded, the Poor might actually have been a legitimate religion. I mean, I see their point that owning too much can get in the way. Except that now almost all of them have houses and furniture and every kind of vehicle. None of them tries to fit the living-room couch on their carts. And you should see some of these carts. They cost more than I make in a year."

"From shocking people," Adel said. "As a professional eyejack."

The comm was silent for a moment. "Are you teasing me, young Adel?"

"No, no." Adel bit back his grin. "Not at all." Even though he knew she couldn't see it, she could apparently *hear* it inflected in his voice. "So you were annoyed at them?"

"I was. Lots of us were. It wasn't only that they were self-righteous hypocrites. I didn't like the way they commandeered the parks just when the rest of us wanted to use them. So I asked myself, how can I shock the Poor and what kind of purse can I make from doing it?"

A new trail diverged from the one they had been following;

Kamilah considered for a moment and then took it. She fell silent for a few moments.

Adel prompted her. "And you came up with a plan."

*—why are we interested in this?—*buzzed plus.

—because we want to get her into bed—

"I did. First I took out a loan; I had to put my house up as collateral. I split two hundred thousand barries across eight hundred cash cards, so each one was worth two hundred and fifty. Next I set up my tent at the annual Poverty Revival at Point Kingsley on the Prithee Sea, which you've never heard of but which is one of the most beautiful places in the Continuum. I passed as one of the Poor, mingling with about ten thousand true believers. I parked a wheelbarrow outside the tent that had nothing in it but a suitcase and a shovel. That got a megagram of disapproval, which told me I was onto something. Just before dawn on the tenth day of the encampment, I tossed the suitcase and shoveled in the eight hundred cash cards. I parked my wheelbarrow at the Tabernacle of the Center and waited with a spycam. I'd painted, 'God Helps Those Who Help Themselves' on the side; I thought that was a nice touch. I was there when people started to discover my little monetary miracle. I shot vids of several hundred of the Poor dipping their hot hands into the cards. Some of them just grabbed a handful and ran, but quite a few tried to sneak up on the wheelbarrow when nobody was looking. But of course, everyone was. The wheelbarrow was empty in about an hour and a half, but people kept coming to look all morning."

Adel was puzzled. "But your sign said they were supposed to help themselves," he said. "Why would they be ashamed?"

"Well, they were supposed to be celebrating their devotion to poverty, not padding their personal assets. But the vids were just documentation, they weren't the sting. Understand that the cards were *mine*. Yes, I authorized all expenditures, but I also collected detailed reports on everything they bought. Everything, as in possessions, Adel. Material goods. All kinds of stuff, and lots of it. I posted the complete record. For six days my web site was one of the most active on the worldnet. Then the local Law Exchange shut me down. Still, even after legal expenses and paying off the loan, I cleared almost three thousand barries."

*—brilliant—*buzzed minus.

*—she got caught—*plus buzzed.

"But this was against the law on Suncast?" said Adel.

"Actually, no." Kamilah kicked at a stone and sent it skittering across the regolith. She trudged on in silence for a few moments. "But I used a wheelbarrow," she said finally, "which LEX ruled was too much like one of their carts—a cultural symbol. According to LEX, I had committed Intolerant Speech. If I had just set the cards out in a basket, the Poor couldn't have touched me. But I didn't and they did. In the remedy phase of my trial, the Poor asked LEX to ship me here. I guess they thought I'd get religion."

"And did you?"

"You don't get to ask all the questions." The tail of her hardsuit darted and the footplate tapped the rear of Adel's suit. "Your turn. Tell me something interesting about yourself. Something that nobody knows."

He considered. "Well, I was a virgin when I got here."

"Something interesting, Adel."

"And I'm not anymore."

"That nobody knows," she said.

*—just trying to shock you—*buzzed plus.

*—bitch—*minus buzzed.

"All right," he said, at last. "I'm a delibertarian."

Kamilah paused, then turned completely around once, as if to get her bearings. "I don't know what that is."

"I have an implant that makes me hear voices. Sometimes they argue with each other."

"Oh?" Kamilah headed off the trail. "About what?"

Adel picked his way after her. "Mostly about what I should do." He sensed that he didn't really have her complete attention. "Say I'm coming out of church and I see a wheelbarrow filled with cash cards. One voice might tell me to grab as many as I can, the other says no."

"I'd get tired of that soon enough."

"Or say someone insults me, hurts my feelings. One voice wants to understand her and the other wants to kick her teeth in. But the thing is, the voices are all me."

"All right then," Kamilah paused, glanced left and then right as if lining up landmarks. "We're here."

*—too bad we can't kick her teeth in—*buzzed minus.

"Where's here?"

"This is the frontside, exactly opposite from where we just were. We should try shutting down again. This might be your lucky spot."

"I don't know if I want to," said Adel. "What am I doing here, Kamilah?"

"Look, Adel, I'm sorry," she said. "I didn't mean to hurt your feelings. I forget you're just a kid. Come over here, let me give you a hug."

"Oh." Adel was at once mollified by Kamilah's apology and stung that she thought of him as a kid.

*—we are a kid—*plus buzzed.

And what kind of hug was he going to get in a hardsuit?

—shut up—

"You're only nine standard older than I am," he said as he brought his suit within robotic arm's reach.

"I know." Her two arms snaked around him. "Turn off your comm, Adel."

This time the *Godspeed* made no objection. When the comm was off, Kamilah didn't bother to speak. She picked up a rock and held it out. Adel waved for her to drop it.

One one thousand, two one thousand, three one thousand, four one thousand, five one thousand six one thousand, seven one . . .

Seven? Adel was confused.

*—we messed up the count—*buzzed minus.

—did not—

He leaned into her and touched her top. "Seven."

"Yes." She paused. "Turn. Off. Lights."

Adel found the control and heard a soft clunk as the firefly docked with his hardsuit. He waved the suit lights off and blacked out the HUD, although he was not in a particularly spiritual mood. The blackness of space closed around them and the sky filled with the shyest of stars. Adel craned in the suit to see them all. Deep space was much more busy than he'd imagined. The stars were all different sizes and many burned in colors: blues, yellows, oranges, and reds—a lot more reds than he would have thought. There were dense patches and sparse patches and an elongated wispy cloud that stretched across his field of vision that he assumed was the rest of the Milky Way.

—amazing—

—but what's going on?—

"Questions?" said Kamilah.

"Questions?" he said under his breath. "Damn right I have questions." When he shouted, he could hear the anger in his voice. "Rocks. Mean. What?"

"Speedy. Slows. Down." She paused. "We. Don't. Know. Why." Another pause. "Act. Normal. More. Later."

—act normal?—

—we're fucked—

"Comm." He screamed. "On."

"Careful," she said. "Adel."

He felt a slithering against his suit as she let go of him. He bashed at the comm switch and brought the suit lights on.

". . . the most amazing experience, isn't it?" she was saying. "It's almost like you're standing naked in space."

"Kamilah . . ." He tried to speak but panic choked him.

"Adel, what's happening," said the *Godspeed*. "Are you all right?"

"I have to tell you," said Kamilah, "that first time I was actually a little scared but I'm used to it now. But you—you did just fine."

"Fine," Adel said. His heart was pounding so hard he thought it might burst his chest. "Just fine."

Day Twelve

Since the *Godspeed* left the orbit of Menander, fifth planet of Hallowell's Star, to begin its historic voyage of discovery, 69,384 of us stepped off her transport stage. Only about ten thousand of us were pilgrims, the rest were itinerant techs and prospective colonists. On average, the pilgrims spent a little over a standard year as passengers, while the sojourn of the colony-builders rarely exceeded sixty days. As it turns out, Sister Lihong Rain held the record for the longest pilgrimage; she stayed on the *Godspeed* for more than seven standards.

At launch, the cognizor in command of the *Godspeed* had been content with a nongendered persona. Not until the 113th year did it present as The Captain, a male authority figure. The Captain was a sandy-haired mesomorph, apparently a native of one of the highest G worlds. His original uniform was modest in comparison to later incarnations, gray and apparently seamless, with neither cuff nor collar. The Captain first appeared on the walls of the library but soon spread throughout the living quarters and then began to manifest as a fetch that could be projected anywhere, even onto the surface. The *Godspeed* mostly used The Captain to oversee shipboard routine but on occasion he would approach us in social contexts. Inevitably he would betray a disturbing knowledge of everything that we had ever done while aboard. We realized to our dismay that the *Godspeed* was always watching.

These awkward attempts at sociability were not well received; The Captain persona was gruff and humorless and all too often presumptuous. He was not at all pleased when one of us nicknamed him Speedy. Later iterations of the persona did little to improve his popularity.

It wasn't until the 332nd year that the stubborn Captain was supplanted by a female persona. The new Speedy impressed everyone. She didn't give orders; she made requests. She picked up on many of the social cues that her predecessor had missed, bowing out of conversations where she was not welcome, not only listening but hearing what we told her. She was accommodating and gregarious, if somewhat emotionally needy. She laughed easily, although her sense of humor was often disconcerting. She didn't mind at all that we called her Speedy. And she kept our secrets.

Only a very few saw the darker shades of the *Godspeed*'s persona. The techs found her eccentricities charming and the colonists celebrated her for being such a prodigious discoverer of terrestrials. Most pilgrims recalled their time aboard with bemused nostalgia.

Of course, the *Godspeed* had no choice but to keep all of us under constant surveillance. We were her charges. Her cargo. Over the course of 1,087 standards, she witnessed six homicides, eleven suicides and 249 deaths from accident, disease, and old age. She took each of these deaths personally, even as she rejoiced in the 268 babies conceived and born in the bedrooms of Dream Street. She presided over 2,018 marriages, 4,089 divorces. She witnessed 29,815,247 acts of sexual congress, not including masturbation. Since she was responsible for our physical and emotional well-being, she monitored what we ate, who we slept with, what drugs we used, how much exercise we got. She tried to defuse quarrels and mediate disputes. She readily ceded her authority to the project manager and team leaders during a colonizing stop but in interstellar space, she was in command.

Since there was little privacy inside the *Godspeed*, it was difficult for Kamilah, Adel, Jarek, Meri, Jonman, and Robman to discuss their situation. None of them had been able to lure Sister out for a suit-to-suit conference, so she was not in their confidence. Adel took a couple of showers with Meri and Jarek. They played crank jams at top volume and whispered in each other's ears as they pretended to make out, but that was awkward at best. They had no way to send or encrypt messages that the *Godspeed* couldn't easily hack. Jonman hit upon the strategy of writing steganographic poetry under blankets at night and then handing them around to be read—also under blankets.

We hear that love can't wait too long,
Go and find her home.
We fear that she who we seek
Must sleep all day, have dreams of night
killed by the fire up in the sky.
Would we? Does she?

Steganography, Adel learned from a whisperer in the library, was the ancient art of hiding messages within messages. When Robman gave him the key of picking out every fourth word of this poem, he read: *We can't go home she must have killed up would.* This puzzled him until he remembered that the last pilgrim to leave the *Godspeed* before he arrived was Upwood Marcene. Then he was chilled. The problem with Jonman's poems was that they had to be written mechanically—on a surface with an implement. None of the pilgrims had ever needed to master the skill of handwriting; their scrawls were all but indecipherable. And asking for the materials to write with aroused the *Godspeed*'s suspicions.

Not only that, but Jonman's poetry was awful.

Over several days, in bits and snatches, Adel was able to arrive at a rough understanding of their dilemma. Three months ago, while Adel was still writing his essay, Jarek had noticed that spacewalking on the surface of the *Godspeed* felt different from the way it had been when he first arrived. He thought his hardsuit might be defective until he tried several others. After that, he devised the test, and led the others out, one by one, to witness it. If the *Godspeed* had actually been traveling at a constant 100,000 kilometers per second, rocks dropped anywhere on the surface would take the same amount of time to fall. However, when she accelerated away from a newly established colony, rocks dropped on the backside took longer to fall than rocks on the frontside. And when she decelerated toward a new discovery . . .

Once they were sure that they were slowing down, the pilgrims had to decide what it meant and what to do next. They queried the library and, as far as they could tell, the *Godspeed* had announced every scan and course change she had ever made. In over a thousand years the only times she had ever decelerated was when she had targeted a new planet. There was no precedent for what was happening and her silence about it scared them. They waited, dissembled as best they could, and desperately hoped that someone back home would notice that something was wrong.

Weeks passed. A month. Two months.

Jonman maintained that there could be only two possible explanations: the *Godspeed* must either be falsifying its navigation reports or it had cut all contact with the Continuum. Either way, he argued, they must continue to wait. Upwood's pilgrimage was almost over; he was scheduled to go home in another two weeks. If the *Godspeed* let him make the jump, then their troubles were over. Hours, or at the most a day, after he reported the anomaly, techs would swarm the transport stage. If she didn't let him make the jump, then at least they would know where they stood. Nobody mentioned a third outcome, although Upwood clearly understood that there was a risk that the *Godspeed* might kill or twist him during transport and make it look like an accident. Flawed jumps were extremely rare but not impossible. Upwood had lost almost five kilos by the day he climbed onto the transport stage. His chest was a washboard of ribs and his eyes were sunken. The other pilgrims watched in hope and horror as he faded into wisps of probability and was gone.

Five days passed. On the sixth day, the *Godspeed* announced that they would be joined by a new pilgrim. A week after Upwood's departure, Adel Ranger Santos was assembled on the transport stage.

———

Sister was horribly miscast as Miranda. Adel thought she would have made a better Caliban, especially since he was Ferdinand. In the script, Miranda was supposed to fall madly in love with Ferdinand, but Sister was unable to summon even a smile for Adel, much less passion. He might as well have been an old sock as the love of her life.

Adel knew why the *Godspeed* had chosen *The Tempest*; she wanted to play Prospero. She'd cast Meri as Ariel and Kamilah as Caliban. Jonman and Robman were Trinculo and Stephano and along with Jarek also took the parts of the various other lesser lords and sons and brothers and sailors. Adel found it a very complicated play, even for Shakespeare.

"I am a fool," said Sister, "to weep when I am glad." She delivered the line like someone hitting the same note on a keyboard again and again.

Adel had a whisperer feeding him lines. "Why do you weep?"

"Stop there." The *Godspeed* waved her magic staff. She was directing the scene in costume. Prospero wore a full-length opalescent cape with fur trim, a black undertunic, and a small silver crown. "Nobody says 'weep' anymore." She had been rewriting the play ever since they started rehearsing. "Adel, have you ever said 'weep' in your life?"

"No," said Adel miserably. He was hungry and was certain he would starve to death before they got through this scene.

"Then neither should Ferdinand. Let's change 'weep' to 'cry.' Say the line, Ferdinand."

Adel said, "Why do you cry?"

"No." She shut her eyes. "No, that's not right either." Her brow wrinkled. "Try 'why are you crying?' "

"Why are you crying?" said Adel.

"Much better." She clapped hands once. "I know the script is a classic but after three thousand years some of these lines are dusty. Miranda, give me 'I am a fool' with the change."

"I am a fool," she said, "to cry when I am glad."

"Why are you crying?"

"Because I'm not worthy. I dare not even offer myself to you—much less ask you to love me." Here the *Godspeed* had directed her to put her arms on Adel's shoulders. "But the more I try to hide my feelings, the more they show."

As they gazed at each other, Adel thought he did see a glimmer of something in Sister's eyes. Probably nausea.

"So no more pretending." Sister knelt awkwardly and gazed up at him. "If you want to marry me, I'll be your wife." She lowered her head, but forgot again to cheat toward the house, so that she delivered the next line to the floor. "If not, I'll live as a virgin the rest of my life, in love with nobody but you."

"We can't hear you, Miranda," said the *Godspeed.*

Sister tilted her head to the side and finished the speech. "You don't even have to talk to me if you don't want. Makes no difference. I'll always be there for you."

"Ferdinand," the *Godspeed* murmured, "she's just made you the happiest man in the world."

Adel pulled her to her feet. "Darling, you make me feel so humble."

"So then you'll be my husband?"

"Sure," he said. "My heart is willing . . . ," he laid his hand against his chest, "and here's my hand." Adel extended his arm.

"And here's mine with my heart in it." She slid her fingers across his palm, her touch cool and feathery.

"And," prompted the *Godspeed.* "And?"

With a sigh, Sister turned her face up toward his. Her eyelids fluttered closed. Adel stooped over her. The first time he had played this scene, she had so clearly not wanted to be kissed that he had just brushed his lips against her thin frown. The *Godspeed* wanted more. Now he lifted her veil and pressed his mouth hard against hers. She did nothing to resist, although he could feel her shiver when he slipped the tip of his tongue between her lips.

"Line?" said the *Godspeed.*

"Well, got to go." Sister twitched out of his embrace. "See you in a bit."

"It will seem like forever." Adel bowed to her and then they both turned to get the *Godspeed's* reaction.

"Better," she said. "But Miranda, flow into his arms. He's going to be your husband, your dream come true."

"I know." Her voice was pained.

"Take your lunch break and send me Stephano and Trinculo." She waved them off. "Topic of the day is . . . what?" She glanced around the little theater, as if she might discover a clue in the empty house. "Today you are to talk about what you're going to do when you get home."

Adel could not help but notice Sister's stricken expression; her eyes were like wounds. But she nodded and made no objection.

As they passed down the aisle, the *Godspeed* brought her fetch downstage to deliver the speech that closed Act III, Scene 1. As always, she gave her lines a grandiloquent, singing quality.

"Those two really take the cake. My plan is working out just great, but I can't sit around patting myself on the back. I've got other fish to fry if I'm going to make this mess end happily ever after."

———

To help Adel and Sister get into character, the *Godspeed* had directed them to eat lunch together every day in the Chillingsworth Breakfasting Room while the other pilgrims dined in the Ophiuchi. They had passed their first meal in tortured silence and might as well have been on different floors of the threshold. When the *Godspeed* asked what they talked about, they sheepishly admitted that they had not spoken at all. She knew this, of course, but pretended to be so provoked that she assigned them topics for mandatory discussion.

The Chillingsworth was a more intimate space than the Ophiuchi. It was cross-shaped; in the three bays were refectory tables and benches. There was a tile fireplace in the fourth bay in which a fetch fire always burned. Sconces in the shapes of the famous singing flowers of Old Zara sprouted from pale blue walls.

Adel set his plate of spiralini in rado sauce on the heavy table and scraped a bench from underneath to sit on. While the pasta cooled he closed his eyes and lifted the mute on his opposites. He had learned back on Harvest that their buzz made acting impossible. They were confused when he was in character and tried to get him to do things that weren't in the script. When he opened his eyes again, Sister was opposite him, head bowed in prayer over a bowl of thrush needles.

He waited for her to finish. "You want to go first?" he said.

"I don't like to think about going home to Pio," she said. "I pray it won't happen anytime soon."

—*your prayers are answered*—buzzed minus.

"Why, was it bad?"

"No." She picked up her spoon but then set it down again. Over the past few days Adel had discovered that she was an extremely nervous eater. She barely touched what was on her plate. "I was happy." Somehow, Adel couldn't quite imagine what happy might look like on Sister Lihong Rain. "But I was much smaller then. When the Main told me I had to make a pilgrimage, I cried. But she has filled with her grace and made me large. Being with her here is the greatest blessing."

"Her? You are talking about Speedy?"

Sister gave him a pitying nod, as if the answer were as obvious as air. "And what about you, Adel?"

Adel had been so anxious since the spacewalk that he hadn't really considered what would happen if he were lucky enough to get off the *Godspeed* alive.

—*we were going to have a whole lot of sex remember?*—buzzed plus.

—*with as many people as possible*—

Adel wondered if Sister would ever consider sleeping with him. "I want to have lovers." He had felt a familiar stirring whenever he kissed her in rehearsal.

"Ah." She nodded. "And get married, like in our play?"

"Well that, sure. Eventually." He remembered lurid fantasies he'd spun about Helell Merwyn, the librarian from the Springs upper school, and his mother's friend Renata Murat and Lucia Guerra who was in that comedy about the talking house. Did he want to marry them?

—*no we just want a taste*—minus buzzed.

"I haven't had much experience. I was a virgin when I got here."

"Were you?" She frowned. "But something has happened, hasn't it? Something between you and Kamilah."

*—we wish—*buzzed plus.

"You think Kamilah and I . . . ?"

"Even though nobody tells me, I do notice things," Sister said. "I'm twenty-six standard old and I've taken courses at the Institute for Godly Fornication. I'm not naïve, Adel."

—fornication?—

"I'm sure you're not." Adel was glad to steer the conversation away from Kamilah, since he knew the *Godspeed* was watching. "So do you ever think about fornicating? I mean in a godly way, of course?"

"I used to think about nothing else." She scooped a spoonful of the needles and held it to her nose, letting the spicy steam curl into her nostrils. "That's why the Main sent me here."

"To fornicate?"

"To find a husband and bring him to nest on Pio." Her shoulders hunched, as if she expected someone to hit her from behind. "The Hard Thumb pressed the Main with a vision that I would find bliss on a threshold. I was your age when I got here, Adel. I was very much like you, obsessed with looking for my true love. I prayed to the Hard Thumb to mark him so that I would know him. But my prayers went unanswered."

As she sat there, staring into her soup, Adel thought that he had never seen a woman so uncomfortable.

*—get her back talking about fornication—*minus buzzed.

"Maybe you were praying for the wrong thing."

"That's very good, Adel." He was surprised when she reached across the table and patted his hand. "You understand me better than I did myself. About a year ago, when Speedy told me that I had been aboard longer than anyone else, I was devastated. But she consoled me. She said that she had heard my prayers over the years and had longed to answer them. I asked her if she were a god, that she could hear prayer?"

Sister fell silent, her eyes shining with the memory.

"So?" Adel was impressed. "What did she say?"

"Speedy is very old, Adel. Very wise. She has revealed mysteries to me that even the Main does not know."

—*she believes*—plus buzzed.

"So you worship her then? Speedy is your god?"

Her smile was thin, almost imperceptible, but it cracked her doleful mask. "Now you understand why I don't want to go home."

"But what about finding true love?"

"I have found it, Adel." Sister pushed her bowl away; she had eaten hardly anything. "No man, no *human* could bring me to where she has brought me."

—*could we maybe try?*—

—*she's not talking about that*—

"So you're never leaving then?" Adel carelessly speared the last spiralini on his plate. "She's going to keep you here for the rest of your life?"

"No." Her voice quavered. "No."

"Sister, are you all right?"

She was weeping. That was the only word for it. This was not mere crying; her chest heaved and tears ran down her cheeks. In the short time he had known her, Adel had often thought that she was on the brink of tears, but he hadn't imagined that her sadness would be so wracking.

"She says something's going to happen . . . soon, too soon and I-I have to leave but I . . ." A strangled moan escaped her lips.

Adel had no experience comforting a woman in pain but he nevertheless came around the table and tried to catch her in his arms.

She twisted free, scattering thrush needles across the table. "Get away." She shot off her bench and flung herself at the wall of the breakfasting room. "I don't want him. Do you hear?" She pounded at the wall with her fists until the sconce shook. "He's nothing to me."

The *Godspeed*'s head filled the wall, her face glowing with sympathy. "Adel,' she said. "You'd better leave us."

"I want you," Sister cried. "It's you I want!"

———

Day Fifteen

Adel sprawled on the camelback sofa and clutched a brocade toss pillow to his chest. He rested his head in the warmth of Meri's lap but, for the first time since they had met, he wasn't thinking of having sex with her. He was trying very hard to think of nothing at all as he gazed up at the clouds flitting across the ceiling of the Blue Salon.

Robman spun his coin at the tikra table. It sang through stacks of particolored blocks that represented the map of the competing biomes, bouncing off trees, whirling over snakes, clattering to a stop by the Verge.

"Take five, put two," said Robman. "I want birds."

"I'll give you flies," said Jonman.

"Digbees and bats?"

"Done."

Jonman spun his coin. "It's not just you, Adel," he said. "Speedy picked Robman and me and Jarek too. Sister didn't want us either."

"Why would she want you two?" said Adel. "You're yoked."

"Not always," said Meri. "Jonman was here a month before Robman."

"But I saw him coming," said Jonman. "Put ought, skip the take."

"She didn't disappear because of you," said Adel.

*—or you either—*buzzed minus.

"Or you either." Meri had been stroking his hair. Now she gave it a short tug. "This has nothing to do with you."

"I made her cry."

"No, *Speedy* did that." Meri spat the name, as if she were daring the *Godspeed* to display. She had not shown herself to them in almost three days.

Robman spun again.

"Speedy wouldn't let her go out of the airlock," said Meri. "Would she?"

"Without a suit?" Robman sipped Z-breeze from a tumbler as he watched his coin dance. "Never."

"Who knows what Speedy will do?" said Adel.

"They're wasting their time," said Jonman. "Sister isn't out there."

"Do you see that," Meri said "or is it just an opinion?"

"Take one, put one," said Robman.

"Which gets you exactly nothing," said Jonman. "I call a storm."

"Then I call a flood." Robman pushed three of his blocks toward

Jonman's side of the board. The tether connecting them quivered and Adel thought he could hear it gurgling faintly.

Jonman distributed the blocks around his biome. "What I see is that she's hiding someplace," he said. "I just don't see where."

Meri slid out from under Adel's head and stood. "And Speedy?" Adel put the pillow on the armrest of the sofa and his head on the pillow.

"She's here," said Jonman. "She's toying with us. That's what she does best."

"At least we don't have to practice her damn play," said Robman.

Adel wanted to wrap the pillow around his ears to blot out this conversation. One of their number had vanished, they were some fifty light-years from the nearest MASTA, and there was something very wrong with the cognizor in command of their threshold. Why weren't the others panicking like he was? "Rehearse," he said.

"What?"

"You don't practice a play. You rehearse it."

Meri told the wall to display the airlock but it was empty. "They must be back already."

"Have some more Z-breeze, Rob," said Jonman. "I can't feel anything yet."

"Here." He thrust the tumbler at Jonman. "Drink it yourself."

Jonman waved it off. "It's your day to eat, not mine."

"You just want to get me drunk so you can win."

"Nothing," said Kamilah, as she entered the salon with Jarek. "She's not out there."

"Thank the Kindly One," said Jarek.

Robman gave Jonman an approving nod. "You saw that."

"Is Speedy back yet?" said Kamilah.

"She hasn't shown herself." Meri had settled into a swivel chair and was turning back and forth nervously.

"Kamilah and I were talking on the way up here," said Jarek. He strode behind Meri's chair and put hands on her shoulders to steady her. "What if she jumped?"

"What if?" Meri leaned her head back to look up at him.

"Adel says she was hysterical," said Kamilah. "Let's say Speedy couldn't settle her down. She's a danger to herself, maybe to us. So Speedy has to send her home."

"Lose your mind and you go free?" Robman spun his coin. "Jon, what are we waiting for?"

"Speedy," said Kamilah. "Is that it? Talk to us, please."

They all looked. The wall showed only the empty airlock.

Adel hurled the pillow at it in a fury. "I can't take this anymore." He scrambled off the couch. "We're in trouble, people."

—be calm—

—tell it—

They were all staring at him but that was fine. The concern on their faces made him want to laugh. "Sister said something was going to happen. This is it." He began to pace around the salon, no longer able to contain the frenzied energy skittering along his nerves. "We have to do something."

"I don't see it," said Jonman.

"No, you wouldn't." Adel turned on him. "You always want to wait. Maybe that was a good idea when all this started, but things have changed."

"Adel," said Meri, "what do you think you're doing?"

"Look at yourselves," he said. "You're afraid that if you try to save yourselves, you'll be fucked. But you know what, people? We're already fucked. It makes no sense anymore to wait for someone to come rescue us."

Adel felt a hand clamp onto his shoulder and another under his buttock. Kamilah lifted him effortlessly. "Sit down." She threw him at the couch. "And shut up." He crashed into the back cushion headfirst, bounced, and tumbled onto the carpet.

Adel bit his tongue when he hit the couch; now he tasted blood. He rolled over, got to his hands and knees and then he did laugh. "Even you, Kamilah." He gazed up at her. She was breathing as if she had just set a record in the 200 meter freestyle. "Even you are perfectly scared." Her medallion spun wildly on its silver chain.

"Gods, Adel." She took a step toward him. "Don't."

Adel muted his opposites then; he knew exactly what he needed to do. "Speedy!" he called out. "We know that you're decelerating."

Meri shrieked in horror. Jonman came out of his chair so quickly that his tether knocked several of the blocks off the tikra board. Kamilah staggered and slumped against a ruby sideboard.

"Why, Adel?" said Jarek. "Why?"

"Because she knows we know." Adel picked himself up off the Berber carpet. "She can scan planets twenty light-years away and you don't think she can see us dropping rocks on her own surface?" He straightened his cape. "You've trapped yourselves in this lie better than she ever could."

"You do look, my son, as if something is bothering you." The *Godspeed*'s fetch stepped from behind the statue of Levia Calla. She was in costume as Prospero.

"What did . . . ?"

"Speedy we don't . . ."

"You have to . . ."

"Where is . . . ?"

The *Godspeed* made a grand flourish that ended with her arm raised high above her head. She ignored their frantic questions, holding this pose until they fell silent. Then she nodded and smiled gaily at her audience.

"Cheer up," she said, her voice swelling with bombast. "The party's almost over. Our actors were all spirits and have melted into air, into thin air. There was never anything here, no soaring towers or gorgeous palaces or solemn temples. This make-believe world is about to blow away like a cloud, leaving not even a wisp behind. We are the stuff that dreams are made of, and our little lives begin and end in sleep. You must excuse me, I'm feeling rather odd just now. My old brain is troubled. But don't worry. Tell you what, why don't you just wait here a few more minutes? I'm going to take a turn outside to settle myself."

The *Godspeed* paused expectantly as if waiting for applause. But the pilgrims were too astonished to do or say anything, and so she bowed and, without saying another word, dissolved the fetch.

"What was that?" said Robman.

"The end of Act IV, scene 1," said Adel grimly.

"But what does it mean?" said Meri.

Jarek put his hand to her cheek but then let it fall again. "I think Adel is right. I think we're . . ."

At that moment, the prazz sentry ship struck the *Godspeed* a mortal blow, crashing into its surface just 40 meters from the backside thruster and compromising the magnetic storage rings that contained the antimatter generated by collider. The sonic blast was deafening as the entire asteroid lurched. Then came the explosion. The pilgrims flew across the Blue Salon like leaves in a storm amidst broken furniture and shattered glass. Alarms screamed and Adel heard the distant hurricane roar of escaping air. Then the lights went out and for a long and hideous moment Adel Ranger Santos lay in darkness, certain that he was about to die. But the lights came up again and he found himself scratched and bruised but not seriously hurt. He heard a moan that he thought might be Kamilah. A man was crying behind an overturned desk. "Is everyone all right?" called Jarek. "Talk to me."

The fetch reappeared in the midst of this chaos, still in costume. Adel had never seen her flicker before. "I'm afraid," said the *Godspeed* to no one in particular, "that I've made a terrible mistake."

The Alien is worshipped on almost all the worlds of the Continuum. While various religions offer divergent views of the Alien, they share two common themes. One is that the Alien gods are—or were once—organic intelligences whose motives are more or less comprehensible. The other is that the gods are absent. The Mission of Tsef promises adherents that they can achieve psychic unity with benign alien nuns who are meditating on their behalf somewhere in the M5 globular cluster. The Cosmic Ancestors are the most popular of the many panspermian religions; they teach that our alien parents seeded earth with life in the form of bacterial stromatolites some 3.7 billion years ago. There are many who hold that humanity's greatest prophets, like Jesus and Ellen and Smike, were aliens come to share the gospel of a loving universe while the Uplift believes that an entire galactic civilization translated itself to a higher reality but left behind astronomical clues for us to decipher so that we can join them someday. It is true that the Glogites conceive of Glog as unknowable and indifferent to humankind, but there is very little discernible difference between them and people who worship black holes.

We find it impossible to imagine a religion that would worship the prazz, but then we know so little about them—or it. Not only is the prazz not organic, but it seems to have a deep-seated antipathy toward all life. Why this should be we can't say: we find the prazz incomprehensible. Even the *Godspeed*, the only intelligence to have any extended contact with the prazz, misjudged it—them—entirely.

Here are a few of the most important questions for which we have no answer:

What exactly are the prazz?

Are they one or many?

Where did they come from?

Why was a sentry posted between our Local Arm and the Sagittarius-Carina Arm of the Milky Way?

Are there more sentries?

And most important of all: what are the intentions of the prazz now that they know about us?

What we can say is this: in the one 1,086th year of her mission, the *Godspeed* detected a communication burst from a source less than a light-year away. Why the prazz sentry chose this precise moment to signal is unknown; the *Godspeed* had been sweeping that sector of space for years and had seen no activity. Acting in accordance with the protocols for first contact, she attempted a stealth scan, which revealed the source as a small robotic ship powered by a matter-antimatter engine. Unfortunately, the prazz sentry sensed that it was being scanned and was able to get a fix on the *Godspeed*. What she should have done at that point was to alert the Continuum of her discovery and continue to track the sentry without making contact. That she did otherwise reflects the unmistakable drift of her persona from threshold norms. Maybe she decided that following procedures lacked dramatic flair. Or perhaps the discovery of the prazz stirred some inexpressible longing for companionship in the *Godspeed*, who was herself an inorganic intelligence. In any event, she attempted to communicate with the prazz sentry and compartmentalized the resources she devoted to the effort so that she could continue to send nominal reports to the Continuum. This was a technique that she had used just once before, but to great effect; compartmentalization was how the *Godspeed* was able to keep her secrets. We understand now that the contact between the two ships was deeply flawed, and their misunderstandings profound. Nevertheless, they agreed to a rendezvous and the *Godspeed* began to decelerate to match course and velocity with the prazz sentry.

⸺

The highboy that killed Robman had crushed his chest and cut the tether that joined him to Jonman. Their blood was all over the floor. Adel had done his best for Jonman, clearing enough debris to lay him out flat, covering him with a carpet. He had tied the remaining length of tether off with wire stripped from the back of a ruined painting, but it still oozed. Adel was no medic but he was pretty sure that Jonman was dying; his face was as gray as his jacket. Kamilah didn't look too bad but she was unconscious and breathing shallowly. Adel worried that she might have internal injuries. Meri's arm was probably broken; when they tried to move her she moaned in agony. Jarek was kicking the slats out of a Yamucha chair back to make her a splint.

"An alien, Speedy?" Adel felt too lightheaded to be scared. "And you didn't tell anyone?" It was as if the gravity generator had failed and at any moment he would float away from this grim reality.

"So where is this fucking prazz now?" Jarek ripped a damask tablecloth into strips.

"The sentry ship itself crashed into the backside engine room. But it has deployed a remote." The *Godspeed* seemed twitchy and preoccupied. "It's in the conservatory, smashing cacti."

"What?" said Adel.

"It has already destroyed my rain forest and torn up my alpine garden."

plus buzzed—*they're fighting with plants?*—

"Show me," said Jarek.

The wall turned a deep featureless blue. "I can't see them; my cameras there are gone." The *Godspeed* paused, her expression uneasy.

—*more bad news coming*—buzzed minus.

"You should know," she said, "that just before it attacked, the prazz warned me that I was infested with vermin and needed to sterilize myself. When I told it that I didn't consider you vermin . . ."

"You're saying they'll come for us?" said Jarek.

"I'm afraid that's very likely."

"Then stop it."

She waved her magic staff disconsolately. "I'm at a loss to know how."

"Fuck that, Speedy." Jarek pointed one of the slats at her fetch. "You think of something. Right now." He knelt by Meri. "I'm going to splint you now, love. It's probably going to hurt."

Meri screamed as he tenderly straightened her arm.

"I know, love," said Jarek. "I know."

—*we have to get out of here*—buzzed minus.

"How badly are you damaged, Speedy?" said Adel. "Can we use the MASTA?"

"My MASTA is operational on a limited basis only. My backside engine complex is a complete loss. I thought I was able to vent all the antimatter in time, but there must have been some left that exploded when the containment failed."

Something slammed onto the level below them so hard that the walls shook.

—*those things are tearing her apart*—

—*looking for us*—

"I've sealed off the area as best I can but the integrity of my life-support envelope has been compromised in several places. At the rate I'm bleeding air into space . . ."

Adel felt another jarring impact, only this one felt as if it were farther away. The *Godspeed's* fetch blurred and dispersed into fog. She reconstituted herself on the wall.

". . . the partial pressure of oxygen will drop below 100 millibars sometime within the next ten to twelve hours."

"That's it, then." Jarek helped Meri to her feet and wiped the tears from her face with his forefinger. "We're all jumping home. Meri can walk, can't you Meri?"

She nodded, her eyes wide with pain. "I'm fine."

"Adel, we'll carry Jonman out first."

"The good news," said the *Godspeed*, "is that I can maintain power indefinitely using my frontside engines."

"Didn't you hear me?" Jarek's voice rose sharply. "We're leaving right now. Jonman and Kamilah can't wait and the rest of us vermin have no intention of being sterilized by your fucking prazz."

"I'm sorry, Jarek." She stared out at them, her face set. "You know I can't send you home. Think about it."

"Speedy!" said Meri. "No."

"What?" said Adel. "What's he talking about?"

"What do you care about the protocols?" Jarek put his arm around Meri's waist to steady her. "You've already kicked them over. That's why we're in this mess."

"The prazz knows where we are," said the *Godspeed*, "but it doesn't know where we're from. I burst my weekly reports . . ."

"Weekly lies, you mean," said Adel.

"They take just six nanoseconds. That's not nearly enough time to get a fix. But a human transmit takes 1.43 *seconds* and the prazz is right here on board." She shook her head sadly. "Pointing it at the Continuum would violate my deepest operating directives. Do you want a prazz army marching off the MASTA stage on Moquin or Harvest?"

"How do we know they have armies?" Jarek said, but his massive shoulders slumped. "Or MASTAs?"

Jonman laughed. It was a low, wet sound, almost a cough. "Adel," he rasped. "I see . . ." He was trying to speak but all that came out of his mouth was thin, pink foam.

Adel knelt by his side. "Jonman, what? You see what?"

"I see." He clutched at Adel's arm. "You." His grip tightened. "Dead." His eyelids fluttered and closed.

—*this isn't happening*—

"What did he say?" said Meri.

"Nothing." Adel felt Jonman's grip relaxing; his arm fell away.

—*dead?*—buzzed plus.

Adel put his ear to Jonman's mouth and heard just the faintest whistle of breath.

minus buzzed—*we're all dead*—

Adel stood up, his thoughts tumbling over each other. He believed that Jonman hadn't spoken out of despair—or cruelty. He had seen something, maybe a way out, and had tried to tell Adel what it was.

*—don't play tikra with Jonman—*buzzed minus*—he cheats—*

*—dead—*plus buzzed*—but not really—*

"Speedy," said Adel, "what if you killed us? What would the prazz do then?"

Jarek snorted in disgust. "What kind of thing is that to . . ." Then he understood what Adel was suggesting. "Hot damn!"

"What?" said Meri. "Tell me."

"But can we do it?" said Jarek. "I mean, didn't they figure out that it's bad for you to be dead too long?"

Adel laughed and clapped Jarek on the shoulder. "Can it be worse than being dead forever?"

*—so dangerous—*buzzed minus.

—we're fucking brilliant—

"You're still talking about the MASTA?" said Meri. "But Speedy won't transmit."

"Exactly," said Adel.

"There isn't much time," said the *Godspeed*.

The Neverending Day

Adel was impressed with how easy it was being dead. The things that had bothered him when he was alive, like being hungry or horny, worrying about whether his friends really liked him, or what he was going to be if he ever grew up—none of that mattered. Who cared that he had never learned the first law of thermodynamics or that he had blown the final turn in the most important race of his life? Appetite was an illusion. Life was pleasant, but then so were movies.

The others felt the same way. Meri couldn't feel her broken arm and Jonman didn't mind at all that he was dying, although he did miss Robman. Adel felt frustrated at first that he couldn't rouse Kamilah, but she was as perfect unconscious as she was when she was awake. Besides, Upwood predicted that she would get bored eventually being alone with herself. It wasn't true that nobody changed after they were dead, he explained, it was just that change came very slowly and was always profound. Adel had been surprised to meet Upwood Marcene in Speedy's pocket-afterlife, but his being there made sense. And of course, Adel had guessed that Sister Lihong Rain would be dead there too. As it turned out, she had been dead many times over the seven years of her pilgrimage.

Speedy had created a virtual space in her memory that was almost identical to the actual *Godspeed*. Of course, Speedy was as real as any of them, which is to say not very real at all. Sister urged the newcomers to follow shipboard routine whenever possible; it would make the transition back to life that much easier. Upwood graciously moved out of The Ranch so that Adel could have his old room back. Speedy and the pilgrims gathered in the Ophiuchi or the Chillingsworth at meal times, and although they did not eat, they did chatter. They even propped Kamilah on a chair to include her in the group. Speedy made a point of talking to her at least once at every meal. She would spin theories about the eating man on Kamilah's medallion or propose eyejack performances Kamilah might try on them.

She also lobbied the group to mount *The Tempest*, but Jarek would have no part in it. Of all of them, he seemed most impatient with death. Instead they played billiards and cards. Adel let Jonman teach him Tikra and didn't mind at all when he cheated. Meri read to them and Jarek played the ruan and sang. Adel visited the VR room but once; the sim made him feel gauzy and extenuated. He did swim 2,000 meters a day in the lap pool, which, although physically disappointing, was a demanding mental challenge. Once he and Jarek and Meri climbed into bed together but nothing very interesting happened. They all laughed about it afterward.

———

Adel was asleep in his own bed, remembering a dream he'd had when he was alive. He was lost in a forest where people grew instead of trees. He stumbled past shrubby little kids and great towering grownups like his parents and Uncle Durwin. He knew he had to keep walking because if he stopped he would grow roots and raise his arms up to the sun like all the other tree people, but he was tired, so very tired.

"Adel." Kamilah shook him roughly. "Can you hear that? Adel!"

At first he thought she must be part of his dream.

—*she's better*—

—*Kamilah*—

"Kamilah, you're awake!"

"Listen." She put her forefinger to her lips and twisted her head, trying to pinpoint the sound. "No, it's gone. I thought they were calling Sister."

"This is wonderful." He reached to embrace her but she slid away from him. "When did you wake up?"

"Just now. I was in my room in bed and I heard singing." She scowled. "What's going on, Adel? The last thing I remember was you telling Speedy you knew we were decelerating. This all feels very wrong to me."

"You don't remember the prazz?"

Her expression was grim. "Tell me everything."

Adel was still groggy, so the story tumbled out in a hodgepodge of the collision and the prazz and the protocols and Robman and the explosion and the blood and the life-support breech and Speedy scanning them into memory and Sister and swimming and tikra and Upwood.

"Upwood is here?"

"Upwood? Oh yes."

—he is?—

—is he?—

As Adel considered the question, his certainty began to crumble. "I mean he was. He gave me his room. But I haven't seen him in a while."

"How long?"

Adel frowned. "I don't know."

"How long have we been here? You and I and the others?"

Adel shook his head.

"Gods, Adel." She reached out tentatively and touched his arm but of course he didn't feel a thing. Kamilah gazed at her own hand in horror, as if it had betrayed her. "Let's find Jarek."

Kamilah led them down the Tulip Stairs, past the Blue and Dagger Salons through the Well Met Arena to the Clarke Airlock. The singing was hushed but so ethereal here that even Jarek and Adel, whose senses had atrophied, could feel it. Sister waited for them just inside the outer door of the airlock.

Although Adel knew it must be her, he didn't recognize her at first. She was naked and her skin was so pale that it was translucent. He could see her heart beating and the dark blood pulsing through her veins, the shiny bundles of muscles sliding over each other as she moved and the skull grinning at him beneath her face. Her thin hair had gone white; it danced around her head as if she were falling.

—*beautiful*—

—*exquisite*—

"I'm glad you're here." She smiled at them. "Adel. Kamilah. Jarek." She nodded at each of them in turn. "My witnesses."

"Sister," said Kamilah, "come away from there."

Sister placed her hand on the door and it vanished. Kamilah staggered back and grabbed at the inner door as if she expected to be expelled from the airlock in a great outrush of air, but Adel knew it wouldn't happen. Kamilah still didn't understand the way things worked here.

They gazed out at a star field much like the one that Adel had seen when he first stepped out onto the surface of the *Godspeed*. Except now there was no surface—only stars.

"Kamilah," said Sister. "you started last and have the farthest to travel. Jarek, you still have doubts. But Adel already knows that the self is a box he has squeezed himself into."

—*yes*—

—*right*—

She stepped backwards out of the airlock and was suspended against the stars.

"Kamilah," she said, "trust us and someday you *will* be perfect." The singing enfolded her and she began to glow in its embrace. The brighter she burned the more she seemed to recede from them, becoming steadily hotter and more concentrated until Adel couldn't tell her from one of the stars. He wasn't sure but he thought she was a blue dwarf.

"Close the airlock, Adel." Speedy strolled into the locker room wearing her golden uniform coat and white sash. "It's too much of a distraction."

"What is this, Speedy?" Jarek's face was ashen. "You said you would send us back."

Adel approached the door cautiously; he wasn't ready to follow Sister to the stars quite yet.

"But I did send you back" she said.

"Then who are we?"

"Copies." Adel jabbed at the control panel and jumped back as the airlock door reappeared. "I think we must be backups."

Kamilah was seething. "You kept copies of us to play with?" Her fists were clenched.

Adel was bemused; they were dead. Who did she think she was going to fight?

"It's not what you think." Speedy smiled. "Let's go up to Blue Salon. We should bring Jonman and Meri into this conversation too." She made ushering motions toward the Well Met and Adel and Jarek turned to leave.

—*good idea*—

—*let's go*—

"No, let's not." With two quick strides, Kamilah gained the doorway and blocked their passage. "If Meri wants to know what's going on, then she can damn well ask."

"Ah, Kamilah. My eyejack insists on the truth." She shrugged and settled onto one of the benches in the locker room. "This is always such a difficult moment," she said.

"Just tell it," said Kamilah.

"The prazz ship expired about three days after the attack. In the confusion of the moment, I'd thought it was my backside engine that exploded. Actually it was the sentry's drive. Once its batteries were exhausted, both the sentry ship and its remote ceased all function. I immediately transmitted all of you to your various home worlds and then disabled my transmitter and deleted all my navigation files. The Continuum is safe—for now. If the prazz come looking, there are further actions I can take."

"And what about us?" said Kamilah. "How do we get home?"

"As I said, you are home, Kamilah. Your injuries were severe but certainly not fatal. Your prognosis was for a complete recovery."

—right—

—makes sense—

"Not that one," said Kamilah. "This one." She tapped her chest angrily. "Me. How do I get home?"

"But Kamilah . . ." Speedy swept an arm expansively, taking in the airlock and lockers and Well Met and the Ophiuchi and Jarek and Adel. ". . . this is your home."

—

The first pilgrim from the *Godspeed* lost during a transmit was Io Waals. We can't say for certain whether she suffered a flawed scan or something interfered with her signal but when the MASTA on Rontaw assembled her, her heart and lungs were outside her body cavity. This was 392 years into the mission. By then, the Captain had long since given way to Speedy.

The *Godspeed* was devastated by Io's death. Some might say it unbalanced her, although we would certainly disagree. But this was when she began to compartmentalize behaviors, sealing them off from the scrutiny of the Continuum and, indeed, from most of her conscious self. She stored backups of every scan she made in her first compartment. For sixty-seven years, she deleted each of them as soon as she received word of a successful transmit. Then Ngong Issonda died when a tech working on Loki improperly recalibrated the MASTA.

Only then did the *Godspeed* understand the terrible price she would pay for compartmentalization. Because she had been keeping the backups a secret not only from the Continuum but also to a large extent from herself, she had never thought through how she might make use of them. It was immediately clear to her that if she resent Ngong, techs would start arriving on her transport stage within the hour to fix her. The *Godspeed* had no intention of being fixed. But what to do with Ngong's scan? She created a new compartment, a simulation of her architecture into which she released Ngong. Ngong did not flourish in the simulation, however. She was depressed and withdrawn whenever the *Godspeed* visited. Her next scan, Keach Soris, arrived safely on Butler's Planet, but Speedy loaded his backup into the simulation with Ngong. Within the year, she was loading all her backups into the sim. But as Upwood Marcene would point out some seven centuries later, dead people change and the change is always profound and immaterial. In less than a year after the sim was created, Ngong, Keach, and Zampa Stackpole stepped out of airlock together into a new compartment, one that against all reason transcends the boundaries of the *Godspeed*, the Milky Way, and spacetime itself.

So then, what do we know about Adel Ranger Santos?

Nothing at all. Once we transmitted him back to Harvest, he passed from our awareness. He may have lived a long happy life or a short painful one. His fate does not concern us.

But what do we know about Adel Ranger Santos?

Only what we know about Upwood Marcene, Kamilah Raunda, Jarek Ohnksen, Merigood Auburn Canada, Lihong Rain, and Jonman Haught Shillaber—which is everything, of course. For they followed Ngong and Keach and Zampa and some forty thousand other pilgrims through the airlock to become us.

And we are they.

SHIVA IN SHADOW

~~~~~~~~~~~

by Nancy Kress

*Nancy Kress, who lives in upstate New York, is the author of twen-
ty-one books, most recently* Nothing Human *and* Crossfire. *Both
are about humanity's future—but with far different premises and outcomes. She is the winner of three Nebulas and one Hugo for her short
fiction. In previous lives she was a calendar model, a fourth-grade
teacher, a college instructor, and an advertising copywriter. Her
"Shiva in Shadow" is that unusual thing, a hard-science science-
fiction story that manages also to be a rich, deep study of fully realized characters under stress in a far-future situation.*

1. SHIP

I WATCHED THE probe launch from the *Kepler's* top-deck observatory,
where the entire Schaad hull is clear to the stars. I stood between Ajit
and Kane. The observatory, which is also the ship's garden, bloomed
wildly with my exotics, bursting into flower in such exuberant profusion that even to see the probe go, we had to squeeze between a seven-
foot-high bed of comoralias and the hull.

"God, Tirzah, can't you prune these things?" Kane said. He
pressed his nose to the nearly invisible hull, like a small child.
Something streaked briefly across the sky. "There it goes. Not that
there's much to see."

I turned to stare at him. Not much to see! Beyond the *Kepler* lay the most violent and dramatic part of the galaxy, in all its murderous glory. True, the *Kepler* had stopped one hundred light-years from the core, for human safety, and dust-and-gas clouds muffled the view somewhat. But, on the other hand, we were far enough away for a panoramic view.

The supermassive black hole Sagittarius A*, the lethal heart of the galaxy, shone gauzily with the heated gases it was sucking downward into oblivion. Around Sag A* circled Sagittarius West, a three-armed spiral of hot plasma ten light-years across, radiating furiously as it cooled. Around *that*, Sagittarius East, a huge shell left over from some catastrophic explosion within the last 100,000 years, expanded outward. I saw thousands of stars, including the blazing blue-hot stars of IRS16, hovering dangerously close to the hole, and giving off a stellar wind fierce enough to blow a long fiery tail off the nearby red giant star. Everything was racing, radiating, colliding, ripping apart, screaming across the entire electromagnetic spectrum. All set against the sweet, light scent of my brief-lived flowers.

Nothing going on. But Kane had never been interested in spectacle.

Ajit said in his musical accent, "No, not much to see. But much to pray for. There go *we*."

Kane snapped, "I don't pray."

"I did not mean 'pray' in the religious sense," Ajit said calmly. He is always calm. "I mean hope. It is a miraculous thing, yes? There go we."

He was right, of course. The probe contained the Ajit-analogue, the Kane-analogue, the Tirzah-analogue, all uploaded into a crystal computer no bigger than a comoralia bloom. "We" would go into that stellar violence at the core, where our fragile human bodies could not go. "We" would observe, and measure, and try to find answers to scientific questions in that roiling heart of galactic spacetime. Ninety percent of the probe's mass was shielding for the computer. Ninety percent of the rest was shielding for the three minicapsules that the probe would fire back to us with recorded and analyzed data. There was no way besides the minicaps to get information out of that bath of frenzied radiation.

Just as there was no way to know exactly what questions Ajit and Kane would need to ask until they were close to Sag A*. The analogues would know. They knew everything Ajit and Kane and I knew, right up until the moment we were uploaded.

"Shiva, dancing," Ajit said.

"What?" Kane said.

"Nothing. You would not appreciate the reference. Come with me, Tirzah. I want to show you something."

I stopped straining to see the probe, unzoomed my eyes, and smiled at Ajit. "Of course."

This is why I am here.

Ajit's skin is softer than Kane's, less muscled. Kane works out every day in ship's gym, scowling like a demon. Ajit rolled off me and laid his hand on my glowing, satisfied crotch.

"You are so beautiful, Tirzah."

I laughed. "We are all beautiful. Why would anyone effect a genetic alteration that wasn't?"

"People will do strange things sometimes."

"So I just noticed," I teased him.

"Sometimes I think so much of what Kane and I do is strange to you. I see you sitting at the table, listening to us, and I know you cannot follow our physics. It makes me sad for you."

I laid my hand on top of his, pushing down my irritation with the skill of long practice. It does irritate me, this calm sensitivity of Ajit's. It's lovely in bed—he is gentler and more considerate, always, than Kane—but then there comes the other side, this faint condescension. *"I feel sad for you."* Sad for me! Because I'm not also a scientist! I am the captain of this expedition, with master status in ship control and a first-class license as a Nurturer. On the *Kepler*, my word is law, with virtually no limits. I have over fifty standard-years' experience, specializing in the nurture of scientists. I have never lost an expedition, and I need no one's pity.

Naturally, I showed none of this to Ajit. I massaged his hand with mine, which meant that his hand massaged my crotch, and purred softly. "I'm glad you decided to show me this."

"Actually, that is not what I wanted to show you."

"No?"

"No. Wait here, Tirzah."

He got up and padded, naked, to his personal locker. Beautiful, beautiful body, brown and smooth, like a slim polished tree. I could see him clearly; Ajit always makes love with the bunk lights on full, as if in sunlight. We lay in his bunk, not mine. I never take either him or Kane to my bunk. My bunk contained various concealed items that they don't, and won't, know about, from duplicate surveillance equipment to rarely used subdermal trackers. Precautions, only. I am a captain.

From his small storage locker, Ajit pulled a statue and turned shyly, even proudly, to show it to me. I sat up, surprised.

The statue was big, big enough so that it must have taken up practically his entire allotment of personal space. Heavy, too, from the way Ajit balanced it before his naked body. It was some sort of god with four arms, enclosed in a circle of flames, made of what looked like very old bronze.

"This is Nataraja," Ajit said. "Shiva dancing."

"Ajit—"

"No, I am not a god worshipper," he smiled. "You know me better than that, Tirzah. Hinduism has many gods—thousands—but they are, except to the ignorant, no more than embodiments of different aspects of reality. Shiva is the dance of creation and destruction, the constant flow of energy in the cosmos. Birth and death and rebirth. It seemed fitting to bring him to the galactic core, where so much goes on of all three."

This explanation sounded weak to me—a holo of Shiva would have accomplished the same thing, without using up nearly all of Ajit's weight allotment. Before I could say this, Ajit said, "This statue has been in my family for four hundred years. I must bring it home, along with the answers to my scientific questions."

I don't understand Ajit's scientific concerns very well—or Kane's—but I know down to my bones how much they matter to him. It is my job to know. Ajit carries within his beautiful body a terrible coursing ambition, a river fed by the longings of a poor family who have sacrificed what little they had gained on New Bombay for this favored son. Ajit is the receptacle into which they have poured so much hope, so much sacrifice, so much selfishness. The strain on that vessel is what makes Ajit's lovemaking so gentle. He cannot afford to crack.

"You'll bring the Shiva statue back to New Bombay," I said softly, "and your answers, too."

In his hands, with the bright lighting, the bronze statue cast a dancing shadow on his naked body.

I found Kane at his terminal, so deep in thought that he didn't know I was there until I squeezed his shoulder. Then he jumped, cursed, and dragged his eyes from his displays.

"How does it progress, Kane?"

"It doesn't. How could it? I need more data!"

"It will come. Be patient," I said.

He rubbed his left ear, a constant habit when he's irritated, which is much of the time. When he's happily excited, Kane runs his left hand through his coarse red hair until it stands up like flames. Now he smiled ruefully. "I'm not much known for patience."

"No, you're not."

"But you're right, Tirzah. The data will come. It's just hard waiting for the first minicap. I wish to hell we could have more than three. Goddamn cheap bureaucrats! At an acceleration of—"

"Don't give me the figures again," I said. I wound my fingers in his hair and pulled playfully. "Kane, I came to ask you a favor."

"All right," he said instantly. Kane never counts costs ahead of time. Ajit would have turned gently cautious. "What is it?"

"I want you to learn to play *go* with Ajit."

He scowled. "Why?"

With Kane, you must have your logic ready. He would do any favor I asked, but unless he can see why, compliance would be grudging at best. "First, because *go* will help you pass the time until the first minicap arrives, in doing something other than chewing the same data over and over again until you've masticated it into tastlessness. Second, because the game is complex enough that I think you'll enjoy it. Third, because I'm not too bad at it myself but Ajit is better, and I think you will be, too, so I can learn from both of you."

And fourth, I didn't say aloud, because Ajit is a master, he will beat you most of the time, and he needs the boost in confidence.

Ajit is not the scientist that Kane is. Practically no one in the settled worlds is the scientist that Kane is. All three of us know this, but none of us have ever mentioned it, not even once. There are geniuses who are easy for the inferior to work with, who are generous enough to slow down their mental strides to the smaller steps of the merely gifted. Kane is not one of them.

"*Go*," Kane says thoughtfully. "I have friends who play that."

This was a misstatement. Kane does not have friends, in the usual sense. He has colleagues, he has science, and he has me.

He smiled at me, a rare touch of sweet gratitude on his handsome face. "Thanks, Tirzah. I'll play with Ajit. You're right, it *will* pass the time until the probe sends back the prelim data. And if I'm occupied, maybe I'll be less of a monster to you."

"You're fine to me," I say, giving his hair another tug, grinning with the casual flippancy he prefers. "Or if you're not, I don't care."

Kane laughs. In moments like this, I am especially careful that my own feelings don't show. To either of them.

2. PROBE

We automatically woke after the hyperjump. For reasons I don't understand, a hyperjump isn't instantaneous, perhaps because it's not really a "jump" but a Calabi-Yau dimension tunnel. Several days ship-time had passed, and the probe now drifted less than five light-years from the galactic core. The probe, power off, checked out perfectly; the shielding had held even better than expected. And so had we. My eyes widened as I studied the wardroom displays.

On the *Kepler*, dust clouds had softened and obscured the view. Here, nothing did. We drifted just outside a star that had begun its deadly spiral inward toward Sag A*. Visuals showed the full deadly glory around the hole: the hot blue cluster of IRS16. The giant red star IRS7 with its long tail distended by stellar winds. The stars already past the point of no return, pulled by the gravity of Sag A* inexorably toward its event horizon. The radio, gamma-ray, and infrared displays revealed even more, brilliant with the radiation pouring from every single gorgeous, lethal object in the bright sky.

And there, too, shone one of the mysteries Kane and Ajit had come to study: the massive young stars that were not being yanked toward Sag A*, and which in this place should have been neither massive nor relatively stable. Such stars should not exist this close to the hole. One star, Kane had told me, was as close to the hole as twice Pluto's orbit from Sol. How had it gotten there?

"It's beautiful, in a hellish way," I said to Ajit and Kane. "I want to go up to the observatory and see it direct."

"The observatory!" Kane said scornfully. "I need to get to work!" He sat down at his terminal.

None of this is true, of course. There is no observatory on the probe, and I can't climb the ladder "up" to it. Nor is there a wardroom with terminals, chairs, table, displays, a computer. We *are* the computer, or rather we are inside it. But the programs running along with us make it all seem as real as the fleshy versions of ourselves on the *Kepler*. This, it was determined by previous disastrous experience in space exploration, is necessary to keep us sane and stable. Human uploads need this illusion, this shadow reality, and we accept it easily. Why not? It's the default setting for our minds.

So Kane "sat" "at" his "terminal" to look at the preliminary data from the sensors. So did Ajit, and I "went" "upstairs" to the observatory, where I gazed outward for a long time.

I—the other "I," the one on the *Kepler*—grew up on a station in the Oort Cloud, Sol System. Space is my natural home. I don't really understand how mud-dwellers live on planets, or why they would want to, at the bottom of a murky and dirty shroud of uncontrollable air. I have learned to simulate understanding planetary love, because it is my job. Both Kane and Ajit come from rocks, Ajit from New Bombay and Kane from Terra herself. They are space scientists, but not real spacers.

No mud-dweller ever really sees the stars. And no human being had ever seen what I saw now, the frantic heart of the human universe.

Eventually I went back downstairs, rechecked ship's data, and then sat at the wardroom table and took up my embroidery. The ancient, irrelevant cloth-ornamenting is very soothing, almost as much so as gardening, although of course that's not why I do it. All first-class Nurturers practice some humble handicraft. It allows you to closely observe people while appearing absorbed and harmless.

Kane, of course, was oblivious to me. I could have glared at him through a magnifying glass and he wouldn't have noticed, not if he was working. Back on the *Kepler*, he had explained in simple terms—or at least as simple as Kane's explanations ever get—why there should not be any young stars this close to the core, as well as three possible explanations for why there are. He told me all this, in typical Kane fashion, in bed. Postcoital intimacy.

"The stars' spectra show they're young, Tirzah. And *close*—SO-2 comes to within eighty AU's of Sag A*! It's *wrong*—the core is incredibly inhospitable to star formation! Also, these close-in stars have very peculiar orbits."

"You're taking it personally," I observed, smiling.

"Of course I am!" This was said totally without irony. "Those young stars have no business there. The tidal forces of the hole should rip any hot dust clouds to shreds long before any stars could form. And if they formed farther out, say one hundred light-years out, they should have died before they got this close in. These supermassive stars only last a few million years."

"But there they are."

"Yes. Why do you still have this lacy thing on? It's irritating."

"Because you were so eager that I didn't have time to get it off."

"Well, take it off now."

I did, and he wrapped my body close to his, and went on fretting over star formation in the core.

"There are three theories. One is that a dust cloud ringing the core, about six light-years out, keeps forming stars, which are then blown outwards again by galactic winds, and then drawn in, and repeat. Another theory is that there's a second, intermediate medium-sized black hole orbiting Sag A* and exerting a counterpull on the stars. But if so, why aren't we detecting its radio waves? Another idea is that the stars aren't really young at all, they're composites of remnants of elderly stars that merged to form a body that only looks bright and young."

I said, "Which theory do you like?"

"None of them." And then, in one of those lightning changes he was capable of, he focused all his attention on me. "Are you all right, Tirzah? I know this has got to be a boring voyage for you. Running ship can't take much of your time, and neither can babysitting me."

I laughed aloud and Kane, having no idea why, frowned slightly. It was such a typically Kane speech. A sudden burst of intense concern, which would prove equally transitory. No mention of Ajit at all, as if only Kane existed for me. And his total ignorance of how often I interceded between him and Ajit, smoothed over tensions between them, spent time calming and centering separately each of these men who were more like the stars outside the ship than either of them were capable of recognizing. Brilliant, heated, intense, inherently unstable.

"I'm fine, Kane. I'm enjoying myself."

"Well, good," he said, and I saw that he then forgot me, back to brooding about his theories.

Neither Kane nor Ajit knows that I love Kane. I don't love Ajit. Whatever calls up love in our hidden hearts, it is unfathomable. Kane arouses in me a happiness, a desire, a completeness that puts a glow on the world because he—difficult, questing, vital—is in it. Ajit, through no fault of his own, does not.

Neither of them will ever know this. I would berate myself if they did. My personal feelings don't matter here. I am a captain.

—◆—

"Damn and double damn!" Kane said, admiringly. "Look at that!"

Ajit reacted as if Kane had spoken to him, but of course Kane had not. He was just thinking aloud. I put down my embroidery and went to stand behind them at their terminals.

Ajit said, "Those readings must be wrong. The sensors were damaged after all, either in hypertransit or by radiation."

Kane didn't reply; I doubt he'd heard. I said, "What is it?"

It was Ajit who answered. "The mass readings are wrong. They're showing high mass density for several areas of empty space."

I said, "Maybe that's where the new young stars are forming?"

Not even Ajit answered this, which told me it was a stupid statement. It doesn't matter; I don't pretend to be a scientist. I merely wanted to keep them talking, to gauge their states of mind.

Ajit said, "It would be remarkable if all equipment had emerged undamaged from the jump into this radiation."

"Kane?" I said.

"It's not the equipment," he muttered. So he had been listening, at least peripherally. "Supersymmetry."

Ajit immediately objected to this, in terms I didn't understand. They were off into a discussion I had no chance of following. I let it go on for a while, then even longer, since it sounded the way scientific discussions are supposed to sound: intense but not acrimonious, not personal.

When they wound down a bit, I said, "Did the minicapsule go off to the *Kepler*? They're waiting for the prelim data, and the minicap takes days to jump. Did either of you remember to record and send?"

They both looked at me, as if trying to remember who I was and what I was doing there. In that moment, for the first time, they looked alike.

"I remembered," Ajit said. "The prelim data went off to the *Kepler*. Kane—"

They were off again.

3. SHIP

The *go* games were not a success.

The problem, I could see, was with Ajit. He was a far better player than Kane, both intuitively and through experience. This didn't bother Kane at all; he thrived on challenge. But his own clear superiority subtly affected Ajit.

"Game won," he said for the third time in the evening, and at the slight smirk in his voice I looked up from my embroidery.

"Damn and double damn," Kane said, without rancor. "Set them up again."

"No, I think I will go celebrate my victories with Tirzah."

This was Kane's night, but the two of them had never insisted on precedence. This was because I had never let it come to that; it's part of my job to give the illusion that I am always available to both, on whatever occasion they wish. Of course, I control, through a hundred subtle signals and without either realizing it, which occasions they happen to wish. Where I make love depends on whom I need to observe. This direct claim by Ajit, connecting me to his *go* victories, was new.

Kane, of course, didn't notice. "All right. God, I wish the minicap would come. I want that data!"

Now that the game had released his attention, he was restless again. He rose and paced around the wardroom, which doesn't admit too much pacing. "I think I'll go up to the observatory. Anybody coming?"

He had already forgotten that I was leaving with Ajit. I saw Ajit go still. Such a small thing—Ajit was affronted that Kane was not affected by Ajit's game victory, or by his bearing me off like some earned prize. Another man would have felt a moment of pique and then forgotten it. Ajit was not another man. Neither was Kane. Stable men don't volunteer for missions like this.

It's different for me; I was bred to space. The scientists were not.

I put down my embroidery, took Ajit's hand, and snuggled close to him. Kane, for the moment, was fine. His restless desire for his data wouldn't do him any harm. It was Ajit I needed to work with.

I was the one who had suggested the *go* games. Good captains are not supposed to make mistakes like that. It was up to me to set things right.

By the time the minicap arrived, everything was worse.

They would not, either of them, stop the *go* games. They played obsessively, six or seven times a day, then nine or ten, and finally every waking minute. Ajit continued to win the large majority of the games, but not all of them. Kane focused his formidable intelligence on devising strategies, and he had the advantage of caring but not too much. Yes, he was obsessed, but I could see that once he had something more significant to do, he would leave the *go* games without a backward glance.

Ajit grew more focused, too. Even more intent on winning, even as he began to lose a few games. More slyly gleeful when he did win. He flicked his winning piece onto the board with a turn of the wrist in which I read both contempt and fear.

I tried everything I could to intervene, every trick from a century of experience. Nothing worked. Sex only made it worse. Ajit regarded sex as an earned prize, Kane as a temporary refreshment so he could return to the games.

One night Ajit brought out the statue of Shiva and put it defiantly on the wardroom table. It took up two-thirds of the space, a wide metal circle enclosing the four-armed dancer.

"What's that?" Kane said, looking up from the game board. "Oh, God, it's a god."

I said quickly, "It's an intellectual concept. The flow of cosmic energy in the universe."

Kane laughed, not maliciously, but I saw Ajit's eyes light up. Ajit said, "I want it here."

Kane shrugged. "Fine by me. Your turn, Ajit."

Wrong, wrong. Ajit had hoped to disturb Kane, to push him into some open objection to the statue. Ajit wanted a small confrontation, some outlet to emphasize his gloating. Some outlet for his growing unease as Kane's game improved. And some outlet for his underlying rage, always just under the surface, at Kane, the better scientist. The statue was supposed to be an assertion, even a slap in the face: *I am here and I take up a lot of your space. Notice that!*

Instead, Kane had shrugged and dismissed it.

I said, "Tell me again, Ajit, about Nataraja. What's the significance of the flames on the great circle?"

Ajit said quietly, "They represent the fire that destroys the world."

Kane said, "Your *turn*, Ajit."

Such a small incident. But deep in my mind, where I was aware of it but not yet overtly affected, fear stirred.

I was losing control here.

Then the first minicap of data arrived.

4. PROBE

Mind uploads are still minds. They are not computer programs in the sense that other programs are. Although freed of biological constraints such as enzymes that create sleep, hunger, and lust, uploads are not free of habit. In fact, it is habit that creates enough structure to keep all of us from frenzied feedback loops. On the probe, my job was to keep habit strong. It was the best safeguard for those brilliant minds.

"Time to sleep, gentlemen," I said lightly. We had been gathered in the wardroom for sixteen hours straight, Kane and Ajit at their terminals, me sitting quietly, watching them. I have powers of concentration equal in degree, though not in kind, to their own. They do not suspect this. It has been hours since I put down my embroidery, but neither noticed.

"Tirzah, not sleep now!" Kane snapped.

"Now."

He looked up at me like a sulky child. But Kane is not a child; I don't make that mistake. He knows an upload has to shut down for the cleansing program to run, a necessity to catch operating errors before they grow large enough to impair function. With all the radiation bathing the probe, the program is more necessary than ever. It takes a few hours to run through. I control the run cues.

Ajit looked at me expectantly. It was his night. This, too, was part of habit, as well as being an actual aid to their work. More than one scientist in my care has had that critical flash of intuition on some scientific problem while in my arms. Upload sex, like its fleshy analogue, both stimulates and relaxes.

"All right, all right," Kane muttered. "Good night."

I shut him down and turned to Ajit.

We went to his bunk. Ajit was tense, stretched taut with data and with sixteen hours with Kane. But I was pleased to see how completely he responded to me. Afterward, I asked him to explain the prelim data to me.

"And keep it simple, please. Remember who you're talking to!"

"To an intelligent and sweet lady," he said, and I gave him the obligatory smile. But he saw that I really did want to know about the data.

"The massive young stars are there when they should not be . . . Kane has explained all this to you, I know."

I nodded.

"They are indeed young, not mashed-together old stars. We have verified that. We are trying now to gather and run data to examine the other two best theories: a fluctuating ring of matter spawning stars, or other black holes."

"How are you examining the theories?"

He hesitated, and I knew he was trying to find explanations I could understand. "We are running various programs, equations, and sims. We are also trying to determine where to jump the probe next—you know about that."

Of course I did. No one moves this ship without my consent. It has two more jumps left in its power pack, and I must approve them both.

"We need to choose a spot from which we can fire beams of various radiation to assess the results. The heavier beams won't last long here, you know—the gravity of the superhole distorts them." He frowned.

"What is it, Ajit? What about gravity?"

"Kane was right," he said, "the mass detectors aren't damaged. They're showing mass nearby, not large but detectable, that isn't manifesting anything but gravity. No radiation of any kind."

"A black hole," I suggested.

"Too small. Small black holes radiate away, Hawking showed that long ago. The internal temperature is too high. There are no black holes smaller than three solar masses. The mass detectors are showing something much smaller than that."

"What?"

"We don't know."

"Were all the weird mass-detector readings in the prelim data you sent back to the *Kepler*?"

"Of course," he said, a slight edge in his voice.

I pulled him closer. "I can always rely on you," I said, and I felt his body relax.

I shut us down, as we lay in each other's arms.

It was Ajit who, the next day, noticed the second anomaly. And I who noticed the third.

"These gas orbits aren't right," Ajit said to Kane. "And they're getting less right all the time."

Kane moved to Ajit's terminal. "Tell me."

"The infalling gases from the circumnuclear disk . . . see . . . they curve here, by the western arm of Sag A West . . ."

"It's wind from the IRS16 cluster," Kane said instantly. "I got updated readings for those yesterday."

"No, I already corrected for that," Ajit said.

"Then maybe magnetization from IRS7, or—"

They were off again. I followed enough to grasp the general problem. Gases streamed at enormous speeds from clouds beyond the circumnuclear disk which surrounded the entire core like a huge doughnut. These streaming gases were funneled by various forces into fairly narrow, cone-like paths. The gases would eventually end up circling the black hole, spiraling inward and compressing to temperatures of billions of degrees before they were absorbed by the maw of the hole. The processes were understood.

But the paths weren't as predicted. Gases were streaming down wrong, approaching the hole wrong for predictions made from all the forces acting on them.

Ajit finally said to Kane, "I want to move the probe earlier than we planned."

"Wait a moment," I said instantly. Ship's movements were *my* decision. "It's not yet the scheduled time."

"Of course I'm including you in my request, Tirzah," Ajit said, with all his usual courtesy. There was something beneath the courtesy, however, a kind of glow. I recognized it. Scientists look like that when they have the germ of an important idea.

I thought Kane would object or ridicule, but something in their technical discussion must have moved him, too. His red hair stood up all over his head. He glanced briefly at his own displays, back at Ajit's, then at the younger man. He said, "You want to put the probe on the other side of Sagittarius A West."

"Yes."

I said, "Show me."

Ajit brought up the simplified graphic he had created weeks ago for me to gain an overview of this mission. It showed the black hole at the center of the galaxy, and the major structures around it: the cluster of hot blue stars, the massive young stars that should not have existed so close to the hole, the red giant star IRS16, with its long fiery tail. All this, plus our probe, lay on one side of the huge, three-armed spiraling plasma remnant, Sagittarius A West. Ajit touched the computer and a new dot appeared on the other side of Sag A West, farther away from the hole than we were now.

"We want to go there, Tirzah," he said. Kane nodded.

I said, deliberately sounding naïve, "I thought there wasn't as much going on over there. And besides, you said that Sag A West would greatly obscure our vision in all wavelengths, with its own radiation."

"It will."

"Then—"

"There's something going on over there now," Kane said. "Ajit's right. That region is the source of whatever pull is distorting the gas infall. We need to go there."

We.

Ajit's right.

The younger man didn't change expression. But the glow was still there, ignited by Ajit's idea and fanned, I now realized, by Kane's approval. I heated it up a bit more. "But, Kane, your work on the massive young stars? I can only move the probe so many times, you know. Our fuel supply—"

"I have a lot of data on the stars now," Kane said, "and this matters more."

I hid my own pleasure. "All right. I'll move the probe."

But when I interfaced with ship's program, I found the probe had already been moved.

5. SHIP

Kane and Ajit fell on the minicap of prelim data like starving wolves. There were no more games of *go*. There was no more anything but work, unless I insisted.

At first I thought that was good. I thought that without the senseless, mounting competition over *go*, the two scientists would cooperate on the intense issues that mattered so much to both of them.

"Damn and double damn!" Kane said, admiringly. "Look at that!"

Ajit reacted as if Kane had spoken to him, but of course Kane had not. He was just thinking aloud. I put down my embroidery and went to stand behind them at their terminals.

Ajit said, with the new arrogance of the *go* wins in his voice, "Those readings must be wrong. The sensors were damaged after all, either in hypertransit or by radiation."

Kane, for a change, caught Ajit's tone. He met it with a sneer he must have used regularly on presumptuous post-grads. "'Must be wrong'? That's just the kind of puerile leaping to conclusions that gets people nowhere."

I said quickly, "What readings?"

It was Ajit who answered me, and although the words were innocuous, even polite, I heard the anger underlying them. "The mass readings are wrong. They're showing high mass density for several areas of empty space."

I said, "Maybe that's where the new young stars are forming?"

Not even Ajit answered this, which told me it was a stupid statement. It doesn't matter; I don't pretend to be a scientist. I merely wanted to keep them talking, to gauge their states of mind.

Ajit said, too evenly, "It would be remarkable if *all* probe equipment had emerged undamaged from the jump into core radiation."

"Kane?" I said.

"It's *not* the equipment." And then, "Supersymmetry."

Ajit immediately objected to this, in terms I didn't understand. They were off into a discussion I had no chance of following. What I could follow was the increasing pressure of Ajit's anger as Kane dismissed and belittled his ideas. I could almost see that anger, a hot plasma. As Kane ridiculed and belittled, the plasma collapsed into greater and greater density.

Abruptly they broke off their argument, went to their separate terminals, and worked like machines for twenty hours straight. I had to make them each eat something. They were obsessed, as only those seized by science or art can obsess. Neither of them would come to bed with me that night. I could have issued an executive order, but I chose not to exert that much trust-destroying force until I had to, although I did eventually announce that I was shutting down terminal access.

"For God's sake, Tirzah!" Kane snarled. "This is a once-in-a-species opportunity! I've got work to do!"

I said evenly, "You're going to rest. The terminals are down for seven hours."

"Five."

"All right." After five hours, Kane would still be snoring away.

He stood, stiff from the long hours of sitting. Kane is well over a hundred; rejuves can only do so much, so long. His cramped muscles, used to much more exercise, misfired briefly. He staggered, laughed, caught himself easily.

But not before he'd bumped the wardroom table. Ajit's statue of Shiva slid off and fell to the floor. The statue was old—four hundred years old, Ajit had said. Metal shows fatigue, too, although later than men. The statue hit the deck at just the right angle and broke.

"Oh . . . sorry, Ajit."

Kane's apology was a beat too late. I knew—with every nerve in my body, I knew this—that the delay happened because Kane's mind was still racing along his data, and it took an effort for him to refocus. It didn't matter. Ajit stiffened, and something in the nature of his anger changed, ionized by Kane's careless, preoccupied tone.

I said quickly, "Ship can weld the statue."

"No, thank you," Ajit said. "I will leave it as it is. Good night."

"Ajit—" I reached for his hand. He pulled it away.

"Good night, Tirzah."

Kane said, "The gamma-ray variations within Sag A West aren't quite what was predicted." He blinked twice. "You're right, I am exhausted."

Kane stumbled off to his bunk. Ajit had already gone. After a long while I picked up the pieces of Ajit's statue and held them, staring at the broken figure of the dancing god.

The preliminary data, Kane had declared when it arrived, contained enough information to keep them both busy until the second minicap arrived. But by the next day, Kane was impatiently demanding more.

"These gas orbits aren't right," he said aloud, although not to either me or Ajit. Kane did that, worked in silence for long stretches until words exploded out of him to no particular audience except his own whirling thoughts. His ear was raw with rubbing.

I said, "What's not right about them?" When he didn't answer, or probably even hear me, I repeated the question, much louder.

Kane came out of his private world and scowled at me. "The infalling gases from beyond the circumnuclear disk aren't showing the right paths to Sag A*."

I said, repeating something he'd taught me, "Could it be wind from the IRS16 cluster?"

"No. I checked those updated readings yesterday and corrected for them."

I had reached the end of what I knew to ask. Kane burst out, "I need more data!"

"Well, it'll get here eventually."

"I want it now," he said, and laughed sourly at himself, and went back to work.

Ajit said nothing, acting as if neither of us had spoken.

I waited until Ajit stood, stretched, and looked around vaguely. Then I said, "Lunch in a minute. But first come look at something with me." Immediately I started up the ladder to the observatory, so that he either had to follow or go through the trouble of arguing. He followed.

I had put the welded statue of Shiva on the bench near clear hull. It was the wrong side of the hull for the spectacular view of the core, but the exotics didn't press so close to the hull here, and thousands of stars shone in a sky more illuminated than Sol had seen since its birth. Shiva danced in his mended circle of flames against a background of cosmic glory.

Ajit said flatly, "I told you I wanted to leave it broken."

With Kane, frank opposition is fine; he's strong enough to take it and, in fact, doesn't respect much else. But Ajit is different. I lowered my eyes and reached for his hand. "I know. I took the liberty of fixing it anyway because, well, I thought you might want to see it whole again and because I like the statue so much. It has so much meaning beyond the obvious, especially here. In this place and this time. Please forgive me."

Ajit was silent for a moment, then he raised my hand to his lips. "You do see that."

"Yes," I said, and it was the truth. Shiva, the endless dance, the endless flow of energy changing form and state—how could anyone not see it in the gas clouds forming stars, the black hole destroying them, the violence and creation outside this very hull? Yet, at the same time, it was a profound insight into the very obvious, and I kept my eyes lowered so no glimpse of my faint contempt reached Ajit.

He kissed me. "You are so spiritual, Tirzah. And so sweet-natured."

I was neither. The only deceptions Ajit could see were the paranoid ones he assumed of others.

But his body had relaxed in my arms, and I knew that some part of his mind had been reassured. He and I could see spiritual beauties that Kane could not. Therefore he was in some sense superior to Kane. He followed me back down the ladder to lunch, and I heard him hum a snatch of some jaunty tune. Pleased with myself, I made for the galley.

Kane stood up so abruptly from his terminal that his eyes glowed. "Oh, my shitting stars. Oh, yes. Tirzah, I've got it."

I stopped cold. I had never seen anyone, even Kane, look quite like that. "Got what?"

"All of it." Suddenly he seized me and swung me into exuberant, clumsy dance. "All of it! I've got all of it! The young stars, the gas orbits, the missing mass in the universe! All shitting fucking *all* of it!"

"Wwwhhhaaatttt . . ." He was whirling me around so fast that my teeth rattled. "Kane, stop!"

He did, and enveloped me in a rib-cracking hug, then abruptly released me and dragged my bruised body to his terminal. "Look, sweetheart, I've got it. Now sit right there and I'm going to explain it in terms even you can understand. You'll love it. It'll love you. Now look here, at this region of space—"

I turned briefly to look at Ajit. For Kane, he didn't even exist.

6. PROBE

"The probe has moved," I said to Ajit and Kane. "It's way beyond the calculated drift. By a factor of ten."

Kane's eyes, red with work, nonetheless sharpened. "Let me see the trajectory."

"I transferred it to both your terminals." Ordinarily ship's data is kept separate, for my eyes only.

Kane brought up the display and whistled.

The probe is under the stresses, gravitational and radiational, that will eventually destroy it. We all know that. Our fleshy counterparts weren't even sure the probe would survive to send one minicap of data, and I'm sure they were jubilant when we did. Probably they treated the minicap like a holy gift, and I can easily imagine how eager they are for more. Back on the ship, I—the other "I"—had been counting on data, like oil, to grease the frictions and tensions between Ajit and Kane. I hoped it had.

We uploads had fuel enough to move the probe twice. After that, and since our last move will be no more than one-fiftieth of a light-year from the black hole at the galactic core, the probe will eventually spiral down into Sag A*. Before that, however, it will have been ripped apart by the immense tidal forces of the hole. However, long before that final death plunge, we analogues will be gone.

The probe's current drift, however, considerably farther away from the hole, was nonetheless much faster than projected. It was also slightly off course. We were being pulled in the general direction of Sag A*, but not on the gravitational trajectory that would bring us into its orbit at the time and place the computer had calculated. In fact, at our current rate of acceleration, there was a chance we'd miss the event horizon completely.

What was going on?

Kane said, "Maybe we better hold off moving the probe to the other side of Sag A West until we find out what's pulling us."

Ajit was studying the data over Kane's shoulder. He said hesitantly, "No . . . wait . . . I think we should move."

"Why?" Kane challenged.

"I don't know. I just have . . . call it an intuition. We should move now."

I held my breath. The only intuition Kane usually acknowledged was his own. But earlier things had subtly shifted. Kane had said, *"Ajit's right. That region is the source of whatever pull is distorting the gas infall."* Ajit had not changed expression, but I'd felt his pleasure, real as heat. That had given him the courage to now offer this unformed—"half-baked" was Kane's usual term—intuition.

Kane said thoughtfully, "Maybe you're right. Maybe the—" Suddenly his eyes widened. "Oh my god."

"What?" I said, despite myself. "What?"

Kane ignored me. "Ajit—run the sims for the gas orbits in correlation with the probe drift. I'll do the young stars!"

"Why do—" Ajit began, and then he saw whatever had seized Kane's mind. Ajit said something in Hindi; it might have been a curse, or a prayer. I didn't know. Nor did I know anything about their idea, or about what was happening with the gas orbits and young stars outside the probe. However, I could see clearly what was happening within.

Ajit and Kane fell into frenzied work. They threw comments and orders to each other, transferred data, backed up sims and equation runs. They tilted their chairs toward each other and spouted incomprehensible jargon. Once Kane cried, "We need more data!" and Ajit laughed, freely and easily, then immediately plunged back into whatever he was doing. I watched them for a long time, then stole quietly up to the observation deck for a minute alone.

The show outside was more spectacular than ever, perhaps because we'd been pulled closer to it than planned. Clouds of whirling gases wrapped and oddly softened that heart of darkness, Sag A*. The fiery tail of the giant red star lit up that part of the sky. Stars glowed in a profusion unimaginable on my native Station J, stuck off in a remote arm of the galaxy. Directly in front of me glowed the glorious blue stars of the cluster IRS16.

I must have stayed on the observation deck longer than I'd planned, because Kane came looking for me. "Tirzah! Come on down! We want to show you where we're moving and why!"

We.

I said severely, gladness bursting in my heart, "You don't show me where we're going, Kane, you ask me. I captain this ship."

"Yeah, yeah, I know, you're a dragon lady. Come on!" He grabbed my hand and pulled me toward the ladder.

They both explained it, interrupting each other, fiercely correcting each other, having a wonderful time. I concentrated as hard as I could, trying to cut through the technicalities they couldn't do without, any more than they could do without air. Eventually I thought I glimpsed the core of their excitement.

"Shadow matter," I said, tasting the words on my tongue. It sounded too bizarre to take seriously, but Kane was insistent.

"The theory's been around for centuries, but deGroot pretty much discredited it in 2086," Kane said. "He—"

"If it's been discredited, then why—" I began.

"I said 'pretty much,'" Kane said. "There were always some mathematical anomalies with deGroot's work. And we can see now where he was *wrong*. He—"

Kane and Ajit started to explain why deGroot was wrong, but I interrupted. "No, don't digress so much! Let me just tell you what I think I understood from what you said."

I was silent a moment, gathering words. Both men waited impatiently, Kane running his hand through his hair, Ajit smiling widely. I said, "You said there's a theory that just after the Big Bang, gravity somehow decoupled from the other forces in the universe, just as matter decoupled from radiation. At the same time, you scientists have known for two centuries that there doesn't seem to be enough matter in the universe to make all your equations work. So scientists posited a lot of 'dark matter' and a lot of black holes, but none of the figures added up right anyway.

"And right now, neither do the orbits of the infalling gas, or the probe's drift, or the fact that massive young stars were forming that close to the black hole without being ripped apart by tidal forces. The forces acting on the huge clouds that have to condense to form stars that big."

I took a breath, quick enough so that neither had time to break in and distract me with technicalities.

"But now you think that if gravity *did* decouple right after the Big Bang—"

"About 10^{-43} seconds after," Ajit said helpfully. I ignored him.

"—then two types of matter were created, normal matter and 'shadow matter.' It's sort of like matter and antimatter, only normal matter and shadow matter can't interact except by gravity. No interaction through any other force, not radiation or strong or weak forces. Only gravity. That's the only effect shadow matter has on *our* universe. Gravity.

"And a big chunk of this stuff is there on the other side of Sag A West. It's exerting enough gravity to affect the path of the infalling gas. And to affect the probe's drift. And even to affect the young stars because the shadow matter-thing's exerting a counterpull on the massive star clouds, and that's keeping them from being ripped apart by the hole as soon as they otherwise would be. So they have time to collapse into young stars."

"Well, that's sort of it, but you've left out some things that alter and validate the whole," Kane said impatiently, scowling.

"Yes, Tirzah, dear heart, you don't see the—you can't just say that 'counterpull'—let me try once more."

They were off again, but this time I didn't listen. So maybe I hadn't seen the theory whole, but only glimpsed its shadow. It was enough.

They had a viable theory. I had a viable expedition, with a goal, and cooperatively productive scientists, and a probability of success.

It was enough.

Kane and Ajit prepared the second minicap for the big ship, and I prepared to move the probe. Our mood was jubilant. There was much laughing and joking, interrupted by intense bursts of incomprehensible jabbering between Ajit and Kane.

But before I finished my programming, Ajit's head disappeared.

7. SHIP

Kane worked all day on his shadow-matter theory. He worked ferociously, hunched over his terminal like a hungry dog with a particularly meaty bone, barely glancing up and saying little. Ajit worked, too, but the quality of his working was different. The terminals both connect to the same computer, of course; whatever Kane had, Ajit had, too. Ajit could follow whatever Kane did.

But that's what Ajit was doing: following. I could tell it from the timing of his accesses, from the whole set of his body. He was a decent scientist, but he was not Kane. Given the data and enough time, Ajit might have been able to go where Kane raced ahead now. Maybe. Or, he might have been able to make valuable additions to Kane's thinking. But Kane gave him no time; Kane was always there first, and he asked no help. He had shut Ajit out completely. For Kane, nothing existed right now but his work.

Toward evening he looked up abruptly and said to me, "They'll move the probe. The uploads—they'll move it."

I said, "How do you know? It's not time yet, according to the schedule."

"No. But they'll move it. If I figured out the shadow matter here, I will there, too. I'll decide that more data is needed from the other side of Sag A West, where the main shadow mass is."

I looked at him. He looked demented, like some sort of Roman warrior who has just wrestled with a lion. All that was missing was the blood. Wild, filthy hair—when had he last showered? Clothes spotted with the food I'd made him gulp down at noon. Age lines beginning, under strain and fatigue and despite the rejuve, to drag down the muscles of his face. And his eyes shining like Sag A West itself.

God, I loved him.

I said, with careful emphasis, "You're right. The *Tirzah upload* will move the ship for better measurements."

"Then we'll get more data in a few days," Ajit said. "But the radiation on the other side of Sag A West is still intense. We must hope nothing gets damaged in the probe programs, or in the uploads themselves, before we get the new data."

"We better hope nothing gets damaged long before that in my upload," Kane said, "or they won't even know what data to collect." He turned back to his screen.

The brutal words hung in the air.

I saw Ajit turn his face away from me. Then he rose and walked into the galley.

If I followed him too soon, he would see it as pity. His shame would mount even more.

"Kane," I said in a low, furious voice, "you are despicable."

He turned to me in genuine surprise. "What?"

"You know what." But he didn't. Kane wasn't even conscious of what he'd said. To him, it was a simple, evident truth. Without the Kane upload, no one on the probe would know how to do first-class science.

"I want to see you upstairs on the observation deck," I said to him. "Not now, but in ten minutes. And *you* announce that you want *me* to see something up there." The time lag, plus Kane's suggesting the trip, would keep Ajit from knowing I was protecting him.

But now I had put up Kane's back. He was tired, he was stressed, he was inevitably coming down from the unsustainable high of his discovery. Neither body nor mind can keep at that near-hysterical pitch for too long. I had misjudged, out of my own anger at him.

He snapped, "I'll see you on the observation deck when *I* want to see you there, and not otherwise. Don't push me around, Tirzah. Not even as captain." He turned back to his display.

Ajit emerged from the galley with three glasses on a tray. "A celebratory drink. A major discovery deserves that. At a minimum."

Relief was so intense I nearly showed it on my face. It was all right. I had misread Ajit, underestimated him. He ranked the magnitude of Kane's discovery higher than his own lack of participation in it, after all. Ajit was, first, a scientist.

He handed a glass to me, one to Kane, one for himself. Kane took a hasty, perfunctory gulp and returned to his display. But I cradled mine, smiling at Ajit, trying with warmth to convey the admiration I felt for his rising above the personal.

"Where did you get the wine? It wasn't on the ship manifest!"

"It was in my personal allotment," Ajit said, smiling.

Personal allotments are not listed nor examined. A bottle of wine, the statue of Shiva . . . Ajit had brought some interesting choices for a galactic core. I sipped the red liquid. It tasted different from the Terran or Martian wines I had grown up with: rougher, more full-bodied, not as sweet.

"Wonderful, Ajit."

"I thought you would like it. It is made in my native New Bombay, from genemod grapes brought from Terra."

He didn't go back to his terminal. For the next half hour, he entertained me with stories of New Bombay. He was a good storyteller, sharp and funny. Kane worked steadily, ignoring us. The ten-minute deadline I had set for him to call me up to the observation deck came and went.

After half an hour, Kane stood and staggered. Once before, when he'd broken Ajit's statue, stiffness after long sitting had made Kane unsteady. That time he'd caught himself after simply bumping the wardroom table. This time he crashed heavily to the floor.

"Kane!"

"Nothing, nothing . . . don't make a fuss, Tirzah! You just won't leave me alone!"

This was so unfair that I wanted to slap him. I didn't. Kane rose by himself, shook his head like some great beast, and said, "I'm just exhausted. I'm going to bed."

I didn't try to stop him from going to his bunk. I had planned on sleeping with Ajit, anyway. It seemed that some slight false note had crept into his storytelling in the last five minutes, some forced exaggeration.

But he smiled at me, and I decided I'd been wrong. I was very tired, too. All at once I wished I could sleep alone this night.

But I couldn't. Ajit, no matter how well he'd recovered from Kane's unconscious brutality, nonetheless had to feel bruised at some level. It was my job to find out where, and how much, and to set it to rights. It was my job to keep the expedition as productive as possible, to counteract Kane's dismissing and belittling behavior toward Ajit. It was my job.

I smiled back at him.

8. PROBE

When Ajit's head disappeared, no one panicked. We'd expected this, of course; in fact, we'd expected it sooner. The probe drifted in a sea of the most intense radiation in the galaxy, much of it at lethal wavelengths: gamma rays from Sagittarius East, X-rays, powerful winds of ionized particles, things I couldn't name. That the probe's shielding had held this long was a minor miracle. It couldn't hold forever. Some particle or particles had penetrated it and reached the computer, contaminating a piece of the upload-maintenance program.

It was a minor glitch. The backup kicked in a moment later and Ajit's head reappeared. But we all knew this was only the beginning. It would happen again, and again, and eventually programming would be hit that couldn't be restored by automatic backup, because the backup would go, too, in a large enough hit—or because uploads are not like other computer programs. We are more than that, and less. An upload has backups to maintain the shadows we see of each other and the ship, the shadows that keep our captured minds sane. But an upload cannot house backups of itself. Even one copy smudges too much, and the copy contaminates the original. It has been tried, with painful results.

Moreover, we uploads run only partly on the main computer. An upload is neither a biological entity nor a long stream of code, but something more than both. Some of the substratum, the hardware, is wired like actual neurons, although constructed of sturdier stuff: thousands of miles of nano-constructed organic polymers. This is why analogues think at the rate of the human brain, not the much faster rate of computers. It's also why we feel as our originals do.

After Ajit's maintenance glitch our mood, which had been exuberant, sobered. But it didn't sour. We worked steadily, with focus and hope, deciding where exactly to position the probe and then entering the coordinates for the jump.

"See you soon," we said to each other. I kissed both Kane and Ajit lightly on the lips. Then we all shut down and the probe jumped.

Days later, we emerged on the other side of Sag A West, all three of us still intact. If it were in my nature, I would have said a prayer of thanksgiving. Instead I said to Ajit, "Still have a head, I see."

"And a good thing he does," Kane said absently, already plunging for the chair in front of his terminal. "We'll need it. And—Ajit, the mass detectors . . . great shitting gods!"

It seems we were to have thanksgiving after all, if only perversely. I said, "What is it? What's there?" The displays showed nothing at all.

"Nothing at all," Ajit said. "And everything."

"Speak English!"

Ajit—I doubt Kane had even heard me, in his absorption—said, "The mass detectors are showing a huge mass less than a quarter light-year away. The radiation detectors—all of them—are showing nothing at all. We're—"

"We're accelerating fast." I studied ship's data; the rate of acceleration made me blink. "We're going to hit whatever it is. Not soon, but the tidal forces—"

The probe was small, but the tidal forces of something this big would still rip it apart when it got close enough.

Something this big. But there was, to all other sensors, nothing there.

Nothing but shadows.

A strange sensation ran over me. Not fear, but something more complicated, much more eerie.

My voice sounded strange in my ears. "What if we hit it? I know you said radiation of all types will go right through shadow matter just as if it isn't there"—*because it isn't, not in our universe*—"but what about the probe? What if we hit it before we take the final event-horizon measurements on Sag A*?"

"We won't hit it," Ajit said. "We'll move before then, Tirzah, back to the hole. Kane—"

They forget me again. I went up to the observation deck. Looking out through the clear hull, I stared at the myriad of stars on the side of the night sky away from Sag A West. Then I turned to look toward that vast three-armed cloud of turning plasma, radiating as it cools. Nothing blocked my view of Sag A West. Yet between us lay a huge, massive body of shadow matter, unseen, pulling on everything else my dazed senses could actually see.

To my left, all the exotic plants in the observatory disappeared.

Ajit and Kane worked feverishly, until once more I made them shut down for "sleep." The radiation here was nearly as great as it had been in our first location. We were right inside Sagittarius A East, the huge expanding shell of an unimaginable explosion sometime during the last 100,000 years. Most of Sag A East wasn't visible at the wavelengths I could see, but the gamma-ray detectors were going crazy.

"We can't stop for five hours!" Kane cried. "Don't you realize how much damage the radiation could do in that time? We need to get all the data we can, work on it, and send off the second minicap!"

"We're going to send off the second minicap right now," I said. "And we'll only shut down for three hours. But, Kane, we are going to do that. I mean it. Uploads run even more damage from not running maintenance than we do from external radiation. You know that."

He did. He scowled at me, and cursed, and fussed with the minicap, but then he fired the minicap off and shut down.

Ajit said, "Just one more minute, Tirzah. I want to show you something."

"Ajit—"

"No, it's not mathematical. I promise. It's something I brought onto the *Kepler*. The object was not included in the probe program, but I can show you a holo."

Somewhere in the recesses of the computer, Ajit's upload created a program and a two-dimensional holo appeared on an empty display screen. I blinked at it, surprised.

It was a statue of some sort of god with four arms, enclosed in a circle of flames, made of what looked like very old bronze.

"This is Nataraja," Ajit said. "Shiva dancing."

"Ajit—"

"No, I am not a god worshipper," he smiled. "You know me better than that, Tirzah. Hinduism has many gods—thousands—but they are, except to the ignorant, no more than embodiments of different aspects of reality. Shiva is the dance of creation and destruction, the constant flow of energy in the cosmos. Birth and death and rebirth. It seemed fitting to bring him to the galactic core, where so much goes on of all three. This statue has been in my family for four hundred years. I must bring it home, along with the answers to our experiments."

"You will bring Shiva back to New Bombay," I said softly, "and your answers, too."

"Yes, I have begun to think so." He smiled at me, a smile with all the need of his quicksilver personality in it, but also all the courtesy and hope. "Now I will sleep."

9. SHIP

The next morning, after a deep sleep one part sheer exhaustion and one part sex, I woke to find Ajit already out of bed and seated in front of his terminal. He rose the moment I entered the wardroom and turned to me with a grave face. "Tirzah. The minicap arrived. I already put the data into the system."

"What's wrong? Where's Kane?"

"Still asleep, I imagine."

I went to Kane's bunk. He lay on his back, still in the clothes he'd worn for three days, smelling sour and snoring softly. I thought of waking him, then decided to wait a bit. Kane could certainly use the sleep, and I could use the time with Ajit. I went back to the wardroom, tightening the belt on my robe.

"What's wrong?" I repeated.

"I put the data from the minicap into the system. It's all corrections to the last minicap's data. Kane says the first set was wrong."

"Kane?" I said stupidly.

"The Kane-analogue," Ajit explained patiently. "He says radiation hit the probe's sensors for the first batch, before any of them realized it. They fired off the preliminary data right after the jump, you know, because they had no idea how long the probe could last. Now they've had time to discover where the radiation hit, to restore the sensor programs, and to retake the measurements. The Kane analogue says these new ones are accurate, the others weren't."

I tried to take it all in. "So Kane's shadow-matter theory—none of that is true?"

"I don't know," Ajit said. "How can anybody know until we see if the data supports it? The minicap only just arrived."

"Then I might not have moved the probe," I said, meaning "the other I." My analogue. I didn't know what I was saying. The shock was too great. All that theorizing, all Kane's sharp triumph, all that tension . . .

I looked more closely at Ajit. He looked very pale, and as fatigued as a genemod man of his youth can look. I said, "You didn't sleep much."

"No. Yesterday was . . . difficult."

"Yes," I agreed, noting the characteristically polite understatement. "Yes."

"Should I wake Kane?" Ajit said, almost diffidently.

"I'll do it."

Kane was hard to wake. I had to shake him several times before he struggled up to consciousness.

"Tirzah?"

"Who else? Kane, you must get up. Something's happened."

"Wh-what?" He yawned hugely and slumped against the bulkhead. His whole body reeked.

I braced myself. "The second minicap arrived. Your analogue sent a recording. He says the prelim data was compromised, due to radiation-caused sensor malfunction."

That woke him. He stared at me as if I were an executioner. "The data's compromised? *All* of it?"

"I don't know."

Kane pushed out of his bunk and ran into the wardroom. Ajit said, "I put the minicap data into the system already, but I—" Kane wasn't listening. He tore into the data, and after a few minutes he actually bellowed.

"No!"

I flattened myself against the bulkhead, not from fear but from surprise. I had never heard a grown man make a noise like that.

But there were no other noises. Kane worked silently, ferociously. Ajit sat at his own terminal and worked, too, not yesterday's tentative copying but the real thing. I put hot coffee beside them both. Kane gulped his steaming, Ajit ignored his.

After half an hour, Kane turned to me. Defeat pulled like gravity at everything on his face, eyes and lips and jaw muscles. Only his filthy hair sprang upward. He said simply, with the naked straightforwardness of despair, "The new data invalidates the idea of shadow matter."

I heard myself say, "Kane, go take a shower."

To my surprise, he went, shambling from the room. Ajit worked a few minutes longer, then climbed the ladder to the observation deck. Over his shoulder he said, "Tirzah, I want to be alone, please. Don't come."

I didn't. I sat at the tiny wardroom table, looked at my own undrunk coffee, and thought of nothing.

10. PROBE

The data from the probe's new position looked good, Kane said. That was his word: "good." Then he returned to his terminal.

"Ajit?" I was coming to rely on him more and more for translation. He was just as busy as Kane, but kinder. This made sense. If, to Kane, Ajit was a secondary but still necessary party to the intellectual action, that's what I was to both of them. Ajit had settled into this position, secure that he was valued. I could feel myself doing the same. The cessation of struggle turned us both kinder.

Kane, never insecure, worked away.

Ajit said, "The new readings confirm a large gravitational mass affecting the paths of both the infalling gas and the probe. The young stars so close to Sag A* are a much knottier problem. We've got to modify the whole theory of star formation to account for the curvatures of spacetime caused by the hole *and* by the shadow mass. It's very complex. Kane's got the computer working on that, and I'm going to take readings on Sag A West, in its different parts, and on stars on the other side of the mass and look at those."

"What about the mass detectors? What do they say?"

"They say we're being pulled toward a mass of about a half million suns."

A half million suns. And we couldn't see it: not with our eyes, nor radio sensors, nor X-ray detectors, nor anything.

"I have a question. Does it have an event horizon? Is it swallowing light, like a black hole does? Isn't it the gravity of a black hole that swallows light?"

"Yes. But radiation, including light, goes right through this shadow matter, Tirzah. Don't you understand? It doesn't interact with normal radiation at all."

"But it has gravity. Why doesn't its gravity trap the light?"

"I don't know." He hesitated. "Kane thinks maybe it doesn't interact with radiation as particles, which respond to gravity. Only as waves."

"How can it do that?"

Ajit took my shoulders and shook them playfully. "I told you—*we don't know*. This is brand-new, dear heart. We know as much about what it will and will not do as primitive hominids knew about fire."

"Well, don't make a god of it," I said, and it was a test. Ajit passed. He didn't stiffen as if I'd made some inappropriate reference to the drawing of Shiva he'd shown me last night. Instead, he laughed and went back to work.

"Tirzah! Tirzah!"

The automatic wake-up brought me out of shutdown. Ajit must have been brought back online a few moments before me, because he was already calling my name. Alarm bells clanged.

"It's Kane! He's been hit!"

I raced into Kane's bunk. He lay still amid the bedclothes. It wasn't the maintenance program that had taken the hit, because every part of his body was intact; so were the bedclothes. But Kane lay stiff and unresponsive.

"Run the full diagnostics," I said to Ajit.

"I already started them."

"Kane," I said, shaking him gently, then harder. He moved a little, groaned. So his upload wasn't dead.

I sat on the edge of the bunk, fighting fear, and took his hand. "Kane, love, can you hear me?"

He squeezed my fingers. The expression on his face didn't change. After a silence in which time itself seemed to stop, Ajit said, "The diagnostics are complete. About a third of brain function is gone."

I got into the bunk beside Kane and put my arms around him.

———

Ajit and I did what we could. Our uploads patched and copied, using material from both of us. Yes, the copying would lead to corruption, but we were beyond that.

Because an upload runs on such a complex combination of computer and nano-constructed polymer networks, we cannot simply be replaced by a backup program cube. The unique software/hardware retes are also why a corrupted analogue is not exactly the same as a stroke- or tumor-impaired human brain.

The analogue brain does not have to pump blood or control breathing. It does not have to move muscles or secrete hormones. Although closely tied to the "purer" programs that maintain our illusion of moving and living as three-dimensional beings in a three-dimensional ship, the analogue brain is tied to the computer in much more complex ways than any fleshy human using a terminal. The resources of the computer were at our disposal, but they could only accomplish limited aims.

When Ajit and I had finished putting together as much of Kane, or a pseudo-Kane, as we could, he walked into the wardroom and sat down. He looked, moved, smiled the same. That part is easy to repair, as easy as had been replacing Ajit's head or the exotics on the observation deck. But the man staring blankly at the terminal was not really Kane.

"What was I working on?" he said.

I got out, "Shadow matter."

"Shadow matter? What's that?"

Ajit said softly, "I have all your work, Kane. Our work. I think I can finish it, now that you've started us in the right direction."

He nodded, looking confused. "Thank you, Ajit." Then, with a flash of his old magnificent combativeness, "But you better get it right!"

"With your help," Ajit said gaily, and in that moment I came close to truly loving him.

They worked out a new division of labor. Kane was able to take the sensor readings and run them through the pre-set algorithms. Actually, Ajit probably could have trained me to do that. But Kane seemed content, frowning earnestly at his displays.

Ajit took over the actual science. I said to him, when we had a moment alone, "Can you do it?"

"I think so," he said, without either anger or arrogance. "I have the foundation that Kane laid. And we worked out some of the preliminaries together."

"We have only one more jump left."

"I know, Tirzah."

"With the risk of radiation killing us all—"

"Not yet. Give me a little more time."

I rested a moment against his shoulder. "All right. A little more time."

He put his arm around me, not in passion but in comradeship. None of us, we both knew, had all that much time left.

11. SHIP

Kane was only temporarily defeated by the contamination of the probe data. Within half a day, he had aborted his shadow-matter theory, archived his work on it, and gone back to his original theories about the mysteriously massive young stars near the hole. He used the probe's new data, which were all logical amplifications of the prelim readings. "I've got some ideas," he told me. "We'll see."

He wasn't as cheerful as usual, let alone as manically exuberant as during the shadow-matter "discovery," but he was working steadily. A mountain, Kane. It would take a lot to actually erode him, certainly more than a failed theory. That rocky insensitivity had its strengths.

Ajit, on the other hand, was not really working. I couldn't follow the displays on his terminal, but I could read the body language. He was restless, inattentive. But what worried me was something else, his attitude toward Kane.

All Ajit's anger was gone.

I watched carefully, while seemingly bent over ship's log or embroidery. Anger is the least subtle of the body's signals. Even when a person is successfully concealing most of it, the signs are there if you know where to look: the tight neck muscles, the turned-away posture, the tinge in the voice. Ajit displayed none of this. Instead, when he faced Kane, as he did during the lunch I insisted we all eat together at the wardroom table, I saw something else. A sly superiority, a secret triumph.

I could be wrong, I thought. I have been wrong before. By now I disliked Ajit so much that I didn't trust my own intuitions.

"Ajit," I said as we finished the simple meal I'd put together, "will you please—"

Ship's alarms went off with a deafening clang. *Breach, breach, breach.*

I whirled toward ship's display, which automatically illuminated. The breach was in the starboard hold, and it was full penetration by a mass of about a hundred grams. Within a minute, the nanos had put on a temporary patch. The alarm stopped and the computer began hectoring me.

"Breach sealed with temporary nano patch. Seal must be reinforced within two hours with permanent hull patch, type 6-A. For location of breach and patch supply, consult ship's log. If unavailability of—" I shut it off.

"Could be worse," Kane said.

"Well, of course it could be worse," I snapped, and immediately regretted it. I was not allowed to snap. That I had done so was an indication of how much the whole situation on the *Kepler* was affecting me. That wasn't allowed, either; it was unprofessional.

Kane wasn't offended. "Could have hit the engines or the living pod instead of just a hold. Actually, I'm surprised it hasn't happened

159

before. There's a lot of drifting debris in this area."

Ajit said, "Are you going into the hold, Tirzah?"

Of course I was going into the hold. But this time I didn't snap; I smiled at him and said, "Yes, I'm going to suit up now."

"I'm coming, too," Kane said.

I blinked. I'd been about to ask if Ajit wanted to go with me. It would be a good way to observe him away from Kane, maybe ask some discreet questions. I said to Kane, "Don't you have to work?"

"The work isn't going anywhere. And I want to retrieve the particle. It didn't exit the ship, and at a hundred grams, there's going to be some of it left after the breach."

Ajit had stiffened at being preempted, yet again, by Kane. Ajit would have wanted to retrieve the particle, too; there is nothing more interesting to space scientists than dead rocks. Essentially, I'd often thought, Sag A* was no more than a very hot, very large dead rock. I knew better than to say this aloud.

I could have ordered Ajit to accompany me, and ordered Kane to stay behind. But that, I sensed, would only make things worse. Ajit, in his present mood of deadly sensitivity, would not take well to orders from anyone, even me. I wasn't going to give him the chance to retreat more into whatever nasty state of mind he currently inhabited.

"Well, then, let's go," I said ungraciously to Kane, who only grinned at me and went to get our suits.

The holds, three of them for redundancy safety, are full of supplies of all types. Every few days I combine a thorough ship inspection with lugging enough food forward to sustain us. We aren't uploads; we need bodily nurturing as well as the kind I was supposed to be providing.

All three holds can be pressurized if necessary, but usually they aren't. Air generation and refreshment doesn't cost much power, but it costs some. Kane and I went into the starboard hold in heated s-suits and helmets.

"I'm going to look around," Kane said. He'd brought a handheld, and I saw him calculating the probable trajectory of the particle from the ship's data and the angle of the breach, as far as he could deduce it. Then he disappeared behind a pallet of crates marked SOYSYNTH.

The breach was larger than I'd expected; that hundred-gram particle had hit at a bad angle. But the nanos had done their usual fine job, and the permanent patch went on without trouble. I began the careful inspection of the rest of the hull, using my handheld instruments.

Kane cursed volubly.

"Kane? What is it?"

"Nothing. Bumped into boxes."

"Well, don't. The last thing I want is you messing up my hold." For a physically fit man, Kane is clumsy in motion. I would bet my ship that he can't dance, and bet my life that he never tries.

"I can't see anything. Can't you brighten the light?"

I did, and he bumped around some more. Whenever he brushed something, he cursed. I did an inspection even more carefully than usual, but found nothing alarming. We met each other back by the hold door.

"It's not here," Kane said. "The particle. It's not here."

"You mean you didn't find it."

"No, I mean it's not here. Don't you think I could find a still hot particle in a hold otherwise filled only with large immobile crates?"

I keyed in the door code. "So it evaporated on impact. Ice and ions and dust."

"To penetrate a Schaad hull? No." He reconsidered. "Well, maybe. What did you find?"

"Not much. Pitting and scarring on the outside, nothing unexpected. But no structural stress to worry about."

"The debris here is undoubtedly orbiting the core, but we're so far out it's not moving all that fast. Still, we should had some warning. But I'm more worried about the probe—when is the third minicap due?"

Kane knew as well as I did when the third minicap was due. His asking was the first sign he was as tense as the rest of us.

"Three more days," I said. "Be patient."

"I'm not patient."

"As if that's new data."

"I'm also afraid the probe will be hit by rapidly orbiting debris, and that will be that. Did you know that the stars close in to Sag A* orbit at several thousand clicks per second?"

I knew. He'd told me often enough. The probe was always a speculative proposition, and before now, Kane had been jubilant that we'd gotten any data at all from it.

I'd never heard Kane admit to being "afraid" of anything. Even allowing for the casualness of the phrase.

I wanted to distract him, and, if Kane was really in a resigned and reflective mood, it also seemed a good time to do my job. "Kane, about Ajit—"

"I don't want to talk about that sniveling slacker," Kane said, with neither interest not rancor. "I picked badly for an assistant, that's all."

It hadn't actually been his "pick"; his input had been one of many. I didn't say this. Kane looked around the hold one more time. "I guess you're right. The particle sublimed. Ah, well."

I put the glove of my hand on the arm of his suit—not exactly an intimate caress, but the best I could do in this circumstance. "Kane, how is the young-star mystery going?"

"Not very well. But that's science." The hold door stood open and he lumbered out.

I gave one last look around the hold before turning off the light, but there was nothing more to see.

The mended statue of Shiva was back on the wardroom table, smack in the center, when Kane and I returned from the hold. I don't think Kane, heading straight for his terminal, even noticed. I smiled at Ajit, although I wasn't sure why he had brought the statue back. He'd told me he never wanted to see it again.

"Tirzah, would you perhaps like to play *go*?"

I couldn't conceal my surprise. "*Go*?"

"Yes. Will you play with me?" Accompanied by his most winning smile.

"All right."

He brought out the board and, bizarrely, set it up balanced on his knees. When he saw my face, he said, "We'll play here. I don't want to disturb the Cosmic Dancer."

"All right." I wasn't sure what to think. I drew my chair close to his, facing him, and bent over the board.

We both knew that Ajit was a better player than I. That's why both of us played: he to win, me to lose. I would learn more from the losing position. Very competitive people—and I thought now that I had never known one as competitive as Ajit—relax only when not threatened.

So I made myself nonthreatening in every way I knew, and Ajit and I talked and laughed, and Kane worked doggedly on his theories that weren't going anywhere. The statue of the dancing god leered at me from the table, and I knew with every passing moment how completely I was failing this already failing mission.

12. PROBE

Kane was gentler since the radiation corruption. Who can say how these things happen? Personality, too, is encoded in the human brain, whether flesh or analogue. He was still Kane, but we saw only his gentler, sweeter side. Previously that part of him had been dominated by his combative intellect, which had been a force of nature all its own, like a high wind. Now the intellect had failed, the wind calmed. The landscape beneath lay serene.

"Here, Ajit," Kane said. "These are the equations you wanted run." He sent them to Ajit's terminal, stood, and stretched. The stretch put him slightly off balance, something damaged in the upload that Ajit and I hadn't been able to fix, or find. A brain is such a complex thing. Kane tottered, and Ajit rose swiftly to catch him.

"Careful, Kane. Here, sit down."

Ajit eased Kane into a chair at the wardroom table. I put down my work. Kane said, "Tirzah, I feel funny."

"Funny how?" Alarm ran through me.

"I don't know. Can we play *go*?"

I had taught him the ancient strategy game, and he enjoyed it. He wasn't very good, not nearly as good as I was, but he liked it and didn't seem to mind losing. I got out the board. Ajit, who was a master at *go*, went back to Kane's shadow-matter theory. He was making good progress, I knew, although he said frankly that all the basic ideas were Kane's.

Halfway through our second game of *go*, the entire wardroom disappeared.

A moment of blind panic seized me. I was adrift in the void, nothing to see or feel or hold onto, a vertigo so terrible it blocked any rational thought. It was the equivalent of a long anguished scream, originating in the most primitive part of my now blind brain: *lost, lost, lost, and alone* . . .

The automatic maintenance program kicked in and the wardroom reappeared. Kane gripped the table edge and stared at me, white-faced. I went to him, wrapped my arms around him reassuringly, and gazed at Ajit. Kane clung to me. A part of my mind noted that some aspects of the wardroom were wrong: the galley door was too low to walk through upright, and one chair had disappeared, along with the *go* board. Maintenance code too damaged to restore.

Ajit said softly, "We have to decide, Tirzah. We could take a final radiation hit at any time."

"I know."

I took my arms away from Kane. "Are you all right?"

He smiled. "Yes. Just for a minute I was . . ." He seemed to lose his thought.

Ajit brought his terminal chair to the table, to replace the vanished one. He sat leaning forward, looking from me to Kane and back. "This is a decision all three of us have to make. We have one minicap left to send back to the *Kepler*, and one more jump for ourselves. At any time we could lose . . . everything. You all know that. What do you think we should do? Kane? Tirzah?"

All my life I'd heard that even very flawed people can rise to leadership under the right circumstances. I'd never believed it, not of someone with Ajit's basic personality structure: competitive, paranoid, angry at such a deep level he didn't even know it. I'd been wrong. I believed now.

Kane said, "I feel funny, and that probably means I've taken another minor hit and the program isn't there to repair it. I think . . . I think . . ."

"Kane?" I took his hand.

He had trouble getting words out. "I think we better send the minicap now."

"I agree," Ajit said. "But that means we send it without the data from our next jump, to just outside the event horizon of Sag A*. So the *Kepler* won't get those readings. They'll get the work on shadow matter, but most of the best things on that already went in the second minicap. Still, it's better than nothing, and I'm afraid if we wait to send until after the jump, nothing is what the *Kepler* will get. It will be too late."

Both men looked at me. As captain, the jump decision was mine. I nodded. "I agree, too. Send off the minicap with whatever you've got, and then we'll jump. But not to the event horizon."

"Why not?" Kane burst out, sounding more like himself than at any time since the accident.

"Because there's no point. We can't send any more data back, so the event horizon readings die with us. And we can survive longer if I jump us completely away from the core. Several hundred light-years out, where the radiation is minimal."

Together, as if rehearsed, they both said, "No."

"*No?*"

"No," Ajit said, with utter calm, utter persuasiveness. "We're not going to go out like that, Tirzah."

"But we don't have to go out at all! Not for decades! Maybe centuries! Not until the probe's life-maintenance power is used up—" Or until the probe is hit by space debris. Or until radiation takes us out. Nowhere in space is really safe.

Kane said, "And what would we do for centuries? I'd go mad. I want to work."

"Me, too," Ajit said. "I want to take the readings by the event horizon and make of them what I can, while I can. Even though the *Kepler* will never see them."

They were scientists.

And I? Could even I, station bred, have lived for centuries in this tiny ship, without a goal beyond survival, trapped with these two men? An Ajit compassionate and calm, now that he was on top. A damaged Kane, gentle and intellectually gutted. And a Tirzah, captaining a pointless expedition with nowhere to go and nothing to do.

I would have ended up hating all three of us.

Ajit took my left hand. My right one still held Kane's, so we made a broken circle in the radiation-damaged wardroom.

"All right," I said. "We'll send off the minicap and then jump to the event horizon."

"Yes," Kane said.

Ajit said, "I'm going to go back to work. Tirzah, if you and Kane want to go up to the observation deck, or anywhere, I'll prepare and launch the minicap." Carefully he turned his back and sat at his terminal.

I led Kane to my bunk. This was a first; I always went to the scientists' bunks. My own, as captain, had features for my eyes only. But now it didn't matter.

We made love, and afterward, holding his superb, aging body in my arms, I whispered against his cheek, "I love you, Kane."

"I love you, too," he said simply, and I had no way of knowing if he meant it, or if it was an automatic response dredged up from some half-remembered ritual from another time. It didn't matter. There are a lot more types of love in the universe than I once suspected.

We were silent a long time, and then Kane said, "I'm trying to remember *pi*. I know 3.1, but I can't remember after that."

I said, through the tightness in my throat, "3.141. That's all I remember."

"Three point one four one," Kane said dutifully. I left him repeating it over and over, when I went to jump the probe to the event horizon of Sag A*.

13. SHIP

The second breach of the hull was more serious than the first.

The third minicap had not arrived from the probe. "The analogues are probably all dead," Kane said dully. "They were supposed to jump to one-twenty-fifth of a light-year from the event horizon. Our calculations were always problematic for where exactly that *is*. It's possible they landed inside, and the probe will just spiral around Sag A* forever. Or they got hit with major radiation and fried."

"It's possible," I said. "How is the massive-young-star problem coming?"

"It's not. Mathematical dead end."

He looked terrible, drawn and, again, unwashed. I was more impatient with the latter than I should be. But how hard is it, as a courtesy to your shipmates if nothing else, to get your body into the shower? How long does it take? Kane had stopped exercising, as well.

"Kane," I began, as quietly but firmly as I could manage, "will you—"

The alarms went off, clanging again at 115 decibels. *Breach, breach, breach . . .*

I scanned the displays. "Oh, God—"

"Breach sealed with temporary nano patch," the computer said. "Seal must be reinforced within one half hour with permanent hull patch, type 1-B, supplemented with equipment repair, if possible. For location of breach and patch supply, consult—" I turned it off.

The intruder had hit the backup engine. It was a much larger particle than the first one, although since it had hit us and then gone on its merry way, rather than penetrating the ship, there was no way to recover it for examination. But the outside mass detectors registered a particle of at least two kilos, and it had probably been moving much faster than the first one. If it had hit us directly, we would all be dead. Instead it had given the ship a glancing blow, damaging the backup engine.

"I'll come with you again," Kane said.

"There won't be any particle to collect this time." Or not collect.

"I know. But I'm not getting anywhere here."

Kane and I, s-suited, went into the backup engine compartment. As soon as I saw it, I knew there was nothing I could do. There is damage you can repair, and there is damage you cannot. The back end of the compartment had been sheared off, and part of the engine with it. No wonder the computer had recommended a 1-B patch, which is essentially the equivalent of "Throw a tarp over it and forget it."

While I patched, Kane poked around the edges of the breach, then at the useless engine. He left before I did, and I found him studying ship's display of the hit on my wardroom screen. He wasn't trying to do anything with ship's log, which was not his place and he knew it, but he stood in front of the data, moving his hand when he wanted another screen, frowning horribly.

"What is it, Kane?" I said. I didn't really want to know; the patch had taken hours and I was exhausted. I didn't see Ajit. Sleeping, or up on the observation deck, or, less likely, in the gym.

"Nothing. Whatever that hit was made of, it wasn't radiating. So it wasn't going very fast, or the external sensors would have picked up at least ionization. Either the mass was cold, or the sensors aren't functioning properly."

"I'll run the diagnostics," I said wearily. "Anything else?"

"Yes. I want to move the ship."

I stared at him, my suit half peeled from my body, my helmet defiantly set on the table, pushing the statue of Shiva to one side. "*Move the ship?*"

Ajit appeared in the doorway from his bunk.

"Yes," Kane said. "Move the ship."

"But these are the coordinates the minicap will return to!"

"It's not coming," Kane said. "Don't you listen to anything I say, Tirzah? The uploads didn't make it. The third minicap is days late; if it were coming, it would be here. The probe is gone, the uploads are gone, and we've got all the data we're going to get from them. If we want more, we're going to have to go after it ourselves."

"Go after it?" I repeated, stupidly. "How?"

"I already told you! Move the ship closer into the core so we can take the readings the probe should have taken. Some of them, anyway."

Ajit said, "Moving the ship is completely Tirzah's decision."

His championship of me when I needed no champion, and especially not in that pointlessly assertive voice, angered me more than Kane's suggestion. "Thank you, Ajit, I can handle this!"

Mistake, mistake.

Kane, undeterred, plowed on. "I don't mean we'd go near the event horizon, of course, or even to the probe's first position near the star cluster. But we could move much closer in. Maybe ten light-years from the core, positioned between the northern and western arms of Sag A West."

Ajit said, "Which would put us right in the circumnuclear disk! Where the radiation is much worse than here!"

Kane turned on him, acknowledging Ajit's presence for the first time in days, with an outpouring of all Kane's accumulated frustration and disappointment. "We've been hit twice with particles that damaged the ship. Clearly we're in the path of some equivalent of an asteroid belt orbiting the core at this immense distance. It can't be any less safe in the circumnuclear disk, which, I might remind you, is only shocked molecular gases, with its major radiation profile unknown. Any first-year astronomy student should know that. Or is it just that you're a coward?"

Ajit's skin mottled, then paled. His features did not change expression at all. But I felt the heat coming from him, the primal rage, greater for being contained. He went into his bunk and closed the door.

"Kane!" I said furiously, too exhausted and frustrated and disappointed myself to watch my tone. "You can't—"

"I can't stand any more of this," Kane said. He slammed down the corridor to the gym, and I heard the exercise bike whirr in rage.

I went to my own bunk, locked the door, and squeezed my eyes shut, fighting for control. But even behind my closed eyelids I saw our furious shadows.

―――

After a few hours I called them both together in the wardroom. When Kane refused, I ordered him. I lifted Ajit's statue of Shiva off the table and handed it to him, making its location his problem, as long as it wasn't on the table. Wordlessly he carried it into his bunk and then returned.

"This can't go on," I said calmly. "We all know that. We're in this small space together to accomplish something important, and our mission overrides all our personal feelings. You are both rational men, scientists, or you wouldn't be here."

"Don't patronize us with flattery," Ajit said.

"I'm sorry. I didn't intend to do that. It's true you're both scientists, and it's true you've both been certified rational enough for space travel."

They couldn't argue with that. I didn't mention how often certification boards had misjudged, or been bribed, or just been too dazzled by well-earned reputations to look below the work to the worker. If Kane or Ajit knew all that, they kept it to themselves.

"I blame myself for any difficulties we've had here," I said, in the best Nurturer fashion. Although it was also true. "It's my job to keep a ship running in productive harmony, and this one, I think we can all agree, is not."

No dissension. I saw that both of them dreaded some long, drawn-out discussion on group dynamics, never a topic that goes down well with astrophysicists. Kane said abruptly, "I still want to move the ship."

I had prepared myself for this. "No, Kane. We're not jumping closer in."

He caught at my loophole. "Then can we jump to another location at the same distance from the core? Maybe measurements from another base point would help."

"We're not jumping anywhere until I'm sure the third minicap isn't coming."

"How long will that be?" I could see the formidable intelligence under the childish tantrums already racing ahead, planning measurements, weighing options.

"We'll give it another three days."

"All right." Suddenly he smiled, his first in days. "Thanks, Tirzah."

I turned to Ajit. "Ajit, what can we do for your work? What do you need?"

"I ask for nothing," he said, with such a strange, intense, unreadable expression that for a moment I felt irrational fear. Then he stood and went into his bunk. I heard the door lock.

I had failed again.

No alarm went off in the middle of the night. There was nothing overt to wake me. But I woke anyway, and I heard someone moving quietly around the wardroom. The muscles of my right arm tensed to open my bunk, and I forced them to still.

Something wasn't right. Intuition, that mysterious shadow of rational thought, told me to lie motionless. To not open my bunk, to not even reach out and access the ship's data on my bunk screen. To not move at all.

Why?

I didn't know.

The smell of coffee wafted from the wardroom. So one of the men couldn't sleep, made some coffee, turned on his terminal. So what?

Don't move, said that pre-reasoning part of my mind, from the shadows.

The coffee smell grew stronger. A chair scraped. Ordinary, mundane sounds.

Don't move.

I didn't have to move. This afternoon I had omitted to mention to Kane and Ajit those times that certification boards had misjudged, or been bribed, or just been too dazzled by well-earned reputations to look below the work to the worker. Those times in which the cramped conditions of space, coupled with swollen egos and frenzied work, had led to disaster for a mission Nurturer. But we had learned. My bunk had equipment the scientists did not know about.

Carefully I slid my gaze to a spot directly above me on the bunk ceiling. Only my eyes moved. I pattern-blinked: two quick, three beats closed, two quick, a long steady stare. The screen brightened.

This was duplicate ship data. Not a backup; it was entirely separate, made simultaneously from the same sensors as the main log but routed into separate, freestanding storage that could not be reached from the main computer. Scientists are all sophisticated users. There is no way to keep data from any who wish to alter it except by discreet, unknown, untraceable storage. I pattern-blinked, not moving so much as a finger or a toe in the bed, to activate various screens of ship data.

It was easy to find.

Yesterday, at 1850 hours, the minicap bay had opened and received a minicap. Signal had failed to transmit to the main computer. Today at 300 hours, which was fifteen minutes ago, the minicap bay had been opened manually and the payload removed. Again signal had failed to the main computer.

The infrared signature in the wardroom, seated at his terminal, was Ajit.

It was possible the signal failures were coincidental, and Ajit was even now transferring data from the third minicap into the computer, enjoying a cup of hot coffee while he did so, gloating in getting a perfectly legitimate jump on Kane. But I didn't think so.

What did I think?

I didn't have to think; I just knew. I could see it unfolding, clear as a holovid. All of it. Ajit had stolen the second minicap, too. That had been the morning after Kane and I had slept so soundly, the morning after Ajit had given us wine to celebrate Kane's shadow-matter theory. What had been in that wine? We'd slept soundly, and Ajit told us that the minicap had come before we were awake. Ajit said he'd already put it into the computer. It carried Kane's upload's apology that the prelim data, the data from which Kane had constructed his shadow-matter thesis, was wrong, contaminated by a radiation strike.

Ajit had fabricated that apology and that replacement data. The actual second minicap would justify Kane's work, not undo it. Ajit was saving all three minicaps to use for himself, to claim the shadow matter discovery for his own. He'd used the second minicap to discredit the first; he would claim the third had never arrived, had never been sent from the dying probe.

The real Kane, my Kane, hadn't found the particle from the first ship's breach because it had, indeed, been made of shadow matter. That, and not slow speed, had been why the particle showed no radiation. The particle had exerted gravity on our world, but nothing else. The second breach, too, had been shadow matter. I knew that as surely as if Kane had shown me the pages of equations to prove it.

I knew something else, too. If I went into the shower and searched my body very carefully, every inch of it, I would find in some inconspicuous place the small, regular hole into which a subdermal tracker had gone the night of the drugged wine. So would Kane. Trackers would apprise Ajit of every move we made, not only large-muscle moves like a step or a hug, but small ones like accessing my bunk display of ship's data. That was what my intuition had been warning me of. Ajit did not want to be discovered during his minicap thefts.

I had the same trackers in my own repertoire. Only I had not thought this mission deteriorated enough to need them. I had not wanted to think that. I'd been wrong.

But how would Ajit make use of Kane's stolen work with Kane there to claim it for himself?

I already knew the answer, of course. I had known it from the moment I pattern-blinked at the ceiling, which was the moment I finally admitted to myself how monstrous this mission had turned.

I pushed open the bunk door and called cheerfully, "Hello? Do I smell coffee? Who's out there?"

"I am," Ajit said genially. "I cannot sleep. Come have some coffee."

"Coming, Ajit."

I put on my robe, tied it at my waist, and slipped the gun from its secret mattress compartment into my palm.

14. PROBE

The probe jumped successfully. We survived.

This close to the core, the view wasn't as spectacular as it was farther out. Sag A*, which captured us in orbit immediately, now appeared as a fuzzy region dominating starboard. The fuzziness, Ajit said, was a combination of Hawking radiation and superheated gases being swallowed by the black hole. To port, the intense blue cluster of IRS16 was muffled by the clouds of ionized plasma around the probe. We experienced some tidal forces, but the probe was so small that the gravitational tides didn't yet cause much damage.

Ajit has found a way to successfully apply Kane's shadow-matter theory to the paths of the infalling gases, as well as to the orbits of the young stars near Sag A*. He says there may well be a really lot of shadow matter near the core, and maybe even farther out. It may even provide enough mass to "balance" the universe, keeping it from either flying apart forever or collapsing in on itself. Shadow matter, left over from the very beginning of creation, may preserve creation.

Kane nods happily as Ajit explains. Kane holds my hand. I stroke his palm gently with my thumb, making circles like tiny orbits.

15. SHIP

Ajit sat, fully dressed and with steaming coffee at his side, in front of his terminal. I didn't give him time to get the best of me. I walked into the wardroom and fired.

The sedative dart dropped him almost instantly. It was effective, for his body weight, for an hour. Kane didn't hear the thud as Ajit fell off his chair and onto the deck; Kane's bunk door stayed closed. I went into Ajit's bunk and searched every cubic meter of it, overriding the lock on his personal storage space. Most of that was taken up with the bronze statue of Shiva. The minicaps were not there, nor anywhere else in his bunk.

I tried the galley next, and came up empty.

Same for the shower, the gym, the supply closets.

Ajit could have hidden the cubes in the engine compartments or the fuel bays or any of a dozen other ship's compartments, but they weren't pressurized and he would have had to either suit up or pressurize them. Either one would have shown up in my private ship data, and they hadn't. Ajit probably hadn't wanted to take the risk of too much covert motion around the ship. He'd only had enough drugs to put Kane and me out once. Otherwise, he wouldn't have risked subdermal trackers.

I guessed he'd hidden the cubes in the observatory.

Looking there involved digging. By the time I'd finished, the exotics lay yanked up in dying heaps around the room. The stones of the fountain had been flung about. I was filthy and sweating, my robe smeared with soil. But I'd found them, the two crystal cubes from the second and third minicaps, removed from their heavy shielding. Their smooth surfaces shed the dirt easily.

Forty-five minutes had passed.

I went downstairs to wake Kane. The expedition would have to jump immediately; there is no room on a three-man ship to confine a prisoner for long. Even if I could protect Kane and me from Ajit, I didn't think I could protect Ajit from Kane. These minicaps held the validation of Kane's shadow-matter work, and in another man, joy over that would have eclipsed the theft. I didn't think it would be that way with Kane.

Ajit still lay where I'd dropped him. The tranquilizer is reliable. I shot Ajit with a second dose and went into Kane's bunk. He wasn't there.

I stood too still for too long, then frantically scrambled into my s-suit.

I had already searched everywhere in the pressurized sections of the ship. Oh, let him be taking a second, fruitless look at the starboard hold, hoping to find some trace of the first particle that had hit us! Let him be in the damaged backup engine compartment, afire with some stupid, brilliant idea to save the engine! Let him be—

"Kane! *Kane!*"

He lay in the starboard hold, on his side, his suit breached. He lay below a jagged piece of plastic from a half-open supply box. Ajit had made it look as if Kane had tried to open a box marked SENSOR REPLACEMENTS, had torn his suit, and the suit sealer nanos had failed. It was an altogether clumsy attempt, but one that, in the absence of any other evidence and a heretofore spotless reputation, would probably have worked.

The thing inside the suit was not Kane. Not anymore.

I knelt beside him. I put my arms around him and begged, cried, pleaded with him to come back. I pounded my gloves on the deck until I, too, risked suit breach. I think, in that abandoned and monstrous moment, I would not have cared.

Then I went into the wardroom, exchanged my tranquilizer gun for a knife, and slit Ajit's throat. I only regretted that he wasn't awake when I did it, and I only regretted that much, much later.

I prepared the ship for the long jump back to the Orion Arm. After the jump would come the acceleration-deceleration to Skillian, the closest settled world, which will take about a month standard. Space physics which I don't understand make this necessary; a ship cannot jump too close to a large body of matter like a planet. Shadow matter, apparently, does not count.

Both Ajit and Kane's bodies rest in the cold of the nonpressurized port hold. Kane's initial work on shadow matter rests in my bunk. Every night I fondle the two cubes which will make him famous— more famous—on the settled Worlds. Every day I look at the data, the equations, the rest of his work on his terminal. I don't understand it, but sometimes I think I can see Kane, his essential self, in these intelligent symbols, these unlockings of the secrets of cosmic energy.

It was our shadow selves, not our essential ones, that destroyed my mission, the shadows in the core of each human being. Ajit's ambition and rivalry. Kane's stunted vision of other people and their limits. My pride, which led me to think I was in control of murderous rage long after it had reached a point of no return. In all of us.

I left one thing behind at the center of the galaxy. Just before the *Kepler* jumped, I jettisoned Ajit's statue of a Shiva dancing, in the direction of Sag A*. I don't know for sure, but I imagine it will travel toward the black hole at the galaxy's core, be caught eventually by its gravity, and spiral in, to someday disappear over the event horizon into some unimaginable singularity. That's what I want to happen to the statue. I hate it.

As to what will happen to me, I don't have the energy to hate it. I'll tell the authorities everything. My license as a Nurturer will surely be revoked, but I won't stand trial for the murder of Ajit. A captain is supreme law on her ship. I had the legal authority to kill Ajit. However, it's unlikely that any scientific expedition will hire me as captain ever again. My useful life is over, and any piece of it left is no more than one of the ashy, burned-out stars Kane says orbit Sag A*, uselessly circling the core until its final death, giving no light.

A shadow.

16. PROBE

We remain near the galactic core, Kane and Ajit and I. The event horizon of Sag A* is about one-fiftieth of a light-year below us. As we spiral closer, our speed is increasing dramatically. The point of no return is one-twentieth of a light-year. The lethal radiation, oddly enough, is less here than when we were drifting near the shadow matter on the other side of Sag A West, but it is enough.

I think at least part of my brain has been affected, along with the repair program to fix it. It's hard to be sure, but I can't seem to remember much before we came aboard the probe, or details of why we're here. Sometimes I almost remember, but then it slips away. I know that Kane and Ajit and I are shadows of something, but I don't remember what.

Ajit and Kane work on their science. I have forgotten what it's about, but I like to sit and watch them together. Ajit works on ideas and Kane assists in minor ways, as once Kane worked on ideas and Ajit assisted in minor ways. We all know the science will go down into Sag A* with us. The scientists do it anyway, for no other gain than pure love of the work. This is, in fact, the purest science in the universe.

Our mission is a success. Ajit and Kane have answers. I have kept them working harmoniously, have satisfied all their needs while they did it, and have captained my ship safely into the very heart of the galaxy. I am content.

Not that there aren't difficulties, of course. It's disconcerting to go up on the observation deck. Most of the exotics remain, blooming in wild profusion, but a good chunk of the hull has disappeared. The effect is that anything up there—flowers, bench, people—is drifting through naked space, held together only by the gravity we exert on each other. I don't understand how we can breathe up there; surely the air is gone. There are a lot of things I don't understand now, but I accept them.

The wardroom is mostly intact, except that you have to stoop to go through the door to the galley, which is only about two feet tall, and Ajit's bunk has disappeared. We manage fine with two bunks, since I sleep every night with Ajit or Kane. The terminals are intact. One of them won't display anymore, though. Ajit has used it to hold a holo he programmed on a functioning part of the computer and superimposed over where the defunct display stood. The holo is a rendition of a image he showed me once before, of an Indian god, Shiva.

Shiva is dancing. He dances, four-armed and graceful, in a circle decorated with flames. Everything about him is dynamic, waving arms and kicking uplifted leg and mobile expression. Even the flames in the circle dance. Only Shiva's face is calm, detached, serene. Kane, especially, will watch the holo for hours.

The god, Ajit tells us, represents the flow of cosmic energy in the universe. Shiva creates, destroys, creates again. All matter and all energy participate in this rhythmic dance, patterns made and unmade throughout all of time.

Shadow matter—that's what Kane and Ajit are working on. I

remember now. Something decoupled from the rest of the universe right after its creation. But shadow matter, too, is part of the dance. It exerted gravitational pull on our ship. We cannot see it, but it is there, changing the orbits of stars, the trajectories of lives, in the great shadow play of Shiva's dancing.

I don't think Kane, Ajit, and I have very much longer. But it doesn't matter, not really. We have each attained what we came for, and since we, too, are part of the cosmic pattern, we cannot really be lost. When the probe goes down into the black hole at the core, if we last that long, it will be as a part of the inevitable, endless, glorious flow of cosmic energy, the divine dance.

I am ready.

THE COLONEL RETURNS
TO THE STARS

~~~~~~

by Robert Silverberg

Among the dozens of novels and hundreds of short stories Robert Silverberg has written during the course of a fifty-year career are such titles as Lord Valentine's Castle, Dying Inside, Nightwings, The Book of Skulls, *and the award-winning novellas "Sailing to Byzantium" and "Born with the Dead." His work has been published everywhere—from France, Spain, and Germany to Egypt, Iran, and Turkey. He has been nominated for more major science-fiction awards than any other writer and is a five-time winner both of the Hugo and the Nebula Awards. In 2004 the Science Fiction Writers of America awarded him its Grand Master designation. Born in New York, Silverberg has lived for many years in the San Francisco area.*

ON THE DAY that the Colonel found himself seized by circumstances and thrust back against his will into active service he had risen early, as usual, he had bathed in the river of sparkling liquid gold that ran behind his isolated villa in a remote corner of the Aureus Highlands, he had plucked a quick handful of dagger-shaped golden leaves from the quezquez tree for the little explosive burst of energy that chewing them always provided, and he had gone for his morning stroll along the glimmering crescent dunes of fine golden powder that ran off down toward the carasar forest, where the slender trunks of the long-limbed trees swayed in the mild breeze like the elongated necks of graceful lammisgazelles. And when the Colonel got back to the villa an hour later for his breakfast the stranger was there, and everything began to change for him in the life that he had designed to be changeless forever more.

The stranger was young—*seemed* young, anyway; one never could really tell—and compactly built, with a tightly focused look about him. His eyes had the cold intensity of a fast-flowing river of clear water; his lips were thin, with deep vertical lines at their sides; his thick, glossy black hair was swept backward against his head like the wings of a raven. The little silver badge of the Imperium was visible on the breast of his tunic.

He was standing on the open patio, arms folded, smiling a smile that was not really much of a smile. Plainly he had already been inside. There was nothing to prevent that. One did not lock one's doors here. The Colonel, looking past him, imagined that he could see the fiery track of the man's intrusive footsteps blazing up from the green flagstone floor. He had entered; he had seen; he had taken note. The Colonel kept about himself in his retirement the abundant memorabilia of a long life spent meddling in the destinies of worlds. In his sprawling house on golden Galgala he had set out on display, for his eyes alone, a vast array of things, none of them very large or very showy—bits of pottery, fossils, mineral specimens, gnarled pieces of wood, coins, quaint rusted weapons, all manner of ethnographic artifacts, and a great number of other tangible reminders of his precise and devastating interventions on those many worlds.

Most of these objects—a scrap of bone, a painted stone, a bit of tapestry, a blunted knife, a tattered banner that bore no emblem, a box of sullen-looking gray sand—had no obvious significance. They would have been baffling to any visitor to the Colonel's Galgala retreat, if ever a visitor were to come, although there had not been any in many years, until this morning. But to the Colonel each of these things had special meaning. They were talismans, touchstones that opened a century and a half of memories. From Eden, from Entrada, from Megalo Kastro, from Narajo of the Seven Pyramids, from snowy Mulano, from unhappy Tristessa, even, and Fenix and Phosphor and some two dozen others out of mankind's uncountable string of planets had they come, most of them collected by the Colonel himself but some by his pinch-faced limping father, the Old Captain, and even a few that had been brought back by his swaggering buccaneer of a grandfather, who had carved a path through the universe as though with a machete five hundred years before him.

The Colonel now was old, older than his father had lived to be and beginning to approach the remarkable longevity of his grandfather, and his days of adventure were over. Having outlived the last of his wives, he lived alone, quietly, seeking no contact with others. He did not even travel any more. For the first two decades after his retirement he had, more from habit than any other motive, gone off, strictly as a tourist, on journeys to this world and that, planets like Jacynth and Macondo and Entropy and Duud Shabeel that he had never found occasion to visit during the course of his long professional career. But then he had stopped doing even that.

In his time he had seen enough, and more than enough. He had been everywhere, more or less, and he had done everything, more or less. He had overthrown governments. He had headed governments. He had survived a dozen assassination attempts. He had carried out assassinations himself. He had ordered executions. He had refused a kingship. He had lived through two poisonings and three marriages. And then, growing old, old beyond the hope of many further rejuvenations, he had put in for retirement and walked away from it all.

When he was young, restless and full of insatiable hungers, he had dreamed of striding from world to world until he had spanned the entire universe, and he had leaped with savage eagerness into the shining maw of each new Velde doorway, impatient to step forth onto the unknown world that awaited him. And no sooner had he arrived but he was dreaming of the next. Now, though, obsessive questing of that sort seemed pointless to him. He had decided, belatedly, that travel between the stars as facilitated by the Velde doorways or by the other and greater system of interstellar transport, the Magellanic one, was too easy, that the ease of it rendered all places identical, however different from one another they might actually be. Travel should involve travail, the Colonel had come to think. But modern travel, simple, instantaneous, unbounded by distance, was too much like magic. Matters had been different for the ancient explorers of ancient Earth, setting out on their arduous voyages of discovery across the dark unfriendly seas of their little planet with almost incomprehensible courage in the face of impossible odds. Those men of so many thousands of years ago, staking their lives to cross uncharted waters in tiny wooden ships for the sake of reaching alien and probably hostile shores on the very same world, had been true heroes. But now—now, when one could go almost anywhere in the galaxy in the twinkling of an eye, without effort or risk, did going anywhere at all matter? After the first fifty worlds, why not simply stay home?

The visitor said, "Your home is fascinating, Colonel." He offered no apology for trespassing. The Colonel did not expect one. With the smallest of gestures he invited the man inside. Asked him, in a perfunctory way, if he had had a good journey. Served him tea on the terrace overlooking the river. Awaited with formal politeness the explanation for the visit, for surely there had to be some explanation, though he did not yet know that it was ultimately going to break the atoms of his body apart once again, and scatter them once more across the cosmos, or he would have shut the man out of his house without hearing another word.

The man's surname was one that the Colonel recognized, one that had long been a distinguished one in the archives of the Imperium. The Colonel had worked with men of that name many years ago. So had his father. Men of that name had pursued his buccaneering grandfather across half the galaxy.

"Do you know of a world called Hermano?" the man asked. "In the Aguila sector, well out toward the Core?"

The Colonel searched his memory and came up with nothing. "No," he said. "Should I?"

"It's two systems over from Gran Chingada. The records show that you spent some time on Gran Chingada ninety years back."

"Yes, I did. But two systems over could be a dozen light-years away," said the Colonel. "I don't know your Hermano."

The stranger described it: an ordinary-sounding world, a reasonably pleasant world-shaped world, with deserts, forests, oceans, flora, fauna, climate. One of six planets, and the only habitable one, around a standard sort of star. Apparently it had been colonized by settlers from Gran Chingada some thirty or forty years before. Its exports were medicinal herbs, precious gems, desirable furs, various useful metals. Three years ago, said the stranger, it had ejected the Imperium commissioners and proclaimed itself independent.

The Colonel, listening in silence, said nothing. But for a moment, only a moment, he reacted as he might have reacted fifty years earlier, feeling the old reflexive stab of cold anger at that clanging troublesome word, *independent*.

The stranger said, "We have, of course, invoked the usual sanctions. They have not been effective." Gran Chingada, itself not the most docile of worlds, had chosen to people its colony-world by shipping it all the hard cases, its most bellicose and refractory citizens, a rancorous and uncongenial crowd who were told upon their departure that if they ever were seen on Gran Chingada again they would be taken to the nearest Velde doorway and shipped out again to some randomly chosen destination that might not prove to be a charming place to live, or even one that was suitable for human life at all. But the Hermano colonists, surly and contentious though they were, had found their new planet very much to their liking. They had made no attempt to return to their mother world, or to go anywhere else. And, once their settlement had reached the point of economic self-sufficiency, they had blithely announced their secession from the Imperium and ceased remitting taxes to the Central Authority. They had also halted all shipments of the medicinal herbs and useful metals to their trading partners throughout the Imperium, pending a favorable adjustment in the general structure of prices and tariffs.

A familiar image had been ablaze in the Colonel's mind since the first mention of Hermano's declaration of independence: the image of a beautiful globe of brilliantly polished silver, formerly flawless, now riven by a dark hideous crack. That was how he had always seen the Imperium, as a perfect polished globe. That was how he had always seen the attempts of one world or another to separate itself from the perfection that was the Imperium, as an ugly crevasse on the pure face of beauty. It had been his life's work to restore the perfection of that flawless silvery face whenever it was marred. But he had separated himself from that work many years ago. It was as though it had been done by another self.

Now, though, a little to his own surprise, a flicker of engagement leaped up in him: he felt questions surging within him, and potential courses of action, just as if he were still on active duty. Those medicinal herbs and useful metals, the Colonel began to realize, must be of considerably more than trifling significance to interstellar commerce. And, over and beyond that, there was the basic issue of maintaining the fundamental integrity of the Imperium. But all that was only a flicker, a momentarily renewed ticking of machinery that he had long since ceased to use. The maintenance of the fundamental integrity of the Imperium was no longer his problem. The thoughts that had for that flickering moment sprung up reflexively within him subsided as quickly as they arose. He had devoted the best part of his life to the Service, and had served loyally and well, and now he was done with all that. He had put his career behind him for good.

But it was clear to him that if he wanted to keep it that way he must be prepared to defend himself against the threat that this man posed, and that it might not be easy, for obviously this man wanted something from him, something that he was not prepared to give.

The stranger said, "You know where I'm heading with this story, Colonel."

"I think I can guess, yes."

The expected words came: "There is no one better able to handle the Hermano problem than you."

The Colonel closed his eyes a moment, nodded, sighed. Yes. What other reason would this man have for coming here? Quietly he said, "And just why do you think so?"

"Because you are uniquely fitted to deal with it."

Of course. Of course. They always said things like that. The Colonel felt a prickling sensation in his fingertips. It was clear now that he was in a duel with the Devil. Smiling, he said, making the expected response, "You say this despite knowing that I've been retired from the Service for forty years." He gestured broadly: the villa, the display of souvenirs of a long career, the garden, the river, the dunes beyond. "You see the sort of life I've constructed for myself here."

"Yes. The life of a man who has gone into hiding from himself, and who lives hunkered down and waiting for death. A man who dies a little more than one day's worth every day."

That was not so expected. It was a nasty thrust, sharp, brutal, intended to wound, even to maim. But the Colonel remained calm, as ever. His inner self was not so easily breached, and surely this man, if he had been briefed at all properly, knew that.

He let the brutality of the words pass unchallenged. "I'm old, now. Hunkering down is a natural enough thing, at my age. You'll see what I mean, in a hundred years or so."

"You're not *that* old, Colonel. Not too old for one last round of service, anyway, when the Imperium summons you."

"Can you understand," the Colonel said slowly, "that a time comes in one's life when one no longer feels an obligation to serve?"

"For some, yes," said the stranger. "But not for someone like you. A time comes when one *wishes* not to serve, yes. I can understand that. But the sense of obligation—no, that never dies. Which is why I've come to you. As I said, you are uniquely fitted for this, as you will understand when I tell you that the man who has made himself the leader of the Hermano rebellion is a certain Geryon Lanista."

Lanista?

It was decades since the Colonel had last heard that name spoken aloud. It crashed into him like a spear striking his breast. If he had not already been sitting, he would have wanted now to sink limply into a seat.

He controlled himself. "How curious. I knew a Geryon Lanista once," he said, after a moment. "He's long dead, that one."

"No," said the stranger. "He isn't. I'm quite sure of that."

"Are we talking about Geryon Lanista of Ultima Thule in the San Pedro Cluster?" The Colonel was struggling for his equilibrium, and struggling not to let the struggle show. "The Geryon Lanista who was formerly a member of our Service?"

"The very one."

"Well, he's been dead for decades. He killed himself after he bungled the Tristessa job. That was probably long before your time, but you could look it all up. He and I handled the Tristessa assignment together. Because of him, we failed in a terrible way."

"Yes. I know that."

"And then he killed himself, before the inquiries were even starting. To escape from the shame of what he had done."

"No. He *didn't* kill himself." Profoundly unsettling words, spoken with quiet conviction that left the Colonel a little dizzied.

"Reliable sources told me that he did."

Calm, the Colonel ordered himself. Stay calm.

"You were misinformed," the visitor said, in that same tone of deadly assurance. "He is very much alive and well and living on Hermano under the name of Martin Bauer, and he is the head of the provisional government there. The accuracy of our identification of him is beyond any doubt. I can show him to you, if you like. Shall I do that?"

Numbly the Colonel signaled acquiescence. His visitor drew a flat metal case from a pocket of his tunic and tapped it lightly. A solid figure of a man sprang instantly into being a short distance away: a stocky, powerfully built man, apparently of middle years, deep-chested and extraordinarily wide through the shoulders, a great massive block of a man, with a blunt-tipped nose, tight-clamped downturned lips, and soft, oddly seductive brown eyes that did not seem to be congruent with the bulkiness of his body or the harshness of his features. The face was not one that the Colonel remembered having seen before, but time and a little corrective surgery would account for that. The powerful frame, though, was something that no surgery, even now when surgery could achieve almost anything, could alter. And the eyes—those strange, haunted eyes—beyond any question they were the eyes of Geryon Lanista.

"What do you think?" the visitor asked.

Grudgingly the Colonel said, "There are some resemblances, yes. But it's impossible. He's dead. I know that he is."

"No doubt you want him to be, Colonel. I can understand that, yes. But this is the man. Believe me. You are looking at your old colleague Geryon Lanista."

How could he say no to that? Surely that was Lanista, here before him. Surely. Surely. An altered Lanista, yes, but Lanista all the same. What was the use of arguing otherwise? Those eyes—those freakishly wide shoulders—that barrel of a chest—

But there was no way that Lanista could be alive.

Clinging to a stubborn certainty that he was beginning not to feel was really solid the Colonel said, "Very well: the face is his. I'll concede that much. But the image? Something out of the files of fifty years ago, tarted up with a few little tweaks here and there to make him look as though he's tried recently to disguise himself? What's here to make me believe that this is a recent image of a living man?"

"We have other images, Colonel." The visitor tapped the metal case again, and there was the stocky man on the veranda of an imposing house set within a luxurious garden. Two small children, built to the same stocky proportions as he, stood beside him, and a smiling young woman. "At his home on Hermano," said the visitor, and tapped the case again. Now the stocky man appeared in a group of other men, evidently at a political meeting; he was declaiming something about the need for Hermano to throw off the shackles of the Imperium. He tapped the case again—

"No. Stop. You can fake whatever scene you want. I know how these things are done."

"Of course you do, Colonel. But why would we bother? Why try to drag you out of retirement with a bunch of faked images? Sooner or later a man of your ability would see through them. But we *know* that this man is Geryon Lanista. We have all the necessary proof, the incontrovertible genetic data. And so we've come to you, as someone who not only has the technical skills to deal with the problem that Lanista is creating, but the personal motivation to do so."

"Incontrovertible genetic data?"

"Yes. Incontrovertible. Shall I show you the genomics? Here: look. From the Service files, sixty years back, Geryon Lanista, his entire genome. And here, this one, from the Gran Chingada immigration records, approximately twenty years old, Martin Bauer. Do you see?"

The Colonel glanced at the images, side by side in the air and identical in every respect, shook his head, looked away. The pairing was convincing, yes. And, yes, they could fake anything they liked, even a pair of gene charts. There wasn't all that much difficulty in that. But to fake so *much*—to go to such preposterous lengths for the sake of bamboozling one tired old man—no, no, the logic that lay at the core of his soul cried out against the likelihood of that.

His last resistance crumbled. He yielded to the inescapable reality. Despite everything he had believed all these years, this man Martin Bauer *was* Geryon Lanista. Alive and well, as this stranger had said, and conspiring against the Imperium on a planet called Hermano. And the Service wanted him to do something about that.

For an instant, contemplating this sudden and disastrous turn of events, the Colonel felt something that wasn't quite fear and not quite dismay—both of them feelings that he scarcely understood, let alone had ever experienced—but was certainly a kind of discomfort. This had been a duel with the Devil, all right, and the Devil had played with predictably diabolical skill, and the Colonel saw that here, in the very first moments of the contest, he had already lost. He had not thought to be beaten so easily. He had lived his life, he had put in his years in the Service, he had met all dangers with bravery and all difficulties with triumphant ingenuity, and here, as the end of it all approached, he had come safely to rest in the harbor of his own invulnerability on this idyllic golden world; and in a moment, with just a few quick syllables, this cold-eyed stranger had ripped him loose from all of that and had tumbled him back into the remorseless torrents of history. He ached to refuse the challenge. It was within the range of possibility for him to refuse it. It was certainly his right to refuse it, at his age, after all that he had done. But—even so—even so—

"Geryon Lanista," the Colonel said, marveling. "Yes. Yes. Well, perhaps this really is him." There was a touch of hoarseness in his tone. —"You know the whole story, Lanista and me?"

"That goes without saying. Why else would we have come to you?"

The odd prickling in the Colonel's fingertips began to give way to an infuriating trembling. "Well, then—"

He looked across the table and it seemed to him that he saw a softening of those icy eyes, even a hint of moisture in them. An upwelling of compassion, was it, for the poor old man who had been so cruelly ensnared in the sanctity of his own home? But was that in any way likely, coming from *this* particular man, who had sprung from *those* ancestors. Compassion had never been a specialty of that tribe. Perhaps they are making them softer nowadays, the Colonel thought, yet another example of the general decadence of modern times, and felt renewed pleasure in the awareness that he was no one's ancestor at all, that his line ended with him. And then he realized that he was wrong, that there was no compassion in this man at all, that those were simply the jubilant self-congratulatory tears of triumph in the other man's eyes.

"We can count on you?" the visitor asked.

"If you've been lying to me—"

"I haven't been lying," said the visitor, saying it in a flat offhanded way that conveyed more conviction than any number of passionate oaths might have done.

The Colonel nodded. "All right. I give in. You win. I'll do what I can do," he said, in a barely audible voice. He felt like a man who had been marched to the edge of a cliff and now was taking a few last breaths before jumping off. "Yes. Yes. There are, I hardly need to say, certain practical details that we need to discuss, first—"

———

There was something dreamlike about finding himself making ready for a new assignment after so many years. He wouldn't leave immediately, of course, nor would the journey to Hermano be anything like instantaneous. The maintenance of the villa during his absence had to be arranged for, and there was the background information of the Hermano situation to master, and certain potentially useful documents to excavate from the archives of his career, and then he would have to make the long overland journey to Elsinore, down on the coast, where the nearest Velde doorway was located. Even after that he still would have some traveling to do, because Gran Chingada and its unruly colony-world Hermano, both of them close to the central sector of the galaxy, were beyond the direct reach of Velde transmission. To complete his journey he would have to shift over to the galaxy's other and greater teleportation system, the ancient and unfathomable one that had been left behind by the people known as the Magellanics.

He had not expected ever to be jaunting across the universe again. The visit to Duud Shabeel, two decades before, had established itself in his mind as the last of all his travels. But plainly there was to be one more trip even so; and as he prepared for it, his mind went back to his first journey ever, the one his ferocious fiery-eyed grandfather had taken him on, in that inconceivably remote epoch when he was ten years old.

He had lived on Galgala even then, though not in the highlands but along the humid coast, where liquid gold came bubbling up out of the swamps. His grandfather had always had a special love for Galgala, the planet that had ruined the value of gold for the entire galaxy. Gold was everywhere there, in the leaves of the trees, in the sands of the desert, in the stones of the ground. Flecks of gold flowed in the veins of Galgala's native animals. Though it had been thousands of years since the yellow metal had passed as currency among humankind, the discovery of Galgala had finished it for all eternity as a commodity of value. But the old pirate who had engendered the Colonel's father was a medieval at heart, and he cherished Galgala for what its gold might have meant in the days when the whole of the human universe was just the little blue world that was Earth. He had made it his headquarters during his privateering career, and when he was old he had gone there to dwell until the end of his days. The Colonel's father, who in his parsimonious pinch-faced way claimed only the honorary title of Captain, was in the Service then, traveling constantly from world to world as need arose and only rarely coming to rest, and, not knowing what to do with the boy who would some day become the Colonel, had sent him to Galgala to live with his grandfather.

"It's time you learned what traveling is like," the old man said one day, when the the boy who would become the Colonel was ten.

He was already tall and sturdy for his age, but he was still only ten, and his grandfather, even then centuries old—no one knew exactly how old he was, perhaps not even he himself—rose up and up beside him like a great tree, a shaggy-bearded tree with furious eyes and long black coils of piratical hair dangling to his shoulders and horrendous jutting cheekbones sharp as blades. The gaunt, bony old man had spent the many years of his life outside the law, the law that the Captain and later the Colonel would serve with such devotion, but no one in the family ever spoke openly of that. And although he had finally abandoned his marauding ways, he still affected the showy costume of his trade, the leather jerkin and the knee-high boots with the tapered tips and the broad-brimmed hat from which the eternally black coils of his long hair came tumbling superabundantly down.

They stood before the doorway, the future Colonel and his formidable grandfather, and the old man said, "When you step through it, you'll be scanned and surveyed, and then you'll be torn apart completely, down to the fragments of your atoms, altogether annihilated, and at the same moment an exact duplicate of you will be assembled at the other end, wherever that may be. How do you like that?"

The old man waited, then, searching for signs of fear or doubt on his grandson's face. But even then the boy understood that such feelings as fear or doubt ought not to be so much as felt, let alone displayed, in the presence of his grandfather.

"And where will we come out, then?" the boy who would be the Colonel asked.

"At our destination," said the old pirate, and casually shoved him toward the doorway. "You wait for me there, do you hear me, boy? I'll be coming along right behind."

The doorway on Galgala, like Velde doorways everywhere in the considerable sector of the galaxy where Velde-system terminals had been established, was a cubicle of black glass, four meters high, three meters wide, three meters deep. Along its inner walls a pair of blacklight lenses stared at each other like enigmatic all-seeing eyes. On the rear wall of the cubicle were three jutting metal cones from which the Velde force emanated whenever a traveler crossed the threshold of the cubicle.

The theory of Velde transmission was something that everyone was taught when young, the way the law of gravity is taught, or the axioms of geometry; but one does not need to study Newton or Euclid very deeply in order to know how to descend a staircase or how to calculate the shortest way to get across a street, and one could make a fifty-light-year Velde hop without any real understanding of the concept that the universe is constructed of paired particles, equal masses of matter and antimatter, and that matter can decay spontaneously into antimatter at any time, but each such event must invariably be accompanied by the simultaneous conversion of an equivalent mass of antimatter into matter somewhere else—anywhere else—in the universe, so that the symmetry of matter is always conserved.

Velde's Theorem had demonstrated the truth of that, long ago, millennia ago, back in those almost unimaginable primeval days when

Earth and Earth alone was mankind's home. Then Conrad Wilf, free-booting physicist, provided a practical use for Velde's equations by showing how it was possible to construct containment facilities that could prevent the normally inescapable mutual annihilation of matter and antimatter, thereby making feasible the controlled conversion of particles into their antiparticles. Matter that was held within a Wilf containment field could be transformed into antimatter and stored, without fear of instant annihilation, while at the same moment a corresponding quantity of antimatter elsewhere in the universe was converted into matter and held in a corresponding Wilf field far away.

But Wilf conversions, contained though they were, still entailed a disconcerting randomness in the conservation of symmetry: when matter was destroyed here and a balancing quantity of antimatter was created elsewhere, *elsewhere* could be at any point at all in the universe, perhaps ten thousand kilometers away, perhaps ten billion light-years; everything was open-ended, without directionality or predictability. It remained for Simtow, the third of the three great pioneers of interstellar transport, to develop a device that tuned the Velde Effect so that the balancing transactions of Wilf conversions took place not randomly but within the confines of a specific closed system with Wilf containment fields at both ends. At the destination end, antimatter was stored in a Wilf containment vessel. At the transmission end, that which was to be transmitted would undergo a Velde transformation into antimatter, a transformation that was balanced, at the designated destination end, by the simultaneous and equivalent transformation of the stored antimatter into a quantity of matter identical to that which had been converted by the transmitter. The last step was the controlled annihilation of the antimatter that had been created at the transmission end, thereby recapturing the energy that had powered the original transmission. The effect was the simultaneous particle-by-particle duplication of the transmission matter at the receiving end.

The boy who would become the Colonel comprehended all this, more or less, at least to the extent of understanding that one was demolished *here* and reassembled instantaneously *there*. He knew, also, of the ancient experiments with inanimate objects, with small animals and plants, and finally with the very much living body of the infinitely courageous pioneering voyager Haakon Christiansen, that showed that whatever went into a transmission doorway would emerge unharmed at its destination. All the same it was impossible for him to avoid a certain degree of uncertainty, even of something not very different from terror, in the moment when his grandfather's bony hand flung him toward the waiting doorway.

That uncertainty, that terror, if that is what it was, lasted only an instant's part of an instant. Then he was within the doorway and, because Velde transmission occurs in a realm where relativistic laws are irrelevant, he found himself immediately outside it again, but he was somewhere else, and it all looked so completely strange that there was no point in being frightened of it.

Where he found himself was a world with a golden-red sun that cast a hard metallic light altogether unlike the cheerful yellow light of Galgala's sun, which was the only sunlight he had ever seen. He was on a barren strip of flat sandy land with a lofty cliff at his back and what looked like a great oceanic expanse of pink mud in front of him. There were no living creatures in sight, no plants, no trees. He had never been in the presence of such utter emptiness before.

That sea of pink mud at whose border he stood stretched out as far as the horizon and, for all he knew, wrapped itself around it and kept going down the other side of the planet. It was indeed an ocean of mud: quivering, rippling mud, mud that seemed almost to be alive. Perhaps it *was* alive, a single living organism of colossal size. He could feel warmth radiating from it. He sensed a kind of sentience about it. Again and again some patch of its surface would begin throbbing spasmodically, and then it would send up odd projections and protuberances that slowly wriggled and writhed like questing tentacles before sinking down again into the huge sluggish mass from which it had arisen. He stared at it for a long while, fascinated by its eerie motions.

After a time he wondered where his grandfather was.

He should have followed instantly, should he not? But it didn't appear that he had. Instead the boy discovered himself alone in a way that was completely new to him, perhaps the only human being on a vast strange planet whose name he did not even know. At least twenty minutes had gone by. That was a long time to be alone in a place like this. He was supposed to wait here; but for how long? He wondered what he would do if, after another hour or two, his grandfather still had not arrived, and decided finally that he would simply step through the doorway in the hope that it would take him back to Galgala, or at least to some world where he could get help finding his way home.

Turning away from the sea, he looked backward and up, and then he understood where it was that his grandfather had sent him, for there on the edge of that towering cliff just in back of him he was able to make out the shape of a monumental stone fortress, low and long, outlined sharply against the glowering greenish sky like a crouching beast making ready to spring. Everyone in the galaxy knew what that fortress was. It was the ancient gigantic ruined building known as Megalo Kastro, from which this planet took its name—the only surviving work of some unknown extinct race that had lived here eight million years ago. There was nothing else like it in the universe.

"What do you say?" his grandfather asked, stepping through the doorway with the broad self-congratulatory smile of someone arriving exactly on time. "Are you ready to climb up there and have a look around?"

It was an exhausting climb. The old man had long legs and a demon's unbounded vitality, and the boy had a ten-year-old's half-developed muscles. But he had no choice other than to follow along as closely as possible, scrambling frantically up the rough stone blocks of the staircase, too far apart for a boy's lesser stride, that had been carved in the face of the cliff. He was breathless by the time he reached the top, fifty paces to the rear of his grandfather. The old man had already entered the ruin and had begun to saunter through it with the proprietorial air of a guide leading a party of tourists.

It was too big to see in a single visit. They went on and on, and still there was no end to its vaulted chambers. "This is the Equinox Hall," his grandfather said, gesturing grandly. "You see the altar down at that end? And this—we call it the Emperor's Throne Room. And this—the Hall of Sacrifices. Our own names for them, you understand. Obviously we'll never know what they really were called." There were no orderly angles everywhere. Everything seemed unstable and oppressively strange. The walls seemed to waver and flow, and though the boy knew it was only an illusion, it was a profoundly troublesome one. His eyes ached. His stomach felt queasy. Yet his heart pounded with fierce excitement.

"Look here," said his grandfather. "The handprint of one of the builders, maybe. Or a prisoner's." They had reached the cellar level now. On the wall of one of the dungeon-like rooms was the white outline of a large hand, a hand with seven fingers and a pair of opposable thumbs, one on each side. An *alien* hand.

The boy who would become the Colonel shivered. No one knew who had built this place. Some extinct race, surely, because there was no known race of the galaxy today that could have done it except the human race—no others encountered thus far had evolved beyond the most primitive level—and mankind itself had not yet evolved when Megalo Kastro had been built. But it was not likely to have been the work of the great unknown race that humans called the Magellanics, either, because they had left their transporter doorways, immensely more efficient and useful than Velde doorways, on every world that had been part of their ancient empire, and there was no Magellanic doorway, nor any trace of one, on Megalo Kastro. So they had never been here. But *someone* had, some third great race that no one knew anything about, and had left this fortress behind, millions of years ago.

"Come," said his grandfather, and they descended and returned to the doorway, and went off to a world with an amber sky that had swirls of blue in it, and a dull reddish sun lying like a lump of coal along the horizon with a second star, brighter, high overhead. This was Cuchulain, said the old man, a moon of the subluminous star Gwydion, the dark companion of a star named Lalande 21185, and they were only eight light-years from Earth, which to the boy's mind seemed just a snap of the fingers away. That amazed him, to be this close to Earth, the almost legendary mother world of the whole Imperium. The air here was thick and soft, almost sticky, and everything in the vicinity of the doorway was wrapped in furry ropes of blue-green vegetation. In the distance a city of considerable size gleamed through the muzzy haze. The boy felt heavy here: Cuchulain's gravity nailed him to the ground.

"Can we go on from here to Earth?" the boy asked. "It's so near, after all!"

"Earth is forbidden," said the old man. "No one goes to Earth except when Earth does the summoning. It is the law."

"But you have always lived outside the law, haven't you?"

"Not this one," his grandfather said, and put an end to the discussion.

He was hurt by that, back then in his boyhood. It seemed unfair, a wanton shutting out of the whole universe by the planet that had set everything in motion for the human race. They should not close themselves off to their descendants this way, he told himself. But years later, looking back on that day with his grandfather, he would take a different view. They are right to keep us out, he would tell himself later. That is how it should be. Earth is long ago, Earth is far away. It should remain like that. We are the galactic people, the people born in the stars. We are the future. They are the past. They and we should not mingle. Our ways are not their ways, and any contact between them and us would be corrupting for both. For better or for worse they have turned us loose into the stars and we live a new kind of life out here in this infinite realm, nothing at all like theirs, and our path must forevermore be separate from theirs.

His grandfather had taken him to Cuchulain only because it was the contact point for a world called Moebius, where four suns danced in the sky, pearly-white triplets and a violet primary. The boy imagined that a world that had a name like Moebius would be a place of sliding dimensions and unexpected twisted vistas, but no, there was nothing unusual about it except the intricacy of the shadows cast by its quartet of suns. His grandfather had a friend on Moebius, a white-haired man as frail and worn as a length of burned rope, and they spent a day and a half visiting with him. The boy understood very little of what the two old men said: it was almost as if they were speaking some other language. Then they moved on, to a wintry world called Zima, and from there to Jackal, and from Jackal to Tycho, and from Tycho to Two Dogs, world after world, most of them worlds of the Rim where the sky was strangely empty, frighteningly black at night with only a few thousand widely spaced stars in view, not the bright, unendingly luminous curtain that eternally surrounded a Core world like Galgala, a wall of blazing light with no break in it anywhere; and then, just as the boy was starting to think that he and the old man were going to travel forever through the Imperium without ever settling down, they stepped through the doorway once more and emerged into the familiar warm sunlight and golden vegetation of Galgala.

"So now you know," his grandfather said. "Galgala is just one small world, out of many."

"How great the Imperium is!" cried the boy, dazzled by his journey. The vastness of it had stunned him, and the generosity of whatever creator it was that had made so many stars and fashioned so many beautiful worlds to whirl about them, and the farsightedness of those who had thought to organize those worlds into one Imperium, so that the citizens of that Imperium could rove freely from star to star, from world to world, without limits or bounds. For the first time in his life, but far from the last, he saw in his mind the image of that flawless silver globe, shining in his imagination like the brightest of all possible moons. His grandfather had worked hard to instill a love for anarchy in him, but the trip had had entirely the opposite effect. "How marvelous that all those different worlds should be bound together under a single government!" he cried.

He knew at once that it was the wrong thing to say. "The Imperium is the enemy, boy," said his grandfather, his voice rumbling deep down in his chest, his scowling face dark as the sky before a thunderstorm. "It strangles us. It is the chain around our throats." And went stalking away, leaving him to face his father, who had come back from a mission in the Outer Sector during his absence, and who, astonishingly, struck him across the cheek when the boy told him where he had been and what he had seen and what his grandfather had said.

"The enemy? A chain about our throats? Oh, no, boy. The Imperium is our only bulwark against chaos," his father told him. "Don't you ever forget that." And slapped him again, to reinforce the lesson. The boy hated his father in that moment as he had never hated him before. But in time the sting of the slaps was gone, and even the memory of the indignity of them had faded, and when the hour came for the boy to choose what his life would be, it was the Service that he chose, and not the buccaneering career of his demonic grandfather.

When the preparations for the start of his journey to rebellious Hermano were complete, the Colonel traveled by regular rail down to the coastal city of Elsinore, where, as he had done so many times in the distant past, he took a room in the Grand Terminus Hotel while the agents of the Imperium worked out his Velde pathway. He had not been in Elsinore for many years and had not thought ever to see it again. Nothing much had changed, he saw: wide streets, bustling traffic, cloudless skies, golden sunlight conjuring stunning brilliance out of the myriad golden flecks that bespeckled the paving-stones. He realized, contemplating now a new offworld journey when he had never expected to make any again, how weary he had become of the golden sameness of lovely Galgala, how eager—yes, actually eager—he was once more to be confronting a change of scene. They gave him a room on the third floor, looking down into a courtyard planted entirely with exotic chlorophyll-based plants, stunningly green against the ubiquitous golden hue of Galgala. Three small purple dragons from some world in the Vendameron system lay twined in a cage at the center of the garden, as always. He wondered if these were the same dragons who had been in that cage the last time, years ago. The Colonel had stayed in this very room before, he was sure. He found it difficult to accept the fact that he was staying in it again, that he was here at the Terminus waiting to make one more Velde jump, after having put his time of traveling so thoroughly behind him. But the cold-eyed emissary from the Imperium had calculated his strategy quite carefully. Whatever vestigial sense of obligation to the Imperium that might still remain in the Colonel would probably not have been enough to break him loose from his retirement in order to deal with one more obstreperous colony. The fact that Geryon Lanista, his onetime protégé, his comrade, his betrayer, was the architect of the Hermano rebellion was another matter entirely, though, one that could not be sidestepped. To allow himself to miss a chance to come face to face with Geryon Lanista after all these years would be to act as though not just his career in the Service but his life itself had come to its end.

The emissary who had come to him at his villa was gone. He had done his work and was on to his next task. Now, at the Grand Terminus

Hotel, the Colonel's liaison man was one Nicanor Ternera, who had the gray-skinned, pudgy-faced look of one who has spent too much of his life in meetings and conferences, and who could not stop staring at the Colonel as though he were some statue of an ancient emperor of old Earth that had unaccountably come to life and walked out of the museum where he was on exhibit.

"These are your papers," Nicanor Ternera told him. "You'll hold formal ambassadorial accreditation as head of a trade legation that's based on Gavial, which as I think you know is a planet of the Cruzeiro system. You will not be going as a representative of the Imperium itself, but rather as a diplomat affiliated with the regional government of the Cruzeiro worlds. As you are already aware, the rebels won't at present allow officials of the Imperium to arrive on Hermano, but they're not otherwise closed to visitors from outside, even during the present period of trade embargo, which they describe as a temporary measure while they await recognition by the Imperium of their independent status."

"They'll wait a long time," said the Colonel. "Especially if they won't allow anyone from the Imperium to go in and explain the error of their ways to them." He glanced at the papers. "For the purpose of this mission my name is Petrus Haym?"

"Correct."

"Lanista will recognize me instantly for who I am. Or is this going to be the sort of mission I'll be doing in disguise?"

"You'll be disguised, to some degree, for the sake of being able to obtain entry. Once you've succeeded in getting access to Hermano as Petrus Haym of Gavial, you can decide for yourself when and how to reveal yourself to Lanista, which beyond any doubt you will at some point find necessary to do in order to bring the mission to a successful conclusion. From that point on you'll be functioning openly as an agent of the Imperium."

"And what leverage am I to have over them?" the Colonel asked.

"The ultimate," said Nicanor Ternera.

"Good," said the Colonel. He had expected no less. He would have accepted no less. Still, it was better to have it offered readily than to have to demand it.

Nicanor Ternera said, "You'll be accompanied on the trip by three genuine government people out of Gavial and another Imperium agent, a woman from Phosphor named Magda Cermak, who'll have the official rank of second secretary to the mission. She's been in the Service for a dozen years and has a good grasp of the entire situation, including your prior relationship with Geryon Lanista."

"You don't think I'd be better off handling this project entirely on my own?"

"It's altogether possible that you could. But we'd rather not take the risk. In any case it's essential to maintain the fiction of a trade delegation at least until you're safely on Hermano and have made contact with Lanista, and a properly plausible delegation involves five or six members, at least." Ternera looked to the Colonel for approval, which he reluctantly gave. "As these documents will show you, the crux of Gavial's issue is Hermano's termination of the export of a drug called cantaxion, the properties of which are beneficial to people suffering from a manganese deficiency, something that's chronic on Gavial. You'll find all the details in the attached documents. Gavial has already asked for an exception to the embargo, which you are now going to try to negotiate. Ostensibly the Hermanans are willing to discuss resumption of cantaxion exports in return for military weapons to be manufactured on Bacalhao, another of the Cruzeiro worlds."

"Which would be, of course, in complete violation of Imperium law, since the Imperium has placed an embargo of its own on doing business with Hermano. Am I supposed to conclude that Gavial is considering rebelling against the Imperium also?"

"Most definitely not. At our strong urging Gavial has indicated that it's at least open to the idea of entering into such transactions, provided they can be kept secret. That doesn't mean it actually would. How far you want to proceed with any of this once you make contact with Lanista himself is entirely up to you, naturally. I doubt that he'll find the idea that this is simply a trade mission very credible, once he realizes that it's you that he's dealing with, but of course that won't matter at that point."

"Of course," said the Colonel, who was already six moves ahead in the game that had to be played once he reached Hermano, and wished that Nicanor Ternera would hand over the rest of the briefing papers and disappear, which eventually he did, though not as swiftly as the Colonel would have preferred.

The first stop on his journey to Hermano was Entrada, where the Service's main operational center was located. Going to Entrada would be to make what could be thought of as a long jump in the wrong direction. Hermano, like Galgala, was a Core world, close to the center of the galaxy, whereas Entrada was one of what had once been called the Inner Worlds, and therefore was actually out on the Rim, because all distances had been measured from Earth in those early days. Earth itself was a Rim world, and Entrada, just a couple of dozen light-years distant from it, was off in the same obscure corner of the galaxy, far from the galactic core, as the original mother planet. But stellar distances had no significant meaning in Velde transmission and Entrada was where the Service had its most important base. Here the Colonel would undergo his transformation into Petrus Haym, diplomat from Gavial.

He had undergone so many transformations in his time that the Service had a better idea of what his baseline self looked like than he did himself. He knew that he was slightly above the median in height, that he was of mesomorphic build with longer-than-average limbs, and that the natural color of his eyes was olive-green. But his eyes had been blue and brown and violet and even scarlet on various occasions, his hair had been tinted every shade in the book and sometimes removed entirely, and his teeth and nose and ears and chin had been subjected to so much modification over the years that he no longer remembered their exact original configuration. When he had retired from the Service they had restored him, so they claimed, to baseline, but he was never entirely sure that the face he saw in the mirror each morning, the pleasant, thoughtful, agreeably nondescript face of a man who was certainly no longer young but nowhere near the end of his days, was really anything like the one that had looked back at him in the days before all the modifications had begun.

The concept of a baseline self was pretty much obsolete, anyway. Short of making fundamental rearrangements in a person's basic skeletal structure—and they were working on that one—it had, for many hundreds of years, been feasible to give anyone any appearance at all. Rebuilds were standard items for everyone, not just operatives of the Service. You could look young or old, benign or cruel, openhearted or brooding, as you wished, and when you tired of one look you could trade it in for another, just as, up to a point, you could roll back the inroads of the aging process by fifty years or so every now and then. That sort of mutability had been available even in the Colonel's grandfather's day, and by now everyone took it for granted. It was only his sheer obstinate perversity of will that had led the Colonel's father to insist on retaining, for the last seventy years of his life, the limp that he had acquired while carrying out an assignment on one of the worlds of the Magnifico system and that he had proudly displayed forever after.

The Colonel hesitated only the tiniest part of a moment when finally he stood before the Elsinore doorway. Some fraction of him still did not want to do this, but it was, he knew, only an extremely small fraction. Then he stepped through and was annihilated instantly and just as instantly reconstituted at the corresponding doorway on Entrada.

It was close to a century since the Colonel had last been to the operations center on Entrada. Entrada was a place he had hoped never to see again. He remembered it as a tropical world, much too hot from pole to pole, humid and jungly everywhere, with two potent white suns that were set close together in the sky and went whirling around each other three or four times a day, giving the appearance of a single weird egg-shaped mass. Only Entrada's great distance from those two sizzling primaries made the planet habitable at all. The Colonel hated its steambath heat, its thick, almost liquid greenish-gold atmosphere, its lunatic profusion of vegetation, the merciless round-the-clock glare of those twin suns. And also it was a world severely afflicted by the presence of a strong lambda field, lambda being a force that had been unknown until the early days of Velde travel. In those days anyone making the transition from a low-lambda world to a high-lambda world found himself knocked flat on his back during a period of adaptation that might stretch across several months. The problem of lambda differential had been conquered over a thousand years ago, but even now some minor effects could be felt by new arrivals to a high-lambda world, a lingering malaise, a sense of spiritual heaviness, that took days or even weeks to shake off.

But the Colonel, having come once more to Entrada despite all expectation, found it easy enough to shrug off all its discomforts. This would be only a brief stop, and there would never be another, of that he was certain beyond all question. He went through it as one goes through a bad dream, waiting for the release that morning brings.

Obsequious Service officers met him at the transit station, greeting him in an almost terrified way, with a kind of heavy-handed stifling reverence, the way one might greet some frightful spectre returned from the tomb, and conveyed him to the operations center, which was ten times the size of the building the Colonel remembered. Once he was inside its windowless mass he might have been on any planet at all: Entrada and all its tropic hyperabundance had no presence within these well-insulated halls.

"Colonel, this is how you are going to look," they told him, and a full-size image of Petrus Haym sprang into view in the air before him.

They had conceived Petrus Haym as a stolid burgher, round-cheeked, complacent, with heavy-lidded sleepy eyes, full lips, a short thick neck, a fleshy body, the very model and essence of what he was supposed to be, a man who had devoted his life to issues of tariff regulation and balances of trade. Indifferently the Colonel gave his approval, offering no suggestions whatever for revisions in the Haym format, though they seemed to be expecting them. He didn't care. The format they had conceived would do. To look like an animated stereotype of a trade commissioner would make it all the simpler for the Colonel to assume the identity he was supposed to take on.

That he would be able to operate convincingly as the accredited leader of a trade delegation from a planet he knew nothing about was not anything that he doubted. He was a quick study. In his time he had assumed all kinds of roles: he had been a priest of the Goddess, an itinerant collector of zoological specimens, an organizer of disenfranchised laborers, a traveling musician, a deeply compassionate counselor to the bereaved, and many other things, whatever was required to fit the task at hand, which was always, ultimately, the engineering of consent. Preserving the integrity of the Imperium had been his constant goal. The Imperium's scope verged on the infinite; so too, then, must his.

When they had done all that they needed to do with him at the operations center, and he had done all that he needed to do as well, he went on to the next stop on his journey, Phosphor, where the rest of his team was awaiting him.

Like many of the worlds of the Imperium, Phosphor was a planet of a multiple-sun system. The Colonel had visited it once before, early in his career, but all he remembered of the visit was that he had gone there to seek out and eliminate a veteran agitator who was living there in exile from his home world and laying plans to return home to engage in a fresh round of destabilizing activities. The Colonel recalled carrying out the job successfully, but the planet itself he had forgotten. Seeing it now, he still did not remember much about his earlier stay there. He had seen so many worlds, after all. Here, a huge cool red sun, old and dying, lay like an angry blemish in the east by day, and a hot blue one that was at least a couple of hundred units away blazed out of the west, bright as a beacon in the sky. Even at night—the unnerving, intensely black night of a Rim world that the Colonel had never learned to like—stray tendrils of light from one sun or the other streamed into view at the hemisphere's darkside edge.

The people of Phosphor did not seem to go in for somatic modification. The likeness they bore toward one another indicated that they seemed to cling almost defiantly to the somatotypes of the original handful of settlers of thousands of years ago, who must predominantly have been short, sinewy, broad-based folk, swarthy-skinned, beady-eyed. Magda Cermak, who was waiting for the Colonel at the Velde station, was the perfect exemplar of her people, a dark-haired sharp-nosed woman who stood only chest-high to the Colonel but who was so solidly planted atop her thick, sturdy legs that a rolling boulder could not have knocked her down. She seemed about fifty, no more than that, and perhaps she actually was. She welcomed the Colonel in an efficient, uneffusive way, addressing him as Petrus Haym, inquiring without real curiosity about his journey, and introducing him to the three delegates from Gavial, two men and a woman, who stood diffidently to one side, a well-nigh invisible trio of pallid bureaucrats, fidgety, self-effacing, like the supernumeraries that in fact they were in the drama to come.

His point of arrival on Phosphor was its capital city, a sprawling, untidy place that bore the ancient historical name of Jerusalem. At the Imperium headquarters there, Magda Cermak provided the Colonel with an update on the activities of Geryon Lanista—Martin Bauer, as he was now—since their paths had last crossed on that ill-starred world, Tristessa, half a century before.

"The one part of the trail we don't have," Cermak said, "covers the period between his escape from Tristessa's companion planet and his arrival in the Aguila sector. The period in the immediate aftermath of the faked suicide, that is. We figure that he spent about twenty years as far out of sight as he could keep himself. Our best guess is that he may have been moving around in the Rim worlds during those years. One informant insists that he even spent a certain amount of time on Earth itself."

"Could that be so?" asked the Colonel.

Magda Cermak shrugged. "There's no way of knowing. He's probably capable of managing it, wouldn't you say? But if he did get to Earth, Earth doesn't know anything about it, and Lanista isn't going to tell us either."

"All right. That's twenty blank years. What about the next thirty?"

"He first turns up under the name of Paul Thurm as a grape farmer on Iriarte, but he doesn't last long there. A legal problem arises, Thurm vanishes, and at that point a couple of years are gone from the record. When we pick up the trail again we find him in one of the Aguila Sector systems as Heinrich Bauer, suppposedly an expert on land reclamation. He spends four years on a planet called Thraka, teaching the locals how to drain swamps, and then he moves on to Alyatta, a world of an adjacent system, where he shows the people how to irrigate a desert."

"A highly versatile man," the Colonel said.

"Very. He's on Alyatta for six or seven years, apparently marrying and having a couple of children and acquiring substantial properties. Then once again he vanishes abruptly, leaving his family behind, and shows up on Gran Chingada, where his name now is *Martin* Bauer. We

don't know the motive for the switch. Something to do with the aban-
donment of his family, perhaps, although why he didn't change the
surname too is hard to understand. Possibly the 'Heinrich' entry was
erroneous all along. Keeping detailed track of a whole galaxy full of
people is only approximately possible, you know. —You have been to
Gran Chingada, I understand."

"A long time ago. It's a rough place."

"It's quieter now. They got rid of their worst malconents thirty
years back."

"Shipping them off to Hermano, two star-systems away, I'm told."

"Correct."

"Was Martin Bauer among those who was sent into exile?"

"No. He emigrated voluntarily, a dozen years ago, after the settlement on Hermano was fairly well established. Supposedly he was
brought in by the plantation owners who grow the herb from which
cantaxion is made, on account of his old specialty, land reclamation.
He became a plantation owner himself in a major way, and involved
himself very quickly in politics there, and before long he had won elec-
tion to the Council of Seven, the oligarchy that was the ruling body on
Hermano before its declaration of independence from the Imperium."

"An oligarchy whose members are *elected*?" said the Colonel.
"Isn't that a little unusual?"

Magda Cermak smiled. " 'Politics' on Hermano doesn't mean that
they have universal suffrage. The richest landowners have run the place
from the beginning. In the days of the Council of Seven, new members
of the Council were chosen by the existing ones whenever a vacancy
developed. It appears that Bauer got very rich very fast and was able
to buy his way onto the Council. From what I hear, he was always an
extremely persuasive man."

"Quite," the Colonel said.

"The last report of the Imperium commissioners before their
expulsion indicates that he quickly made himself the dominant figure
on it. He was the one, as I expect you've already guessed, who maneuvered Hermano into breaking with the Imperium."

"And what is he now, King of Hermano? Emperor of Hermano?"

"First Secretary of the Provisional Government is his title. He and four other members of the old Council of Seven make up the provisional government."

"An oligarchy of five being more manageable than an oligarchy of seven, I suppose. The next phase in the process being the replacement of the provisional government with an even more manageable one-man dictatorship."

"No doubt," said Magda Cermak.

She had more to tell him, little details of Martin Bauer's life on Hermano—he had married again, it seemed, and had had another set of children, and lived in monarchical splendor on a great estate on the southern coast of Hermano's one settled continent. The Colonel paid no more attention to what she was saying than professional courtesy required. It came as no surprise to hear that Geryon Lanista was looking after himself well. That had always been a specialty of his.

What occupied the center of the Colonel's attention was the fact of the rebellion on Hermano itself. That the person formerly known as Geryon Lanista was the instrument by which that rebellion had come about concerned him only in an incidental way now; it was a purely personal datum that had succeeded nicely in entangling him, at a time when he had thought he had completely shed his identity as a functionary of the Service, in this enterprise. If he could settle the score with Geryon Lanista after all this time, so be it. That would not be a trivial thing, but it was nevertheless a peripheral one. It was the existence of the rebellion, rather than Lanista's involvement in it, that had in these recent days brought powerful old emotions up from the center of the Colonel's being, had reawakened in him that sense of the necessity of protecting the Imperium that had been the essential driving factor of his personality through his entire adult life.

A rebellion was an act of war, nothing else. And in a galaxy of many thousands of inhabited worlds war could not be allowed to come back into existence.

There had been strife once, plenty of it, in the early years of the great galactic expansion. There had been trade wars and there had been religious wars and there had been real wars, in which whole worlds had been destroyed. The immensity of the spaces that separated one planet from another, one solar system from another, one stellar cluster from another, meant nothing at all in a civilization in which the far-flung Velde system and the even more expansive network of Magellanic gateways rendered travel over unthinkable distances a simpler and faster and safer process than a journey from one city to the next on the same continent had been in that era, many thousands of years in the past, when all of mankind had been confined to a single small world of the galaxy.

In those ancient days war between cities, and then between states when states had evolved, had been commonplace events. Schoolchildren on a million worlds still studied the history and literature of Earth as if they themselves were citizens of that little planet. They would not be able to find Earth's sun on a chart of the skies if they searched for thirty centuries, but they could recite the names of a dozen or more of Earth's famous wars, going back even into dim prehistory to the oldest war of all, the great war between the Greeks and the Trojans, when men had fought with clanging swords.

That had been a small war fought by great men. Later, millennia later, when humanity had spilled forth into all the galaxy, had come great wars fought by small men, wars not between tiny cities but between worlds, and there had been raging chaos in the stars, terrible death, terrible destruction. And then the chaos had at last burned itself out and there had come peace, fragile at first, then more certain. The galaxy-spanning institution known as the Imperium maintained that peace with iron determination.

The Imperium would not allow war. The age of chaos was over forever. That was universally understood, understood by all—or nearly all—

"Well, then, shall we start out on our way to Hermano, and get on with the job?" said the Colonel, when Magda Cermak had finished her briefing at last.

The first segments of the Velde system had been constructed at a time when Earth was all there was to the human galaxy and no one seriously expected that the multitudinous stars of the galactic center would ever come within mankind's reach. Though Velde transmission itself was nonrelativistic, the setting up of the original system had had to be carried out under the constraints of the old Einsteinian rules, in which the speed of light was the limiting velocity.

And so, piece by piece, the necessary receiving equipment was put in place by conventional methods of delivery on one after another of the so-called Inner Worlds, those that orbited stars lying within a sphere a hundred light-years in diameter with Earth at its center. Even though the equipment was shipped out aboard vessels traveling close to the Einsteinian limit, unmanned starships journeying outward with great sails unfurled to the photonic winds, finding potentially habitable worlds, releasing robots that would set the Velde receivers in position, then going on to the next world and the next, extending the highway of receiving stations from one star system to another, it took centuries to get the job done. And by then the Magellanics' transit system had been discovered, impinging—just barely—on the tiny segment of the galaxy where Earth had managed to set up its little network of Velde stations.

Nobody knew how old the Magellanic system was, nor who had built it, nor even how it worked. That their builders had originated in the nearby galaxy known as the Greater Magellanic Cloud was only a guess, which somehow everyone had embraced as though it were a proven fact. They might just as readily have come from the Andromeda galaxy, or the great spiral galaxy in Eridanus, or some other stellar cluster ten or twelve billion light-years away, whose component stars and all the inhabitants of its many worlds had perished back in the ungraspable remoteness of the distant past. No one knew; no one expected to find out. The only thing that was certain was that the so-called Magellanics had traveled freely through the galaxy that one day would be mankind's, roaming it some unknowable number of years ago, using a system of matter transmission to journey from world to world, and that among the artifacts they had left behind on those worlds were their matter-transmitters, still in working order, apparently designed to function through all of eternity to come.

They operated more or less as the Velde transmitters did—you stepped through *here* and came out *there*—but whether they worked on similar principles was also something that was unknowable. There was nothing to analyze. Their doorways had no moving parts and drew on no apparent power source. Certain brave souls, stumbling upon these doorways during the early days of exploration on the outer worlds of humanity's sphere of expansion, had stepped through them and emerged on other planets even farther out, and eventually some working knowledge of the network, which doorway led to what other world, had been attained. How many lives had been lost in the course of attaining that knowledge was another thing that could never be known, for only those explorers who had survived their trips through the doorways could report on what they had done. The others—instantly transported, perhaps, to some other galaxy, or to the heart of a star, or to a world of intolerable gravitational force, or one whose doorway had been surrounded, over the millennia, by a sea of molten lava—had not been able to send back useful information about their trips.

By now, though, humankind had been making use of the Magellanic doorways for upwards of ten thousand years. The usable routes had all been tested and charted and the doorways had played a determining role in mankind's expansion across immense galactic distances that otherwise might not have been crossed until some era unimaginably far off in the future. The little sphere of planets that once had been known as the Inner Worlds was now thought of as the Rim, out there on the edge of galactic civilization; Earth, the primordial world where everything had begun, had become almost a legend, unvisited and shrouded in myth, that had very little reality for most of the Imperium's trillions of citizens; the essential life of galactic mankind long ago had moved from the Rim to the close-packed worlds of the Core. Though Velde stations still were an important means of travel within local sectors of the galaxy, and new Velde links were being constructed all the time, most long-hop travel now was carried out via the Magellanic system, which required no input of energy and maintained itself free of cost to those who used its gateways. The Colonel's journey to Hermano would involve the use of both systems.

The first jump took him via Velde transmission from Phosphor to nearby Entropy, a world that the Colonel had visited as a tourist forty years before, in the early days of his retirement. He did not remember it as a particularly interesting place. He had gone there only to gain access to the Magellanic doorway on Trewen, fifty light-years away, where he could leap across the galaxy to lovely Jacynth, his intended destination back then.

Entropy was no more interesting now: a yellow-green sun, mild weather, a few small cities, three big moons dangling in a row across the daytime sky. Magda Cermak preceded him there, and his three Gavial associates followed along behind. When the whole group was assembled they did a Velde hop to Trewen, now as before a virtually uninhabited world, cool and dry and bleak, notable only because the Magellanics had chosen to plant one of their doorways on it. Transit agents from the Service were waiting there to conduct the Colonel and his party to the doorway, which was tucked away within a deep cave on a rocky plateau a few hundred meters from the Velde station.

It seemed like only the day before yesterday that the Colonel had made his previous visit to this place. There on the right side of the cave was the sleek three-sided doorway, tapering upward to a sharp point, framing within itself a darkness so intense that it made the darkness of a Rim-world night seem almost inconsequential. Along each of its three sides was a row of gleaming hieroglyphs, an incomprehensible message out of a vanished eon. The doorway was wide enough for several to go through at a time. The Colonel beckoned the three Gavial people through first, and then stepped through himself, with Magda Cermak at his side. There was no sensation of transition: he walked through the darkness and came out of another doorway on Jacynth, one of the most beautiful of all worlds, as beautiful, almost, as lost Tristessa: a place of emerald meadows and a ruby-red sky, where great trees with feathery silver leaves and scarlet trunks sprang up all about them and a milky waterfall went cascading down the side of an ebony mountain that rose in serried pinnacles just ahead. The Colonel would have been happy to end the journey at that point and simply remain on Jacynth, where even the most troubled soul could find contentment for a while, but there was no hope of that, for more Service personnel awaited him there to lead him on to the next doorway, and by day's end the Colonel had arrived on Gavial of the Cruzeiro system, halfway across the galaxy from that morning's starting point at the Grand Terminus Hotel on Galgala.

Not even a Colonel in the Service was able to know everything about every one of the worlds of the Imperium, or even very much about very many of them. The galaxy was simply too big. Before the dark-haired intruder had enmeshed him in this undertaking the Colonel had been aware of Cruzeiro only because it was that rare thing, a solar system that had more than one world—four, in fact—that was inhabitable by human beings without extensive modification. Of Gavial itself, or its neighbor Bacalhao, or the other two worlds of the Cruzeiro system, he knew nothing at all. But now he was going to be masquerading as a native of the place, no less, and so he needed to acquire some firsthand familiarity with it. He had carried out the usual sort of research in the days before leaving home, and that had given him all the background on Gavial that he needed, though not a fully three-dimensional sense of what sort of world it was. For that you had to spend a little time there. He did know how large Gavial was, though, its climatic and geographical details, the history of its colonization, its major products, and a host of other things that he was probably not going to need to draw upon during his stay on Hermano, but which, simply by being present in some substratum of his mind, would allow him to make a convincing pretense of being Gavialese. As part of that he had learned to speak in the thick-tongued Gavialese way, spitting and sputtering his words in a fashion that accurately mimicked the manner of speech of his three Gavialese companions.

At first Magda Cermak, who spoke Galactic with the sharp-edged precision that seemed to be typical of the natives of Phosphor, could be seen smothering laughter every time the Colonel began to speak.

"Is it so comic, then?" he asked her.

"You sound like a marthresant," she said, giggling.

"Remind me of what a marthresant is," said the Colonel.

It was, she explained, one of her world's marine mammals, a huge ungainly creature with a wild tangle of bristly whiskers and long flaring tusks, which made coarse whooping snorts that could be heard half a kilometer away when it came up for air. Saying that he sounded like a marthresant did not appear to be a compliment. But he thanked her gravely for the explanation and told her that he was happy that his accent provided her with a little reminder of home.

That seemed to amuse her. But perhaps she was wondering whether she had offended him, for she made a point of telling him that she found his own accent, the accent of Galgala, extremely elegant.Which obliged the Colonel to inform her that his accent was not Galgalan at all, that he had lived on Galgala only during his boyhood and in the years since his retirement, and that in the years between he had spent so much time on so many different worlds, counterfeiting so many different accents, that he had lost whatever his original manner of speech had been. What he normally spoke now was actually a kind of all-purpose pan-Galactic, a randomly assorted mixture of mannerisms that would baffle even the most expert student of linguistics.

"And will you have some Gavialese in the mix when this is all over?" she asked.

"Perhaps nothing worse than a little snorting and whooping around the edges of the consonants," he told her, and winked.

She appeared to be startled by his sudden playfulness. But it had emerged only in response to hers, when she had begun giggling over his accent. The Colonel had been aware from the first that she felt an almost paralyzing awe for him, which she had been attempting to conceal with great effort. Nothing unusual about that: he was a legendary figure in the Service, already famous throughout the galaxy long before she was born, the hero of a hundred extravagantly risky campaigns. Everyone he had come in contact with since taking on this assignment had regarded him in that same awestricken way, though some had been a little better at hiding it than others.There were times, looking back at all he had done, that he almost felt a twinge of awe himself. The only one who had seemed immune to the power of his fame was the cold-eyed man who had gone to him in the first place, someone, obviously, who was so highly placed in the modern Service that he was beyond all such emotion. All the others were overwhelmed by the accumulated grandeur of his reputation. But it would only make things more difficult all around as this project unfolded if Magda went on thinking of him as some sort of demigod who had condescended to step down from the heavens and move among mortals again this one last time. He was relieved that she was professional enough to shake some of that off.

They remained on Gavial for a week while he soaked up the atmosphere of the place, did a little further research, and endured a round of governmental banquets and tiresome speeches that were designed to help him believe that he really *was* a trade representative from this planet whose only purpose in visiting Hermano was to get the flow of a vitally needed medicine going again. By the time that week was nearing its end Magda's attitude toward him had loosened to the extent that she was able to say, "It must be strange to think that in a few days you're finally going to get a chance to come face to face with the man you hate more than anyone else in the universe."

"Lanista? I don't even know if that's really him, over there on Hermano."

"It is. There's no question that it is."

"The Service says he is, and says it has the proof, but I've had too much experience with the way the Service creates whatever evidence it needs to buy a hundred percent of anything the Service claims. But suppose that *is* Lanista on Hermano. Why do you think I would hate him? I don't even know what the word means, really."

"The man who was working against you behind your back on one of your most important projects, and who, when things were heading toward an explosion that he himself had set up, went off without giving you a word of warning that you were very likely to get killed? What do you call that, if not treachery?"

"Treachery is exactly what I would call it, indeed," said the Colonel.

"And yet you don't hate him for that?" She was floundering now.

"I told you," the Colonel said, trying to choose his words with great care, "that 'hate' isn't a word I understand very well. Hate seems so useless, anyway. My real concern here is that I could have misjudged that man so completely. I *loved* him, you know. I thought of him almost as a son. I brought him into the Service, I taught him the craft, I worked with him on a dozen jobs, I personally insisted on his taking part in the Tristessa thing. And then—then—then he—he—"

His throat went dry. He found himself unable to continue speaking. He was swept by feelings that he could only begin to comprehend.

Magda was staring at him in something close to horror. Perhaps she feared that she had pushed into territory that she had had no right to be exploring.

But then, as though trying to repair whatever damage she had caused, she pressed desperately onward.

"I didn't realize that you and Lanista were actually that—close. I thought he was just your partner on an assignment. Which would be bad enough, selling you out like that. But if in fact he was almost like—your—"

She faltered.

"My protégé," the Colonel said. "Call him my protégé." He went to the window and stood with his back to her, knotting his hands together behind him. He wished he had never let this conversation begin.

The sun, Cruzeiro, was starting to set, an unspectacular yellowish sun tinged with pale pink. A hard-edged crescent moon was edging upward in the sky. Behind it lay two sharp points of brilliant light, two neighboring worlds of this system. Bacalhao and Coracao, their names were. He thought that Bacalhao was the one on the left, but wasn't entirely sure which was which. You could usually see them both in the twilight sky here. The odd names, he supposed, were derived, as so many planetary names were, from one of the ancient languages of Earth, a world where, so it was said, they had had a hundred different languages all at once, and people from one place could scarcely understand what people from another place were saying. It was a wonder they had been able to accomplish anything, those Earthers, when they wouldn't even have been able to make themselves understood if they went as much as five hundred kilometers away from home. And yet they had managed to make the great leap out into space, somehow, and to spread their colonies over thousands of solar systems, and to leave their words behind as the names of planets, although no one remembered any more what most of those words once meant.

"My protégé," he said again, without turning to face her. "Who betrayed me, yes. That has always mystified me, that he would have done such a thing. But do I hate him for it? No."

Yes, he told himself. *Of course you do.*

Tristessa. A magical place, the Colonel had once thought. On Tristessa your eye encountered beauty wherever it came to rest. He remembered everything about it down to the finest detail: the sweet fragrance of its soft, moist atmosphere, the bright turquoise/emerald glory of its double sun, the throngs of magnificent winged reptiles soaring overhead, the glistening smoothness of the big, round white pebbles, like the eggs of some prehistoric monster, that formed the bed of the clear rushing stream that ran past his lodging. The pungent flavor of a triangular yellow fruit that dangled in immense quantities from nearby trees. The many-legged crablike things, glossy black carapaces crisscrossed with jagged blood-red streaks, that roamed the misty forests searching in the dark rich loam for food, and looked up from their foraging to study you like solemn philosophers with a multitude of faceted amber eyes.

Its name, someone had told him once, was derived from a word of one of the languages of ancient Earth, a word that carried a connotation of "sadness," and certainly sadness was appropriate in thinking of Tristessa now. But how could they have known, when giving such a melancholy name to such a beautiful world, what sort of destiny was awaiting it five thousand years in the future?

For the Colonel, who was in the late prime of his career as an arch-manipulator of worlds, the Tristessa affair had begun as a routine political intervention, the sort of assignment he had dealt with on more occasions than he could count. He saw no special challenge in it. He expected that Geryon Lanista, whom he had been grooming for a decade or so to be his successor in the Service, would do much of the real work; the Colonel would merely supervise, observe, confirm in his own mind that Lanista was fully qualified to take things over from him.

Tristessa, lovely, underpopulated, economically undeveloped, had a companion world, Shannakha, less than thirty million kilometers away. Shannakha had been settled first. Its climate, temperate rather than tropical, wasn't as appealing as Tristessa's, nor was its predominantly sandy, rocky landscape anywhere near as beautiful. But it offered a wider range of natural resources—pretty little Tristessa had nothing much in the way of metals or fossil fuels—and it was on Shannakha that cities had been founded and an industrial economy established. Tristessa, colonized by Shannakha a few hundred years later, became the holiday planet for its neighbor in the skies. Shannakha's powerful merchant princes set up plantations where

Tristessa's abundant fruits and vegetables could be raised and shipped to eager markets on the other world, and created great estates for themselves in the midst of those plantations; Shannakha's entrepreneurs built grand resort hotels for middle-class amusement on the beautiful island archipelagoes of Tristessa's tropical seas; and thousands of less fortunate Shannakhans settled on Tristessa to provide a labor force for all those estates, plantations, and hotels. It all worked very well for hundreds of years, though of course it worked rather better for the absentee owners on Shannakha than it did for their employees on Tristessa, since the Shannakhans prohibited any kind of ownership of Tristessan real estate or other property by Tristessans, kept payrolls as low as possible, and exported all profits to Shannakha.

But, as any student of history as well informed as the Colonel was would certainly know, the unilateral exploitation of one world by another does not work well forever, any more than the unilateral exploitation of one city or state by another had worked well in that long-ago era when all the human race was confined to that one little world called Earth. At some point a malcontent will arise who will argue that the assets of a place belong to the people who dwell in that place, and should not be tapped for the exclusive benefit of a patrician class living somewhere else, far away. And, if he is sufficiently persuasive and charismatic, that malcontent can succeed in finding followers, founding a movement, launching an insurrection, liberating his people from the colonial yoke.

Just that was in the process of happening when the Colonel was called in. Tristessa's charismatic malcontent had arisen. His name was Ilion Gabell; he came from a long line of farmers who raised and grew the agreeably narcotic zembani leaf that was the source of a recreational drug vastly popular on Shannakha; and because his natural abilities of leadership were so plainly manifest, he had been entrusted by a group of the plantation owners with the management of a group of adjacent zembani tracts that stretched nearly halfway across Tristessa's primary continent. That, unfortunately for the plantation owners, gave him access to clear knowledge of how profitable the Tristessa plantations really were. And now—so reliable informants had reported—he was on the verge of launching a rebellion that would break Tristessa free of the grasp of its Shannakhan owners. It was the Colonel's assignment to keep this from happening. He had chosen Geryon Lanista to assist him.

Lanista, who was fond of exploring both sides of an issue as an intellectual exercise, said, "And why, exactly, should this be any concern of the Imperium? Is it our job to protect the economic interests of one particular group of landowners against its own colonial employees? Are we really such conservatives that we have to be the policemen of the status quo all over the universe?"

"There would be wider ramifications to a Tristessa uprising," the Colonel said. "Consider: this Ilion Gabell gives the signal, and in a single night every Shannakhan who happens to be on Tristessa is slaughtered. Such things have occurred elsewhere, as you surely know. The Imperium quite rightly deplores wholesale murder, no matter what virtuous pretext is put forth for it. Next, a revolutionary government is proclaimed and transfers title to all Shannakhan-owned property on Tristessa to itself, to be held in the name of the citizenry of the Republic of Tristessa. What happens after that? Will Shannakha, peace-loving and enlightened, simply shrug and say that inasmuch as war between planets is illegal by decree of the Imperium, it therefore has no choice but to recognize the independence of Tristessa, and invites the Tristessans to enter into normal trade relationships with their old friends on the neighboring world?"

"Maybe so," said Lanista. "And that might even work."

"But the downside—"

"The downside, I suppose, is that it would send a signal to other planets in Tristessa's position that a rebellion against the established property interests can pay off. Which will create a lot of little Tristessa-style uprisings all over the galaxy, one of which might eventually explode into actual warfare between the mother world and its colony. Therefore a great deal of new toil for the Service will be required in order to keep those uprisings from breaking out, in which case it might be better to snuff out this one before it gets going."

"It might indeed," said the Colonel. "Now, the opposite scenario—"

"Yes. Shannakha, infuriated by the expropriation of its properties on Tristessa, retaliates by sending an armed expedition to Tristessa to get things under control. Thousands of Tristessans die in the first burst of hostilities. Then a guerrilla war erupts as Gabell and his insurrectionists are driven underground, and in the course of it the plantations and resorts of Tristessa are destroyed, perhaps with unusually ugly ecological consequences, and many additional casualties besides. Shannakha wrecks its own economy to pay for the war and Tristessa is ruined for decades or centuries to come. And at the end of it all we either wind up with something that's worse than the status quo ante bellum, Shannakha still in charge of Tristessa but now perhaps unable to meet the expense of rebuilding what was there once, or else with two devastated planets, Tristessa independent but useless and Shannakha bankrupt."

"And therefore—" the Colonel said, waiting for the answer that he knew would be forthcoming.

Lanista provided it. "Therefore we try to calm Ilion Gabell down and negotiate the peaceful separation of Tristessa and Shannakha by telling Gabell that we will obtain better working conditions for his people, while at the same time leading the Shannakhans to see that it's in their own best interest to strike a deal before a revolution can break out. If we can't manage that, I'd say that the interests of Tristessa, Shannakha, and the Imperium would best be served by suppressing Ilion Gabell's little revolution out of hand, either by removing him permanently or by demonstrating to him in a sufficiently persuasive way that he stands no chance of success, and simultaneously indicating to the Shannakhans that they'd better start treating the Tristessans a little more generously or they're going to find themselves faced with the same problem again before long, whether the revolution is led by Gabell or by someone else with the same ideas. Yes?"

"Yes," said the Colonel.

So it was clear, then, what they had to try to achieve, and what they were going to do to achieve it. All scenarios but one led to a violent outcome, and violence was a spreading sore that if not checked at its source could consume an entire civilization, even a galactic one. The problems on Tristessa, which were easily enough identified, needed to be corrected peacefully before a worse kind of correction got under way. The Colonel was as skillful an operative as there was and Geryon

Lanista was nearly as shrewd as he was, and he still had all the energy of youth, besides. Why, then, had it all gone so terribly wrong?

And then it was time at last to make the last jump in the sequence, the one from Gavial to Hermano, where, despite all that the Colonel had believed for the last fifty years, Geryon Lanista was very much alive and at the head of his own insurrectionist government.

Despite the general trade embargo, the Velde link between Hermano and certain worlds of the galaxy, such as Gavial, was still operational. Only the wildest of insurrectionists would take the rash step of cutting themselves completely off from interstellar transit, and Lanista was evidently not that wild. Velde connections required two sets of tuned equipment, one at each end of any link, and once a planet chose to separate itself from Velde travel it would need the cooperation of the Imperium to reestablish the linkage. Lanista hadn't cared to risk handing the Imperium a unilateral stranglehold over his planet's economy. There had been other rebellions, as he of all people would have known very well, in which the Imperium had picked a time of its own choosing to restore contact once it had been broken off by the rebels.

The Colonel was completely composed as they set out on this final hop of the long journey. He searched for anxiety within himself and found none. He realized that it must have been destined all along that before the end of his life he would once again come face to face with Geryon Lanista, so that there might be a settlement of that troublesome account at last.

And why, he asked himself, should there be any immediate cause for anxiety? For the moment he was Petrus Haym, emissary plenipotentiary from the Cruzeiro system to the provisional government of independent Hermano, and Lanista was Martin Bauer, the head of that provisional government. Whatever meeting there was to be between the two of them would be conducted, at least at first, behind those masks.

Hermano, the Colonel saw at once, was no Tristessa. Perhaps he had arrived in this hemisphere's winter: the air was cool, even sharp, with hardly any humidity at all. He detected a hint of impending snow in it. The sky had a grayish, gloomy, lowering look. There was an odd acrid flavor to the atmosphere that would require some getting used to. The gravity was a little above Standard Human, which was going to exacerbate the task of carrying the extra flesh of Petrus Haym.

Everything within immediate view had a thrown-together, improvised appearance. The area around the Velde station was one of drably utilitarian tin-roofed warehouses, with an unprepossessing medium-sized town of low, anonymous-looking buildings visible in the distance against a backdrop of bleak stony hills. Tufts of scruffy vegetation, angular and almost angry-looking, sprang up here and there out of the dry, sandy soil. There was nothing to charm the eye anywhere. The Colonel reminded himself that this planet had been settled only about forty years before by a population of exiles and outcasts. Its people probably hadn't found time yet for much in the way of architectural niceties. Perhaps they had little interest in such things.

Somber-faced port officials greeted him in no very congenial way, addressing him as Commissioner Haym, checking through his papers and those of his companions, and unsmilingly waving him and his four companions aboard a convoy of antiquated lorries that took them down a ragged, potholed highway into town. Alto Hermano, the place was called. A signpost at the edge of town identified it grandiosely as the planetary capital, though its population couldn't have been much over twenty or thirty thousand. The vehicles halted in a stark open square bordered on all four sides by identical five-story buildings with undecorated mud-colored brick facades. An official who introduced himself as Municipal Procurator Tambern Collian met them there. He was a gray-eyed unsmiling man, just as dour of affect as everyone else the Colonel had encountered thus far here. He did not offer the expectable conventional wishes that Commissioner Haym had had an easy journey to Hermano nor did he provide pleasantries of any other sort, but simply escorted the delegation from Cruzeiro into one of the buildings on the square, which turned out to be a hotel, grimly functionalist in nature, that the government maintained for the use of official visitors. It was low-ceilinged and dim, with the look of a third-class commercial hotel on a backwater world. Municipal Procurator Collian showed the Colonel to his quite modest suite without apologies, indifferently wished him a good evening, and left, saying he would call again in the morning to begin their discussions.

Magda Cermak's room was adjacent to his. She came by to visit, rolling her eyes, when the Municipal Procurator was gone. The coolness of their welcome plainly hadn't been any cause of surprise to her, but she was irritated all the same. A dining room on the ground floor of the hotel provided them with a joyless dinner, choice of three sorts of unknown meat, no wine available of any kind. Neither of them had much to say. Their hosts were all making it very clear that Hermano was a planet that had declared war on the entire universe. They were willing to allow the delegation from the Cruzeiro system to come here to try to work out some sort of trade agreement, since they appeared to see some benefit to themselves in that, but evidently they were damned if they were going to offer the visitors much in the way of a welcome.

Municipal Procurator Collian, it developed, was to be Commissioner Haym's primary liaison with the provisional government. Precisely what Collian's own role was in that government was unclear. There were times when he seemed to be just the mayor of this starkly functional little city, and others when he appeared to speak as a high functionary of the planetary government. Perhaps he was both; perhaps there was no clear definition of official roles here at the moment. This was, after all, a provisional government, one that had seized power only a few years before from a previous government that had itself been mostly an improvisation.

It was clear, at any rate, that First Secretary Bauer himself did not plan to make himself a party to the trade talks, at least not in their initial stages. The Colonel did not see that as a problem. He wanted a little time to take the measure of this place before entering into what promised to be a complex and perhaps dangerous confrontation.

Each morning, then, the Colonel, Magda, and the three Gavialese would cross the plaza to a building on the far side that was the headquarters of the Ministry of Trade. There, around a squarish conference table of the sort of inelegant dreary design that seemed especially favored by the Hermanan esthetic, they would meet with Municipal Procurator Collian and a constantly shifting but consistently unconvivial assortment of other Hermanan officials to discuss the problem of

Hermano's embargo on all foreign trade, and specifically its discontinuation of pharmaceutical exports to Gavial that Gavial regarded as vital to the health of its citizens,

The factor behind the unconviviality soon became clear. The Hermanans, a prickly bunch inexperienced in galactic diplomacy, apparently were convinced that Commissioner Haym and his companions were here to accomplish some sort of trickery. But the Hermanans had no way of knowing that and had been given no reason to suspect it. And the faintly concealed animosity with which they were treating the visitors from Gavial would surely get in the way of reaching any agreement on the treaty that the Gavialese had ostensibly come here to negotiate, a treaty that would be just as beneficial to Hermano as it would to Gavial.

So it became the Colonel's immediate job—in the role of Petrus Haym, envoy from the Cruzeiro system, not as a functionary of the Imperium—to show the Hermanans that their own frosty attitude was counterproductive. For that he needed to make himself seem to be the opposite of deceitful: a good-hearted, willingly transparent man, open and friendly, a little on the innocent side, maybe, not in any way a fool but so eager to have his mission end in a mutually advantageous agreement that the Hermanans would think he might allow himself to be swayed into becoming an advocate for the primary interests of Hermano. Therefore, no matter the provocation, he was the soul of amiability. The technicians of the Service had designed him to look stout and sleepy and unthreatening, and he spoke with a comic-opera Gavialese accent, which was helpful in enabling him to play the part of an easy mark. He spoke of how much he longed to be back on Gavial with his wife and children, and he let it be perceived without explicitly saying so that for the sake of an earlier family reunion he might well be willing to entertain almost any proposal for a quick settlement of the negotiations. He made little mild jokes about the discomforts of his lodgings here and the inadequacies of the food to underscore his desire to be done with this job and on his way. When one of the authentic Gavialese betrayed some impatience with the seeming one-sidedness of the talks in their early stage, Commissioner Haym rebuked him good-naturedly in front of the Hermanans, pointing out that Hermano was a planet that had chosen an exceedingly difficult road for itself, and needed to be given the benefit of every doubt. And gradually the Hermanans began to thaw a bit.

The sticking point in the discussions was Hermano's request that the Cruzeiro worlds serve as Hermano's advocate before the Imperium in its quest for independence. What the Cruzeiro people knew, and Hermano probably knew it as well, was that the Imperium was never going to permit any world to secede. The only way that Gavial was going to get the pharmaceuticals that it wanted from Hermano, and for Hermano to get the weapons it wanted from the Cruzeiro worlds, was for the two groups to cook up a secret and completely illegal deal between them, in utter disregard not just of the wishes of the Imperium but of its laws.

Gavial had already signaled, disingenuously, that it was willing to do this—urged on by the Imperium, which had pledged that it would provide them with a continued supply of cantaxion in return for its cooperation. But Hermano, perhaps because it quite rightly was mistrustful of Gavial's willingness to enter into a secret illegal deal or perhaps because of the obstinate naivete of its leaders, was continuing to hold out for official recognition by Gavial and the other Cruzeiro worlds of Hermanan independence.

By prearrangement the Colonel and Magda Cermak took opposite positions on this issue. Magda—stolid, brusque, rigid, unsmiling—bluntly told the Hermanan negotiators the self-evident truth of the situation, which was that Gavial was not going to align itself with the Hermanan independence movement because nobody's requests for independence from the Imperium were ever going to get anywhere, that the Imperium would never countenance any kind of official recognition of any member world's independence. Such a thing would set a wholly unacceptable precedent. It was out of the question; it was scarcely worth even discussing. If Gavialese recognition of Hermanan independence was the price of reopening trade relations between Gavial and Hermano, she said coldly, then the Gavialese trade delegation might as well go home right now.

Meanwhile her associate, Commissioner Haym—genial, placid, undogmatic, a trifle lacking in backbone, maybe, and therefore readily manipulable—sadly agreed that getting the Imperium to allow a member world, no matter how obscure, to pull out of the confederation would be a very difficult matter to arrange, perhaps impossible. But he did point out that that it was the belief of the rulers of Gavial that the current philosophy of the Imperium was strongly nonbelligerent, that the Central Authority was quite eager to avoid having to launch military action against unruly members. For that reason, Commissioner Haym suggested, certain highly influential officials in the government of Gavial felt that the Imperium might be willing under the right circumstances to forget about Hermano entirely and look the other way while Hermano went right on regarding itself as independent. "I am not, you realize, speaking on behalf of the Imperium," Commissioner Haym said. "How could I? I have no right to do that. But we of Gavial have been given to understand that the Imperium is inclined toward leniency in this instance." The essential thing was that Hermano would have to keep quiet about its claim to independence, though it could go on behaving as though it were independent all the same. That is, in return for that silence, Commissioner Haym indicated, the Central Authority might be willing to overlook Hermano's refusal to pay taxes to it, considering that those taxes were a pittance anyway. And Hermano would be free to strike whatever private deals with whatever Imperium worlds it liked, so long as it kept quiet about those too— such as, he said, the proposed weapons-for-drugs arrangement that would get a supply of cantaxion flowing to Gavial once again and allow Hermano to feel capable of protecting itself against possible Imperium aggression.

Commissioner Haym communicated these thoughts to Procurator Collian at a time when Magda Cermak was elsewhere. Demanding immediate independence, he reiterated, was probably going to achieve nothing. But independence for Hermano might just be achievable in stages. Accepting a kind of de facto independence now might well clear the way for full independence later on. And he offered—unofficially, of course—Gavial's cooperation in persuading the Imperium to leave Hermano alone while it went on along its present solitary way outside the confederation of worlds.

Collian looked doubtful. "Will it work? I wonder. And how can you assure me the cooperation of your planet's government when not even your own colleague Commissioner Cermak is in agreement with you on any of this?"

"Ah, Commissioner Cermak. Commissioner Cermak!" Commissioner Haym favored Procurator Collian with a conspiratorial smile. "A difficult woman, yes. But not an unreasonable one. She understands that our fundamental goal in coming here, after all, is to restore trade between Gavial and Hermano by any means possible. Which ultimately should be Hermano's goal, too." Commissioner Haym allowed a semblance of craftiness to glimmer in his heavy-lidded eyes. "This is, of course, a very ticklish business all around, because of the Imperium's involvement in our dealings. You and I understand how complicated it is, eh?" A wink, a nudge of complicity. "But I do believe that your planet and mine, working toward our mutual interests, can keep the Imperium out of our hair, and that Gavial will stand up for Hermano before the Imperium if we commissioners bring back a unanimous report. And do you know how I think I can swing her over to the position that you and I favor?" he asked. "If I could show her that we have the full backing of First Secretary Bauer—that he sees the plan's advantages for both our worlds, that he wholeheartedly supports it—I think we can work out a deal."

Municipal Procurator Collian seemed to think that that was an interesting possibility. He proposed that Commissioner Haym quickly prepare a memorandum setting forth all that they had discussed between themselves, which he could place before the First Secretary for his consideration. Commissioner Haym, though, replied mildly that Municipal Procurator Collian did not seem to have fully understood his point. Commissioner Haym was of the opinion that he could most effectively make his thoughts clear to the First Secretary during the course of a personal meeting. Collian was a bit taken aback by that. The evasive look that flitted across his chilly features indicated that very likely one was not supposed to consume the time of the First Secretary in such low-level things as meetings with trade commissioners. But then—the Colonel watched the wheels turning within the man—Collian began, so it seemed, to appreciate the merits of letting First Secretary Bauer have a go at molding with his own hands this extremely malleable envoy from Gavial. "I'll see what I can do," he said.

Not all of Hermano was as bleak as the area around the capital city, the Colonel quickly discovered. The climate grew moister and more tropical as he headed southward, scraggy grasslands giving way to forests and forests to lush jungles in the southernmost region of the continent, the one continent that the Hermanans had managed to penetrate thus far. The view from the air revealed little sign of development in the southern zone, only widely scattered plantations, little isolated jungle domains, separated from one another by great roadless swaths of dense green vegetation. He did not see anything amounting to continuous settlement until he was nearly at the shores of the ocean that occupied the entire southern hemisphere of this world, stretching all the way to the pole. Here, along a narrow coastal strip between the jungle and the sea, the elite of Hermano had taken up residence.

First Secretary Bauer's estate was situated at the midpoint of that strip, on a headland looking out toward the green, peaceful waters of that southern sea. It was expectably grand. The only surprising thing about it was that it was undefended by walls or gates or even any visible guard force: the road from the airstrip led straight into the First Secretary's compound, and the estate-house itself, a long, low stone building rising commandingly on the headland in a way that reminded the Colonel of the fortress at Megalo Kastro, seemed accessible to anyone who cared to walk up to its door.

But the Colonel was taken instead to one of the many outbuildings, a good distance down the coastal road from the First Secretary's villa itself, and there he was left in comfortable seclusion for three long days. He had a five-room cottage to himself, with a pretty garden of flowering shrubs and a pleasant view of the sea. No one kept watch over him, but even so it seemed inappropriate and perhaps unwise to wander any great distance from his lodgings. His meals were brought to him punctually by silent servants: seafood of various kinds, mainly, prepared with skill and subtlety, and accompanied by pale wines that were interestingly tangy and tart. A small library had been provided for him, mostly familiar classics, the sort of books that Geryon Lanista had favored during their years of working together. He inspected the garden, he strolled along the beach, he ventured a short way into the dense forest of scrubby little red-leaved trees with aromatic bark on the inland side of the compound. The air here was soft and had a mildly spicy flavor, not at all bitter like the air up at Alto Hermano. The water of the sea, into which he ventured ankle-deep one morning, was warm and clear, lapping gently at the pink sands. Even the strong pull of this world's gravity was less oppressive here, though the Colonel knew that that was only illusion.

On the fourth day the summons to the presence of the First Secretary came to him.

The dispassionate tranquility that had marked the Colonel's demeanor since his departure from Gavial remained with him now. He had brought himself to his goal and whatever was fated to happen next would happen; he faced all possibilities with equanimity. He was taken into the great villa, conveyed down long silent hallways floored with gleaming panels of dark polished wood, led past huge rooms whose windows looked toward the sea, and delivered, finally, into a much smaller room, simply furnished with a desk and a few chairs, at the far end of the building. A man who unquestionably was Geryon Lanista waited for him there, standing behind the desk.

He was greatly altered, of course. The Colonel was prepared for that. The face of the man who stood before him now was the one he had seen in the solido that the dark-haired visitor had shown him in his villa on Galgala, that day that now seemed so long ago: that blunt-tipped nose, those downturned lips, the flaring cheekbones, the harsh jutting jaw, all of them nothing like the features of the Geryon Lanista he once had known. This man looked only to be sixty or so, and that too was unsurprising, though actually Lanista had to be close to twice that age; but no one ever looked much more than sixty anymore, except those few who preferred to let a few signs of something approaching their true age show through to the surface. Lanista had had every reason to transform himself beyond all recognition since the debacle on Tristessa. The surprising thing, the thing that forced the Colonel for an instant to fight against allowing an uncontrolled reaction to make itself visible, was how easy it was for him to see beyond the cosmetic transformations to the real identity behind them.

Was it the hulking frame that gave him away, or the expression of the eyes? Those things had to be part of it, naturally. Very few men were built on such a massive scale as Lanista, and not even the canniest of cosmetic surgeons could have done anything about the breadth of those tremendous shoulders and that huge vault of a chest. His stance was Lanista's stance, the rock-solid stance of a man of enormous strength and physical poise: one's habitual way of holding one's body could not be unlearned, it seemed. And the eyes, though they were brown now and the Colonel remembered Lanista to have had piercingly blue ones, still had that eerie, almost feminine softness that had given such an odd cast to the old Lanista's otherwise formidably masculine face. Surely a surgeon could have done something about that. But perhaps one had tried, and even succeeded, and then the new eyes had come to reveal the innate expression of Lanista's soul even so, shining through inexorably despite everything: for there were the veritable eyes of Geryon Lanista looking out at him from this unfamiliar face.

The eyes—the stance—and something else, the Colonel thought, the mere intangible presence of the man—the inescapable, unconcealable essence of him—

While the Colonel was studying Martin Bauer and finding Geryon Lanista behind the facade, Martin Bauer was studying Commissioner Petrus Haym, giving him the sort of close scrutiny that any head of state trying to evaluate a visiting diplomat of whom he intended to make use could be expected to give. Plainly he was reading Petrus Haym's bland meaty face to assure himself that the Gavialese commissioner was just as obtuse and pliable as the advance word from Procurator Collian had indicated. The precise moment when Lanista made the intuitive leap by which he saw through the mask of Commissioner Petrus Haym to the hidden Colonel beneath was difficult for the Colonel to locate. Was it when the tiniest of muscular tremors flickered for an instant in his left cheek? When there was that barely perceptible fluttering of an eyelid? That momentary puckering at the corner of his mouth? The Colonel had had a lifetime's training in reading faces, and yet he wasn't sure. Perhaps it was all three of those little cues that signalled Lanista's sudden stunned realization that he was in the presence of the man he had looked to as his master and mentor, or perhaps it was none of them; but somewhere in the early minutes of this encounter Lanista had identified him. The Colonel was certain of that.

For a time neither man gave any overt indication of what he knew about the other. The conversation circled hazily about the ostensible theme of an exchange of arms for medicine and how that could be arranged in conjunction with Hermano's desire to break free from the political control of the Central Authority of the Imperium. The Colonel, as Haym, took pains to radiate an amiability just this side of buffoonery, while always drawing back from full surrender to the other man's wishes. Lanista, as Bauer, pressed Haym ever more strongly for a commitment to his cause, though never quite pouncing on him with a specific demand for acquiescence. Gradually it became clear to the Colonel that they were beginning to conduct these negotiations in the voices of Lanista and the Colonel, not in those of First Secretary Bauer and Commissioner Haym. Gradually, too, it became clear to him that Lanista was just as aware of this as he was.

In the end it was Lanista who was the one who decided to abandon the pretense. He had never been good at biding his time. It had been his besetting flaw in the old days that a moment would always come when he could no longer contain his impatience, and the Colonel saw now that no surgery could alter that, either. Commissioner Haym had been moving through the old circular path once more, asking the First Secretary to consider the problems that Gavial faced in weighing its need for cantaxion against the political risks involved in defying the decrees of the Central Authority, when Lanista said abruptly, in a tone of voice far more sharply focused and forceful than the woolly diplomatic one he had been using up until then, "Gavial doesn't have the slightest intention of speaking up for us before the Imperium, does it, Colonel? This whole mission has been trumped up purely for the sake of inserting you into the situation so you can carry out the Imperium's dirty work here, whatever that may be. Am I not right about that?"

"Colonel?" the Colonel said, in the Haym voice.

"Colonel, yes." Lanista was quivering, now, with the effort to maintain his composure. "I can see who you are. I saw it right away. —I thought you had retired a long time ago."

"I thought so too, but I was wrong about that. And I thought you were dead. I seem to have been wrong about that too."

———

For half a century the Colonel had lived, day in, day out, with the memories of his last two weeks on the paradise-world that Tristessa once had been. Like most bad memories, those recollections of the Tristessan tragedy, and his own narrow escape from destruction, had receded into the everyday background of his existence, nothing more now than the dull, quiet throbbing of a wound long healed, easily enough ignored much of the time. But in fact the wound had never healed at all. It had merely been bandaged over, sealed away by an act of sheer will. From time to time it would remind him of its existence in the most agonizing way. Now the pain of it came bursting upward once again out of that buried part of his consciousness in wave upon wave.

He was back on Tristessa again, waiting for Lanista to return from his mission to Shannakha. Lanista had gone to the companion world ten days before, intending to see the minister who had jurisdiction over Tristessan affairs and make one last effort to head off the conflict between the two planets that had begun to seem inevitable. He was carrying with him documents indicating that the Tristessa colonists were ready to launch their rebellion, and that only the promulgation by Shannakha of a radical program of economic reform could now avoid a costly and destructive struggle. Recent developments on Shannakha had given rise to hope that at least one powerful faction of the government was willing to offer some significant concessions to the Tristessan colonists. The Colonel, meanwhile, was holding talks with Ilion Gabell, the rebel leader, in an attempt to get him to hold his uprising off a little while longer while Lanista worked out the details of whatever concessions Shannakha might offer.

Gabell's headquarters were on the floating island of Petra Hodesta, five hundred hectares of grasses thick as hawsers that had woven themselves tightly together long ago and broken free of the mainland. The island, its grassy foundation covered now with an accretion of soil out of which a forest of slender blue-fronded palms had sprouted, circled in a slow current-driven migration through the sparkling topaz waters of Tristessa's Triple Sea, and Gabell's camp was a ring of bamboo huts along the island's shore. The Colonel had arrived five days earlier. He had a good working relationship with Gabell, who was a man of commanding presence and keen intelligence with a natural gift for leadership, forty or fifty years old and still in the first strength and flourish of his early manhood. The Colonel had laid out in great detail and more than customary forthrightness everything that Lanista had gone to the mother world to request; and Gabell had agreed to wait at least until he saw what portion of the things Lanista was asking for would be granted. He was not a rash or hasty man, was Gabell. But he warned that any kind of treachery on Shannakha's part would be met with immediate and terrible reprisals.

"There will be no treachery," the Colonel promised.

Petra Hodesta's wandering route now was taking it toward the northernmost of Triple Sea's three lobes, the one adjacent to Gespinord, the Tristessan capital province. Since Lanista was due back from Shannakha in a few more days, it was the Colonel's plan to go ashore on the coast of Gespinord and make his way by airtrain to the main Velde terminal, two hundred kilometers inland at the capital city, to await his return. But he was less than halfway there when the train came spiraling down to its track with the sighing, whistling sound of an emergency disconnect and someone in uniform came rushing through the cars, ordering everyone outside.

Tristessa was under attack. Without warning Shannakhan troops had come pouring through every Velde doorway on the planet. Gespinord City, the capital, had already been taken. All transit lines had been cut. The Colonel heard distant explosions, and saw a thick column of black smoke rising in the north, and another, much closer, to the east. They were hideous blotches against the flawless emerald-green of the Tristessan sky; and there in the west the Colonel saw a different sort of blemish, the harsh dark face of stark stony Shannakha, low and swollen and menacing on the horizon. What had gone wrong up there? What—even while they were in the midst of delicate negotiations—had led the Shannakhans to break the fragile peace?

The train had halted at some provincial station bordered on both sides by rolling crimson meadows. Somehow the Colonel found a communications terminal. Reaching Lanista on Shannakha proved impossible: no outgoing contact with other worlds was being allowed. But against all probability he did manage to get a call through to the rebel headquarters on Petra Hodesta, and, what was even less probable than that, Ilion Gabell himself came to the screen. His handsome features now had taken on a wild, almost bestial look: the curling golden mane was greasy and disheveled, the luminous, meditative eyes had a frenzied glaze, his lips were drawn back in a toothy grimace. He gave the Colonel a look of searing contempt. "No treachery, you said. What do you call this? They've invaded us everywhere at once. Without warning, without any declaration of hostilities. They must have been planning it for years."

"I assure you—"

"I know what your assurance is worth," Gabell said. "Well, mine is worth more. The reprisals have already begun, Colonel. And as for you—"

A blare of visual static sliced across the screen and it went black. "Hello?" the Colonel shouted. "Hello? Hello?"

The stationmaster, bald and plump and nearly as wild-eyed as Gabell had looked, appeared from a back room. The Colonel identified himself to him. He gaped at the Colonel in amazement and blurted, "There's an order out for your arrest. You and that other Imperium agent, both. You're supposed to be seized by anyone who finds you and turned over to the nearest officers of the republic."

"What republic is that?"

"Republic of Tristessa. Proclaimed three hours ago by Ilion Gabell. All enemies of the republic are supposed to be rounded up and—"

"Enemies of the republic?" the Colonel said, astonished. He wondered if he was going to have to kill him. But the plump stationmaster clearly had no appetite for playing policeman. He let his eye wander vaguely toward the open door to his left and shrugged, and made an ostentatious show of turning his attention away from the Colonel, busying himself with important-looking papers on his desk instead.

The Colonel was out through the door in a moment.

He saw no option but to make his way to the capital and find whatever was left of the diplomatic community, which no doubt was attempting to get off Tristessa as quickly as possible, and get himself off with them. Something apocalyptic was going on here. The sky was black with smoke in every direction, now, and the drumroll of explosions came without a break, and frightful tongues of flame were leaping up from a town just beyond the field on his left. Was the whole planet under Shannakhan attack? But that made no sense. This place was Shannakha's property; destroying it by way of bringing it back under control was foolishness.

Gabell had spoken of reprisals. Was *he* the one behind the explosions?

It took the Colonel a week and a half to cover the hundred kilometers from the train station to the capital, a week and a half of little sleep and less food while he traversed a zigzag route through the devastated beauty of Gespinord Province, dodging anyone who might be affiliated with the rebels. That could be almost anybody, and was likely to be nearly everybody. A woman who gave him shelter one night told him of what the rebels were doing, the broken dams and torched granaries and poisoned fields, a war of Tristessa against itself that would leave the planet scarred for decades and worse than useless to its Shannakhan masters. At dawn she came to him and told him to go; he saw men wearing black rebel armbands entering the house on one side as he slipped away from it on the other.

He had three more such narrow escapes in the next four days. After the last of them he stayed away from inhabited areas entirely. He hurt his leg badly, slogging across a muddy lake. He cut his hand on a sharp palm frond and it became infected. He ate some unknown succulent-looking fruit and vomited for a day and a half. Skulking northward through swamps and over fresh ash heaps still warm from the torching, he started to experience the breaking down of his innate unquenchable vitality. The eternal self-restoring capacity of his many-times-rejuvenated body was no longer in evidence. A great weariness came over him, a sense of fatigue that approached a willingness to cease all striving and lie down forever. That was a new experience for him, and one that shocked him. He began to feel his true age and then to feel older than his true age, a thousand years older, a million. He was ragged and dirty and lame and his throat was perpetually parched and there was a pounding against the right side of his skull in back that would not stop; and as he grew weaker and weaker with the passing days he began to think that he was going to die before much longer, not from some rebel's shot but only from the rigors of this journey, the fever and the chill and the hunger. He cursed Geryon Lanista a thousand times. Whatever Lanista had been up to on Shannakha, could he not have taken a moment to send his partner on Tristessa some warning that everything was on the verge of blowing up? Evidently not.

And then, at last, he stumbled into Gespinord City, where uniformed soldiers of Shannakha patrolled every street. He identified himself to one of them as a representative of the Imperium, and was taken to a makeshift dormitory in a school gymnasium where members of the diplomatic corps were being given refuge. There were about a dozen of them from five or six worlds, consular officials, mainly, who in ordinary times looked after the interests of tourists from their sectors of the galaxy that were holidaying on Tristessa. All the tourists were long gone, and the few officials who remained had stayed behind only to supervise the final stages of the evacuation of the planet. One of them, a woman from Thanda Bandanareen, saw to it that the Colonel was washed and fed and medicated, and afterward, when he had rested awhile, explained that the Tristessan Authority, which was the name under which the invaders from Shannakha were going, had ordered all outworlders to leave Tristessa at once. "I've been shipping people out for five days straight," she said, and the Colonel perceived for the first time that she was not much farther from exhaustion than he was himself. "There's no time to set coordinates. You go to the doorway and you step through and you work things out for yourself on the other side. Are you ready to go?"

"Now?"

"The sooner I get the last few stragglers out of here, the sooner I can go myself."

She led him to the doorway and, offering a word or two of thanks for her help, he entered its Velde field, a blind leap to anywhere, and came out, to his relief, on that glorious planet, Nabomba Zom, identifiable instantly by the astounding scarlet sea before him, which was shimmering with a violet glow as the first blue rays of morning struck its surface. There, in a guest lodge of the Imperium at the base of pale green mountains soft as velvet, the Colonel learned from a fellow member of the Service what had taken place on Shannakha.

It seemed that Geryon Lanista had badly overplayed his hand. For the sake of persuading the Shannakhans to adopt a more lenient Tristessa policy, Lanista had shown them forged documents indicating that Ilion Gabell's revolutionary army would not simply launch a rebellion on Tristessa if concessions weren't granted but would invade Shannakha itself. The Shannakhans had taken this fantasy seriously, much *too* seriously. Lanista had meant to worry them with it, but instead he terrified them; and in a frantic preemptive overreaction they hurriedly shipped an invading army to Tristessa to bring the troublesome colonists to heel. The worst-case scenario that Lanista had foreseen as a theoretical possibility, but did not seem to believe could happen, was going to occur.

The Colonel shook his head in disbelief. That Lanista—his own protégé—would have done anything so stupid was next to impossible to accept; that he would have done so without telling him that he had any such crazy tactic in mind was an unpardonable breach of Service methodology. That he had not sent word to the fellow officer whom he had left behind in harm's way on Tristessa that events in this planetary system had begun to slide toward a ghastly cataclysm as a result of his bizarrely clumsy maneuver was unforgivable for a different reason.

It seemed Gabell had been anticipating an invasion from Shannakha and had had a plan all ready for it: a scorched-earth program by which everything on Tristessa that was of value to Shannakha would be destroyed within hours after the arrival of Shannakhan invaders. One overreaction had led to another; by the end of the first week of war Tristessa was utterly ruined. Between the furious destructiveness of the rebels and the brutal repression of the rebellion by the invaders that had followed, nothing was left of Tristessa's plantations, its great estates, its hotels, its towns and cities, but ashes.

"And Lanista?" the Colonel asked leadenly. "Where is he?"

"Dead. By his own hand, it would seem, though that isn't a hundred percent certain. Either he was trying to get away from Shannakha in a tremendous hurry and accidentally made a mess out of his Velde coordinates, or else he deliberately scrambled up the coding so that he wouldn't be reassembled alive at his destination. Whichever it was, there wasn't very much left of him when he got there."

"You really believed I was dead?" Lanista asked.

"I *hoped* you were dead. I *wanted* you to be dead. But yes, yes, I believed you were dead, too. Why wouldn't I? They said you had gone into a doorway and come out in pieces someplace far away. Considering what you had managed to achieve on Shannakha, that was a completely appropriate thing to have done. So I accepted what they told me and I went on believing it for the next fifty years, until some bastard from the Imperium showed up at my house with proof that you were still alive."

"Believe me, I thought of killing myself. I imagined fifty different ways of doing it. Fifty *thousand*. But it wasn't in me to do a thing like that."

"A great pity, that," the Colonel said. "You allowed yourself to stay alive and you lived happily ever after."

"Not happily, no," said Lanista.

He had fled from Shannakha in a desperate delirious vertigo, he told the Colonel: aware of how badly awry it all had gone, frantic with shame and grief. There had been no attempt at a feigned suicide, he insisted. Whatever evidence the Service had found of such a thing was its own misinterpretation of something that had nothing to do with him. Fearing that the truth about the supposed Tristessan invasion would emerge, that the Shannakhans would discover that he had flagrantly misled them, he had taken advantage of the confusion of the moment to escape to the nearest world that had a Magellanic doorway and in a series of virtually unprogrammed hops had taken himself into some shadowy sector of the Rim where he had hidden himself away until at last he had felt ready to emerge, first under the Heinrich Bauer name, and then, as a result of some kind of clerical error, as *Martin* Bauer.

In the feverish final hours before the Shannakhan invasion began

he had, he maintained, made several attempts to contact the Colonel on
Tristessa and urge him to get away. But all communications lines
between Shannakha and its colony-world had already been severed,
and even the Imperium's own private communications channels failed
him. He asked the Colonel to believe that that was true. He *begged* the
Colonel to believe it. The Colonel had never seen Geryon Lanista begging for anything, before. Something about the haggard, insistent look
that came into his eyes made his plea almost believable. He himself
had been unable to get any calls through to Lanista on Shannakha; perhaps the systems were blocked in the other direction too. That was not
something that needed to be resolved just at this moment. The Colonel
put the question aside for later consideration. For fifty years the
Colonel had believed that Lanista had deliberately left him to die in the
midst of the Tristessa uprising, because he could not face the anger of
the Colonel's rebuke for the clumsiness of what he had done on
Shannakha. Perhaps he didn't need to believe that any longer. He
would prefer not to believe it any longer; but it was too soon to tell
whether he was capable of that.

"Tell me this," he said, when Lanista at last had fallen silent.
"What possessed you to invent that business about a Tristessan invasion of Shannakha in the first place? How could you ever have imagined it would lead to anything constructive? And above all else, why
didn't you try the idea out on me before you went off to Shannakha?"

Lanista was a long while in replying. At length he said, in a flat,
low, dead voice, the voice of a headstrong child who is bringing himself to confess that he has done something shameful, "I wanted to surprise you."

"What?"

"To surprise you and to impress you. I wanted to out-Colonel the
Colonel with a tremendous dramatic move that would solve the whole
crisis in one quick shot. I would come back to Tristessa with a treaty
that would pacify the rebels and keep the Shannakhans happy too, and
everything would be sweetness and light again, and you would ask me
how I had done it, and I would tell you and you would tell me what a
genius I was." Lanista was looking directly at the Colonel with an
unwavering gaze. "That was all there was to it. An idiotic young sub-

238

altern was fishing for praise from his superior officer and came up with a brilliant idea that backfired in the most appalling way. The rest of my life has been spent in an attempt to atone for what I did on Shannakha."

"Ah," the Colonel said. "That spoils it, that last little maudlin bit at the end of the confession. 'An attempt to atone'? Come off it, Geryon. Atoning by starting up a rebellion of your own? Against the Imperium, which you once had sworn to defend with your life?"

Icy fury instantly replaced the look of intense supplication in Lanista's eyes. "We all have our own notions of atonement, Colonel. I destroyed a world, or maybe two worlds, and since then I've been trying to build them. As for the Imperium, and whatever I may have sworn to it—"

"Yes?"

"The Imperium. The Imperium. The universal foe, the great force for galactic stagnation. I don't owe the Imperium a thing." He shook his head angrily. "Let it pass. You can't begin to see what I mean. —The Imperium has sent you here, I gather. For what purpose? To work your old hocus-pocus on our little independence movement and bring me to heel the way you were trying to do with Ilion Gabell on Tristessa?"

"Essentially, yes."

"And how will you do it, exactly?" Lanista's face was suddenly bright with expectation. "Come on, Colonel, you can tell me! Consider it the old pro laying out his strategy one more time for the bumptious novice. Tell me. Tell me. The plan for neutralizing the revolution and restoring order."

The Colonel nodded. It would make no real difference, after all. "I can do two things. The evidence that you are Geryon Lanista and that you were responsible for the catastrophic outcome of the Tristessa rebellion is all fully archived and can quickly be distributed to all your fellow citizens here on Hermano. They might have a different view about your capability as a master schemer once they find out what a botch you made out of the Tristessa operation."

"They might. I doubt it very much, but they might. —What's the other thing you can do to us?"

"I can cut Hermano off from the Velde system. I have that power. The ultimate sanction: you may recall the term from your own Service days. I pass through the doorway and lock the door behind me, and Hermano is forever isolated from the rest of the galaxy. Or isolated until it begs to be allowed back in, and provides the Imperium with proof that it deserves to be."

"Will that please you, to cut us off like that?"

"What would please me is irrelevant. What would have pleased me would have been never to have had to come here in the first place. But here I am. —Of course, now that I've said all this, you can always prevent me from carrying any of it out. By killing me, for example."

Lanista smiled. "Why would I want to kill you? I've already got enough sins against you on my conscience, don't I? And I know as well as you do that the Imperium could cut us off from the Velde system from the outside any time it likes, and would surely do so if its clandestine operative fails to return safely from this mission. I'd wind up in the same position but with additional guilt to burden me. No, Colonel, I wouldn't kill you. But I do have a better idea."

The Colonel waited without replying.

"Cut us off from the Imperium, all right," Lanista said. "Lock the door, throw away the key. But stay here on the inside with us. There's no reason for you to go back to the Imperium, really. You've given the Imperium more than enough of your life as it is. And for what? Has serving the Imperium done anything for you except twisting your life out of shape? Certainly it twisted mine. It's twisted everybody's, but especially those of the people of the Service. All that meddling in interstellar politics—all that cynical tinkering with other people's governments—ah, no, no, Colonel, here at the end it's time for you to give all that up. Start your life over here on Hermano."

The Colonel was staring incredulously, wonderingly, bemusedly.

Lanista went on, "Your friends from Gavial can go home, but you stay here. You live out the rest of your days on Hermano. You can have a villa just like mine, twenty kilometers down the coast. The perfect retirement home, eh? Hermano's not the worst place in the universe to live. You'll have the servants you need. The finest food and wine. And an absolute guarantee that the Imperium will never bother you again. If you don't feel like retiring, you can have a post in the government here, a very high post, in fact. You and I could share the top place. I'd gladly make room for you. Who could know better than I do what a shrewd old bird you are? You'd be a vital asset for us, and we'd reward you accordingly. —What do you say, Colonel? Think it over. It's the best offer you'll ever get, I promise you that."

It was easiest to interpret what Lanista had said as a grotesque joke, but when the Colonel tried to shrug it away Lanista repeated it, more earnestly even than before. He realized that the man was serious. But, as though aware now that this conversation had gone on too long, Lanista suggested that the Colonel return to his own lodgings and rest for a time. They could talk again of these matters later. Until then he was always free to resume the identity of Petrus Haym of the Gavialese trade mission, and to go back to his four companions and continue to hatch out whatever schemes they liked involving commerce between Gavial and the Free Republic of Hermano.

He was unable to sleep for much of that night. So many revelations, so many possibilities. He hadn't been prepared for that much. None of the usual adjustments would work; but toward dawn sleep came, though only for a little while, and then he awoke suddenly, drenched in sweat, with sunlight pouring through his windows. Lanista's words still resounded in his mind. *The Imperium has twisted your life out of shape,* Lanista had said. Was that so? He remembered his grandfather saying, hundreds of years ago—thousands, it felt like—*The Imperium is the enemy, boy. It strangles us. It is the chain around our throats.* The boy who would become the Colonel had never understood what he meant by that, and when he came to adulthood he followed his father, who had said always that the Imperium was civilization's one bulwark against chaos, into the Service.

Well, perhaps his father had been right, and his grandfather as well. He had strapped on the armor of the Service of the Imperium and he had gone forth to do battle in its name, and done his duty unquestioningly throughout a long life, a very long life. And perhaps he had done enough, and it was time to let that armor drop away from him now. What had Lanista said of the Imperium? *The universal foe, the great force for galactic stagnation.* An angry man. Angry words. But there was some truth to them. His grandfather had said almost the same thing. An absentee government, enforcing conformity on an entire galaxy—

On that strange morning the Colonel felt something within him breaking up that had been frozen in place for a long time.

"What do you say?" Lanista asked, when the Colonel had returned to the small office with the desk and the chairs. "Will you stay here with us?"

"I have a home that I love on Galgala. I've lived there ever since my retirement."

"And will they let you live in peace, when you get back there to Galgala?"

"Who?"

"The people who sent you to find me and crush me," Lanista said. "The ones who came to you and said, *Go to a place called Hermano, Colonel. Put aside your retirement and do one more job for us*. They told you that a man you hate was making problems for them here and that you were the best one to deal with him, am I not right? And so you went, thinking you could help the good old Imperium out yet again and also come to grips with a little private business of your own. And they can send you out again, wherever else they feel like sending you, whenever they think you're the best one to deal with whatever needs dealing with."

"No," the Colonel said. "I'm an old man. I can't do anything more for them, and they won't ask. After all, I've failed them here. I was supposed to destroy this rebellion, and that won't happen now."

"Won't it?"

"You know that it won't," the Colonel said. He wondered whether he had ever intended to take any sort of action against the Hermano rebels. It was clear to him now that he had come here only for the sake of seeing Lanista once again and hearing his explanation of what had happened on Shannakha. Well, now he had heard it, and had managed to persuade himself that what Lanista had done on Shannakha had been merely to commit an error of judgment, which anyone can do, rather than to have sought to contrive the death of his senior officer for the sake of covering up his own terrible blunder. And now there was that strange sensation he was beginning to feel, that something that had been frozen for fifty years, or maybe for two hundred, was breaking up within him. He said, "Proclaim your damned independence, if you like. Cut yourselves off from the Imperium. It makes no difference to me. They should have sent someone else to do this job."

"Yes. They should have. —Will you stay?"

"I don't know."

"We're no longer of the Imperium and neither are you."

Lanista spoke once again of the villa by the sea, the servants, the wines, the place beside him in the high administration of the independent world of Hermano. The Colonel was barely listening. It would be easy enough to go home, he was thinking. Lanista wouldn't interfere with that. Hop, hop, hop, and Galgala again. His lovely house beside that golden river. His collection of memorabilia. The souvenirs of a life spent in the service of the Imperium, which is a chain about our throats. Home, yes, home to Galgala, to live alone within the security of the Imperium. The Imperium is the enemy of chaos, but chaos is the force that drives evolutionary growth.

"This is all real, what you're offering me?" he asked. "The villa, the servants, the government post?"

"All real, yes. Whatever you want."

"What about Magda Cermak and the other three?"

"What do you want done with them?"

"Send them home. Tell them that the talks are broken off and they have to go back to Gavial."

"Yes. I will."

"And what will you do about the doorways?"

"I'll seal them," Lanista said. "We don't need to be part of the Imperium. There was a time, you know, when Earth was the only world in the galaxy, when there was no Imperium at all, no Velde doorways either, and somehow Earth managed to get along for a few billion years without needing anything more than itself in the universe. We can do that too. The doorways will be sealed and the Imperium will forget all about Hermano."

"And all about me, too?" the Colonel asked.

"And all about you, yes."

The Colonel laughed. Then he walked to the window and saw that night had fallen, the radiant, fiery night of the Core, with a million million stars blazing in every direction he looked. The doorways would be sealed, but the galaxy still would be out there, filling the sky, and whenever he needed to see its multitude of stars he needed only to look upward. That seemed sufficient. He had traveled far and wide and the time was at hand, was more than at hand, for him to bring an end to his journeying. Well, so be it. So be it. No one would ever come looking for him here. No one would look for him anywhere; or, if looking, would never find. At the Service's behest he had returned to the stars one last time; and now, at no one's behest but his own, he had at last lost himself among them forever.

KEEPSAKES

~~~~~~~~~~~~

by Mike Resnick

Mike Resnick, an Ohio resident, is the author of more than forty science fiction novels, 150 stories, and two screenplays, and has edited more than thirty anthologies. He is the winner of four Hugo Awards and a Nebula, and has won other major awards in the United States, France, Spain, Japan, Croatia, and Poland. Resnick has traveled widely in Africa, and from his experiences there he has derived many of his best-known works, such as the Hugo-winning story "Kirinyaga" and its popular sequels. His latest novel is The Return of Santiago. *Here he handles the theme of a challenging galactic mystery with his characteristic lightness of touch and swiftness of narrative pace.*

THEY CAME LIKE a plague, blown on the galactic winds.

No one knew where they came from, no one knew where they were going, no one even knew for sure if they were human. One day they would appear and offer their services, and sometime later they would leave, their coffers filled to overflowing with broken dreams and shattered hopes. Oh, they were paid in currency, lots of it—but what they really traded in was misery.

They had many names, some of their own devising, some not. The one that stuck was the Star Gypsies.

It was my job to hunt them down. Of course, no one told me what to do when I caught them, because they usually hadn't broken any laws. Hearts, yes; dreams, absolutely. But laws? Not often, if at all.

They gave me an assistant. Well, actually, they gave me a lot of assistants, but the one I'm referring to was Jebediah Burke, because he's the one this story is about.

He was a young man, was Jebediah, young and handsome and eager to make a name for himself, to right wrongs and rescue damsels in distress, to make the galaxy a better place, to do all the things you really think are possible before Life starts peeling away your romantic illusions. He had a thick shock of wavy brown hair that never stayed in place but always looked like the wind was blowing through it. He was tall and lanky, but he moved gracefully. His eyes were a pale blue; I know you can't characterize a pair of eyes, but to me they always seemed to be open and trusting. Now that I think of it, I can't remember him ever blinking.

I don't know why he joined the service. He'd been to school and graduated with honors. There were a hundred other things he could have done, more lucrative and certainly less frustrating, but like I said, he had a young man's thirst to see new worlds, and a young man's urge to make a difference. He was such a friendly, decent young man that the old hands refrained from telling him that none of us would ever make a difference, that Man had spent quite a few thousand years trying to protect his neighbors from themselves, and we sure as hell didn't have much to show for it except some resentful neighbors.

I still remember his first day on the job. He'd already found his desk in the huge office when I showed up, and was poring over all the material we had accumulated on the Star Gypsies. He had pulled up holographic interviews with victims, transcripts, financial records, anything he could access.

We got the introductions over with, and I left him to study the face of the enemy. Except, of course, that he couldn't find it. Finally he walked over to me.

"Excuse me, sir," he began.

"Forget the sir," I said. "I'm just Gabe."

"I feel awkward calling you by your first name, sir," he said.

"Get over it. The last thing I need if we're on an undercover assignment is someone calling me sir."

"I'll try to remember that, sir . . . I mean Gabe."

"It shouldn't be hard," I said. "It's a Biblical name, just like yours."

"Jebediah isn't Biblical, Gabe."

"Okay," I said. "One's Biblical and one *sounds* Biblical. That's close enough. Now, what's your problem?"

"The Star Gypsies."

"They're the whole department's problem," I noted wryly. "Just what particular facet of them is bothering you?"

He frowned. "I must be asking the computer the wrong questions," he said. "I can find out everything they've done—well, everything that's been reported, anyway—but I can't find any hard information on *them*. I can't even find out what they look like."

I couldn't resist a smile. "Now you know why we welcomed you with open arms."

"You mean *nobody* knows?" he said in disbelief. "How can that be? Surely the victims gave you descriptions!"

"We have more descriptions than we know what to do with," I said. "They're not worth the powder to blow them to hell."

"I don't understand, sir."

"Gabe."

"Gabe," he amended.

"To humans, they look like men. To the inhabitants of Komornos, they look like Komornans. To a Mullutei, they look like Mollutes."

"They're shape-changers?"

"We don't know what the hell they are," I admitted. "They've been around for close to ninety years, and we still don't have any idea." I sighed. "They were here before I got here, and they'll be here after you and I are both in the grave. Welcome to the service; at least you're not lacking job security."

He seemed to stare right through me at some fixed point in space only he could see. For a moment I thought he'd actually gone into some kind of trance, or perhaps that he was seriously reconsidering his choice of careers, but then he relaxed and rejoined the here and now.

"Ninety years, and we've never captured one," he said. "Now that's a challenge."

"That's a pit of quicksand," I corrected him.

"Maybe you just need fresh eyes, Gabe."

"Fresh eyes?" I repeated, wondering what the hell he was talking about.

"Maybe you just need someone who looks at the problem from a different angle."

I didn't want to discourage him his first morning on the job, so I allowed that maybe a pair of fresh eyes could spot what we'd all been missing. Then I went back to reading the day's reports, while he returned to his desk and learned what more he could about the Star Gypsies, most of it second-, third-, and even fourth-hand accounts and tall tales.

At noon I stopped by and invited him out to lunch.

"I think I'd be better off staying here and learning what I can," he said.

"Come on," I said. "They've been around longer than we've both been alive. Another hour won't hurt."

He shrugged, deactivated his computer, got to his feet, and followed me out the door. We took the slidewalk to the corner, stepped onto a crosswalk, and let it carry us to Romeo's, which is the restaurant most of our people hang out at when they're on the planet.

"It's amazing," said Jebediah as we sat down at a table in the corner and the holographic menu suddenly appeared in midair, rotating gently so we could both read it.

"Romeo's?" I repeated. "It's just a lunch shop."

"No," he said, looking around. "I mean, any one of *them* could be a Star Gypsy."

"They could," I agreed. "But most of them are your coworkers."

He frowned disapprovingly. "They're all humans. Everyone I saw in the office this morning was human."

"The department is only about 40 percent human," I explained. "But most of the nonhumans can't metabolize our food, so they eat at their own restaurants."

"We should probably join them every now and then to show solidarity."

I shook my head. "You wouldn't want to go back to work for a day or two after seeing what they eat."

"I didn't notice any of them in the office."

"They're in the building," I said. "We try to accommodate their needs, whether it's chlorine or methane or 200 degrees Fahrenheit."

"I'd like to speak to some of them, to get their take on the Star Gypsies."

"It's all there in the computer," I told him.

"I'd rather do it face-to-face," he said, "unless you have some objection to that."

"Be my guest," I said. "I suppose two-thirds of them actually *have* faces, and you'll figure out where the rest are hiding their ears and mouths."

He was silent for a moment. "Do you think you've ever seen one, Gabe?"

"An alien? Every day."

"I mean a Star Gypsy."

"Probably. I really couldn't say."

"What do you suppose they really want?" he asked.

"Most days I think they want to drive me crazy."

"That was a serious question," said Jebediah.

"That was an almost-serious answer," I replied. "Beyond that, I don't know what the hell they want. Why does their only goal seem to be making people miserable? Why don't they just rob some banks and be done with it? If they're going to walk away with everything a man holds dear, why not finish the job and kill him?" I sighed. "You start questioning motivations and you could run smack-dab into Eternity."

He shook his head. "Every sentient being has a motivation," he said with conviction.

"Figure theirs out and we just might make you the head of the department the next morning," I said.

"Maybe I will," he half-promised.

I looked at the temperature. It was 28 degrees Celsius. And getting warmer.

"Maybe it'll snow tomorrow, too," I said.

———

Well, it didn't snow, but there was a change. Not in the weather; the weather on Goldenrod never changes. But we got word that the Star Gypsies had been on New Rhodesia, and had made off with "the usual."

I figured Jebediah might as well see what we were up against, so I gave him a couple of hours to pack and meet me at the spaceport. He was waiting for me when I got there.

"I tried to find New Rhodesia on a star map, and I couldn't," he announced as we walked out to the ship.

"Officially it's Beta Draconis IV," I said. "But the inhabitants call it New Rhodesia, and that's good enough for me."

"Are they human?"

"The colonists are. There are some remnants of the native race, but I gather we won't be running into them."

"Shy?"

"Decimated," I replied. "Not every world welcomed us with open arms."

He looked his disapproval. I wanted to explain to him that you can't be a hero if you don't have some enemies to conquer, and that actually the enemies in this star cluster had proven a little easier to conquer than most, but I decided not to. Young idealists have enough disillusionments in store for them; why rush the revelations?

We reached the ship and stopped.

"This is it?" said Jebediah, hands on hips, studying it.

"This is it."

"We're not going to keep our identities secret in this thing," he said. "Maybe we should get one that doesn't display all the departmental insignia."

"We don't have any," I said. "Besides, there won't be anyone there to frighten away. If the Star Gypsies aren't gone yet, I guarantee they'll be gone by the time we get there."

"How do you know?" asked Jebediah.

"Because they always are."

We took the airlift up to the ship's hatch. I set the navigational computer for the Beta Draconis system and ordered it to alert me when we got within half a light-year, and then, since it would be a dull twenty-hour trip even at light speeds, Jebediah and I lay down in pods in the Deepsleep Chamber.

It awakened us eighteen hours later, as programmed. I was famished, as I always am when I come out of Deepsleep, and so was

Jebediah. We made our way to the galley, ordered up a couple of meals, and ate in silence.

Then Jebediah got up and carefully inspected every inch of the ship. He never said a word, never touched a thing, just looked and mentally catalogued. I decided that it was a shame his thoroughness was wasted on our particular quest.

Finally he sat back down.

"Tell me what we know about the situation," he said. I noticed that "Please," "Gabe," and even "sir" had vanished from his vocabulary, but of course he was now an old-timer in his second full day on the job.

"New Rhodesia's a farming world," I said. "It supplies food to eleven nearby planets, most of them mining worlds, plus a couple of scientific outposts out in the Horatius system's asteroid belt."

"What's New Rhodesia's population?"

"Humans, maybe 800. Natives, and I have no idea what they call themselves or what we call them, about 400,000, maybe a little more."

"Eight hundred," he repeated. "I'm surprised the Star Gypsies had even heard of it."

"That's the kind of place they specialize in," I said.

"What happened there?"

"They had their wettest season on record," I answered. "The ground got saturated, the harvesting machines couldn't work because they kept sinking into the mud, and the crops were in danger of rotting where they stood. Most of the colonists are mortgaged up to the hilt, and they couldn't make it through a single season without a harvest." I paused and lit a smokeless cigar. "Then one day the Star Gypsies showed up and offered to work the fields—for a price, of course."

"And did they?"

"Oh, yes," I said. "They always deliver on their promises. From what I can tell, they worked in shifts, around the clock, day in and day out, until every last field was harvested."

"And then?"

"And then they took their payment and left—or if they haven't left yet, they'll be gone before we show up."

"What kind of payment?"

"That's the question no one ever asks up front," I said ruefully.

"Oh, they'll have demanded money, of course, and the farmer will be happy to pay it—and if that's all they wanted, we could disband the department and go catch murderers and extortionists."

"What do you *think* they got along with the money?" persisted Jebediah.

"Why guess?" I said. "We'll be there in a few hours, and then we'll know."

He fell silent, and I could tell from his expression that something was still troubling him, so I asked him about it.

"I don't understand any of this," he said. "They don't steal anything. They don't physically harm anyone. Whatever they got paid, people have agreed to their terms in advance. So why are we chasing after them? What laws have they broken?"

"None."

"Then—"

"When you go to war, do you do it because someone has broken a law?" I said. "No, you do it because a force of the enemy, however large or small, has committed actions that are detrimental to the people you are charged with protecting. This is pretty much the same thing."

It didn't sound all that convincing, even to me, and he sure as hell didn't look convinced.

"Look, kid," I said, "they trade in heartbreak and misery. I don't really care if it's legal or not, and neither do the people who pay us. Our job is to stop them by any means available."

"Even if they're not breaking any laws?"

"Even so."

He shook his head. "There's got to be more to it than that. You don't spend the resources of an entire governmental department tracking them down just because you disapprove of them."

"Disapprove is an understatement," I responded.

"I'm trying to understand, Gabe," he said. "I've heard rumors and old wives' tales about the Star Gypsies, but I couldn't find any justification in our files for going after them. They do what they promise to do, they don't rob anyone. Are you sure the complaints aren't cases of the biter-bit?"

"Biter-bit?" I repeated, puzzled. It wasn't an expression I'd heard before.

"People who thought they'd outwitted them, who thought they were getting the better of a bargain, and then found out they hadn't."

"There's a lot of biting that goes on," I acknowledged. "And the Star Gypsies do all of it."

"I'm not trying to start an argument, Gabe," he said. "But if I'm going to devote a goodly portion of my life to hunting down the Star Gypsies, I want to be sure I'm on the right side—and so far I'm not convinced."

"Tell you what," I said. "Talk face-to-face with some of their victims, and then if you want a transfer, I'll agree to it and sign the papers. Fair enough?"

"Yes, that's fair enough."

He didn't say another word until we touched down on New Rhodesia nine hours later. He just sat and stared at the various screens and panels around the ship, and I could tell he was wondering what this had to do with making the galaxy a better place. I almost wished for his sake that he wasn't about to find out.

—————

New Rhodesia was like a giant mudball. It had been raining for three months solid, and it was still raining when we touched down at the tiny spaceport. The air was thick with moisture, and the proximity of the yellow sun made the world uncomfortably warm.

The department made sure there was an airbus waiting for us. We hopped in, grateful for the air-cooled and dehumidified compartment. The bus levitated a couple of feet above the ground and the robot driver's head swiveled 180 degrees until it was facing us.

"May I have your destination, please?" it asked in a dull grating monotone.

"Yeah," I said. "Jacob Ellsworth's farm. Do you know where it is, or do you need coordinates?"

"All human locations are entered in my data banks," it said.

"Good. We want the farmhouse. If there's more than one dwelling, take us to the largest one."

"We shall arrive in eleven minutes and twenty-three seconds," announced the robot as the airbus raced forward.

"I know you don't have to watch the road, that the vehicle has dozens of sensors, and that you're just an extension of it," I said. "But I'd still feel a lot more comfortable if you turned your head around and watched the road."

The robot swiveled its head back without another word.

"Jacob Ellsworth," said Jebediah. "He's the one who filed the complaint?"

"Indirectly," I said.

"Indirectly?"

"You'll see."

We drove past a couple of huge farms that hadn't been harvested. The smell of the rotting vegetation even penetrated our compartment, and you could see the stuff bent in half from its own water-burdened weight, with mold starting to spread all over what remained of it.

Then we came to a neat flat field, maybe 4,000 hectares, everything picked clean, fresh furrows in the ground, and I knew we'd reached the Ellsworth farm.

"How come only this one was harvested?" asked Jebediah.

"Maybe the other farmers knew better than to deal with the Star Gypsies," I said. "Or maybe there were only enough of them to work a few farms this time. They don't all travel together, you know. In fact, I hear they've started showing up in the Albion and Quinellus Clusters in the past few months."

We drove alongside a pasture filled with mutated cattle, huge but placid animals standing some twelve feet at the shoulder, chewing their cud and staring at us with lackluster eyes. Off in the distance I could see some other animals, not from Terran stock, in a pair of smaller pastures.

And then we were at the house. I wasn't surprised to see a police vehicle in front of it. Nearby was a medical vehicle; the two robot attendants stood motionless at its doors, not bothering to acknowledge our—or even New Rhodesia's—existence.

Jebediah and I got out of the airbus and walked up to the front door. It scanned our retinas, and since it had no record of us it refused to open but immediately informed any occupants of our presence. A moment later a uniformed officer ordered the door to dilate and let us in. He was short and stocky, starting to lose his hair, and there were sweat stains all over his shirt, possibly due to exertion, more likely just from the heat and the humidity. He looked familiar, but I couldn't place him.

"Hi, Gabe," he said, extending his hand. "It's been a long time."

"It sure has," I said, shaking his hand and wondering who he was.

"Ben Paulson," he said when he realized I couldn't come up with his name. "You were my first boss."

"Oh, sure," I said. "Now I remember. You used to have a little more hair and a little less stomach. Meet Jebediah Burke, your replacement ten or fifteen times removed."

"Please to meet you, Jebediah," he said. "Been on the job long?"

"Just a couple of days," said Jebediah.

"Good luck," said Paulson. "You're going to need it. Not everyone can last as long as Gabe." He laughed humorlessly. "Not anyone, now that I think of it."

"You're the one who discovered him?" I asked.

"Yeah," said Paulson. "Isn't that a bitch? Quit the department, move out to the boonies where I'll never have to deal with the Star Gypsies again, and the bastards pick *my* planet." He snorted disgustedly. "I should have kept working for you—it paid better." He paused for a moment, remembering the old days. "Nah. They'd have locked me away in an asylum by now."

"I take it Ellsworth was dead when you found him?" I said.

He nodded an affirmative. "At least I didn't have to watch," said Paulson. "The medical robot says he'd been dead for almost a day before anyone noticed he wasn't answering his messages. I'll get a precise time of death back at the infirmary—we're too small a world to have a real bona fide hospital—but I've kept him here in case you want to look at him."

"No, that won't be necessary," I said.

"I'd like to see him," interjected Jebediah.

"Help yourself," said Paulson. "He's in the vehicle out front—the one with the two robots."

"Is there a code word?" asked Jebediah as he reached the door.

"No, just climb in and see what you need to see. They're not programmed to stop you."

Jebediah went out, and Paulson turned to me. "He's very young."

"We all were once."

"These damned Star Gypsies can age you fast." He shook his head sadly. "Too bad, an earnest young man like that."

"You might as well wait until he gets back. Then you won't have to repeat everything."

"Won't he take your word for it?"

"Not this week," I said.

"He will soon," said Paulson knowingly.

"Is there anything to drink in the kitchen?" I asked.

"No booze in the entire house," he said. "I put on some coffee about half an hour ago, if that's your style."

"This guy, this Ellsworth, he left a bubble, right?"

"Right."

"Well, I'd rather see it with some alcohol, but I suppose coffee's better than nothing."

I followed him into the kitchen and had just ordered the machine to pour my coffee when Jebediah came back into the house, and entered the kitchen. It was all he could do to keep from saluting.

"A single wound to the temple," he announced. "I'd say death was instantaneous."

"It was," agreed Paulson.

"It looks self-inflicted," continued Jebediah, "but we can't be sure at this point."

"Yes, we can," said Paulson. "Follow me, gentlemen."

He led us to the main parlor, opened up a small case with his official insignia on it, and withdrew a translucent bubble about an inch in diameter.

"This was rigged to begin playing the minute someone walked into this room," he said. "You can examine it when we're done, but I need it back. It's evidence."

I nodded. "Okay, play it."

He activated the globe, and suddenly a full-sized three-dimensional Ellsworth stood facing a recording device that no one could see.

"I am Jacob Ellsworth," said the simulacron, and you didn't have to be a genius to see that the man was obviously distraught. "I just want to leave a record so someone will know what happened." He started to say something. The words wouldn't come out. He cleared his throat and began again.

"My crops were rotting in the field when *they* came. I don't know if they were human or not. They *looked* like men. They said they'd heard about our problems here on New Rhodesia, and had come to help. I explained the situation, that the ground was so wet we couldn't work it. They offered to harvest our crops by hand, mine and Hiram Morton's. Hiram said no, that he wouldn't have any truck with them, but I was desperate. Last year's crop wasn't that good, and I had a pair of notes due on the farm."

He'd been going pretty good for a moment there, but now he started choking off his words again.

"They asked me how much I owed on the notes, and I told them. Then they asked what the crop would be worth if I could get it to market, and I told them that too. And they named a price that would even allow me a small profit after I paid off my debts. The only other thing they wanted in addition to the money we'd agreed upon was a single keepsake of their time on New Rhodesia, a book of their choosing from my house. I couldn't see anything wrong with that, and I agreed."

And now the tears began running down his scrawny cheeks.

"Tell Hiram Morton I should have listened to him." He stared at the lens. "They did what they said they'd do, and I paid them. And then they took their keepsake."

He paused, struggling to put together the words.

"I'm not like most farmers. I'm not tied to the land. I don't love the soil. The only thing in my life I've ever loved was Elizabeth, my wife. We were married for forty-three years. She died six years ago."

And now he glared furiously into the lens.

"They took the only book of holographs of her that I owned! I told them that they couldn't have it, that they could have anything else in the house. But they said this was the only book they wanted. I tried to stop them, but I'm an old man and they threw me down and ripped it from my hands and left with it."

The tears began again.

"And now I'll never see her again. Already I'm having trouble remembering exactly what the lines and curves of her face were like, the color of her eyes, the shape of her lips. In another week or another month it'll be completely gone. Those bastards stole the only memory I want, the only thing I ever loved!"

He raised a laser pistol to his left temple.

"Find them and do to them what they did to me."

Then he fired the gun, and his image vanished.

We were silent for a moment. I'd seen it, or something like it, more times than I cared to remember, but it was a new experience for Jebediah, and I could tell he was upset. I felt sorry for the kid; he was finally realizing just what it was that we were up against, and it disturbed him, probably more than anything had ever disturbed him before.

Finally Paulson spoke up. "I looked through the place before you got here," he said. "The man was a bibliophile. He had a first of Charles Dickens from almost 1,700 years ago. He had an inscribed copy of Jason Boorman from the 24th century A.D., and a first of Tanblixt's Canphorian poetry from the 9th century G.E. Those three books alone could have bought just about any farm on this planet. And they wouldn't take any of them." He turned to Jebediah. "They visited 143 farms. Twenty-eight owners turned them away; 115 are busy wishing they had—those that are still in any condition to wish, anyway." He paused, and I could see the pain reflected on his face. "This world will never be the same again. Oh, they'll still grow crops, but people don't get over something like this. It was a nice place to live until now. I suppose I'll stick around for a few months, and then I'll be off to some other world the Star Gypsies haven't visited yet, and hope I die of old age before they discover it."

"I'm still trying to figure out why they wanted the holos of his wife," said Jebediah, frowning.

"Because *he* wanted them. They take whatever's most valuable to you, especially if it has no value to anyone else. They work for cash, but mostly they take their pay in pain and remorse." Paulson looked like he was about to spit, then remembered he was inside. "What kind of twisted minds take pleasure in that?"

"There must be a reason," insisted Jebediah, who was clearly shaken. "Why would they bring such misery to a man who had trusted them and kept his bargain and hadn't done them any harm?"

"There comes a point where you stop worrying about why evil beings do something, and you concentrate on stopping them," said Paulson. He turned to me. "That is, if you're as tough as Gabe here. Me, I couldn't face one more victim. That's why I quit."

"How long were you with the department?" asked Jebediah.

"Maybe a year, maybe a little more. Too damned long." He turned to me. "How about you, Gabe?"

"Too damned long," I said.

"You still remember your first experience with them?" he asked.

"It's not the kind of thing you ever forget," I said.

I could still see it plain as day, the tortured countenance of the orange-skinned fur-covered Bedorian. He was as unlike a human as you could get in every way but one—his grief. A storm was coming, a storm such as Bedore VII hadn't seen in a century or more. His brood-house needed reinforcement or it would blow away and leave all his offspring exposed to the elements before they were old enough to cope with them. The Star Gypsies showed up like magic and offered to work on his broodhouse, and extracted their usual fee—local currency, plus one small artifact that was unique to Bedore VII. He agreed, they did the work, they paid him—and then they took the artifact, a small piece of stone called a *rlymph*. It just looked like a stone to me, and, I'm sure, to them, but to the Bedorian it was a religious token that guaranteed that his brood, some 150 strong, would eventually find their way to the afterlife. In his mind—and who's to say he was wrong?—they had condemned his brood to wander eternally in limbo with no possibility of ever joining him or his mates in a Bedorian paradise. I spent the rest of the week visiting close to a hundred other Bedorians; every story was the same.

"Are you all right?" asked Jebediah, reaching out to touch my shoulder, and I realized I'd been motionless for a couple of minutes while the scene played through my mind again.

"Yeah, I'm fine," I said. "It's been twenty-seven years, but I can still feel it like it was this morning."

"And from that day to this, did you ever find anyone who was pleased to have dealt with the Star Gypsies?" said Paulson.

I shook my head. "No one." I turned to Jebediah. "As their reputation spread, a lot of people refused to hire them. Now they concentrate mainly on little out-of-the-way worlds like this one. And even when they don't try to hide who they are, there are always some people who think they can outsmart them, and some people who are so desperate they'll agree to anything. Then they find out exactly what it is they've *really* agreed to." I smiled ironically. "You might feel the same way. You agreed to join the department, and now you're finding out exactly what we're up against. If it was just one farmer here and one banker there and one alien elsewhere, it wouldn't be worth our time—but it's three dozen here and two hundred there and a thousand some other place."

"I'd heard rumors," he said. "But I didn't realize . . ." He let the words trail off.

"Everyone's heard rumors," said Paulson. "Most people don't believe them. That's why the Star Gypsies can function."

"They're sentient beings. No sentient being brings this kind of misery to other sentient beings without a reason," he said firmly.

"You never heard of a sadist?" asked Paulson.

"I never heard of a race of them," Jebediah shot back. He turned back to me. "Have they some grievance against the Republic or perhaps a local planetary government?"

"If they have, they've never voiced it."

"Did they object to being colonized?"

"You're barking up the wrong tree," said Paulson. "We don't even know where they come from."

"They must have a planet or a headquarters where they store all the things they've taken," said Jebediah.

"You know what I think?" said Paulson. "I think those things are as worthless to them as they are to everyone but the original owners. My guess is that they jettison them the moment they break out of orbit."

I'd heard all these theories before from dozens of men on my staff, so I began looking around. "I don't suppose they left any more clues than usual?"

"None," said Paulson. "Wouldn't matter anyway. We don't have a holo, a retinagram, a fingerprint, a DNA record, anything, on any of them."

"It would be a start," said Jebediah sternly, clearly annoyed at the officer's pessimism.

"I like your attitude, young man," said Paulson. "Don't let our failures deter you. You know you're going to hunt them down where everyone else has failed, and I salute you."

"Then why do you make it sound so sarcastic?" asked Jebediah.

"Because they've even robbed me," answered Paulson seriously. "I was just like you when I went to work for the department. It took them less than a year to rob me of something I once valued—my faith in my ability to put an end to the pain they bring. I hope they don't take the same thing away from you."

Not this week, I thought. *Maybe in a month or a year, but not this week. After all, he's only seen one victim.*

He saw more in the next few weeks.

There was the Ragobad, a race that lived in symbiosis with a little animal called a *lasphine.* The Ragobad had spent years building a complex system of burrows beneath the inhospitable exterior of Helena II. Due to earthquakes caused by sudden tectonic activity, the system had collapsed, and, right on schedule, the Star Gypsies showed up to help rebuild it. They did a hell of a job on it, too. All it cost the 823 Ragobadim who agreed was cash—and their *lasphine* symbiotes.

There was Homer Padoupolas, who lived alone on the mining world of Cassandra with his pet *braque,* a doglike creature from Alpha Bednares V. He'd had it for close to twenty years and lavished all his affection on it. (You can see this one coming, can't you?) The Star Gypsies repaired his broken mining machines and helped him make his monthly quota. What they took for their efforts was 30 percent of his profits—and his *braque.*

There was Cold Steel, the outstanding cloned racehorse from the 27th century A.D. His owner had promised that 90 percent of the colt's winnings would be donated to his church if God would just cure his daughter of her terminal disease—and God, or something very like Him, stepped in and did just that. Cold Steel won race after race, and became the most famous and popular horse in the galaxy, known far and wide as The Horse That Raced for God. Then one day he went lame, and no veterinarian could cure him . . . but the Star Gypsies knew what to do and made him sound again for a cash fee—and for the ugly little goat that lived in the stall with him and kept him company. Cold Steel never took another lame step, never won another race, and the owner's church soon found out that 90 percent of nothing is nothing.

On and on it went, the litany of misery and regret. We interviewed two men who had been sure they could outsmart the Star Gypsies, who haggled and narrowed down the definition of the keepsakes they would have to relinquish—and all they proved was that sometimes even you yourself don't know what your most valued possession is. It might be nothing more than an old coffee mug or a recording of a song or a lace handkerchief or a toy left over from your childhood, something as trivial as that—until it is taken from you and you realize that you'd give everything you have to get it back.

And you also know deep in your soul that once having been visited by the Star Gypsies, you will never see them again.

Things were quiet for the next month. That didn't mean the Star Gypsies weren't as active as usual, just that no one was willing to report them. Some of their victims were ashamed to tell us the value they put on whatever they'd lost. Some just gave up and didn't want to go on living. Most of them knew that they could report what happened and we'd go through all the motions, but we'd never retrieve what had been taken.

Jebediah's first experience with the Star Gypsies had motivated him. He was still at his desk every night when I went home, and he was there every morning when I showed up for work. He watched every interview we had with every victim who'd been willing to talk to us. He crossed-checked every report on planets that were facing natural disasters, or economic crises, or anything else that might attract the Star Gypsies.

When I sat down at my desk at the beginning of his sixth week on the job, he walked over to me, and I could see he was disturbed.

"What's up?" I asked.

"They're driving me crazy," he said.

"They have that propensity," I agreed.

He looked at me with pained, puzzled eyes. "Why do they do what they do, Gabe? One sick mind I could understand, but why does an entire race go out of its way to ruin so many lives? What makes them that way?"

"You answer that and we're halfway to catching them," I replied.

"We're missing something," he said. "I can't believe what they do brings them pleasure."

"Why not?" I shot back. "The casebooks are full of psychopaths who got pleasure by inflicting pain."

He shook his head. "You're talking about individuals," he said. "No *race* can take pleasure from it."

"This race does."

"They don't," he said with total conviction.

I found myself wishing that I was as sure of anything in my life as he was of that. "Why not?" I said. "All the evidence says they do."

"Because it's against all logic for rational beings to take pleasure from bringing unhappiness to others."

"I don't know about that," I said. "We felt pretty good about winning the war against the Sett. The Canphorites were overjoyed when they conquered the Vostinians. Back when we were still Earthbound, I'm sure the Sioux felt happy about slaughtering General Custer."

"Those were military actions, taken to redress a real or imagined wrong," said Jebediah. "We haven't wronged the Star Gypsies. As far as I can tell, we didn't even know they existed a century ago."

"That doesn't mean we haven't harmed them or their planet without even knowing that we did it," I said. "We could have destroyed one of their military convoys by mistake, or crashed into their holiest shrine, or accidentally spread a virus against which they have no defense all over their home world."

"No," he said adamantly.

"Why not?"

"Because they're a sentient race, and this is not the reaction of a sentient race to a real or imagined abuse."

"So you say," I replied dubiously.

"All right, there's a better reason," he continued. "Even if we've unknowingly committed every act you mentioned, then their grievance is against the race of Man. But they've brought misery to over a dozen races, maybe more that we don't yet know about—and some of them aren't members of the Republic and have no social or economic ties to us."

I had to admit I hadn't considered that. Maybe there was something to the concept of fresh eyes after all.

"All right, I concede the point," I said. "But that doesn't put us any closer to understanding why they behave as they do. It just eliminates one possible explanation for it."

"If we can eliminate enough we'll narrow it down," said Jebediah. "And once we know why they're the way they are, we'll be able to stop them." He paused again. "We can't allow them to keep bringing such pain to their victims."

"I take it that means you've decided to stay in the department?"

He nodded an affirmative. "When I was a young man," he began, as if he was anything else, "I dreamed of battling the pirates who plague the spaceways, or rescuing beautiful young women from a variety of fates, each worse than death. They were glorious, romantic dreams . . ." The words trailed off and he looked at some fixed point in time and space that only he could see. "But you know something? People survive piracy, and they even survive fates worse than death—but nobody survives the loss of their most treasured memory. Of course I'm staying. This is where I belong." He paused, then continued after a moment. "This weekend I watched holos of more than two hundred victims describing their lives after their dealings with the Star Gypsies. I'll live with the memories of those interviews—and I'll never be rid of *my* memories until I can make sure no one else will be robbed of theirs."

"Well, it sounds like you've found your life's work."

"I hope not."

"I don't understand," I said, puzzled. "You just said—"

"If I'm here for a lifetime, that means we won't have solved the problem. I plan to stay with the department *until* I stop them."

"I felt that way once myself," I said.

"You still must," he noted. "You're still here."

"Where would I go and what would I do?" I replied. "I don't know that I'll ever catch one of them, and I'm pretty much convinced that I'll never find a way to stop them, but I can't just turn my back on the problem, not after seeing the damage they do. It's a war, but the collateral damage isn't shattered buildings and burnt-out vehicles; it's shattered memories and burnt-out dreams, and I think in the long run that kind of devastation is worse."

He stared at me for a long moment. "That's very interesting," he said. "I've been working with you for almost two months now. At first I thought you were just a cynical man marking time until he could retire on his pension."

"And now?"

"Now I think you're a cynical man who still wants to stop the Star Gypsies."

"Of course I do. But you have to insulate yourself emotionally, or you become Ben Paulson and eventually you run off to be the entire police force on an outpost world that's never had a crime."

"How do you drown out the misery?" he asked.

"We each have our own way. How does a doctor who deals with incurable diseases go home and lead a normal life away from his hospital? You make whatever adjustments you have to make. As far as I'm concerned, Ben Paulson, and half a hundred other Ben Paulsons, are victims the same as if they'd been visited by the Star Gypsies, because they never learned to protect their emotions." I looked at him. "How about you? Are you going to be able to protect yourself?"

"Yes," he said. "I'm going to catch them."

I couldn't remember for sure, but I'd almost have bet I'd said those very words twenty-seven years ago, before I grew up and lost something important along the way.

Our first break came three days later, and from the unlikeliest source.

Our computers were programmed to pick up and report any activity that might imply the presence of the Star Gypsies. Sooner or later they did—but it was always after the fact, after the deals had been made and the seemingly innocent payments had been extracted and the

Star Gypsies had gone back to wherever it was they came from.

But this time it wasn't one of the computers at all. It was a sub-space radio message from a small news organization on the colony world of Branson III.

I was sitting at my desk, going over reports from a dozen worlds at the edge of the cluster, when Jaimie Kwamo walked up to me, an odd expression on her face.

"Yeah, what is it?" I said.

"There's something I think you ought to hear," she said.

"Okay. What is it?"

"It's on Channel 173."

"Is it private?" I asked.

"Hardly."

"Then pipe it in so everyone can hear it," I told her.

She hit the controls, and suddenly the shaky, static-filled image of a middle-aged woman's face appeared to float a couple of feet above every desk in the office. Little flashes of light kept appearing and disappearing, but all it meant was that the signal was weak. It wasn't an especially memorable face; the skin was smooth, the eyes dark, the hair black and pulled back into the cone that was so popular on the more sophisticated worlds toward the Core.

"Hello," said the image, and the voice was also fuzzy and static-filled. "I hope I'm contacting the right place. My name is Omira Maspoli, and I work for the Branson Beacon, a local newsdisk." The image began breaking up, and we waited until it stabilized. "Among my other duties here, I am in charge of the fraud investigation division. Prior to transferring to the Branson system, I worked on Matusadona II." That brought quite a reaction in the office. Matusadona was almost legendary in our department.

"I was there when the tidal wave hit and the Star Gypsies came. The devastation from both was staggering. The planet recovered only from the tidal wave." She paused for effect, then spoke again. "That is why I have contacted you. This morning I received the following electronic query."

She leaned over and read from a small screen.

"Dear Omira Maspoli:

"My daughter is graduating from the University of Durastanti IV in nineteen Standard days. I own one ship, and it is not functioning. I'm no mechanic, and I have no idea what's wrong with it. It cost all my savings to pay for my daughter's tuition, and I simply cannot afford to buy a new ship or even repair the one I own. I can't even pay for passage on a spaceliner. I am a widow, and my daughter is all that I've got. I was afraid that I had no option but to remain at home and miss the most important day of her life, but yesterday a group of men suddenly showed up at my house. They told me they'd heard my ship had mechanical problems, and that they were itinerant mechanics, traveling from world to world looking for work. I explained that I have very little money to spend, and that the best estimate I'd gotten from the spaceship company was 32,000 credits. They offered to repair it for 3,000 Maria Theresa dollars, which as you know comes to less than 10,000 credits. It sounds almost too good to be true, but I'm really desperate. I told them I'd give them my answer later today. My question is: what legal recourse have I if they do a poor job and have moved on to the next world before I'm ready to leave for the Durastanti system?"

Omira Maspoli's image looked up from what she had been reading.

"If these *are* the Star Gypsies, I've seen what they can do, and I urge you to take prompt action. If not, I apologize for taking up your time."

The image vanished.

"Contact her immediately and find out how I can get in touch with the woman who wrote that message!" I said.

"I've got it already," said Jebediah. "She fed it into our computer at the time of transmission."

Suddenly the name and code appeared simultaneously on all our screens.

"Harriet Meeker," announced Jaimie. She uttered a terse string of commands to the computer. "Okay, Gabe—you're clear to send."

"This message is for Harriet Meeker," I said, looking into the transmission lens and pronouncing each word carefully since I figured that whatever was causing the static would be working both ways. "My name is Gabriel Bola, and your missive to Omira Maspoli was forwarded to my department. I am attaching my ID, which you can check with any government department on Branson.

"The men offering to repair your spaceship may be exactly what they appear to be, or they may be something very different and far more sinister. I need to ask you one question, and if the answer is yes, make no bargains, sign no contracts, and contact me immediately. The question is simply this: have they asked for any form of payment, no matter how seemingly trivial, above and beyond the 3,000 Maria Theresa dollars you mentioned to Omira Maspoli?"

"That's it?" asked Jaimie.

"That's it."

"Okay, it's sent. I'll resend it in a minute and route it through our station on Pinto. There should be less chance of it breaking up that way."

"Fine," I said. "Keep a channel open around the clock, and tell anyone we've got within fifty light-years of Branson III to monitor that channel, in case the static prevents her answer from getting through here." I got to my feet and turned to Jebediah. "You've got twenty minutes to round up your gear and meet me at the spaceport."

"You're going out there before you get your answer?" asked Jaimie.

"If we wait for an answer, what do you think we'll find when we get there?" I said.

"You're right, of course," she said with a grimace. "If she responds, what do I tell her?"

"Tell her to stall them, to say that she's got some money coming in. But she's a moral woman and she won't enter into an agreement with them until she knows she can keep her end of the bargain."

"And if they cut their price?"

"They won't," I said, walking to the door.

"What makes you so sure?" asked Jebediah as he joined me.

"They've never had to," I said. "Why do you suppose so many people who should know better deal with them? Because their offer is almost irresistible."

"Some people say no," he noted.

"Not many," I replied. "And like I say, the Star Gypsies don't bargain. Say no and they're on their way—and then you get to spend the rest of your life wishing you hadn't sent them away."

The irony of it wasn't lost on him. "So they deal in regrets even when you say no."

"That's right."

"Do you think your message will reach her in time?" asked Jebediah as we left the building and hopped the expresswalk.

"Probably."

"Will she listen?"

"Oh, she'll listen," I said. "But like she says, it's the biggest day in her daughter's life, and 3,000 Maria Theresa dollars is such a reasonable price."

"So you don't think she'll send them packing?" he persisted.

"Would you?" I asked.

⸺

Branson III was a lovely little world with a temperate climate, a trio of freshwater oceans dotted with hundreds of islands, even a couple of impressive-looking snow-capped mountain ranges. There were no sentient native races, but evolution had taken a number of adventurous twists, and the planet had originally been opened up and operated as a safari world. Then the game had been shot out (it doesn't take as long as you think), protected parks were created for the multitudes of endangered species, and diamond pipes were discovered. The mining companies moved in, and they were followed by the support networks. The mines were played out in less than a century, but a number of towns still remained, going about their daily business, making Branson III one of the thousands of unexceptional worlds in the Republic that paid most of their taxes, obeyed most of their laws, and made as few political waves as possible. It seemed as nice a place to live as any other—until the Star Gypsies put it on their itinerary.

"How could the Star Gypsies know?" asked Jebediah as we stood in line at Passport Control. "This isn't a world with a widespread disaster, natural or otherwise, where your computer could pull up the information about a tidal wave or an earthquake or a typhoon. This is just one woman who can't afford to repair her ship."

"They always know," I said.

"They couldn't even have learned by intercepting Omira Maspoli's message," he continued. "She didn't send it until *after* they'd visited Harriet Meeker."

"If it *is* the Star Gypsies."

"Do you doubt it?"

"No," I said. "Not really."

"Neither do I."

I stepped up to the passport kiosk.

"Welcome to Branson III," intoned the robotic officer. "How long will you be on the planet?"

"Probably less than a day," I answered.

"I have scanned your passport, and it is free of all restrictions. I have approved you for entry and given you a three-day visa. If you wish to stay longer, please report to the Office of Immigration and Tourism, which can extend your visa for six more days at no charge. Our local currency is Far London pounds; we also accept Maria Theresa dollars, New Punjab rupees, and Republic credits. The gravity is 97.28 percent Earth Standard, and the planetary day is 22.17 Standard hours. Have you any questions?"

"No."

"Enjoy your stay on Branson III," said the robot, and began asking the same questions of Jebediah, who was standing directly behind me.

When we had cleared Customs and were admitted to the lobby of the spaceport, a small, well-dressed man approached me.

"Hi, Gabe," he said.

"Hi, Wolf," I replied. "Jebediah, meet Wolfgang Spora, our man in this sector. Wolf, this is Jebediah Burke."

"Pleased to meet you, Jebediah," said Wolf.

"How many men have we got here?" I asked him.

"I have twenty-five posted around the spaceport," he replied. "We've got another dozen keeping the Meeker house under observation. By the time we got to the little port where she keeps her ship, the work had already been done on it, but I left five men there in case they come back for any tools or anything they might have left behind."

"Okay, that sounds pretty thorough. Meeker doesn't know she's being watched?"

He shook his head. "I don't want her peeking into the bushes or peering at the neighbor's roof if she starts getting nervous. If I can pick up signals like that, the Star Gypsies sure as hell can."

"How can we get to her house?" I asked.

"I'll take you," offered Wolf. "I've got a vehicle just beyond the exit."

"No," I said. "*They* might be watching the house, too. I want to take public transportation—and it'll just be Jebediah and me. She's only expecting two of us, and I don't want her to look surprised or curious when we show up, just in case."

He looked disappointed, but he was too much of a pro to question my orders. "After you walk out of the spaceport," he said, "just summon a public transport courtesy vehicle. It'll be programmed with the address of every Branson III resident. There aren't all that many of them, well under half a million." He paused. "Do you want me to stay here or join my men out by the house?"

"I'd rather you stayed here," I said. "The less movement we have around her place, the better. And if they get by me, they still have to find a way off the planet. How are we doing on the private ports?"

"There are five of them around the planet. I've got men at each of them, and I have some police ships in orbit in case they get past us on the ground."

"You seem to have everything under control," I said. "I can't think of anything else, at least not at the moment. I'll contact you on the gamma frequency if I need to speak to you."

"Good luck," he said. "I'm trying not to get excited, but I have a feeling this time we've got 'em!"

"Let's hope," I said.

Jebediah and I walked to the exit, hopped a sleek-looking airbus, and ordered it to take us to Harriet Meeker's place. In a few minutes we were gliding through a charming little village that looked like it could almost have existed back on old Earth itself. It was filled with stone cottages and picket fences and colorful gardens. Of course, the stone was a facade over the titanium structures, the fences were capable of vaporizing any unwanted intruders, and the gardens were tended by robots, but you didn't think of that on first viewing. It just looked small and peaceful and old-fashioned.

After another minute we came to a stop in front of one of the cottages, and the vehicle informed us that we had reached the Meeker residence. We got off, walked up to the front gate, identified ourselves to the Spy-Eye hidden inside the bolt, waited until the gate swung open, and walked up to the front door. It scanned our retinas and bone structures, instantly tied in to the spaceport computer and matched its findings to our passports, then informed the owner of our presence and waited for her to order it to let us in.

A rather frail-looking woman, clearly at the far end of middle age, stood in the main room and invited us in.

"Good morning," I said. "I'm Gabe Mola and this is my assistant, Jebediah Burke. Did you receive the message I sent you yesterday from Goldenrod?"

"Yes, I did, Mr. Mola," she said. "I found it quite unsettling. What is going on?"

"Hopefully nothing," I said. "Did I contact you in time?"

"If you mean, had I entered into an agreement with these itinerant mechanics, no, you did not contact me in time. If you mean have they completed the work and asked for payment, the answer is: not yet."

I could see the excitement on Jebediah's face. Six weeks on the job and he might actually get to see a Star Gypsy, something I hadn't managed in twenty-seven years.

"What was the exact payment they requested?" I asked.

"As I told Omira Maspoli, they asked for 3,000 Maria Theresa dollars, and I agreed to that amount."

"And what else?"

"How did you know even yesterday that there would be something else?" she asked.

"There always is."

"Are they criminals, then?" she asked. Suddenly a look of apprehension appeared on her face. "Does this mean they won't fix my ship and I won't be able to go to my daughter's graduation after all?"

"They'll fix your ship," I said. "They always deliver what they promise."

"*That's* a relief!" she exclaimed. "You had me scared for a moment there, Mr. Mola."

"You still haven't answered my question," I said. "What else did they ask for?"

"Oh, something small and trivial," she said. "Just some little keepsake."

"Did they identify it?"

"No," said Harriet Meeker. "They said they'd choose it later, when they finish their work on the ship and present their bill. But I don't understand why you've come all the way from Goldenrod. They even wrote into the contract that it can't have a market value of more than fifty credits."

"And they'll be coming here to the house for their payment?"

"That's what they said," she replied. "I'd be just as happy to pay them at the bank or the spaceport, but they'll want to choose their keepsake, and they can't do that if they don't come to the house."

"Do you mind if we wait here to meet them?" I asked.

"I knew it!" she said, and I thought she was about to burst into tears. "They've done something wrong and you're going to arrest them and I'll never get to Durastanti!"

"We're going to *prevent* them from doing something wrong," I replied, trying to sound reassuring.

"Who are they?" she demanded. "What have they done?"

"Have you ever heard of the Star Gypsies?" I asked.

"Just rumors and legends. Are you trying to say that they really exist?"

"They exist, all right," I replied. "You entered into a contract with them."

"Those nice men who are fixing my ship?" she said. "I don't believe it!"

"I'm sorry you feel that way," I said, "because that's who they are."

"Even if you're right, you yourself said they always do what they promise to do," she said stubbornly. "And they promised to repair my ship for 3,000 Maria Theresa dollars."

"And a keepsake," said Jeremiah.

"A trivial one."

He looked at me, as if to say: *How much do you want to tell her?*

It was a problem. I didn't want to keep any facts from her. After all, she was their target, and we were here to protect her. But she was so grateful that the Star Gypsies were going to make it possible for her to fly to Durastanti that I was afraid she might actually try to warn them off if she thought we meant them any harm. I considered all my options, and finally hit on a solution that I thought would satisfy everyone.

"I know you don't want us to wait for them here, and I think I know why," I said. "What if I promise that if they break their bargain or if your ship doesn't function for any reason, my department will see to it that you get to your daughter's graduation at no cost to yourself?"

"Do you mean it?" she asked suspiciously.

I repeated my pledge into my pocket computer, sealed it with my thumbprint, transmitted a copy of it to Omira Maspoli, another to headquarters on Goldenrod, and printed out a copy that I handed to Harriet Meeker.

She read it carefully, then looked up. "All right, Mr. Mola. You and Mr. Burke can stay. May I get you something to eat or drink?"

"Just some coffee or soft drinks," I said.

"I don't drink coffee myself," she said. "It will take me a few minutes to reprogram the robot chef."

"We're in no hurry," I assured her.

I looked out the window as she left the room. I couldn't see any sign of the Star Gypsies or of our own men.

"Her yard's a mess, and the house needs cleaning," said Jebediah softly when she reached the kitchen. "She doesn't have a robot, at least not a functioning one. She's going to cook and clean up after us herself."

"I know," I said. "But the alternative is going out to a restaurant— and I'm not going to be somewhere else when they arrive." I patted the pulse gun I carried under my armpit, a nervous habit I'd picked up over the years to assure myself that I really hadn't left it on the dresser or in the office.

"It's still there," said Jebediah, staring at me.

"What are you carrying?" I asked him.

"The usual—a burner and a screecher," he replied, referring to his laser and sonic pistols.

Harriet reentered the room a moment later, carrying two mugs of black coffee on a tray.

We each took a sip. It tasted like swampwater.

"This is very good," lied Jebediah. "Is it Antarean?"

"Bransonian—we grow it here ourselves," she said with a touch of pride. "And how do you like it, Mr. Mola?"

"Memorable," I said, hoping it wouldn't have me racing to the bathroom all night long.

"May I ask a question?" she said.

"Certainly."

"What have the Star Gypsies actually done? Who have they robbed?"

"Officially, no one."

She sighed deeply. "I'm so tired of you bureaucrats and your secrets."

It's not my *secrets they're after,* I thought. Aloud I said: "How many of them came here?"

"Three the first time they appeared. Then seven when they returned and I agreed to their terms."

"All Men?" asked Jebediah.

"No, there were two women."

"I meant the race of Man?"

"They appeared to be."

"Appeared?" I repeated.

"They just . . . well, there are all kinds of minor mutations now that we've spread throughout the galaxy and lived in different environments for generations."

"And how did these differ from you and me?" I asked.

"They didn't, not really," she said. "There are probably some tiny differences, but now that I think about it, there's nothing I can truly pinpoint."

"Did you notice anything unusual about their manner of speaking, perhaps? The timber of their voices, the way they pronounced words or strung them together?"

She thought for a moment, then shook her head. "No. I don't mean to mislead you, Mr. Mola. I've been under a lot of strain because of my situation, and perhaps I was imagining some minor differences that don't really exist."

"There are differences, all right," I said.

"What do you mean?" she asked.

"I mean that after all these years, we still don't know what they are."

"They're Men."

"No," said Jebediah. "If there's one thing we're pretty sure of, it's what they aren't."

"You must be mistaken," she insisted. "I know who I spoke to."

"There's no sense arguing," I said. "We'll see for ourselves when they arrive."

"They were *Men,*" she muttered. Then: "I think I'll go into the kitchen and supervise the robot." She headed off to begin preparing our dinner.

"I feel sorry for her," said Jebediah, "having to put on an act like this."

"She doesn't have to," I said. "She *chooses* to. And you'd feel a lot sorrier for her if we showed up after the Star Gypsies got what they wanted."

"I know," he agreed. "Still, I—"

Suddenly he tensed.

"What is it?" I asked.

"I just saw someone outside."

"One of them or one of us?"

"We'll know soon enough," he said, and I noticed he had loosened his tunic to make it easier to reach his weapons.

I called Harriet in from the kitchen and told her to order the door to open.

Two men and a woman entered. One of the men was tall, ash blond, slender, with piercing blue eyes. The other was burly and muscular, bald on the top, graying on the sides, with a prominent nose and a receding chin. The woman was in her early twenties, with short dark hair, narrow staring dark eyes, no jewelry or cosmetics that I could spot, maybe a few pounds overweight.

They didn't look at all surprised to see Jebediah and me standing there.

"The ship is ready," announced the taller man.

"We're friends of the family," I said, stepping forward. "I hope you don't mind if we inspect it before you're paid."

"You're no friend of anyone, Gabriel Mola," he replied. "But we stand behind our work. You are welcome to look at it."

"You know my name?"

"We know all about you," he said easily.

"Certainly more than you know about us," said the second man.

"Not for lack of trying," I said. "I've been waiting a long time to meet you."

"And now you have," said the woman. "I hope we haven't disappointed you."

"I'll let you know," I said. "After we've had a nice long talk back on Goldenrod."

"We're not going to Goldenrod," said the tall man.

"I wouldn't bet my last credit on that," I said, pulling out my pulsar and signaling Jebediah to produce his burner.

"Put those away," said the woman with no show of fear. "You know by now that we don't possess any weapons."

"Having it in my hand increases my comfort level," I said. "I want you to know that escape is out of the question. The house is surrounded, and I've got men at every public and private spaceport on the planet."

"We have no intention of leaving until we've been paid," said the tall man. He turned to Harriet Meeker. "Your ship has been repaired. Are you prepared to fulfill your obligation?"

"If it's been repaired, you'll be paid," I said. "You might use it as a retainer for a good lawyer. You're going to need one."

"I wasn't speaking to you, Gabriel Mola. We made a bargain, and we kept our end of it. Are you advising Harriet Meeker to renege on her commitment?"

"I told you: if the ship works, she'll deposit the money in an escrow fund that will be made available to you if and when we release you."

"That is only part of her obligation," said the tall man. "There is also the matter of a keepsake."

"I don't believe you've been listening to me at all," I said. "Let's get down to business. Will you surrender yourselves to our custody?"

"Of course not," said the tall man. "What laws have we broken?"

"We'll discuss it on Goldenrod," I said.

"I told you: we're not going to Goldenrod," he said. "At least, not as your prisoners. The day may come when we decide to pay it a visit, but that day is still far off."

I couldn't figure it out. I had all the aces. Jebediah and I had our weapons trained on them. They had to know I wasn't lying about the house being surrounded, surely they were aware that my men were all over the spaceports, and still they showed no sign of apprehension. It was as though they simply didn't understand the helplessness of their situation.

"It is *you* who doesn't understand the situation," said the tall man, echoing my unspoken words.

"So you're telepaths," I said, only half-surprised. "Do you just receive, or do you send too?"

"One or the other," said the woman with a smile.

"If you can read my mind, you know that you haven't got a chance of escaping, so don't make this any more difficult than it has to be."

The tall man turned to Harriet once more. "I ask you one last time, Harriet Meeker: will you honor your bargain with us?"

She looked at me questioningly. "What should I do, Mr. Mola?" she said.

"I've already told you," I said to him. "If the ship works, you'll get your money."

"I think you know that we don't care about the money," said the tall man.

"And I think you know I don't give a damn what you care about," I said. I waved the pulsar at them. "Let's get going."

Jeremiah stepped over and positioned himself front of Harriet, in case things started getting out of hand.

"That is your final word on the subject?"

"That's right."

"You are a foolish man, Gabriel Mola," he said. "I expected better of you."

"We all have to learn to live with disappointment," I said sardonically.

"No," he said firmly. "Only some of us do."

And suddenly the tall man was no longer there, and I was looking at an exact duplicate of myself. I blinked furiously, but nothing changed. Then I was aware that there were two Jebediahs and two Harriet Meekers in the room.

I didn't know if they were shape-changers, or if they were simply exercising some kind of mind control, but it didn't matter. They were even more dangerous than I'd thought.

"Gabe?" said one of the Jeremiahs uncertainly. "What do I do?"

"Help me, Gabe!" said the other in the identical voice. "There are two of you!"

"If you can't figure it out, shoot both of us!" I said. "Now that we know what they can do, we can't allow them to get away!"

"And aim straight!" said my double in my voice.

The Jebediah on my left tried to raise his burner. I could see his muscles tightening, I could see the sweat pouring down his face, but his hand didn't rise as much as a centimeter. I figured I was going to have to shoot both Jebediahs—and suddenly I found that I couldn't move either.

And now my mirror image stood in front of me and smiled again.

"Do you still think we won't walk right out of here?" he said. He took my pocket computer from my tunic, logged onto the gamma frequency, and spoke into it. "Hi, Wolf," he said, and even his inflections were my own. "False alarm. They really *are* just a bunch of itinerant mechanics. Call it off; we'll join you at the spaceport in an hour or so."

He broke the connection, and put the computer into his own pocket, while I wondered how he planned to dispose of our bodies.

"Nobody's killing anyone today, Gabriel Mola," he said in response to my thought. "You may be my prey, but you're not my enemy."

"The hell I'm not!" I grated.

"You know our history," he said. "Has one of us ever physically harmed one of you?"

"You have other ways."

He smiled again, almost regretfully, I thought. "Now there you have me," he admitted.

He walked over to Harriet, who also was obviously unable to move. "And now, Harriet Meeker, it is time to complete our agreement. I know you meant us no harm, so I will not hold Gabriel Mola and Jebediah Burke's presence against you—but I will insist that you keep your end of the bargain. Gabriel Mola has promised us our money, and we will assume that he is a man of honor and will keep his word. We will contact him later with instructions as to its disposition." He paused. "There remains only the valueless keepsake."

He nodded to the other "Harriet," who began walking around the room, touching books, shelves, vases, paintings, a clock, a holo machine. Suddenly she seemed drawn to the bedroom, and she disappeared into it, emerging a moment later with a battered old hairbrush.

"No!" cried Harriet. "Not that! Take anything else you want!"

The false Harriet handed the brush to my double, who held it up and examined it. "Even new, I doubt that this would sell for as much as ten credits. Yes, this will complete your obligation to us, Harriet Meeker."

"Please!" she said, tears streaming down her face.

"And now I think it's time to take our leave of you," he continued, handing the brush to the female. He placed a hand on my shoulder and stared into my eyes. "You and I shall never see each other again, Gabriel Mola, but I am glad we have finally had this opportunity to meet." He turned to Jebediah. "You carry a heavy burden, Jebediah Burke. Protect it well."

At first I thought it was just an insult meant for me, that I was his burden. Then I saw the surprise on Jebediah's face and realized that *he* knew what they were talking about even if I didn't.

And then, as quickly as they had come, they were gone.

The three of us stood motionless for another half hour. I asked Harriet about the hairbrush, but every time I mentioned it she began crying, and finally I gave up.

Then we were able to move again, and I knew the Star Gypsies were off the planet.

We were debriefed for three full days when we got back to Goldenrod, but it didn't help much. Knowing that they could appear to be anyone didn't make spotting them any easier, and knowing they could read your thoughts didn't help you to protect those thoughts. The only change came when the government doubled the department's budget and added seventy-five Men and aliens to the staff.

Then came a rigorous series of physical and mental tests to make sure the Star Gypsies hadn't infiltrated the department. Somehow I knew we wouldn't turn up any of them, and in the end we didn't.

"Why would they come here anyway?" said Jebediah. "We never act, we only react. They don't have any need to misdirect us."

"It's just a matter of touching all the bases," I said. "Probably nothing we do will make a difference, but we can't take the chance."

"I know," he said. "We should have shot one of them when we had the opportunity. At least we could have turned him over to our scientists and maybe learned how to spot them."

"The Republic frowns on cold-blooded murder," I said.

"The Republic's never been up against anyone or anything with these abilities," replied Jebediah.

"You're not thinking it through," I pointed out. "How are you going to kill a creature that can read your thoughts and knows what you're going to do as soon as you yourself know?"

"If I decide when he's twenty feet away, he's not going to be able to stop me."

"Unless walls can prevent him from reading thoughts, he'll know before he opens the door, in which case he either won't open it or he'll be prepared. Besides, any way you cut it, that's murder."

He sighed deeply. "I suppose you're right. I just hate to see what they do to their victims. The fact that they're willing victims doesn't matter; they don't know what they're going to have to give up."

"Anyway," I said, "the only way we're ever going to stop them is to figure out *why* they do what they do. Even if the department sanctioned a couple of shootings, what would we get from it? Two corpses, and maybe a way to spot them. It wouldn't stop them from visiting world after world and looking for work."

"As far as I can tell, they've never made a deal for straight cash," said Jebediah. "It's got to be the trinkets."

"Of course it is. But *why*? That's the question I've been asking myself ever since I left the Navy and came to work here."

"You were in the Navy before you put in twenty-seven years here? You don't look that old."

"I wasn't there long. Just under two years. Got my leg blown off in the Sett War. Ever since, I've been walking around on one the government gave me."

"I never noticed."

"No reason why you should have. It's not the handicap it once was. Hell, Marcus Quintoby was the best-paid Murderball player on the planet last year, and he's got two prosthetic arms."

We spoke a little longer, and then we got word that a team of Star Gypsies had struck again, if "struck" is the right word, out in the Corinda system. It was too late to do anything about it, but we dutifully went to the ship and set off for Corinda.

The Belage were a race of sentient marsupials, tripedal and covered from head to toe with bright orange down, that lived on Corinda IV. The world had been growing warmer and more arid for eons, and all of their water came from deep wells. The well supplying a local infirmary had collapsed. If it wasn't fixed within a solar day the patients were going to suffer; if it wasn't fixed in three days at the outside most of them were going to die.

The Star Gypsies showed up, made their usual seemingly generous offer, and had the well open and the walls reinforced in just under a day. But they had signed their contract with the entire staff of the infirmary, and by the time we got there it was difficult to tell who was suffering more, the patients or the doctors.

We asked the usual questions, got the usual answers, made the usual fruitless search for clues as to where the Star Gypsies might be going next, and finally we left, glad to get away from the misery.

We'd just gotten clear of Corinda IV's stratosphere and were about to switch to light speeds when a subspace message came over the radio. Three human miners were stranded in the asteroid belt between the sixth and seventh planets of the Churchill system. Their ship had broken down and they'd sent out an SOS. There was a rescue ship on the way, but it would take a Standard day to get there, and we could reach them in six hours. We would help them if we could, of course—

but more to the point, this seemed a perfect opening for the Star Gypsies. Maybe, with a little luck, we could be waiting for them.

Headquarters fed the coordinates into the navigational computer, we reached multiples of light speed, and then it was just a matter of waiting until we arrived. There was no sense entering a Deepsleep pod, not for a six-hour journey. We checked our weaponry, ate a light lunch, and waited for the trip to end.

About twenty minutes before we reached our destination we got another message. The miners had finally managed to get their ship running again, and it was limping toward port on the colony world of Greenwillow, which was two systems away.

"What do you think?" I asked Jebediah. "Do you want to try it anyway?"

"If they didn't hear the message, they won't know the ship isn't there. We've got the coordinates. If we can touch down on the asteroid before they show up, there's no reason why they shouldn't think we're the miners."

"Until they land," I said. "It's that damned telepathy." I considered our options, and realized that we really didn't have any. We were just about there, and if I didn't plan to confront them until they were unable to read my thoughts, I was never going to see them again. "Yeah, let's go for it."

We braked to light speeds in eighteen minutes and began weaving our way through the asteroid belt. I took over manual control and finally got Churchill Asteroid 1783-B—our destination—in my viewscreen when it happened. A tiny piece of solar debris—it couldn't have been the size of a tin can—ripped through the ship's hull and power pack. Had we been standing still it would have bounced off, but it had picked up speed in its orbit and we were still going about 75 percent of light speed, and it just tore right through nuclear pile and the power thrusters.

"Shit!" I muttered as the ship started spinning out of control.

"What happened?" asked Jebediah, clutching the arms of his chair.

"Some piece of space garbage," I said. "A rock, an iceball, something."

"How much trouble are we in?"

"If I can maneuver to where I can land on one of the asteroids, we'll be all right. If we keep spinning through the belt, sooner or later we're going to crash into something a lot bigger than what hit us."

It took me about two minutes to slowly bring the ship out of its spin. 1783-B was behind us, but I saw another asteroid about 90,000 miles up ahead, and I figured if I could slow us down enough that was our best chance. The braking system was sluggish, and the ship wanted to spin again, but somehow I managed to get it under control.

"Brace yourself!" I said. "We're going to make it, but I can't promise a soft landing."

Soon the asteroid filled the entire viewscreen. I tried to set us down tail-first, but the controls weren't responding, and finally I settled for sliding in belly-first. It was damned lucky there were no baby mountains on that piece of rock, because we slid close to three miles before we finally came to a stop.

"Are you okay?" I asked.

"I can't vouch for my heart rate or blood pressure," said Jebediah, "but nothing's broken."

"Settle for it. Forty-five seconds ago I'd have given odds against our surviving it."

He smiled. "I'm glad you didn't tell me that earlier."

I checked the instrument panel. "We've still got problems," I said.

"Oh?"

"The radio's gone, and I have a feeling the ship's skin has been compromised. We're losing oxygen. We'd better climb into our spacesuits."

"What kind of oxygen supply do they carry?" he asked.

"About half a day."

"And how long before the ship's out of air?"

"At the rate we're losing it, maybe four hours."

I could tell what he was thinking. I could do the math myself. Four hours and half a day. Sixteen Standard hours. It was going to take the rescue ship twenty-four Standard hours start to finish, and even if it hadn't turned back—and there was no reason for it to still be on its way—it would arrive two hours after we'd run through all our air.

"We won't get into the suits until we have to," I said. "That'll buy us a little more time to see if we can get the radio working."

It was a fantasy. Even if we did get the radio functioning, there simply weren't any Republic worlds close enough to reach us in time. Oh, our signal might be picked up by a ship in transit—in fact, that was our only hope—but the odds weren't good, and they got longer every minute that the radio wasn't working.

After an hour I knew we'd never be able to fix it. Maybe a better mechanic could, but fixing broken subspace radios just wasn't one of my specialties, and Jebediah knew even less about them than I did.

"Ah, well," I said, finally sitting down. "It hasn't been that bad a life, I suppose. I'm just sorry it has to end before I finish my work."

"Have you got any kids, Gabe?" asked Jebediah.

"A son," I said. "I haven't seen him in, oh, ten or eleven years. My wife left me—I guess I didn't exactly keep the job's frustrations to myself—and he went with her." I paused. "He was a nice enough kid. I left him almost everything in my will."

"Almost?"

I pulled a small packet out of my breast pocket. "Everything but this. This I don't share with anyone."

"What is it?"

I opened it and held it up for him to see. "The Medal of Courage, from the Sett War."

"Was that when you lost your leg?" he asked.

"Yeah. I saved seven members of my squad and lost a leg. I think it was a good trade. So did the Navy."

"I'm impressed," said Jebediah. "I've never seen one of these before."

"They don't give a lot of them out."

"You should be very proud."

"It was a long time ago," I said. "Doesn't seem to make much difference at this particular minute." I paused and considered my life. On the whole, it came out a plus. Not a real big one, but a plus. "Still, I don't have any regrets—except for never catching one of the Star Gypsies. How about you?"

"There's a lot of things I planned to do," he said. "Somebody else will have to do them, I guess."

"That's the future," I said. "Any regrets about the past?"

"Just one."

"And that is?"

"A regret."

Well, if he didn't want to talk about it, I wasn't going to make him. I figured we had maybe fifteen hours to get our thoughts in order and try to go out with a little dignity.

He kept fiddling with the instruments. Some were working, some weren't. The important one—the radio—was stone-cold dead. I thought it was getting warmer. It could have been my imagination, or it could have been the oxygen seeping out. I decided not to get into the suit until I had to, or maybe not even get into it at all. When you've lived fifty-two years, what's another twelve hours—especially twelve hours of slow suffocation.

"I've never made a will," said Jebediah suddenly. "I just didn't figure I'd need one this soon. I suppose I ought to write one down so whoever finds us can deliver it to the authorities. Not that I own that much."

"It could be centuries before they find us," I said. "The whole system's uninhabited, and no one knows where we are." A thought occurred to me, and I chuckled.

"What so funny?"

"If you've got any money in the market or the bank, it could be worth millions by the time we're discovered. Too bad you won't have any descendants to collect it."

"It does make a will seem kind of silly, doesn't it?" he agreed.

"Leave it to your favorite church or political party," I said. "Someone will find a use for it."

"I suppose so." He turned to reach for the microphone to dictate his will to the computer. He sat perfectly still for a moment, staring at the small screen in front of his chair, then turned to me with a curious expression on his face.

"What's the matter?" I asked, wondering what else *could* go wrong.

"You said the Churchill System's uninhabited, right?"

"Right."

"And you never got off a radio message?"

"You know I didn't."

"Well, there's a ship approaching," he said.

"Are any of the weapon systems working, I wonder?" I said. "We could fire a near-miss to attract its attention."

"We won't have to. It's not flying by; it's slowing down."

I activated the main viewscreen. He was right. There *was* a small silver ship approaching us.

"I can't see its insignia," I said.

"What difference does it make?"

"If they've spotted us, they can probably tell we're disabled," I said, pulling out my pulse gun. "I hope they're here to help, but just in case they've come to rob us, let's be ready for them. Maybe we can disable them and take over their ship."

He pulled out his burner and screecher and laid them on the console next to him.

"Did you ever see a ship like this?" he asked as it came still closer.

"No," I admitted. "They must be aliens. There are no ships like that in the Republic."

"It's awfully small," he noted. "It looks like a one-man job."

"At any rate, he'll never fit both of us into it, even if he's got Samaritan impulses," I said.

The ship was now hovering less than a mile above us, and it began lowering gracefully to the surface of the asteroid. For a moment it looked like it would land on top of us, but it missed us by inches.

Then we heard—well, *felt*—things being done to our hatch. It continued for a few minutes, and then I heard something I never expected to hear on an airless world: someone was knocking gently on the hatch door.

I ordered the hatch to open, but it was yet another piece of our equipment that wasn't functioning. I trained my pulse gun on it, then gestured for Jebediah to open it manually.

He did so, then stepped back as it swung inward.

A middle-aged woman with clear blue eyes, graying brown hair, and a muscular body entered. She was wearing some kind of all-purpose coverall, rather than a spacesuit, so I knew our ship was now connected to hers, or she'd never have been able to move between them.

She looked around briefly, then focused on me.

"I'm pleased to meet you too," she said wryly, and I realized I was pointing the pulse gun at her. I lowered it, but kept it in my hand.

"Who are you?" I asked.

"Do you want the truth or a fairy tale?" she replied.

"You're one of *them*, aren't you?"

"And you're Gabriel Mola and he's Jebediah Burke," she said.

"How did you know we were here?"

"Is that really important?" she said.

"I'd like to know before we die."

"You will. But I thought you might prefer to live."

"Did you have something to do with our ship's problems?" asked Jebediah.

"Of course not," she replied. "I know you don't believe me, but we really aren't vicious sadists."

"Do your fellow Gypsies know you're here?"

"They do now."

"And you're here to rescue us?"

"Well, that's what we have to discuss."

I uttered a harsh laugh. "How many millions of credits is this going to cost?"

"You're really not worth very much as a human being, Gabriel Mola," she said. "You hunt us for no reason, you persecute us even though we have never broken any of your laws, you warn people not to enter into honest and open negotiations with us. No, you are simply not a valuable member of your race. I think I will charge you one Republic credit to save your life."

"What's the catch?" I said.

"There's no catch. One credit, and a keepsake to remember you by." She smiled at me. "Payable upon demand after the job is completed."

"I saw your ship on my screen," I said. "You can't possibly fit both of us on it with you."

"That was my offer to *you*," she said. Then she turned to Jebediah. "I will save you for free, Jebediah Burke. No money, no keepsake."

"Why?" he asked suspiciously. "You people never work for free."

"You have qualities."

"What qualities?"

"We will discuss them aboard my ship."

"There's something wrong here, something I'm missing," he said. "If you're going to save us one at a time, take Gabe first."

"I don't want him," she said firmly.

"I won't leave him here to die."

"If he'll agree to my terms, he will be rescued."

"And if not?"

"Then he will die alone and unmourned," she said. "His name will be forgotten, his body will never be found, and it will be as if he had never existed. Is that really the fate you wish for your friend?"

"Then save him first," repeated Jebediah adamantly.

"Don't be a fool, Jebediah," I said. "Go with her while you've got a chance."

"I'm not deserting you," he replied.

She turned back to me. "Do not argue with him. He will come of his own free will when the time arrives. Do you and I have a deal, Gabriel Mola?"

"One credit?"

"And a keepsake."

"What the hell," I said. "If I die here, none of my keepsakes will do me any good. Yeah, you've got a deal." I turned to Jebediah. "If I don't make it back, I want you to give every single thing in my apartment away, or burn it or atomize it, before you let her get her hands on any piece of it."

"I'm not going anywhere until you do," he insisted.

She walked over and extended her hand. "I prefer a written contract, but under the current conditions, I will settle for a handshake. Have we got a deal, Gabriel Mola?"

I shook her hand. It felt just like a real woman's. "We have a deal. Now, how are you going to pull this off?"

"I will take Jebediah Burke with me. This will give you almost two more hours of oxygen. Someone will be here to take you away before it has run out." She paused. "Try not to be too hostile to them, Gabriel Mola. After all, they *will* be saving your life."

"This doesn't mean I'll stop hunting you down," I said.

"I think perhaps a credit was too high a value to place upon you," she said. Then she shrugged. "Still, a bargain's a bargain."

She walked back to the hatch and turned to us again—and suddenly we weren't looking at a middle-aged woman anymore. Somehow she had become a lithe, slender girl, probably still in her teens, with dark sad eyes, long wavy honey-colored hair. She looked young and innocent, untouched by life.

"Come, Jebediah Burke," she said in a voice that perfectly matched her body. "It is time for us to leave."

"Oh, God!" murmured Jebediah. "How could you know? I put her out of my mind!"

"You have lied to yourself," said the Star Gypsy. "She is the most prominent image in your mind."

"Don't do this to me!" said Jebediah. "I lost you once. I've made my peace with the universe. Don't make me do it again!"

"You've lost me, and now you've found me," she said.

"Who is she?" I asked.

A tortured expression spread across his face. "Her name is Serafina. We were going to be married." He forced out the words. "And I killed her."

"It wasn't your fault," she said. "The police cited the other vehicle."

"I was so busy looking at you instead of the road I never saw it coming at us," he said. "*That* makes it my fault."

She reached a hand out toward him. "I forgive you."

He tried to look away from her, but he couldn't.

"Come with me, Jebediah," she purred. "Time is running out."

He stood as if hypnotized. "You're not Serafina," he managed to say.

"I will be Serafina for you for as long as you wish," she said, backing out through the hatch. "Come, Jebediah."

"Gabe, I . . ." The words caught in his throat.

"Go on," I said. "You can't do us any good by staying here."

He seemed to resist for another second. Then, with a sound that was halfway between a sigh and a sob, he followed her into her ship. A moment later the hatch closed, and I watched them take off on the viewscreen.

For the next two hours I wondered if she would keep her bargain. The interior of the ship grew uncomfortably warm, and breathing became an effort. I was about to climb into my spacesuit when a ship, larger than the last one, dropped down gently right next to mine. There were five Star Gypsies on it. They attached our ships, opened the hatch, and very politely told me to enter their vessel.

We took off a moment later. They offered me food and drink, which I refused, and pleasant conversation, which I found ridiculous under the circumstances. It took us a couple of hours at light speeds to reach Greenwillow, where they touched down at a small private space-port and let me off.

"Where's Jebediah Burke?" I asked, looking around at the empty landing field.

"He'll return to you when he's ready to," said the one who seemed to be their leader.

"How do I know you haven't killed him?"

He seemed amused. "You know more about us than anyone else. Have we ever killed anyone?"

"No," I admitted. "But why do you do the things you do?"

"Why do you eat?" he responded. "Why do you breathe?"

"What the hell kind of answer is that?" I demanded. "Are you try-ing to tell me that you're compelled to bring heartbreak and misery wherever you go?"

"We are not the enemy, Gabriel Mola."

"Then who is?"

A look of infinite sadness crossed his handsome countenance. Then the hatch closed, and a moment later the ship took off.

———

I got in touch with the department's closest office, which was on Hesporite III, reported what had happened, and waited while they sent a ship for me.

When I got back to Goldenrod, I half expected Jebediah to be wait-ing for me, but he hadn't shown up. I put out a Priority Search order for him and transmitted it not only throughout my department but to every police department in the entire Quinellus Cluster. Nobody had seen him, nobody knew anyone who had seen him, and after a year I finally had to face the fact that the Star Gypsies had committed their first murder. I hoped he had enjoyed his last few minutes or hours of life with his pseudo-Serafina.

The Star Gypsies seemed to get bolder. Oh, except for Jebediah their crimes were no different, but they seemed to anticipate every trap we laid for them. Prior to this they had confined themselves to small outpost and colony worlds, but now they began operating on the more populous worlds as well. The situation was always the same: there was work that had to be done, they appeared almost by magic, they did the job for an incredibly low price—and an incredibly high one.

I thought I had a couple of them trapped on Daedalus IV, but they simply waited until my reinforcements showed up, took the shapes of the first two men to arrive, and walked out in the confusion. I took a shot at one of them in a dingy Tradertown on the Inner Frontier world of Covenant, but he ducked into a deserted building and I never saw him again, though I examined every inch of it.

I directed half a hundred searches for their home world, but it was no use. No one knew what they really looked like when they weren't busy looking like someone else, so there was no way to tell whether we'd found it or not.

The job was really getting me down, so much so that I was thinking of taking early retirement. I just couldn't take much more of the misery I saw and the frustration I felt. If I'd thought drinking or drugging every night would have helped I'd have done it, but I knew the problem would still be there the next morning.

Then one evening, toward the end of summer, I stopped by my usual restaurant for dinner, and decided to walk home rather than ride one of the express slidewalks. It was dark when I finally got there, and I was surprised to see a light in my window. I could have sworn I'd turned the lights out when I left in the morning.

I approached the door carefully, pulse gun in hand. I uttered the combination, waited for the door to dilate, then stepped through—and found myself facing Jebediah Burke.

"I can't believe my eyes!" I said, putting my gun away. "I gave you up for dead almost three years ago!"

"How are you, Gabe?" he said easily.

"Shocked," I replied, making no effort to hide my delight at seeing him. "What are you doing here?"

He looked around the angular living room. "I've been admiring the paintings on your wall," he said. "And your library. It's been a long time since I've seen a real book."

"How the hell did you get in here? That's a state-of-the-art lock on the front door."

"I learned a lot of tricks from the Star Gypsies."

"How did you get away from them?" I asked.

"That's what we have to talk about," said Jebediah.

"You've learned something about them!" I said excitedly.

"I've learned everything about them."

I walked over to my favorite easy chair, ordered it to hover a few inches above the floor, and sat down. "Tell me about it."

"That's what I'm here to do."

"Start with your escape," I said.

"I didn't escape," said Jebediah.

"I don't understand."

"I know. But you will." He summoned a hard-backed chair, waited a few seconds for it to arrive from the corner, and sat down a few feet away from me. "Let me begin by saying that they weren't lying to you. They've never broken a law."

"No," I said. "They just break hearts and destroy dreams."

He nodded. "Yes, often they do. It can't be helped."

"Of course it can be helped," I shot back. "They don't have to rob their victims."

"They didn't rob anyone, Gabe. They never forced anyone to make a bargain, and they never took anything that hadn't been promised to them."

"Come off it!" I said. "You sound like one of them."

"That's not surprising," he said.

I reached for my pulse gun again. "Are you telling me you've joined them?" I demanded.

"Put it away, Gabe," he said with no show of fear. "Do you want answers or do you want blood?"

"I haven't decided."

"I'm all through talking until you choose one or the other."

He folded his arms across his chest and waited patiently. He knew that after thirty-one years of chasing the Star Gypsies, I wanted the answers. Finally I muttered a curse and put my gun back in its holster.

"That's better," said Jebediah.

"Talk," I said. "And it better be good."

"The first thing you have to understand about them, Gabe, is that they're aliens, with all that the word implies."

"I know."

"You *don't* know," he said emphatically. "You think you do, but they appear as humans, they speak flawless Terran, they do the same work that Men do, they accept payment in Republic currency, and you think of them as human. Cruel and unfeeling, to be sure, but human just the same."

"That's what they are," I said.

"That's what I thought, too. But I was wrong, just as you are."

"Go on. I'm listening."

"I know you are. I just hope you're *hearing*."

"Spare me your word games and get on with it," I said.

"All right. The Star Gypsies have been blessed with a number of abilities. You've seen many of them, and I'm sure you're aware of others. But they are also cursed with a defect, one that probably outweighs all the virtues." He paused. "They have no emotions. They can't *feel*."

"What are you talking about?"

"Just what I said. They are incapable of generating emotions. But they are not incapable of appropriating the emotions of others. They realized both this lack and this ability when they first came into contact with an alien race. They saw how empty their lives were, and they went about solving the problem."

"And the only emotion they seek is misery?" I said. "I'm not buying it."

"No, Gabe. They don't seek misery. They don't take all those keepsakes to make the owners miserable. They take them because through means that are all but incomprehensible even to me, they can assimilate the love, the happiness, the tenderness, the fond memories that are associated with them. That's what they're after: a sense of love and joy, even a borrowed one. They know the pain they bring. That's why they work so cheap; they're trying to make up for it. And they know most people will get over the loss sooner or later. But without these objects, they themselves would go through life eating, sleeping, working, but never feeling a thing."

He fell silent for a moment while I considered what he had said.

"If that's true, I sympathize with them," I said at last. "But I don't sympathize enough to let them bring emotional pain to members of every other race in the cluster."

"Is it really so terrible, given the alternative?"

"You've spoken to their victims," I said. "What do you think?"

"I think it's an unfair universe," said Jebediah, "and that in the long run the best you can do is choose the lesser of two evils."

"They've brainwashed you," I said.

"I went with them of my own free will," he said. "I can leave whenever I want—but I don't want to."

"You think you joined them willingly, but you were chosen, kid," I said. "That Star Gypsy appeared as your Serafina because they could read your mind. They not only found her there, but they saw that you were young and impressionable, and that you could tell them how I think, how the department functions."

"No!" he insisted. "I've joined them because I want to help them."

"I thought you wanted to help their victims."

"Everyone has to make choices," said Jebediah. "They're not always easy. I've made mine."

"Have you thought about what's going to happen to you when they no longer have any use for you?" I continued. "You've turned your back on your own kind. You're not one of us any more. You've joined the people that cause us pain and misery. We'll never take you back."

"I don't want to come back," he said. "All my life I've wanted a purpose. Now I've got one. They were getting clumsy. You found them on Branson III, and again on Daedalus IV and Covenant. They needed someone to direct them."

"So you didn't just *join* them," I said accusingly. "You're *leading* them."

"Somebody has to, or sooner or later the department is going to start killing them. You're a reasonable man, Gabe, and I truly don't think you'd stoop to murder, especially now that you know why they take what they do—but others would, and once it started there'd be no stopping it."

"So what do you and I do now?" I asked.

"Now we complete a final piece of business, and then we go our separate ways."

"All right," I said. "But after tonight I'll be coming after you."

"You'll never find me."

"That won't stop me from trying," I promised him. "Now what's this business you're talking about?"

"Four years ago a Star Gypsy saved your life. The agreement was that payment would be made sometime after the job was completed. I'm here to collect it."

I took a coin from my pocket and tossed it to him.

"This is a five-credit piece," he said.

"It's the smallest I've got. Tell them they can keep the change."

"No," he said, pulling four one-credit coins out of a pocket and handing them to me. "A deal is a deal. We never accept more than a contract calls for."

"All right," I said. "Now we're done. Get out."

"We're not quite done," he said. "You still owe us a keepsake."

I waved an arm around the apartment. "Choose one and leave."

"It's not on a shelf or in a drawer, Gabe," he said. "It's in your pocket."

"What are you talking about?"

"Your Medal of Courage. That's the keepsake we want."

"You go to hell!" I yelled.

"You made a deal, Gabe. Nobody forced you to."

"Take anything else and I'll give you a week's head start before I go hunting for you."

"We don't want anything else. You're an honorable man, Gabe. We expect you to keep your word."

"I didn't make that deal with you," I said. "I made it with a Star Gypsy who looked like a girl you once knew. When she shows up and demands payment, I'll turn it over to her."

For a moment I thought he was going to try to take the medal from me, but then he shrugged and walked to the door.

"Tell her I'll be waiting," I said.

He walked out of the apartment, and that was the last I saw of Jebediah Burke, who gave up his own hopes and dreams to help the Star Gypsies steal theirs.

He was a basically decent young man, probably better than most, filled with idealism. He wanted to make the galaxy a better place, and he found a race that managed to engage his services and his loyalty. But you don't help one man or one race by harming another, especially when you take those very private things they hold most dear.

I said we'd never take him back, but I didn't mean it. I hope someday he'll realize that and come back. Of course we'll forgive him his transgressions, because that's the way we're made. The Star Gypsies have one major advantage over us in this undeclared war: we're each capable of harming innocent parties, but only we regret it, and only we try to avoid it. It's strange, but I've never thought of compassion as a problem before.

I don't know if we can win with that kind of handicap, but I know it's why we've got to try.

INVESTMENTS

~~~~~~~~~~

by Walter Jon Williams

Walter Jon Williams, who is an author, traveler, kenpo fiend, and scuba maven, lives with his wife, Kathleen Hedges, on an old Spanish land grant in the high desert of New Mexico, and is the author of nineteen novels and two collections of shorter works. After an earlier career as a writer of historical novels, he switched to science fiction, and first attracted serious public attention with his 1986 novel Hardwired. *His later titles include* Days of Atonement, Aristoi, Metropolitan, *and the novella "Wall, Stone, Craft," which was nominated for the Hugo, Nebula, and World Fantasy Awards. In 2001 his novella "Daddy's World" won a Nebula. "Investments," a story that builds quietly to one of the most explosive climaxes—in the most literal sense of the term—that science fiction has seen in many an eon, is set in the far future of Williams's Dread Empire's Fall, a series that began with* The Praxis *and continued in* The Sundering.

THE CAR SPED south in the subtropical twilight. The Rio Hondo was on Lieutenant Severin's right, a silver presence that wound in and out of his perceptions. As long as he stayed on the highway the rental car, which knew Laredo better than he did, implemented its own navigation and steering, and Severin had nothing to do but relax, to gaze through the windows at the thick, vine-wrapped trunks of the cavella trees, the brilliant plumage of tropical birds, the occasional sight of a hovercraft on the river, its fans a deep bass rumble as it carried cargo south to the port at Punta Piedra. Overhead, stars began to glow on either side of the great tented glittering arc of Laredo's accelerator ring. The silver river turned scarlet in the light of the setting sun.

The vehicle issued a series of warning tones, and Severin took the controls as the car left the highway. Severin drove through an underpass, then up a long straight alley flanked by live oaks, their twisted black limbs sprawled like the legs of fantastic beasts. Overhead arced a series of formal gateways, all elaborate wrought-iron covered with scrollwork, spikes, and heraldic emblems, and each with a teardrop-shaped light that dangled from the center of the arch and cast pale light on the path. Beyond was a large house, two stories wrapped with verandahs, painted a kind of orange-rust color with white trim. It was covered with lights.

People strolled along the verandahs and on the expansive lawns. They were dressed formally, and Severin began to hope that his uniform was sufficiently well tailored so as not to mark him out. Practically all the other guests, Severin assumed, were Peers, the class that the conquering Shaa had imposed on humanity and other defeated species. It was a class into which Severin had not been born, but rather one to which he'd nearly been annexed.

At the start of the recent war Severin had been a warrant officer in the Exploration Service, normally the highest rank to which a commoner might aspire. As a result of service in the war he'd received a field promotion to lieutenant, and suddenly found himself amid a class that had been as remote from him as the stars that glimmered above Laredo's ring.

He parked in front of the house and stepped from the car as the door rolled up into the roof. Tobacco smoke mingled uneasily in the air with tropical perfume. A pair of servants, one Terran, one Torminel, trotted from the house to join him. The Torminel wore huge darkened glasses over her nocturnal-adapted eyes.

"You are Lieutenant Severin?" the Torminel asked, speaking carefully around her fangs.

"Yes."

"Welcome to Rio Hondo, my lord."

Severin wasn't a lord, but all officers were called that out of courtesy, most of them being Peers anyway. Severin had got used to it.

"Thank you," he said. He stepped away from the car, then hesitated. "My luggage," he said.

"Blist will take care of that, my lord. I'll look after your car. Please go up to the house, unless of course you'd prefer that I announce you."

Severin, who could imagine only a puzzled, awkward silence in the moments following a servant announcing his presence, smiled and said, "That won't be necessary. Thank you."

He adjusted his blue uniform tunic and walked across the brick apron to the stairs. Perhaps, he thought, he should have brought his orderly, but in his years among the enlisted ranks he'd got used to looking after his own gear, and he never really gave his servant enough work to justify his existence.

Instead of taking his orderly with him to Rio Hondo, he'd given the man leave. In the meantime Severin could brush his own uniforms and polish his own shoes, something he rarely left to a servant anyway.

Severin's heels clacked on the polished asteroid material that made up the floor of the verandah. A figure detached itself from a group and approached. Severin took a moment to recognize his host, because he had never actually met Senior Captain Lord Gareth Martinez face-to-face.

"Lieutenant Severin? Is that you?"

"Yes, lord captain."

Martinez smiled and reached out to clasp Severin's hand. "Very good to meet you at last!"

Martinez was tall, with broad shoulders, long arms, and big hands; he had wavy dark hair and thick dark brows. He wore the viridian-green uniform of the Fleet, and at his throat was the disk of the Golden Orb, the empire's highest decoration.

Severin and Martinez had been of use to each other during the war, and Severin suspected that it had been Martinez who had arranged his promotion to the officer class. He and Severin had kept in touch with one another over the years, but all their communication had been through electronic means.

Martinez was a native of Laredo, a son of Lord Martinez, Laredo's principal Peer, and when he'd returned to his home world, he'd learned that Severin was based on Laredo's ring and invited him to the family home for a few days.

"You've missed dinner, I'm afraid," Martinez said. "It went on most of the afternoon. Fortunately you also missed the speeches."

Martinez spoke with a heavy Laredo accent, a mark of his provincial origins that Severin suspected did him little good in the drawing rooms of Zanshaa High City.

"I'm sorry to have missed your speech anyway, my lord," Severin said in his resolutely middle-class voice.

Martinez gave a heavy sigh. "You'll get a chance to hear it again. I give the same one over and over." He tilted his chin high and struck a pose. "'The empire, under the guidance of the Praxis, contains a social order of unlimited potential.'" The pose evaporated. He looked at Severin. "How long are you on the planet?"

"Nearly a month, I think. *Surveyor* will be leaving ahead of *Titan,* while they're still loading antihydrogen."

"Where's *Surveyor* bound, then?"

"Through Chee to Parkhurst. And possibly beyond even that . . . the spectra from Parkhurst indicate there may be two undiscovered wormholes there, and we're going to look for them."

Martinez was impressed. "Good luck. Maybe Laredo will become a hub of commerce instead of a dead end on the interstellar roadway."

It was a good time to be in the Exploration Service. Founded originally to locate wormholes, stabilize them, and travel through them to discover new systems, planets, and species, the Service had dwindled during the last thousand years of Shaa rule as the Great Masters lost their taste for expanding their empire. Since the death of the last Shaa and the war that followed, the Convocation had decided again on a policy of expansion, beginning with Chee and Parkhurst, two systems that could be reached through Laredo, and which had been surveyed hundreds of years earlier without any settlement actually being authorized.

The Service was expanding to fill its mandate, and that meant more money, better ships, and incoming classes of young officers for Severin to be senior to. The Exploration Service now offered the possibility of great discoveries and adventure, and Severin—as an officer who had come out of the war with credit—was in a position to take advantage of such an offer.

A Terran stepped out of the house with a pair of drinks in his hand. He strongly resembled Martinez, and he wore the dark red tunic of the Lords Convocate, the six-hundred-odd member committee that ruled the empire in the absence of the Shaa.

"Here you are," he said, and handed a drink to Martinez. He looked at Severin, hesitated, and then offered him the second glass.

"Delta whisky?" he asked.

"Thank you." Severin took the glass.

"Lieutenant Severin," Martinez said, "allow me to introduce you to my older brother, Roland."

"Lord convocate," Severin said. He juggled the whisky glass to take Roland's hand.

"Pleased you could come," Roland said. "My brother has spoken of you." He turned to Martinez. "Don't forget that you and Terza are pledged to play tingo tonight with Lord Mukerji."

Martinez made a face. "Can't you find someone else?"

"You're the hero," Roland said. "That makes your money better than anyone else's. You and my lord Severin can rehash the war tomorrow, after our special guests have left."

Martinez looked at Severin. "I'm sorry," he said. "There are people here concerned with the Chee development, and it's the polite thing to keep them happy."

Since the Chee development was the settlement of an entire planet, and the special guests were presumably paying for it, Severin sympathized with the necessity of keeping them happy.

"I understand," he said.

Roland's eyes tracked over Severin's shoulder, and he raised his eyebrows. "Here's Terza now."

Severin turned to see a small group on the lawn, an elegant, black-haired woman in a pale gown walking hand-in-hand with a boy of three, smiling and talking with another woman, fair-haired and pregnant.

"Cassilda's looking well," Martinez remarked.

"Fecundity suits her," said Roland.

"Fecundity and a fortune," Martinez said. "What more could a man ask?"

Roland smiled. "Pliability," he said lightly, then stepped forward to help his pregnant wife up the stairs. Martinez waited for the other woman to follow and greeted her with a kiss.

Introductions were made. The black-haired woman was Lady Terza Chen, heir to the high-caste Chen clan and Martinez's wife. The child was Young Gareth. The light-haired woman was Lady Cassilda Zykov, who was apparently not an heir but came with a fortune anyway.

"Pleased to meet you," Severin said.

"Thank you for keeping my husband alive," Terza said. "I hope you won't stop now."

Severin looked at Martinez. "He seems to be doing well enough on his own."

Lady Terza was slim and poised and had a lovely, almond-eyed face. She put a hand on Severin's arm. "Have you eaten?"

"I had a bite coming down in the skyhook."

She drew Severin toward the door. "That was a long time ago. Let me show you the buffet. I'll introduce you to some people and then—" Her eyes turned to Martinez.

"Tingo with Mukerji," Martinez said. "I know."

She looked again at Severin. "You don't play tingo, do you?"

Bankruptcy doesn't suit me, he thought.

"No," he said, "I'm afraid not."

<hr>

Terza took Martinez's arm in both her own and rested her head on his shoulder. "It was time you came home," she said. "I've never seen you with your own people."

He looked at her. "You're my people, now," he said.

Terza had spent most of her pregnancy on Laredo, but without him: that had been wartime, with the Convocation in flight from the capital and Martinez fighting with the Fleet. After that, with the rebels driven from Zanshaa and the war at an end, the family had reunited in the High City to bask in the cheers of a thankful population. Chee and Parkhurst had been opened to settlement under Martinez patronage. Roland had been co-opted into the Convocation.

Now, three years later, the cheers of the High City had faded.

Enmity on the Fleet Control Board kept Martinez from command of a ship or any meaningful assignments. Terza led an active life that combined a post at the Ministry of Right and Dominion with a full schedule of High City diversions: receptions, balls, concerts, exhibitions, and an endless round of parties. Martinez was feeling more and more like his wife's appendage, trailed around from one event to the next.

The choice was stark: either go home or write his memoirs. Sitting down to write the story of his life, like an old man at the end of his days with nothing to offer to the empire but words, was an image he found repellent. He arranged for passage to Laredo on the huge transport *Wi-hun*, and embarked his family and their servants.

Before he left, Martinez applied to be appointed Lord Inspector of the Fleet for Laredo, Chee, and Parkhurst, thus giving his journey an official pretext. The appointment was approved so quickly that Martinez could only imagine the joy on the Fleet Control Board at the news that Senior Captain Martinez had been willing, for once, to settle for a meaningless task.

The appointment kept him on the active list. It gave him the authority to interfere here and there, if he felt like interfering. Maybe he would interfere just to convince himself that the postwar arrangement hadn't made him irrelevant.

"Captain Martinez! Lady Terza! Are you ready for tingo?"

Martinez decided that he wouldn't submerge into irrelevance just yet, not as long as games of tingo were without a fifth player.

"Certainly, Lord Mukerji," he said.

Lord Mukerji was a short, spare Terran with wiry gray hair, a well-cultivated handlebar mustache, and all the social connections in the worlds. He had been brought in as the President of the Chee Development Company in order to provide the necessary tone. Opening two whole worlds to settlement was beyond the financial capabilities even of the staggeringly rich Lord Martinez, and outside investors had to be brought in. It had to be admitted that the Peers and financiers of the High City preferred to hear about investment opportunities in tones more congenial to their ears than those uttered in a barbaric Laredo accent.

And Lord Mukerji had certainly done his job. Investment had

poured into the company's coffers from the moment he'd begun spreading his balm on the moneyed classes. Important Peer clans were signed on to become the official patrons of settlers, of cities, or even of entire industries. Company stock was doing well on the Zanshaa Exchange, and the bonds were doing even better.

Martinez and Terza took their seats as a tall figure loomed above the table. "Do you know Lord Pa?" Mukerji said.

"We've met only briefly, before dinner," Martinez said.

Lord Pa Maq-fan was a Lai-own, a species of flightless birds, and was the chairman of a privately held company that was one of the prime contractors for the Chee development. From his great height he looked at Terza and Martinez with disturbing blood-red eyes and bared the peg teeth in his short muzzle. "All Lai-own know Captain Martinez," he said. "He saved our home world."

"Very kind of you to say so," Martinez said as Lord Pa settled his keel-like breastbone into his special chair.

He was always heartened when people remembered these little details.

"I haven't kept people waiting, I hope." Lady Marcella Zykov hastened into her place at the table. She was a first cousin of Roland's bride, Cassilda, and the chief of operations for the Chee Company, having been put in place to look after the money the Zykov clan was putting into the venture. She was a very short, very busy woman in her thirties, with a pointed face and auburn hair pulled into an untidy knot behind her head, and she absently brushed tobacco ash off her jacket as she took her place.

"Shall we roll the bones, then?" Lord Mukerji said.

All players bet a hundred zeniths. The bones were rolled, and they appointed Marcella the dealer. She ran the tiles through the sorting machine and dealt each player an initial schema.

"Discard," said Terza, who sat on her right, and removed the Three Virtues from her schema.

"Claim," said Lord Mukerji. He took the Three Virtues into his schema and smiled beneath his broad mustaches. He waited for Marcella to be dealt a new tile, then touched a numbered pad on the table. "Another two hundred," he said.

Martinez thought it was a little early in the game to raise, but he paid two hundred for a new tile just to see where the game would go. Two rounds later, when Lord Mukerji doubled, Martinez and Terza both dropped out. The game was won by Lord Pa, who had quietly built a Tower that he promptly dropped onto Lord Mukerji's Bouquet of Probity.

"Roll the bones," said Mukerji.

The bones decided to make Mukerji the dealer. As he ran the tiles through the sorting machine, Marcella looked up from the table.

"Will you be traveling to Chee, Captain Martinez?"

"I'm Lord Inspector for Chee," Martinez said, "so I'll be required to inspect the skyhook, the station, and the other Fleet facilities."

"And Parkhurst as well?"

"There's nothing in the Parkhurst system at the moment but a Fleet survey vessel. I can wait for it to return."

"I can offer you transport on the *Kayenta,*" Marcella said, "if you can leave in twenty days or so." She turned to Terza. "That way Lady Terza can accompany you without the discomforts of a Fleet vessel or a transport."

Martinez was pleasantly surprised. He'd been planning on booking a ride on one of the giant transports heading to Chee—they carried immigrants as well as cargo and had adequate facilities for passengers—but *Kayenta* was the Chee Company's executive yacht, with first-class accommodations and a crew that included a masseur and a cosmetician.

He turned to Terza, who seemed delighted by the offer. "Thank you," he said. "We'll definitely consider the option."

"Are you going out to Chee yourself, Lady Marcella?" Mukerji asked.

"Yes. They're beginning the new railhead at Corona, and Lord Pa and I will need to consult with Allodorm."

Martinez caught the surprise that crossed Terza's face, surprise that was swiftly suppressed. Terza took up her tiles.

"Is that Ledo Allodorm?" she asked.

Lord Pa's blood-red eyes gazed at her from across the table. "Yes," he said. "Do you know that gentleman?"

"Not personally," Terza said, as she looked down at her tiles. "His name came up, I don't know where."

Martinez noted with interest that his wife wore the serene smile that experience told him was a sure sign she was telling less than the truth.

"Shall we roll the bones?" asked Lord Mukerji.

Mukerji doubled three times on the first three rounds and drove everyone else out of the game. Martinez realized he'd found his way into a very serious and potentially expensive contest, and began to calculate odds very carefully.

Terza won the following game with the Six Cardinal Directions. Lord Pa won the next. Marcella the game after. Then Lord Pa, then Martinez with a Bouquet of Delights over Lord Mukerji's Crossroads.

"Roll the bones," Lord Mukerji said.

Lord Pa took another game, then Terza, and Marcella won three games in a row. In the next game, the bones rolled six, so the stakes were doubled and the bones rolled again, and this time proclaimed Martinez dealer. He discarded Two Sunsets, only to have Lord Mukerji claim it, which argued that Lord Mukerji was aiming at filling a Bouquet of Sorrows. Mukerji in his turn was dealt, and discarded, a South, which Martinez claimed to add to his East and Up to make three of the Six Cardinal Directions. On subsequent turns, Martinez was dealt a South, needing only a North and a Down for six. Mukerji claimed Four Night Winds, doubled, kept a tile he was dealt, doubled, was dealt and discarded Two Ancestors, and doubled again anyway. Terza and Lord Pa dropped out of the game during the doubling, turning over their tiles to reveal unpromising schemas.

Martinez looked at the total and felt his mouth go dry. He received a generous allowance from his father, but to continue the game would be to abuse his parent severely.

His worried contemplation of the score made him a critical half-second late when Marcella, dropping out of the game, made her final discard, a Down.

"Claim," Mukerji said.

Mukerji had claimed the tile simply to thwart him. Martinez, the word already spilling from his lips, had no choice but to let Mukerji take the tile he badly needed to complete his hand.

"Double," Mukerji said, his eyes gleaming.

Martinez looked at his schema, then scanned the discards and the tiles of the players who had dropped out of the betting. Neither of the two Norths was revealed, and neither was the second Down.

He looked at his own tiles again. Beside the Directions he had Three and Four Ships, a Sunlit Garden, and a Road of Metal. If he got Two or Five Ships, he'd have a Small Flotilla. A Flotilla plus the Cardinal Directions equaled a Migration.

He scanned the discards and reveals again, and saw singletons of Two and Five Ships, which meant other Ships were still in the sorting machine.

Or already in Lord Mukerji's schema.

Martinez decided it was worth the risk.

Without speaking Martinez dealt himself another tile. It was Four Ships, and he discarded it. Lord Mukerji ignored it and took another tile, which he discarded.

Five Ships. Martinez claimed it, discarded his Road of Metal, then dealt himself another tile, which he discarded.

He was suddenly aware that the room had fallen silent, that others stood around him, watching. Roland watched from amid the spectators with a frown on his face, and Cassilda with her hands pressed protectively over her growing abdomen. Lord Pa's red eyes were obscured by nictitating membranes. Marcella was frozen in her seat, but her hands formed little fists and her knuckles were white.

Terza, on his right, had the serene smile that she wore to conceal her thoughts, but he saw the tension crimping the corners of her eyes.

Lord Mukerji was dealt and discarded a tile, and then Martinez dealt himself an Angle, which he discarded.

"Claim," Mukerji said in triumph.

He laid down his completed Bouquet of Sorrows, then added the Angle to his Point and his Coordinate, making a Geometry. His grin broadened beneath the spreading mustache as he pushed the odd Down into the discard pile.

"That's a game for me, then," he said.

"Claim," said Martinez.

He turned over his tiles to reveal the incomplete Migration, which he completed by adding the Down and discarding his Sunlit Garden. From the room he heard a collective exhalation of breath.

He looked at Mukerji, who was suddenly very white around the eyes. "That's a limit schema," Mukerji said.

Honesty compelled Martinez to speak. "And the bones came up six, if you remember, so the limit is doubled. And I'm dealer, so that doubles again."

Lord Mukerji surveyed the table, then slowly leaned backwards into his chair, draping himself on the chair back as if he were a fallen flag.

"What *is* the limit?" Martinez heard someone ask.

"Ten thousand," came the reply.

"Fucking amazing," said the first.

"Well played," said Lord Mukerji. "I do believe you let me have that Cardinal Direction on purpose."

"Of course," Martinez lied.

Mukerji held out his hand. "You must give me an opportunity for revenge," he said.

Martinez took the hand. "Later tonight, if you like."

There was applause from the crowd as the two clasped hands.

"I need to visit the smoking lounge," Marcella said, and stood.

Martinez rose from the table. His head spun, and his knees felt watery. Terza rose with him and took his arm.

"That was terrifying," she murmured.

"Ten thousand doubled twice," Martinez breathed. "For forty we could buy a small palace in the High City."

"We already *have* a small palace."

"I could have lost it tonight." He passed a hand over his forehead.

Roland loomed up at his other elbow. "That was well judged," he said.

"Thank you."

"But you were lucky."

Martinez looked at him. "I *am* lucky," he said. If he weren't, he wouldn't have been a senior captain before he was thirty.

"Just so you don't go counting on it." A mischievous light glowed in Roland's eyes. "You're not taking up tingo as a substitute for the excitement of combat, are you?"

"Combat's easier," Martinez said. He looked at his brother. "That isn't true, by the way."

"I know."

A thought passed through Martinez's mind. "Mukerji wasn't playing with *our* money, was he?"

"You mean the Company's? No. His presidency is ceremonial; he doesn't have access to the accounts. He doesn't even take a salary."

Martinez raised an eyebrow.

"Oh," Roland said, "we gave him lots of *stock*. If the Chee Company does well, so does he."

"He may have to sell some of his stock after tonight."

Roland shook his head. "He can afford a lot of nights like this."

"How many, I wonder," Terza said. She stroked Martinez's arm. "I should make sure Gareth's got to bed. If you're all right?"

"I could use a drink."

"Absolutely not," Roland said. "Not if you're committed to an evening of high play."

Martinez let go a long breath. "You've got a point."

Terza smiled, patted his arm, and went in search of the children. Martinez went to the bar with Roland, ordered an orange juice, and poured it over ice.

Roland ordered champagne. "You don't have to rub it in," Martinez said, and turned to find Severin at his elbow.

"You're finding your way all right?" he asked.

"Yes. There's a Cree band tuning in the ballroom. I'll dance."

"Good."

"I hear you've done something spectacular at tingo. Everyone's talking about it."

Martinez felt a tingle of vanity. "I made a mistake early on," he said, "but I calculated the odds correctly in the end."

He explained the play as he made his way back to the parlor. They came to Mukerji, who was speaking with Lord Pa. "If the geologist's report was in error, then it must be done again, of course," he said. "I'm sure Cassilda will—" He broke off, then looked at Martinez.

"Lord captain," he said. "Shall we resume the game?"

"We seem to be without a few players as yet," Martinez said. "May I introduce Lieutenant Severin? He saved the empire at Protipanu, and saved *me* a few months later, during the battle there."

Pa looked down from his great height, nictitating membranes clearing his red eyes as he gazed at Severin with studious intensity. "I don't recall any of that in the histories," he said.

"The wrong people *wrote* the histories," Martinez said. Those same people had decided to keep Severin's contribution to the war a secret. He had used a trick of physics to physically move a wormhole out from under a Naxid squadron, and since the empire depended for its very existence on the wormholes that knit its systems together, the censors had decided not to remind people that such a thing could be done.

"In any case, lord lieutenant, I am pleased to meet you," said Pa to Severin.

"So am I," Mukerji said. His long mustache gave a twitch. "You wouldn't care to join us for a game of tingo?"

"Thank you, my lord," Severin said, "but I don't play."

"Don't play tingo?" Mukerji said, blinking with apparent astonishment. "What *do* you do in those officers' clubs or wardrooms or whatever you call them?"

"Mostly I do paperwork," Severin said.

"Perhaps we should actively search for a fifth player," Martinez said. "I'm not certain that Terza will return from putting Gareth to bed anytime soon."

He spoke quickly. He knew that, as someone promoted from the ranks, Severin was unlikely to possess the large private income normal for most officers. Very possibly the unfortunate man was forced to live on his pay. A game of tingo played for high stakes wasn't simply unwise for a man like Severin, it was impossible.

Best to get him off the hook as quickly as possible.

Pa and Mukerji went in search of a tingo player, and Martinez asked Severin about his last voyage, several months in which *Surveyor* had been in the Chee system, making one rendezvous after another with asteroids, strapping antimatter-fueled thrusters onto the giant rocks, and sending them on looping courses to Wormhole Station One, where they were used to balance the mass coming into the system on the huge freighters. The task was both dull and dangerous, a risky combination, but the voyage had been successful and the wormhole station wouldn't need any more raw material for a year or more.

"Fortunately the mass driver on Chee's moon is taking over the job of supplying the wormhole stations," Severin said, "so we're available for other duties."

"Excellent. Your voyage was uneventful otherwise?"

"Our skipper's good," Severin said. "No one on the trip tore so much as a hangnail."

"Do I know him?" Martinez asked.

"Lord Go Shikimori. An old Service family."

Martinez considered, then shook his head. "The name's not familiar."

Marcella returned from the smoking lounge brushing ash from her jacket. Pa and Mukerji arrived with an elderly, fangless Torminel named Lady Uzdil.

"I seem to be caught up in the game," Martinez told Severin. "My apologies."

"I think I hear music," Severin said.

"Enjoy."

What *did* Severin do with himself in his ship's wardroom? Martinez wondered. He probably couldn't afford most of an officer's amusements.

And judging by his uniform, he couldn't afford much of a tailor, either.

Martinez settled in to play tingo. Lady Uzdil seemed to be shedding: the air was full of graying fur. Martinez played conservatively, which meant that he frequently allowed himself to be driven out of a round by Mukerji's insistent doubling. He held firm when fortune gave him good tiles, though, and managed a modest profit on top of the forty thousand he'd won earlier. Lord Pa did very well, Cassilda well enough, and Lady Uzdil lost a modest amount. It was Mukerji who lost heavily, plunging heavily on one bad venture after another. Though he didn't run afoul of any limit schemas, and he didn't lose another High

City palace, Martinez calculated that he lost at least the value of a sumptuous country villa—and not one on Laredo, either, but on Zanshaa.

After two hours Martinez considered that he'd done his duty in giving Mukerji a chance to win his money back, and left the game. Mukerji protested, but Cassilda and Pa were happy with their winnings and left the game as well.

"I'm glad he doesn't have any financial control in the Chee Company," Martinez told Terza later, when he was abed. "Not if he runs a business the same way he gambles."

"I'm sure he has no idea whatever of how to run a business," Terza said as she approached the bed. "That's what Marcella's for." She wore a blue silk nightgown, and had bound her long black hair with matching blue ribbon into a long tail that she wore over one shoulder. The look gave her a pleasing asymmetry. Martinez reached out one of his big hands and stroked her hip with the back of his knuckles.

Their marriage had been arranged by their families, one of Roland's more elaborate and insistent conspiracies. Martinez felt free to resent Roland's interference, but he had decided long ago not to resent Terza.

"What about Ledo Allodorm?" he asked.

Terza's almond eyes widened faintly. "You noticed?" she asked.

"I saw you react to the name. I doubt the others know you well enough to have seen what I did."

"Move over. I'll tell you what I know."

Martinez made room on the bed. Terza slipped beneath the covers and curled on her side facing Martinez. Her scent floated delicately through his perceptions.

"I found out about Allodorm when I was asked to review some old contracts left over from the war," she said. The Ministry of Right and Dominion, where she was posted, was the civilian agency that encompassed the Fleet, and dealt with issues of contracts, supply, Fleet facilities, budgets, and support.

"Allodorm is a Daimong from Devajjo, in the Hone Reach," she continued. "During the war he received a contract to build four—or was it five?—transport vessels for the Fleet. The war ended before he could deliver the ships, and the contract was canceled."

"So what did he do?" Martinez asked. "Convert the transports to civilian purposes? That would be allowed, wouldn't it, if the government didn't want them anymore?"

Terza frowned. "There was an allegation that he never built the ships at all."

Martinez blinked. "He took the money and did *nothing*?"

"Other than commission some architects, print some stationery, and recruit some staff and some high-priced legal talent, no." She looked thoughtful. "It was possible to make a calculation that the war would be over before he had to deliver. If we won, the contracts would be canceled; and if the Naxids won, they wouldn't care if he'd started work or not."

"Didn't the Investigative Service climb all over Allodorm's operation? Couldn't the ministry at least have asked for its money back?"

Terza offered a mild shrug. "After the war the IS was involved in purging rebels and their sympathizers, and didn't spare a thought for the people who were supposed to be on *our* side. When the file finally came across my desk I recommended an investigation, but the ministry decided against it. I don't know why; it's possible that Allodorm is politically protected."

"So now Allodorm is on Chee, and Marcella and Lord Pa are traveling to consult with him."

"Maybe he's a subcontractor."

"That doesn't speak well for the prospect of the Chee Company's balance sheet."

"The Chee Company may be all right," Terza pointed out. "It's Lord Pa and the Meridian Company that's the prime contractor. If anyone's being gouged, it's probably them."

"Either way, it's my family's money." He shifted closer to Terza's warmth and she rested her head on his shoulder and put an arm across his chest. "*Our* balance sheet has improved anyway. What shall we do with Mukerji's cash?"

He could sense her amusement. "Buy something preposterous, I suppose. You've always talked about taking up yachting."

Martinez felt a twinge of annoyance. "They wouldn't let me into the Seven Stars or the Ion Club," he said. "A provincial can't get past their august doors, no matter how many medals he's won." He kissed Terza's forehead. "Or how many high-placed ministry officials he's married."

"So join a lesser club," Terza said, "and beat the pants off the Seven Stars in every match."

Martinez grinned at the ceiling. "That's not a half-bad idea," he said.

He felt Terza's warm breath on his neck as she spoke. "Is this the room you lived in as a child?"

"Yes, as a matter of fact. Same furniture, too, but the model Fleet ships that I hung from the ceiling are gone. And so are the uniform guides to the various academies that I'd tacked up on the walls."

Her low chuckle came to his ear. "So joining the Fleet was *your* idea, I take it."

"Oh yes. I had a lot of romantic ideas—must have got those from my mother. And my father didn't mind, because in the Fleet at least I'd learn some useful skills."

He remembered, before the war, when speaking with—with a certain person, a woman he preferred not ever to think about, a woman with pale hair and milky skin and blazing green eyes—he'd expressed his frustration at being in a meaningless service, a club not unlike the Seven Stars but less useful, a club devoted to ritual and display and serving the limitless vanity of its commanders.

The war had changed that, at least for a while.

What hadn't changed, apparently, were the politically connected contractors who gouged the government while delivering shoddy, late, or nonexistent work.

That, he supposed, was the government's business. What concerned Martinez was that if Allodorm were stealing money now, he was no longer stealing it just from the government, but the Martinez family.

That, of course, had to stop.

Terza pressed closer to Martinez on the bed. She kissed his cheek. "I wonder," she said, "if when you were a boy in this bed, you ever imagined—"

Martinez sat up, displacing Terza's head and arm. "Comm," he said. "Wall display: on."

The chameleon-weave fabric of the display normally matched the geometric pattern of the wallpaper, but now it brightened into a video screen displaying the Martinez crest. "Comm: search," Martinez said. "Ledo plus Allodorm plus Meridian plus Company. Begin."

In half a second data flashed on the screen. Martinez chose the first listing, and saw a page from the Meridian Company's official prospectus of the Chee development. He absorbed the information.

"Allodorm's chief engineer for the Meridian Company," he said. "He's in charge of all their projects on Chee. *All* of them."

He turned to Terza and saw her pensive expression. "Something wrong?" he said.

A serene smile crossed her face, the one he knew for its falsity.

"Nothing at all," she said.

———

"Daddy says I'm a genius. Daddy says I'm going to do great things."

"I'm sure you are," said Severin.

"I'm going to smash Naxids." The dark-haired child raised a hand over his head. In his fist was a toy warship. He flung it on the polished asteroid material of the verandah. "*Bang!*"

"Good shot," Severin observed.

He'd grown up in a family with a pair of younger sisters, and knew how to keep a young child entertained. Lord Gareth Chen—who bore his father's first name but the surname of his mother, who was the Chen heir and ranked higher—picked up the warship and flung it again. Wet explosive sounds came from his pursed lips.

"But what if the Naxids come from *this* direction?" Severin asked, and leaned out of his metal whitewashed chair to threaten the boy's flank.

"*Bang!*"

"Or from here?" The other flank.

"*Bang!*"

"Or here?" Overhead.

"*Bang!*"

Lord Gareth the Younger was at a stage of life where this could go on for quite a while before he got bored. Having nothing better to do, Severin was content to continue the game, though his thoughts were elsewhere.

He had awakened that morning with a dream clinging to his memory like a shroud. In the dream he had been driving up the oak alley toward the house, beneath the series of iron arches, and somehow one of the arches had transformed itself into a proscenium, and he'd stepped through the proscenium onto a stage that was the house.

The house had been covered with lights, and a party had been underway. The guests glittered in fine clothes and uniforms. Severin knew none of them. Their conversation was strangely oblique, and Severin kept feeling that he could understand them if only he listened a little harder. At some point he discovered that they were not people at all, but automata, smiling and glimmering as they spoke words that had been preprogrammed by someone else.

In the dream Severin hadn't found this discovery horrifying, but intensely interesting. He wandered through the party listening to the conversation and admiring the brilliance of the puppets' design.

When he woke he was still under the spell of the dream. He breakfasted alone on the terrace—apparently his hosts were not yet awake—and he found himself thinking about the strange conversations that he'd heard, and trying to work out the obscure story behind them.

He thought about going back to bed and hoping to pick the dream up where it had left off, but at this point Gareth Junior arrived, and the battle with the Naxids began.

He was rescued in time by Martinez, who came out of the house and lunged at his son, scooping him up in both arms and whirling him overhead as the child shrilled his laughter.

Following Martinez from the house came his older brother, Roland, who carried a cup of coffee in one hand. Both wore civilian clothes, which made Severin more conscious than usual of his shabby uniform.

"I suppose it won't be long before I'm behaving like that," Roland said as he watched Martinez twirling his son.

"I suppose it won't," Severin said.

Roland sipped coffee. Martinez tucked his son under one arm and turned to Severin. "Has the boy prodigy been bothering you?"

"He's been mashing Naxids, mostly."

Martinez grinned. "Exercising tactical genius, eh? Just like his father!" Young Gareth still under his arm, Martinez sprinted into the house as the child waved his fists and laughed aloud.

"Perhaps I *won't* behave like that, after all," Roland decided.

Martinez returned a few moments later, having delivered his offspring to the nursemaid. He combed his disordered hair with his fingers and dropped into the whitewashed metal chair next to Severin.

"I saw you dancing last night," he said. "With a curly-haired girl."

"Lady Consuelo Dalmas," Severin said.

"Consuelo." Martinez blinked. "I thought she looked familiar. I used to see her older sister, when we were all, ah, much younger."

"She's invited me to a garden party tomorrow afternoon."

Martinez smiled. "Have a good time."

"I will." He considered offering a resigned sort of sigh and decided against it. "Of course," he added, "sooner or later either she or her parents will discover that I'm not a Peer, and have no money, and then I won't see her again." Severin clasped his hands between his knees. "But then I'm used to that."

Martinez gave him an unsettled look. "You're not regretting your promotion, I hope."

"No." Severin considered. "But it's made me aware of how many locked doors there are, doors that I once had no idea even existed."

"If there's anything I can do to open them . . ." Martinez ventured.

"Thank you. I'm not certain there's anything that can be done."

"Unless we have another war," Roland said. "Then all bets are off."

Smiling lightly to himself, Roland walked to the verandah rail and looked out into the oak alley, raising his head at the honeyed scent of the o-pii flowers floating on the morning breeze. "Consuelo's not right for you anyway, if you don't mind my saying so," he said. "Too young, too much a part of the fashionable set. What you need is a comely widow, or a young woman married to a dull old husband."

Martinez looked at him. "You don't have anyone in mind, do you?"

"Let me put my mind to it."

Martinez gave Severin an uneasy look. "Better make your wishes plain. Roland has disturbing success as a matchmaker."

There was something in the air, Severin felt, some history between the brothers that made this an uncomfortable moment.

"I'm only here for a month," Severin said.

"Narrow window of opportunity," Roland said. "I'll see what I can do."

"Apropos conspiracy," Martinez said, "do you know anything about Allodorm, Meridian Company's chief engineer?"

"I've met him on Chee Station," Severin said. "Though I haven't conspired with him."

"I haven't met him at all," Roland said. He turned around, eyes mild as he contemplated his brother. "I appreciate your confidence in my omniscience, but what I really do is look after family interests in the Convocation. I'm not really connected to the Chee development business."

"Terza thinks that Allodorm's a swindler," Martinez said. "And if she's right, he's in a perfect place to walk off with a lot of our money."

Roland absorbed this with a distracted frown. "What does Terza know, exactly?"

"During the war, he took the money to build five ships and then didn't build them."

Severin felt a moment of shock. As an officer in government service he was familiar enough with waste and theft, but five whole missing ships seemed extreme.

There was a moment of silence, and then Roland turned to Severin.

"I'd appreciate your discretion," he said.

"Certainly," Severin said.

"There may not be anything in this," Roland said.

"Of course," Severin said.

He found himself fascinated by the interactions in this household, the delicate play between the decorated Fleet officer and his politician brother. Since his promotion he'd had the opportunity to observe several Peer families, and none had been quite like this one.

"I wish I knew who hired Allodorm," Martinez said pensively.

"Lord Pa, presumably," Roland said. "The question is whether Lord Pa know about the Fleet ships, or cared if he did." He pulled another of the metal chairs toward Severin and sat. "Would you tell us about this Allodorm?"

Severin shrugged. "He's a Daimong. Youngish, I think, though with Daimong it's hard to tell. When *Surveyor* first docked at Chee Station, he was on hand to make sure we got everything we needed. I thought that was very good of him."

"Were you treated well?" Roland asked.

"Yes. Since I'm the exec, the lord captain assigned me to work with Allodorm, and it was first-class all the way. Supplies came aboard within hours of submitting our requests. The victuals were fresh. Allodorm put one of the worker hostels at Port Vipsania at the disposal of our liberty crew, and he hosted a dinner for the officers."

"Nothing odd?" Martinez asked. "Nothing a little off-center in the way the station's run?"

"Other than it being first-class, no," Severin said. "In the Exploration Service we're used to things being more worn and shabby—it's not like we've got the Fleet's prestige or budget—but everything on Chee Station was new and shiny and efficient. The facilities were bigger than they needed, but then there are plans to expand."

The brothers contemplated this. "I don't suppose we should tell our father."

"What would we tell him? We've got dozens of inspectors on Chee anyway—what can he do that they can't?"

Martinez gave a little shrug. "Not get bribed?" he said.

"Father's supposed to open the meeting of the Petitioners' Council in something like fifteen days." Roland gave a tight little smile. "If he abandons his task and goes charging off to Chee on the *Ensenada* to expose the wicked, that's all the warning Allodorm or anyone else is going to need. Everything would be tidied up by the time he gets there."

"And you?"

"I'm not going anywhere until Cassilda has our baby, after which the whole family will leave for Zanshaa so that I can sit in Convocation."

Martinez sighed. "I'm the Lord Inspector, aren't I? I suppose it's up to me to inspect."

Severin thought again about the two brothers. They knew each other well, they worked together deftly, they had a shared history and vocabulary. It occurred to Severin, however, that perhaps they didn't like each other.

"Lady Liao," Roland said suddenly.

Martinez looked at him. "Beg pardon?"

Roland turned to Severin. "Lady Liao, wife of Lord Judge Omohundro. She's perfect for you. Her husband's on the ring tied up in a long series of hearings, and I'm sure she's looking for amusement."

Severin could do nothing but stare. *Can you* do *that?* he wanted to ask.

Roland looked at him. "Shall I invite her to tea?" he said.

"We are holding at five minutes," said Lord Go Shikimori, captain of the *Surveyor*.

"Holding at five minutes, my lord," said Severin.

Surveyor awaited final permission from Ring Control to launch on its mission through Chee and Parkhurst to the possible wormholes beyond. Encircled by the round metal hoops of his acceleration cage, Severin glanced down at the pilot's board before him—it was he who would steer *Surveyor* from the ring and into the great emptiness beyond, not that the job was particularly difficult.

The lights of the pilot's board glittered on the ring Severin wore on the middle finger of his right hand. Nine small sapphires sparkled around a central opal. The ring had been a parting gift from Lady Liao, one sapphire for each night she and Severin had spent together.

For a moment he was lost in reverie, memories of smooth cool sheets, silken flesh, Lady Liao's subtle scent. Wind chimes that saluted the dawn on the balcony outside her room.

Lord Roland Martinez, he thought, was very, very smart.

"Message from Ring Control, my lord," reported Lord Barry Montcrief, who sat at the comm board—he had the drawling High City accent that Lord Go preferred as the official voice of his ship. "Permission granted to depart the station en route to Chee system."

"Resume countdown," the captain said.

"Countdown resumed," said Warrant Officer Lily Bhagwati, who sat at the engines station.

"Depressurize boarding tube. Warn crew for zero gravity."

"Depressurizing boarding tube." Alarms clattered through the ship. "Zero gravity alarm, my lord."

Severin checked his board, took the joysticks in his hands, rotated them. "Maneuvering thrusters gimbaled," he said. "Pressure at thruster heads nominal."

"Boarding tube depressurized."

"Withdraw boarding tube," said the captain.

"Boarding tube . . . " Waiting for the light to go on. " . . . withdrawn, my lord."

"Electrical connections withdrawn," said Bhagwati. "Outside connectors sealed. Ship is on 100 percent internal power."

"Data connectors withdrawn," said Lord Barry. "Outside data ports sealed."

"Main engines gimbaled," said Bhagwati. "Gimbal test successful."

"Hold at ten seconds," said the captain. "Status, everyone."

All stations reported clean boards.

"Launch in ten," Lord Go said. "Pilot, the ship is yours."

"The ship is mine, my lord." Severin released and clenched his hands on the joysticks.

The digit counter in the corner of his display counted down to zero. Lights flashed.

"Clamps withdrawn," he said. "Magnetic grapples released."

Severin suddenly floated free in his webbing as *Surveyor* was cast free of Laredo's accelerator ring. *Surveyor* had been moored nose-in, and the release of centripetal force from the upper ring, which was spinning at seven times the rate of the planet below, gave the ship a good rate of speed that carried it clear of any potential obstacles.

Severin checked the navigation display anyway, and saw no threats. He thumbed buttons on his joysticks and engaged the maneuvering thrusters. An increase in gravity snugged him against his chest harness. He fired the thrusters several more times to increase the rate at which *Surveyor* was withdrawing from the ring.

323

It was very illegal to fire *Surveyor*'s main antimatter engines, with their radioactive plumes, anywhere near the inhabited ring. Severin needed to push the ship past the safety zone before *Surveyor* could really begin its journey.

Again Severin checked the navigation displays. He could see the Chee Company yacht *Kayenta* outbound for Wormhole Station Two, carrying Martinez and Lady Terza to the newly opened planet. *Surveyor* would follow in their wake, fourteen days behind. A chain of cargo vessels were inbound from Station One, many of them carrying equipment or settlers for Chee, all of them standing on huge pillars of fire as they decelerated to their rendezvous with the ring. The closest was still seven hours away.

The only obstacle of note was the giant bulk of the *Titan,* which orbited Laredo at a considerable distance for reasons of safety. *Titan* was full of antimatter destined for Chee and Parkhurst, and even though the antimatter was remarkably stable—flakes of antihydrogen suspended by static electricity inside incredibly tiny etched silicon shells, all so tiny they flowed like a thick fluid—nevertheless if things went wrong the explosion would vaporize a chunk of Laredo's ring and bring the rest down on the planet below.

It would be a good thing for *Surveyor* to stay well clear of *Titan.*

Severin looked at the point of light on the display that represented *Titan* and wondered about the conversation he'd had with Martinez and his brother, the one where Allodorm's name had first been raised. *Titan* was a Meridian Company ship leased long-term by the Exploration Service. The growing settlements on Chee required antimatter to generate power, and as yet had no accelerator ring. Cree Station, with its skyhook that ran cargo to the surface, required power as well.

The wormhole stations at both Chee and Parkhurst, with their colossal mass drivers that kept the wormholes stable, required an enormous output of power.

Since Chee could not as yet generate its own antimatter, it had been decided to ramp up antihydrogen production on Laredo's ring, fill *Titan* with the results, and move the whole ship to a distant parking orbit around the newly settled planet, on the far side of Chee's largest moon so that even if the unthinkable happened and *Titan* blew, none of the energetic neutrons and furious gamma rays would reach Chee's population. When one of Chee's installations needed antihydrogen, they'd send a shuttle to *Titan* and collect some. By the time *Titan* had been depleted, an accelerator ring—a small one, not the vast technological wonder that circled all of Laredo—would have been built in Chee orbit.

Severin wondered if it truly made economic sense to use *Titan* that way, or whether it was a complex scheme to fill Allodorm's coffers.

Surveyor finally reached the limit of Laredo's safety zone, and Severin rotated the ship onto a new heading, his couch sliding lightly within the rings of his acceleration cage.

"We are on our new heading, my lord," Severin said. "Two-two-zero by zero-zero-one absolute. Mission plan is in the guidance computer."

"I am in command," Lord Go called.

"The lord captain is in command," Severin agreed. He took his hands off the joysticks.

"Engines, fire engines," the captain said. "Accelerate at two point three gravities."

Severin felt a kick to his spine and his acceleration couch swung within its cage as the gravities began piling on his chest.

"Accelerating at two point three gravities," Bhagwati said. "Course two-two-zero by zero-zero-one absolute."

They would accelerate hard until they'd achieved escape velocity from Laredo, then slacken for most of the journey to a single gravity, going to harder accelerations for an hour out of each watch.

Severin looked at the displays and saw *Kayenta* again, outbound and approaching the wormhole that would take it to Chee. It was a pity that *Surveyor* wouldn't travel to Chee, but merely pass through the system on its way to Parkhurst and the possible new wormholes. A pity not only because Severin wouldn't see Martinez and Terza again, but because he'd probably never find out how the Allodorm thing worked out.

He'd just have to find something else to amuse him for the next few months, and he thought he knew what it was.

He'd been unable to entirely forget the dream he'd had at Rio

Hondo, and he'd loaded his personal data foil with articles on puppets, puppeteers, marionettes, automata, shadow puppets, and recordings of performances.

People on long voyages found many ways to occupy their hours. Some gambled, some drank, some drew into themselves. Some concentrated obsessively on their work. Some watched recorded entertainments, some had affairs with other crew members, some played musical instruments. Some worked as hard as they could at making everyone else on the ship miserable.

Perhaps, Severin thought, he would be the first to plan a puppet theater.

Certainly it was a field that seemed to have a lot of room to expand.

"Are you all on virtual?" asked the astronomer Shon-dan. "I'm transmitting the outside cameras on Channel Seventeen."

"Comm: Channel Seventeen." Terza's soft voice came to Martinez's ears from the nearest acceleration couch.

Martinez was already on the correct channel, his head filled with the stars as viewed from the *Kayenta* as it passed the final moments of its twenty-day acceleration out of the Laredo system. The virtual cap he wore to project the image onto his visual centers was lighter than the Fleet issue, which required earphones and microphone pickups, and he sensed other differences as well: the depth of field was subtly different, a bit flatter, perhaps because the civilian rig required less precision.

The stars were thrown like a great wash of diamonds across the midnight backdrop, silent and steady and grand. They were the home stars under which Martinez had spent the first half of his life, and his mind naturally sought the familiar, comforting constellations in their well-known places. Laredo's own star, this far out, was hardly brighter than other bright stars. The software had been instructed to blot out *Kayenta*'s brilliant tail so as to avoid losing the stars by contrast, and the result was a flickering, disturbing negative blot occupying one part of the display, a void of absolute darkness that seemed to pursue the ship.

Martinez and Terza were in *Kayenta*'s main lounge, the softly scented center of the yacht's social life, and were now twenty days out from Laredo. Shon-dan, an astronomer from the Imperial University of Zarafan who had come aboard as Marcella's guest, was about to show the reason why an astronomical observatory had been placed on Chee Station, and why she had spent months journeying here.

"Ten seconds," Shon-dan said. "Eight. Five."

Kayenta was traveling too fast for Martinez to see the wormhole station as the ship flashed past, or the wormhole itself, the inverted-bowl-of-stars that was their destination. The transition itself was instantaneous, and the star field changed at the same instant.

A vast, lush globe of stars suddenly blazed across Martinez's perceptions, occupying at least a third of the sky, the stars so packed together they seemed nearly as dense as glittering grains of sand stretched along an ocean shore. Martinez felt himself take an involuntary breath, and he heard Terza's gasp. The closer Martinez looked, the more stars he saw. There seemed to be vague clouds and structures within the globe, each made up of more and more brilliants, but Martinez couldn't tell whether the clouds actually existed or were the results of his own mind trying to create order in this vast, burning randomness, seeking the familiar just as it had sought out constellations in Laredo's sky.

Gazing into the vast star-globe was like drifting deeper and deeper into a endless sea, past complex, ill-defined shoals that on closer inspection were made up of millions of coral structures, while the structures themselves, looked at with greater care, were found to be composed of tiny limestone shells, and the shells themselves, on examination, each held tiny specks of life, a kind of infinite regression that baffled the senses.

"Now you see why we've built the observatory." Shon-dan's voice, floating into Martinez' perceptions, was quietly triumphant. "Of all the wormholes in the empire, this one leads to a system that's closest to the center of a galaxy. This is our best chance to observe how a galactic core is structured. From here we can directly observe the effects on nearby stars of the supermassive black hole at the galaxy's center."

With an effort of will Martinez shifted his attention away from the glowing globe to the rest of the starry envelope that surrounded *Kayenta*. By comparison with Laredo the entire sky was packed with stars, with an opalescent strip that marked the galaxy's disk spiraling out into endless space. The Chee system was actually within the galactic core, though on its periphery, and stars on all sides were near and burning bright. Chee's own star, Cheemah, shone with a warm yellow light, but other nearby stars equaled its fire.

"The stars here are very dense," Shon-dan said, "though not as dense as they are further in. The Chee system has seven stars—or maybe eight, we're not sure—and the orbits are very complex."

"Do we actually know which galaxy we're in?" Terza asked.

"No. We're scanning for Cepheids and other yardsticks that might give us an indication, but so far we haven't found enough to make certain of anything. We could be anywhere in the universe, of course, and anywhere within a billion years of where we started."

Martinez heard footfalls enter the room, then the voice of Lord Pa. "Looking at the stars?" he said. "You'll get tired of them soon enough. Between the galactic core and the other six stars in Chee's system, there's no true night on the planet, and we've had to install polarizing windows on all our workers' dormitories just so our people can get some rest. I've just stopped looking at the sky—galactic centers are nasty violent places, and the less we have to do with them, the better."

"Stars are packed pretty closely here, true enough, my lord." Shon-dan's deference to a wealthy Peer did not quite disguise her disagreement. Clearly she was not about to tire of gazing at this sky anytime soon.

"I'm going to sit and play a game of cinhal," Lord Pa said. "Don't let me disturb you."

Martinez returned his attention to the great, glowing galactic core while he heard Lord Pa shuffle to a table, then give it the muted commands to set up a game.

"So far you're only seeing the light in its visible spectrum," Shon-dan said. "I'm going to add some other spectra in a moment. There will be some false colors. I'll try to fix those later." Martinez heard the Lai-own give a few muted commands, and then the galactic core shifted from a pearly color to a muted amber, and the great sphere was suddenly pierced through by an enormous lance of light, shimmering and alive, a giant pillar that seemed to stretched from the foundations of the universe to its uttermost heaven.

Martinez gave an involuntary cry, and he heard Terza's echo.

"Yes." Triumph had again entered Shon-dan's voice. "That's the beam of relativistic particles generated by the galaxy's supermassive black hole. If you look closely, you'll see it has fine structure—we didn't expect that, and we're working on theories of the phenomenon, but so far we don't have an explanation."

In his virtual display Martinez coasted closer to the great burning pillar of energy, and he saw the pillar pulse with light, saw strands of opalescent color weave and shift as they were caught in some vast incomprehensible flow of power, a hypnotic dance of colossal force.

For the next hour Shon-dan showed Martinez and Terza features within the galactic core, including the four giant stars now in a swift death spiral around the central black hole. "The black hole is feeding now," he said. "Sometimes the supermassive black holes are actively involved in devouring neighboring stars and sometimes they aren't. We don't know why or how they shift from one state to another."

"Nasty, as I said," said Lord Pa. "I have to say that I prefer nature a good deal less chaotic and destructive. I like games with rules. I like comfortable chairs, compound interest, and a guaranteed annual profit. I prefer not to think of some cosmic accident about to jump out of hiding and suck all my comforts right out of the universe."

"We're perfectly safe from the black hole, my lord," Shon-dan said. "We're nowhere near the danger zone."

Martinez quietly turned off the virtual display to take a look at Lord Pa. He sat in a Lai-own chair that cradled his breastbone, and was bent over the room's game board. The light from the display shone up on his face, on the short muzzle and deep red eyes.

Behind Pa the yellow chesz wood panels, inset with red enjo in abstract designs, glowed in the recessed lights of the lounge. A heavy crystal goblet sat near one hand, filled with Lai-own protein broth.

Comforts, Martinez thought. *Guaranteed profit.* Right.

"Perhaps we should break for now," Shon-dan said. He had noticed Martinez leaving the virtual display.

"Thank you," Terza said. "That was breathtaking. I hope we can do it again."

"I'd be delighted," Shon-dan said, rising. She was a Lai-own, with golden eyes, and wore a formal academic uniform of dark brown with several medals of scholastic distinction. She was young for all her honors, and the feathery side-hairs on her head were still a youthful brown.

"We have another twenty-three days to Chee," she said, "and the stars will be there the entire time."

"Perhaps tomorrow," Martinez said.

He rose from his couch and walked to the bar, where he poured himself a brandy. He idled toward Lord Pa, who was still bent over his game. Martinez scanned the board, spotted at once the move that Lord Pa should make, and began to point it out before he decided not to.

On the twentieth day of the voyage, *Kayenta*'s passengers were beginning to get on each other's nerves a little.

The first part of the trip had been as pleasant and social as possible, given that Martinez suspected one of the party of stealing from his family. Marcella, Lord Pa, Martinez, Terza, and Shon-dan had dined together each day. Tingo and other games had been suggested, but interest in gambling waned after it became clear that Terza and Martinez weren't interested in playing for high stakes, and that Shon-dan's academic salary didn't allow her to play even for what passed for small change amid Peers.

The conversation during and after meals had ranged far and wide, though Terza had cautioned Martinez about raising the kind of questions he burned to ask, detailed questions about the financial arrangements between the Cree and Meridian companies. "It will sound like an interrogation," she said.

Martinez confined himself to a few mild queries per day, beginning with broad questions about the progress of the Chee settlements, then going into more detail as the conversation developed. Marcella and Pa seemed pleased enough to talk about their work, and Martinez found himself genuinely interested in the technical details, though Martinez made a point of breaking off when he saw a slight frown on Terza's face, or felt the soft touch of her hand on his thigh.

Shon-dan talked about astronomical subjects. Martinez told his war stories. Terza avoided the subject of her work at the Ministry, but spoke of High City society, and brought out her harp and played a number of sonatas.

But now, by the twentieth day, the conversations had grown a little listless. Marcella spent much time in her cabin, working on Cree Company business, smoking endless cigarettes, and playing spiky, nerve-jabbing music that rattled her cabin door in its frame. Lord Pa received and sent detailed memoranda to his crews on Cree, and otherwise spent a lot of time puzzling over his game board.

Martinez sent frequent videos to his son—the three months aboard *Wi-hun* with a small and lively child had been challenging enough for all concerned, so Young Gareth had been left on Laredo with his nursemaid and his doting grandparents. The videos that Martinez received in return were full of excitement, for Lord Martinez had introduced his grandson to his collection of vintage automobiles, and had been roaring around on his private track with Young Gareth as a passenger.

"Gareth's favorite is the Lodi Turbine Express," Martinez told Terza. "At his age I liked that one myself, though I liked the Scarlet Messenger better." And then, at her look, said, "My father hasn't had an accident yet, you know."

"I'll try to be reassured," Terza said. She had just come from her dressing room, where she'd prepared for bed: her black hair had been brushed till it glowed and then tied with ribbon, and her face was scrubbed of cosmetics and softly sheened with health. Over her nightgown she wore a bed jacket that crackled with gold brocade.

After Shon-dan's astronomical exhibition they'd retired to their suite, glossy light behl wood paneling veined in blood-red, a video screen in a lacy Rakthan frame, a bathtub hacked out of a single block of chocolate-brown marble and which—to avoid gooseflesh on entering—was warmed by hidden heating elements of a vaguely sonic nature.

"My father could have worse hobbies," Martinez pointed out. "Racing pai-car chariots, say."

Her eyes narrowed. "I'll try to keep that in mind, too."

Twenty days on the small vessel had, perhaps, begun to unravel slightly the serenity that Terza carried with her, the unearthly tranquility that Martinez had come to admire as her greatest accomplishment. He rose from his chair and stood behind her, his big hands working through the crisp silk of her jacket to loosen her shoulder muscles. She sighed and relaxed against him.

"You miss Gareth, don't you?" he asked.

"Yes. Of course."

"So do I."

They had not spent so much time apart from the boy since he had been born.

"This has got to be dull for you," Martinez said. "Maybe we should have left you on Laredo."

"Dull?" Her tone was amused. "Reviewing contracts in hopes of discovering hidden felonies? Surely not."

He smiled. "Won't it be exciting if you actually find one?"

"But I won't find one. Not in the contracts. Lawyers have been all over the contracts to make sure no hint of impropriety will be found. If there's anything to be found, it will be in interpretation and practice."

He hadn't been able to obtain any of the contracts that the Cree Company had signed with their prime contractor—neither he nor Terza nor Roland were officers of the company. But in his capacity as Lord Inspector he'd acquired the entire file of the dealings the Meridian Company had with the Fleet, for building Fleet installations on Cree and in Cree orbit. But Martinez hadn't enough experience to understand the contracts particularly well, and so Terza had been pressed into the job.

"Escalator clauses are always suspect, and the contracts have plenty of them," Terza said. "On a big job there are always a thousand places to hide illegitimate expenses, and *this* job is literally as big as a planet. Meridian is allowed to revise the estimates if unexpected conditions cause their own costs to rise, and there are *always* unexpected conditions. A little to the right, please."

Martinez obliged. "Surely they can't jack up their expenses forever," he said.

"No. In the case of the Fleet contracts, the local Fleet representative has to agree that the rises are justified."

"According to the records she almost always did," Martinez said.

"And now she's received her captaincy and has been posted to the Fourth Fleet, so I won't be able to ask her any questions."

Amusement returned to Terza's voice. "I'm sure that if you saw her, she would of course immediately inform you of any unjustified cost overrides that she'd personally approved. I think you're better off with the new commander. He won't be obliged to defend his predecessor's expenses." She stretched, raising her arms over her head, torquing her spine left and right. Martinez could feel the muscles flex beneath his fingertips.

He left off his massage as she bent forward, flexing her spine again, pressing her palms to the deep pile carpet. She straightened, sighed, turned to face him.

"Thank you," she said. She put her arms around him, pillowed her head on his chest. "This could still be a pleasant vacation, you know."

I've been on vacation for three years, he wanted to say. Digging around in old Fleet construction contracts was the most useful thing he'd done in ages.

But he knew what Terza meant. "I'll try to remember to look at the stars now and again," he said.

Her arms tightened around him. "I had thought we might make good use of the time."

Martinez smiled. "I have no objection."

Terza drew her head back, her dark eyes raised to his. "That's not *entirely* what I meant," she said. "I thought we might give Gareth a brother or sister."

A rush of sensation took his breath away. Martinez's marriage had been arranged, not an uncommon phenomenon among Peers—and in Martinez's case, Roland had arranged the marriage with a crowbar. For all that Martinez had genuinely wanted a child, Young Gareth had been arranged as well. Martinez knew perfectly well that Terza had been lowering herself to marry him—Lord Chen required significant financial help from the Martinez clan at the time—and Martinez had always wondered just what Terza had thought of the long-armed provincial officer she'd been constrained, on only a few hours' acquaintance, to marry.

Wondered, but never asked. He never asked questions when he

knew the answers might draw him into sadness.

He had watched with increasing pleasure as Terza floated into his life, supported by that quality of serenity that was, perhaps, just a bit too eerily perfect. He had never been completely certain what might happen if Lord Chen, his finances recovered, ordered his daughter to divorce. It was always possible that she would leave her marriage with the same unearthly tranquility with which she'd entered it. He had never known precisely what was going on behind that composed, lovely face.

Until now. A second child was not part of the contract between their families.

He and Terza were writing their own codicil to the contract, right now.

"Of course," Martinez said, when he got his breath back. "Absolutely. At once, if possible."

She smiled. "At once isn't quite an option," she said. "I'll have to get the implant removed first. *Kayenta*'s doctor can do it, or we can wait till we get to Chee." She kissed his cheek. "Though I'd hate to waste the next twenty-three days."

Kayenta's doctor was a sour, elderly Lai-own who had scarcely been seen since the beginning of the journey, when he gave the obligatory lecture about weightlessness, acceleration, and space-sickness. Whatever the quirks of his personality, however, he was presumably competent at basic procedures for interspecies medicine.

"I think you should see the old fellow first thing tomorrow," Martinez said. "But that doesn't mean we should waste tonight."

Her look was direct. "I hadn't intended to," she said.

Hours later, before the forenoon watch, Martinez woke from sleep with a start, with a cry frozen on his lips. Terza, her perfect tranquility maintained, slept on, her head pillowed on his chest.

He hadn't had one of these dreams in at least two months. For a moment, blinking in the darkness of *Kayenta*'s guest suite, he had seen not Terza's black hair spread on his chest, but hair of white gold, framing a pale face with blazing emerald eyes.

His heart thundered in his chest. Martinez could hear his own breath rasping in his throat.

There were other reasons why he hadn't inquired what Terza thought of their marriage.

He had his own secrets. It seemed only fair that he allow Terza to keep hers.

The cable of the elevator descended from geostationary orbit, a line that disappeared into the deep green of the planet's equator like a fishing line fading into the sea. On the approach, what the monitors showed Martinez of the elevator itself was a pale gray tower of shaped asteroid and lunar material, the massive counterweight to the cable. The tower terminated in a series of sculpted peaks that looked like battlements, but which were actually a kind of jigsaw mechanism to lock additional weights into place should they be needed.

Ships docked at the elevator terminus at the base of the tower, in zero gravity. Passengers then traveled down a weightless tube to the hub of the residential and commercial areas of the station, where they could shift laterally to either one of two fat rotating wheels of white laminate that contained living quarters for workers, Fleet personnel, Shon-dan's astronomers, and anyone in transit from Chee to anywhere else.

Martinez thanked Marcella and Lord Pa for the ride on *Kayenta* before they left the ship, since he knew that once he transferred to the station, the awesome role of Lord Inspector would descend on him, and a long series of rigid protocols would take place.

Which in fact they did. As soon as Martinez floated out of the docking tube, one white-gloved hand on the guide rope that had been strung from the tube into the bay, he heard the bellow of petty officers calling the honor guard to attention, and the public address system boomed out "Our Thoughts Are Ever Guided by the Praxis," one of the Fleet's snappier marching tunes.

The honor guard were all Lai-own Military Constabulary in full dress, with the toes of their shoes tucked under an elastic strap that had been stretched along the deck to keep everyone properly lined up in zero gravity. Standing before them, braced at the salute, was Lieutenant Captain Lord Ehl Tir-bal, who commanded the station, and his staff.

Lord Ehl was young, and short for a Lai-own—he and Martinez could almost look level into one another's eyes. Lord Ehl introduced his staff, and then turned to the cadaverous civilian who stood behind the party of officers.

"My lord," he said, "may I introduce Meridian Company's chief engineer, Mister Ledo Allodorm."

"Mister Allodorm," Martinez said, and nodded.

"An honor to meet you, my lord." Allodorm's face, like those of all Daimong, was permanently fixed in the round-eyed, open-mouthed stare that a Terran could read either as surprise or terror or existential anguish. His voice was a lovely tenor that sounded like a pair of trumpets playing in soft harmony, and Martinez could see his soft mouth parts working behind the gray, fixed bony lips as he spoke.

Martinez performed a ritual inspection of the honor guard, after which Martinez, Terza, their servants and and their baggage were loaded into a long, narrow viridian-green vehicle that would carry them to their lodging. Lord Ehl and Allodorm both joined them, and Ehl pointed out the features of the station as, on little puffs of air, the vehicle rose and began its journey down the docking bay.

The post of Chee's station commander was Lord Ehl's first major assignment, and his delight in his new command showed. He pointed out the features of the station, which was fresh and glossy and, to Martinez's mind, rather overdesigned. Every feature, from the cargo loaders to the computer-operated ductwork on the air vents, was of the largest, brightest, most efficient type available.

"The air purifying and circulation systems are custom designed," Ehl said. "So is the power plant."

"We didn't just take a thousand-year-old design off the shelf," Allodorm said. "Everything on this station was rethought from basics."

Custom design is very expensive, Martinez thought. "It's very impressive," he said. "I'm not used to seeing new stations."

"The first new station in nine hundred years," Allodorm said. "And now that the Convocation's begun opening new systems to expansion, we can expect to see many more."

"You've done all this in a little over two years," Martinez said. "That's fast work."

And awfully fast for such custom work. Perhaps, he thought, it wasn't custom after all.

How would anyone know? No one had built an orbital station in eons. You could take an old standard design and change a few minor specifications and call it custom work.

All he knew was that, even if the circulation system was custom designed, the air smelled the same as it did on every other station he'd ever been on.

The vehicle jetted down the connecting tube to the hub of the two wheels, where it entered a large elevator and began to descend toward the living areas. "You'll be the first occupant of the Senior Officers' Quarters," Ehl said. "There will be a full staff on hand to look after you. Please let one of them—or me—know if anything is unsatisfactory."

Gravity began to tug with greater insistence at Martinez's inner ear. "Thank you, lord elcap," Martinez said. "I'm sure everything will be satisfactory."

One full gravity had been restored by the time the elevator reached the main level of Wheel Number One. The staff of the Senior Officers' Quarters were lined up by the exit, as if for inspection. Ehl gave an order, and the staff scurried to the vehicle to unload the luggage and to help Terza and Martinez from their seats. The luggage was placed on motorized robot carts, and Martinez and Terza walked followed by the carts and Lord Ehl and the staff and Allodorm.

"My lord," Allodorm said, "I hope you and Lady Terza will accept the hospitality of the Meridian Company, two nights from now. The company's executive and engineering staff would be honored to meet you."

"We'd be delighted," Martinez said.

Lord Ehl and the Fleet officers on station were dining with him tomorrow night, and he'd already been sent a rather ambitious schedule involving trips to various Fleet installations. He recognized Ehl's plan well enough, which was to keep him so busy going from place to place, viewing one engineering wonder after another, and receiving toast after toast at banquets, that he would have precious little time to do any actual inspections. There wasn't necessarily anything sinister in this scheme—it was the sort of thing Martinez might do himself, were he in charge of an installation and saw a Lord Inspector bearing down on him.

Ahead was the bright new corridor, curving only slightly upward, walls that looked as if they were made of pale ceramic, lighting recessed into the tented ceiling. Martinez looked down at the polymerized flooring beneath their feet. It was a dark gray and rubbery, giving slightly under his shoes, the standard flooring for an installation of this type.

"There was some confusion with this flooring, as I recall?" Martinez asked. His review of the Fleet contracts had told him that much.

"Yes, Lord Inspector, there was," Allodorm said in his beautiful voice. "A consequence of our *not* rethinking something—we hadn't worried about anything so basic as station flooring. But when we looked at the standard station flooring we'd ordered, we found that it was inadequate to the stresses of a developing station, the vehicle traffic and weights we'd have to move along in these corridors. We'd have to replace it all within ten years, and of course we couldn't afford to shut down the station to do that, not with our deadlines. So we had to special order new flooring from Zarafan, and ship it out by high-gee express."

"That Torminel crew must have knocked years off their lives getting it here," Ehl said, and made a deliberate, shivering motion of his hands—his hollow-boned species abhorred high gravities.

"Well," said Martinez, "at least the problem was corrected."

He tried to sound offhand, and he wondered how he could get underneath the flooring to take a look at it.

The Senior Officers' Quarters were as overdesigned as the rest of the station, with dark wood paneling and polished brass fittings. Aquaria glowed turquoise along the walls, filled with exotic fish from the planet below, and below the tall ceilings hung chandeliers that looked like ice sculptures. Everything smelled new. Ehl and Allodorm retired to allow their visitors to "recover from the rigors of the journey," as if traveling forty-three days by private yacht were as taxing as crossing a mountain range on the back of a mule.

That left Terza and Martinez alone in the entrance hall, standing on the wood parquet that formed a map of the empire, with Chee a small disk of green malachite and Zanshaa, the capital, a blood-red garnet.

They looked at each other. "They've given us separate bedrooms," Terza said.

"I noticed."

"I'll have Fran move my things into your room, if that's all right."

"Please," Martinez said. "That huge room would be lonely without you."

Their palace in Zanshaa High City didn't have bedrooms as large. The Fleet must have paid a pretty penny for these accommodations, but on the other hand the Fleet wasn't exactly known for depriving its officers of their comforts.

There was an hour or so before dinner. Martinez had his orderly, Alikhan, find him some casual civilian clothes, and he changed and left his quarters through the kitchen entrance, surprising the cooks who were preparing his meal.

This was a free hour on his schedule. He might as well make use of it.

He walked to one of the personnel elevators, then went to the unfinished wheel. He found an area still under construction, where Torminel workers straddled polycarbon beams just beyond portable barriers, working on pipes and ducts, and the flooring waited on huge spools taller than a Lai-own. Martinez quietly made some measurements, then ventured across the barriers to the point where the flooring dropped away to reveal an expanse of plastic sheeting, followed by open beams and the workers.

If the Torminel noticed Martinez making his measurements, they gave no sign. Martinez finished his task and returned to his quarters.

"Not custom-made, not at all," Martinez said over dinner. "They're just laying a second layer of the standard flooring over the first." He raised a glass and sipped some of the Fleet's excellent emerald Hy-oso wine. "The Meridian Company's pocketing the money for all that flooring."

"I'd suggest not," Terza said. "I think the flooring exists. That express ship came out here with *something*. I think the flooring's been diverted to another project, one owned one hundred percent by the Meridian Company."

"I wonder how many people *know*," Martinez said.

"Quite a few, probably," Terza said. "Not the work gangs, who I imagine just do what they're told. You can't do corruption on this scale without a good many people figuring it out. But I'm sure the company keeps them happy one way or another."

"Does Lord Ehl know, I wonder?" Martinez asked. "He'd have to be remarkably incurious not to notice what's happening with the flooring, but perhaps he *is* incurious."

Terza gave Martinez a significant look. "I suggest you not ask him," she said.

Martinez looked at his plate and considered his roast fristigo lying in its sauce of onions and kistip berries. The berries and vegetables were fresh, a delight after forty-three days without—the settlements must have got agriculture underway. "I wish we knew who owns the Meridian Company. But it's privately held, and the exchanges don't know because it's not publicly traded . . ." He let the thought fade away. "As Lord Inspector I could demand the information, but I might not get it, and it's an indiscreet way of conducting an investigation."

"Lord Pa must be one of the owners, and very likely the whole Maq-fan clan is involved," Terza said. "But unless we get access to the confidential records of whatever planet the company's chartered on, we're sunk . . . " She looked thoughtful. "You know, I *could* find out."

Martinez turned to her. "How?" he said.

"Meridian does business with the Fleet, and law requires them to give the Ministry a list of their principal owners. The names are supposed to remain confidential, but—" She gazed upward into a distant corner of the room. "I'm trying to think who I could ask."

"Your father," Martinez pointed out. "He's on the Fleet Control Board, he should have the authority to get the information."

Terza shook her head. "He couldn't do it discreetly. An inquiry from the Control Board is like firing an antimatter missile from orbit." She smiled. "Or like a command from a Lord Inspector. People would notice." She gazed up into the corner again for a long moment.

"Bernardo, then," she decided. "He's got access and is reasonably discreet. But I'll owe him a *big* favor."

"Ten days for the query to get to Zanshaa," Martinez said. "Another ten days for the answer to return."

The communication would leap from system to system at the speed of light, but Martinez still felt a burning impatience at the delay.

A smile quirked its way across Terza's face. "I've never seen you work before. Half the time you're frantic with impatience, and the rest of the time you're marching around giving orders like a little king. It's actually sort of fascinating."

Martinez raised his eyebrows at this description of himself, but said, "I hope you can manage to sustain the fascination a little longer."

"I think I'll manage."

Martinez reached across the corner of the table to take her hand. Terza leaned toward him to kiss his cheek. Her voice came low to his ear. "My doctor once told me that a woman's at her most fertile in the month following the removal of her implant. I think we've proved him right. For the second time."

He felt his skin prickle with sudden heat as delight flared along his nerves. "Are you sure?" he asked.

"Well, no," Terza said, "I'm not. But I feel the same way I felt last time, and I think experience counts in these things."

"It definitely should," Martinez said.

Fecundity, he thought. What more could a man want?

———

"The harbor looks a little bare," Martinez said. He sat, awaiting breakfast, beneath an umbrella on the terrace of the Chee Fishing Club, where he had been given an honorary membership, and where he and Terza were staying. No Fleet accommodation on the ground had been judged worthy of a Lord Inspector, and the only deluxe lodgings on the planet were at the club—conveniently owned by Martinez's father, a part of a sport-fishing scheme.

"The commercial fishing boats are out, and the shuttles aren't coming in any longer," the manager said. He was a Terran, with a beard dyed purple and twined in two thin braids. He wore a jacket with padded shoulders and of many different fabrics, all in bright tropical colors, stitched together in a clashing melee of brilliant pigment. Martinez hadn't seen anyone else similarly dressed, and he suspected the manager's style was peculiar to him alone.

Steam rose as the manager freshened Martinez's coffee. "Without the shuttles we've just got a small fishing fleet and just a few sport boats," he said, "though more will come in time. We can build up an enormous fishery here—though we may have to export most of the catch, since everyone here ate nothing but fish for the first year and a half, and they're all sick of it."

Martinez gazed down a lawn-green slope at three bobbing boats dwarfed by the huge gray concrete quay against which they were moored. Two flew Fishing Club ensigns, and another a private flag, probably that of an official in the Meridian or Chee companies. Across the harbor was the town of Port Vipsania, named after one of Martinez's sisters, and beyond that, stretching up into the sky, was the cable that ran to geosynchronous orbit and Chee Station.

Port Vipsania, like all the early settlements, was built on the sea, because before the skyhook had gone into operation the previous year, workers and their gear had been brought to the planet in shuttles powered by chemical rockets, shuttles that had landed on the open water and then taxied to a mooring. Supplies, too, had been dropped into the sea in unmanned containers braked with retro-rockets, then towed to shore by workers in boats. The huge resinous containers, opened, also served as temporary shelters and warehouses.

Once the skyhook could bring people and cargo from orbit at much less expense, the shuttles were largely discontinued, though Port Gareth, in the north and as yet unconnected to the expanding rail network, was still supplied by shuttles and containers dropped down from orbit.

A bare three years after the opening of the planet to exploitation, the Chee settlements were growing with incredible speed, fueled by even more incredible amounts of capital. The investment was vast, and as the work had only begun the inflow of capital would have to continue. Lord Mukerji's work in attracting ceaseless investment was vital, as was the work of many lesser envoys, and of course the work of Lord Martinez himself, raising funds from his own considerable resources.

The resources of a whole planet were more than enough to repay any investment over time, but the scale of the payouts ran in years, and mismanagement and theft were still dangers to the Chee Company. If investor confidence were lost the company could go bankrupt whether it owned a planet or not . . .

"I'd like to see a fleet of boats on that quay," Martinez said.

"So would I," the manager said. "The business would be a lot better." He grinned. "And after all the trouble building that quay, I'd like to see it in use."

"Trouble?" Martinez asked.

"They shipped down the wrong kind of cement for that pier," the manager said. "They need De-loq cement, that sets underwater and is immune to salt-water corrosion. But they sent down the ordinary stuff, and a special shipment had to be made from Laredo."

"What did they do with the other cement?" Martinez asked.

"Condemned," the manager said. "They couldn't use it. Ah— here's your breakfast."

Martinez's breakfast arrived, a grilled fish with needle-sharp teeth, a pair of eyes on each end, and plates of armor expertly peeled back from the flesh. Martinez's eyes rose from the fish to Port Vipsania, to the rows of white concrete apartments that held the Meridian Company's workers.

"Pity they couldn't find a use for it," he said.

Martinez found that he couldn't resist the lure of the town his father had named after him. After ten days on Chee, Martinez escaped the endless round of formal banquets and receptions by taking a Fleet coleopter to Port Gareth, north in the temperate zone.

The coleopter carried him over land that was a uniform green— while the oceans thronged with a staggering variety of fish, life on land was primitive and confined to a few basic types: the only fauna were worms and millipedes, and plants were confined to molds, fungus, and a wide variety of fern, some as tall as a two-storied building.

All of which were going to face stiff competition, as alien plants and animals were being introduced in abundance. Herds of portschen, fristigo, sheep, bison, and cattle had been landed and allowed more or less to run wild. Without any predators to cull their numbers, the herds were growing swiftly.

Vast farms, largely automated, had also been set up in the interior, upriver from the settlements, or along the expanding railroads. Because no one yet knew what would grow, the farms were simply planting *everything,* far more than the population could conceivably need. If things went reasonably well, the planet could become a grain exporter very quickly and start earning a bit of profit for the Chee Corporation.

Within a couple of centuries, it was calculated, the only native plants a person would see would probably be in a museum.

The coleopter bounded over a range of mountains that kept Port Gareth isolated from the rest of the continent, then dropped over a rich plain that showed rivers of gleaming silver curling amid the green fern forest. The coleopter fell toward a green-blue ocean that began to creep over the horizon, and then began to fly over cultivated fields, the sun winking off the clear canopies of the harvesters.

Port Gareth was very possibly outside the mandate of a Lord Inspector, as it contained no Fleet installations, but Martinez had decided that the railroad that would connect the town to the settlements farther south was a matter of state security, and therefore of interest to the Fleet.

The turbine shrouds on the ends of the aircraft's wings rotated, and the craft began to descend. On the edge of the pad was yet another reception committee.

The coleopter's wide cargo door rolled open. Martinez took off his headset, thanked the pilot, and stepped out onto the landing pad. The brisk wind tore at his hair. As Alikhan stepped from the coleopter with Martinez's luggage, the reception committee advanced behind the Lady Mayor, a client of the Martinez family who Martinez vaguely remembered from childhood. She was a Torminel, whose gray and black fur was more suitable to the bracing climate of Port Gareth than to the tropics of Port Vipsania.

In short order Martinez was introduced to the Mayor's Council, and the local representatives of the Meridian and Chee companies, and then a familiar figure stepped forward from the long, teardrop-shaped car.

"Remember me, my lord?" the man leered.

Martinez could hardly forget. Ahmet had been a rigger on *Corona*, Martinez's first command. He had spent a considerable portion of the commission under arrest or doing punishment duty; and the rest of his time had been occupied with running illegal gambling games, brewing illicit liquor, and performing the occasional bit of vandalism.

"Ahmet," Martinez said. "You're out of the Fleet, I see."

This was only good news for the Fleet.

"I'm a foreman here on the railroad project," Ahmet said. "When I heard you were coming, I told everyone I knew you, and asked to be part of the welcoming committee." With one sleeve he buffed the shiny object pinned to his chest. "I still have the *Corona* medal, as you see. I've been assigned as your guide and driver."

To Martinez, their employment of Ahmet in a position of responsibility was proof enough of criminal negligence or worse. But he smiled as stoutly as he could, said "Good to see you," and was then carried off toward his lodging in the Mayor's Palace, after which he would endure yet another banquet. He had a healthy respect for himself that some considered conceit, but even so he was beginning to grow weary of all these meals in his honor.

Still, he was pleased to discover a statue of himself in the main square, looking stern and carrying the Golden Orb. He was less pleased to see a pump jack in the overgrown green park behind the statue, its flywheel spinning brightly in the sun.

"What's that?" he asked. "Petroleum?"

"Yes," the Lady Mayor said. "We found it close to the surface here—lucky, otherwise we couldn't have brought it up with the equipment we've got."

"What do you use it for?"

"Plastics. We'll have a whole industry running here in a few years."

"How is the railroad progressing?"

The railroad would eventually connect Port Gareth to the south: supersonic trains would speed north from the skyhook, bringing migrants and supplies, and carrying away produce and plastic products for export. The rails were being laid from each end toward a common center, and would meet somewhere in the mountains.

"There were some delays last month," the Lady Mayor said. "But the track's still ahead of schedule."

"Delays?" Martinez said. "There's nothing the Fleet can do to expedite matters, is there?"

"Very kind, but no. It turned out that the early geologists' reports were incorrect, or maybe just incomplete. The engineers encountered a much harder layer of rock than they'd expected, and it held up the work for some time."

Martinez decided that though he didn't know much about geology, he was going to learn.

Next morning Martinez rose early, took the cup of coffee that his orderly handed him, and called Ahmet.

"I'd like to get up to the railhead," he said. "Can you do it?"

"Absolutely, my lord."

"I also don't want a fuss. I'm tired of delegations. Can we go, just the two of us, with you as my guide?"

Martinez sensed a degree of personal triumph in Ahmet's reply. "Of course, lord captain! That's easier than anything!"

The ride to the railhead was made on a train bringing out supplies, and Martinez spent the ride in the car reserved for the transport crews. He wore civilian clothes and heavy boots, which he thought disappointed Ahmet, who wanted a fully dressed military hero to show off to his colleagues. As it was, Martinez had to put up with Ahmet's loud reminiscences of the *Corona* and the battle of Hone-bar, which managed to imply that Martinez, under Ahmet's brilliant direction, had managed to polish off the Naxids in time for breakfast.

"That's when we swung onto our new heading and dazzled the Naxids with our engine flares, so they couldn't see our supports," Ahmet said, and then gave Martinez a confidential wink. "Isn't that right, my lord?"

"Yes," Martinez said. And then, peering out the window, "What's up ahead?"

The track for the supersonic train was necessarily nearly straight and quite level. It approached the mountains on huge ramps, built by equally huge machines and pierced with archways for rivers and future roads. Terraces had been gouged into mountains to provide the necessarily wide roadbed, and tunnels bored through solid rock. The gossamer-seeming bridges that spanned distant valleys were, on closer inspection, built of trusses wider than a bus and cables the thickness of Martinez's leg. The trains themselves, floating on magnetic fields above the rails, would be equipped with vanes that canceled out their sonic shockwave, but even so the tunnels had to be lined with baffles and sound suppressors to keep the mountain from being shaken down.

At the railhead Martinez was treated to a view of the giant drilling machine that bored the tunnel, and the other machines that cleared the rubble, braced the tunnel, and laid the track. The machines were sophisticated enough, and their operators experienced enough, that everyone seemed confident that their tunnel would meet the northbound crews, coming from the other side of the mountain, well ahead of schedule.

"So we can earn that big completion bonus from the Chee Company," Ahmet grinned. "Isn't that right, my lord?"

"Good for you," Martinez said. He waited for a moment alone with Ahmet before he asked the next question.

"Wasn't there a big delay a month or so ago? Can we stop there on our way back?"

Ahmet gave Martinez a wink. "Let me talk to the engine driver."

They took a ride back on a small engine that was shuttling rails to the construction site, and the Lai-own driver was amenable to a brief delay. "Marker 593," Ahmet told him, and the engine slowed and braked. Ahmet, an electric lantern in his hand, hopped off into the dark tunnel, and Martinez heard a splash.

"Careful, my lord," Ahmet said. "It's a bit damp here."

Martinez lowered himself to the roadbed and followed the bobbing lantern. Upheaval of the mountain range had tipped the geologic strata nearly vertical here. "They called it a pluton, or a laccolith, or something like that," Ahmet said. "Whatever it is, it's damn hard. The drill couldn't get through it. There it is." He brandished the lantern.

A deep gray stripe lay along the strata, a river of mica flecks gleaming in the lantern like a river of stars. "That's *it*?" Martinez asked. He could span the layer with his two arms. Whatever this was, it wasn't a pluton.

"Yes, my lord. They had to do a redesign of the drill head."

Couldn't they blast it? Martinez bit back the question.

Of course they could have blasted, he thought; but explosives wouldn't have added a hefty enough overcharge. Then Martinez remembered, during the party held in his honor at Rio Hondo, a conversation between Lords Pa and Mukerji. Something about the geologist's report . . .

Suddenly Martinez wondered if Mukerji—the plunging gambler—had been the Chee Company official responsible for approving the cost overruns. He was president of the company, after all; very possibly he could approve such things.

But Mukerji had never been to Chee—the requests would have had to chase him all over the empire as he went off on his quests for funds. Mukerji had never been to Chee, and wouldn't have been available to fill most spending requests.

Unless . . . unless Mukerji was part of the conspiracy. Receiving payments from the conspirators in order to relieve his gambling debts.

"Interesting," Martinez said.

Ahmet's eyes glittered in the lamplight, the admiration of one thief and confidence man for a job well and professionally done. "Fascinating," he said, "isn't it? Geology?"

The question was how to reveal to Eggfont the relationship between Lord Mince and Lady Belledrawers. If Eggfont was told by the valet Cadaver, that would tell Eggfont something about Cadaver that for the present should remain hidden. Yet how else could Eggfont find out in time for the Grand Ball . . . ?

A token, Severin thought. A mysterious token, which Eggfont would understand but which would be opaque to anyone else. But introduced by *who*?

Severin tapped Lady Liao's ring on the arm of his couch in slow accompaniment to his thoughts. He had to admit that his invention was flagging. It was three hours past midnight in *Surveyor*'s official twenty-nine-hour day, and Severin was tired. He could call for a cup of coffee from the wardroom, he supposed, but that would mean waking up someone.

Perhaps Severin should put his puppet show aside and find something else to occupy his thoughts. Commanding the ship, for instance.

Surveyor's control room featured the usual stations, for navigation, for controlling the engines, for communications, for the captain and the pilot and the sensor tech. Each station featured a couch balanced carefully in its acceleration cage, and each couch was equipped with a hinged control board that could lock down in front of the occupant.

At the moment the sensor station was occupied by a very bored Warrant Officer Second Class Chamcha, and the screen that occupied his desultory attention wasn't tuned to the spectacular starscapes of Chee's system, but to a game called Mindsprain, which he was losing through inattention. The sensor station had only been crewed because regulations required it, just as regulations required someone at the engine station, at the moment Lily Bhagwati, another at communications—Signaler Trainee Jaye Nkomo—and yet another, qualified to stand watches, in the captain's couch—Severin himself.

Severin's watch had finished the hour out of each watch for hard acceleration, and breakfast was still hours away. Severin's attention drifted vaguely over the smiling pictures of Lord Go's family that the captain had attached to the command board—the captain was lenient that way, and each station in the control room was decorated with personal items belonging to the various crew who served at that station. Pictures of family, notes from loved ones, paper flowers, jokes, poems, pictures of actors and singers and models, someone pretty to dream about when you were three months away from the nearest ring station.

Severin realized that he'd been staring for many minutes at Lord Go's family, the smiling wife and waving children, proud parents, the pet dog and the stuffed Torminel doll. He raised his head, shook it violently to clear his mind, and scanned the other stations. Nothing seemed to warrant his attention. No alarms sounded, no violent colors flashed on the displays.

He called up Warrant Officer Chamcha's game onto his own display, saw the comprehensive rate at which Chamcha was losing, and sighed. Perhaps when Chamcha conceded, he'd challenge Chamcha to a game of hyper-tourney, or something. Anything to keep awake.

While waiting for Chamcha's position to collapse he called up the navigation screen. *Surveyor,* heading straight from Wormhole One to

Wormhole Two, was well outside of the normal trade routes that ended at Chee.

No navigational hazards threatened.

Severin looked at Chamcha. Hadn't he lost *yet?*

Something flashed on the sensor screens, and Severin looked down at his display, just as the lights and the display itself went off, then on . . .

"Status check!" Severin shouted, as the lights dimmed, then flashed bright again.

Warrant Officer Lily Bhagwati gave a sudden galvanic leap on her acceleration couch. There were shrill panicky highlights in her voice. "Power spike on Main Bus One! Spike on Main Bus Two!"

Severin's fingers flashed to his display, tried to get the ship's system display onto his board.

The lights went off, then returned. The image on Severin's displays twisted, slowed.

How very interesting, he thought distinctly.

"Breaker trip on Main Bus One!" Bhagwati said. "Main engine trip! Emergency power!"

Whatever was happening to the ship was happening too fast for Bhagwati's reports to keep up. Automatic circuits were responding to protect themselves faster than the Terran crew could possibly act. Severin did catch the words "main engine trip" and had time to register their impact before the all-pervading rumble of the engine ceased, and he began to drift free of his couch.

He reached for his webbing to lash himself in and every light and every display in the room went dark, leaving him in pitch blackness save for the afterimage of his displays slowly fading from his retinas.

"Emergency Circuit One breaker trip!" Bhagwati shouted unnecessarily.

In the ensuing silence Severin heard the distant whisper of the ventilation slowly fade, like the last sigh of a dying man.

This never happens, he told himself.

And because it never happened, there were no standard procedures to follow. An absolutely cold startup of all ship systems, including the ones that had been mysteriously damaged?

This also *never happens,* he thought.

"Everyone stay in your cages!" he said. "I don't want you drifting around in the dark."

He tapped Lady Liao's ring on the arm of his couch while he tried to think what to do next. Little flickers of light, like fireflies, indicated here and there where battery-powered flashlights waited in their chargers. They weren't intended for emergencies, since the emergency lighting wasn't supposed to fail, but rather for getting light into odd corners of the displays that were undergoing repair.

The flickering lights were inviting. Severin thought he should probably get a flashlight.

"I'm going to get a light," he said. "Everyone else stand by."

His fingers released the webbing that he'd never quite fastened down. Then he unlocked his display and pushed it above his head, out of the way, a maneuver that also pushed him more deeply into his couch. Now free, he reached out, found one of the struts of his cage, and tugged gently till his head and torso floated free of the cage.

With careful movements, he jackknifed to pull his legs out of the cage, a movement that rolled the cage slightly. He straightened his body and his feet contacted the floor.

He couldn't push off the floor to approach the flashlights: that would send him the wrong way. Instead he flung the acceleration cage with both hands, a movement that sent the cage spinning on all three axes while he drifted gently to the nearest wall. Severin reached out a hand and snagged the handle on the battery charger.

He became aware that he was breathing hard. Even this little exertion had taxed him.

There was a distant thump. Then another. Severin realized that someone outside the control room was pounding on the heavy shielded door, slowly and with great deliberation.

He released the flashlight from the charger that was designed to hold it at high gee. He turned it on and flashed it over the control room.

Three sets of eyes stared back at him. The others were awaiting his orders.

From outside the command room door, Severin began to hear the muffled sound of screams.

Screams could still be heard faintly through the door.

Severin shone his light on Chamcha long enough for the sensor operator to work his way out of his cage and push across the room toward another flashlight. Then he turned to the problem of the door. He pulled and locked down a handgrip installed for the purpose, then—floating on the end of the handgrip—opened an access panel, removed a light alloy crank, and inserted it into the door mechanism. With one hand on the grip, the flashlight stuck to the wall on an adhesive strip, and a foot braced against the bottom of an instrument panel, Severin began to crank the door open.

The screams had stopped. Severin didn't know whether to be encouraged by that or not.

By the time Severin had cranked open the heavy door he was puffing and throwing off beads of sweat that floated like drops of molten gold in the light. The control room crew clustered around him, hanging by fingertips onto cage struts or instrument displays, and their lights were turned to the outside corridor. Severin heard a series of gasps, and the single cry, "Lord captain!"

Severin looked out and saw Lord Go hanging weightless in the flashlight beams. He was wearing turquoise satin pajamas. His skin had turned bright red, and his eyes were hidden amid scarlet swellings. Large blisters were forming on his face and hands. His expression was slack.

Burns, Severin thought. But he saw no fire and could smell no burning.

"My lord!" Severin called. With one hand still on the grip, he swung himself toward Lord Go, reached out, and took his captain's hand. Another crew member, he saw, was hovering motionlessly a short distance down the corridor, and from the golden hair that floated in the absence of gravity he knew it was Lady Maxine Wellstone, the ship's junior lieutenant.

Severin drew Lord Go toward him by the hand, and his stomach queased at the slippery way the captain's flesh felt under his fingers—it felt *unattached,* as if he could peel the skin from Lord Go's hand like taking off a glove. He tried to brake Lord Go as gently as he could and brought him to a motionless halt just inside the door.

"Bhagwati," he said. "Tether the lord captain to an acceleration cage or something. Try not to touch him."

"Yes, my lord."

"Nkomo, go find the doctor and bring her here."

Surveyor's doctor was no doctor at all, but a Pharmacist First Class. She would have to do.

"Very good, my lord," Nkomo said. He made an agile dive into the corridor over Severin's head, and Severin pushed off to Nkomo's acceleration cage, where Lily Bhagwati was tethering Lord Go to a cage strut with her belt. Severin held himself a short distance from his captain's face, and tried not to look too closely at the scalded, weeping flesh.

"My lord," he said, "do you know what happened?"

Bloody eyes moved beneath the swollen lids. Lord Go sounded as if he were trying to talk past a tongue twice its normal size.

"Don't . . . know," he said.

"Was there a fire?"

"No . . . fire." Lord Go gave a long sigh. "Hurts," he said.

Severin bit his lip. "You're in pain, my lord?"

"Hurts," the captain said again.

"The doctor's on his way."

"Don't know," Lord Go said again, and then fell silent, lids falling on his dull eyes. His breathing was harsh. Severin looked at Bhagwati and saw his own anxiety mirrored in her wide brown eyes.

He had to get the ship working again.

"Right," he said. "Bhagwati, Chamcha, check the main breakers. We've got to get power on." He remembered the flash of blonde hair in the corridor outside. "I'm going to check on Lieutenant Wellstone."

He pushed off the floor with his fingers and drifted into the corridor outside. He tried not to look at Wellstone's burned, tortured face as he touched her neck in search of a pulse.

There was none. When he returned to the control room, he felt a tremor in his hands.

"My lord," Chamcha said as Severin returned to the command cage. "My lord, it's radiation."

Severin's heart turned over. He turned to Chamcha. "You were monitoring the sensors. Did you see the spectra?"

"I saw spikes, but I didn't get a clear idea of what was happening before everything blew out." Chamcha licked his lips. "But it's got to be radiation, my lord, not a fire. It's the only explanation."

Severin felt a cold finger touch his heart. Chamcha was right.

There were several areas on the ship that had heavy radiation shielding. The control room, and also engine control. There were also hardened radiation shelters where the crew could hide in the event of a solar flare, but they were small and crowded, and unless there was a radiation alert the crew never slept there.

"We'll look at the recordings once we get power," Severin said. "Get busy with the breakers."

"Yes, my lord."

Radiation, Severin thought. But what kind? And from what? They were alone in space, in transit from one wormhole to another, bypassing the one inhabited planet in the system. There were no other planets nearby, no stations, no other ships.

The electronic failures could be explained in terms of a solar flare. The fast protons fired out of a solar flare had a deadly habit of actually traveling along electric field lines until they could find something to blow up. But a solar flare so massive that it could knock out all electric systems in a ship the size of *Surveyor,* plus seriously irradiate any unshielded crew, and do it all in a very few seconds, had to be a solar flare larger than any recorded in history.

A solar flare so huge it might be ripping the atmosphere off Chee right now.

Such a flare, however, seemed very unlikely. Normally under a radiation alert the crew had plenty of time to get into their cramped shelters. Plus, *Surveyor* when underway generated an electric field from metallic strips planted along its resinous hull, a field intended to help repel any high-energy charged particles coming their way.

Which left uncharged particles . . .

"My lord!" Bhagwati called. She'd pulled her head out of a access hatch, and her face was angry. "These breakers are slagged. Whatever hit them destroyed them before they could even trip. We can't just reset them, they have to be replaced."

"Get replacements, then," Severin said.

Severin turned as he caught the gleam of a light dancing in the corridor outside. A grey-haired woman floated past the doorway, and reached out one hand to snag the doorsill in passing. The woman halted and drew her body into the control room, and Severin recognized Engineer First Class Mojtahed.

"Reporting, my lord," Mojtahed said. She was a burly, middle-aged, pot-bellied woman with her hair trimmed short and a prominent mole on one cheek. Severin felt relief at the very sight of her: at least one of the two principal engineers had been in the shielded engine control station when *Surveyor* had been hit.

"What's the situation?" Severin asked.

"A power spike tripped the engine," Mojtahed said. "We've reset breakers, and replaced some others, and I've ordered the engine countdown started. We're at something like twenty minutes."

"You've got enough power for that?"

"Emergency batteries are good, so far." She glanced around the darkened control room, and realized that Severin wasn't in any position to be able to command the ship, and wouldn't be for a while.

"We can stop the countdown at any point," she said.

"Hold at one minute, then."

"Yes, my lord."

Severin looked at her. "How many were in engine control with you?"

A hard sadness settled onto her face. "Minimum engine crew on this watch, my lord. Two."

That gave Severin at least seven people he knew of who had been in hardened areas of the ship when the radiation hit.

Seven, out of a crew of thirty-four.

Mojtahed hesitated for a moment, then spoke. "May I speak with you privately, my lord?"

"Yes." Severin turned to Chamcha and Bhagwati, who were still hovering by the access panel. "Bring the breakers," he said.

The two crewmen made their way out. Severin turned to Mojtahed. "Yes?" he said.

Mojtahed pushed off from the door and brought herself to a stop a short distance from Severin. She glanced at Lord Go, and her face hardened. She turned to Severin and spoke almost angrily.

"Have you considered that we may have just been attacked?"

"No," Severin said, though he was unsurprised by the question. His thoughts hadn't yet stretched to that possibility, but they would have reached it in time.

"Gamma rays and fast neutrons," Mojtahed said. "That's what we'd get with a missile burst."

"We saw no signs of a missile incoming," Severin said. "No missile flares, nothing on radar. And there's no sign of a fireball."

"A missile could have been accelerated to relativistic velocities outside the system, then shot through a wormhole at us."

Severin thought about this. "But *why?*" *Surveyor* wasn't a military ship, or particularly valuable, and it was engaged in crossing a system from one wormhole to another, outside any trade routes. As the target for the opening salvo of a war, *Surveyor* hardly rated.

"Why," Mojtahed repeated, "and who."

Severin's mind raced. "If it's an attack, the first thing we need to do is get a message to Chee Station and to the wormhole relay station for passage outside. We've got to do that before we light the engine, before we maneuver, before *anything.* Because if an enemy detects a sign of life, they may finish us off."

Mojtahed took in a breath, held it for a moment between clenched teeth, then let it out in a big, angry sigh. "If they're attacking the likes of us, I don't hold much hope for Chee Station or the wormhole relay station."

The silence had reached into its third second when Nkomo stuck her head through the door.

"Doctor's dead, my lord. I looked for her assistant and—" Nkomo hesitated. "He's no better off than the captain."

"Thank you," Severin said, but Nkomo wasn't done.

"Lieutenant Wellstone's dead in the corridor just outside, my lord," she said as she came into the control room. "And I checked in Lieutenant Montcrief's cabin, and he's in his rack. He's alive, but I can't wake him."

"Thank you," Severin said again. He turned to Mojtahed. "Get back to engine control and lock yourself in, just in case we're hit again. I'll concentrate on getting communications geared up before anything else."

"Very good, my lord." Mojtahed began to push off, then paused. "Could it have been *Titan?*" she asked. "If *Titan* blew, we'd get a hell of a lot of radiation."

Mojtahed's theory would have explained everything so conveniently that Severin hated to dispose of it.

"Not unless *Titan* was nearby," he said, "and it wasn't. *Titan* isn't even in the system yet."

Mojtahed apparently regretted the loss of her hypothesis as much as Severin. "Too bad, my lord." she said, and then another idea occurred to her. "Could it be something in nature? We're close to the core of this galaxy. Could something have blown up in the galactic center and the radiation just reached us?"

"I don't know," Severin said. "I don't think so, but I don't know."

Mojtahed pushed off the acceleration cage lightly, with her fingers. Even so that was enough to cause the cage to roll, and Lord Go, tethered to it, woke with a gasp.

"Hurts!" he cried, and Severin's nerves gave a leap. He pulled himself closer to his captain.

"Medicine's on its way, my lord."

"Hurts!"

Afraid to disturb Lord Go again, Severin let go of the cage and touched the deck with one shoe. He pushed toward a wall, pushed off again, and snagged the doorsill.

"We're going to the pharmacy," Severin told Nkomo. "Then we're going to start looking after the crew."

On Nkomo's face was a look that combined anxiety and relief. "Yes, my lord," she said.

Severin looked at the body of Lieutenant Wellstone. "Let's get her in her cabin," he said, and he and Nkomo carried the body a short distance down the corridor. They put Wellstone in her rack, then raised the netting at the sides to keep her from floating away.

On their way to the pharmacy they encountered Bhagwati and Chamcha returning with boxes of replacement electric parts. Severin told them to try to get the comm station working first, then led aft through a bulkhead. The pharmacy was in a shielded area of the ship: if the pharmacist had only been at her duty station instead of asleep in her rack, she would have survived.

Two crew had come to the pharmacy in their agony, but had been unable to open the locked door. One was unconscious now, and the other curled in a ball, whimpering. Severin used his lieutenant's key to open the pharmacy door and then the medicine locker. He pulled out a med injector, then began looking through the neatly labeled white plastic boxes slotted into the heavy metal frames that guarded the contents against heavy accelerations. He found Phenyldorphin-Zed, pulled out one of the boxes, and handed it to Nkomo. He took another box, opened it, slotted a vial into the injector, and stuffed the rest of the vials into one of the leg pockets of his coveralls.

Severin switched the med injector on. A tone sounded. Colors flickered on the display. A tiny bubble of air rose in the clear vial, and the injector flashed an analysis of the contents and a range of recommended doses.

The software in the injectors was as idiot-proof as the Exploration Service could manage. He dialed a dose

He floated toward the nearest of the two crew, the one that whimpered with each breath, and he anchored his feet against the frame of the pharmacy door, pulled the woman toward him, and gently tipped her chin back with his fingers. He placed the med injector against her neck, waited for the display to signal that he'd placed the injector correctly, and fired a dose straight into her carotid.

The woman's eyelids fell. The whimpering stopped, and her breathing grew regular. Severin floated to the unconscious recruit and treated him likewise. Then he offered the injector to Nkomo.

"You go to the female recruits' quarters and then take care of the petty officers. I'll look after the male recruits, the warrant officers, the lieutenant, and the captain."

Nkomo looked at the med injector without touching it, her dark eyes wide. "What about doses? What about—?"

"The highest recommended dose," Severin said. "I've already set it on the injector."

Nkomo didn't move. "Isn't that dangerous, my lord? Because these people are so sick, I mean."

Severin felt a sudden blaze of hatred for Nkomo. Nkomo was going to make him voice a thought that he hated himself for thinking, let alone for speaking out loud. The anger showed in his voice, and it made Nkomo start and stare at him.

"Nkomo," he said, "does it look to you as if the quality of life for these people is going to improve anytime soon?"

Nkomo was cautious. "Ah—no, my lord."

"They're *dying*," Severin said. "We can't do anything about it except try to make them more comfortable. If you give someone an accidental overdose, then as far as I'm concerned that's *fine*. It just means that she won't have to spend days dying in agony. But use whatever dose you want, I don't give a damn."

He held out the injector again. Nkomo hesitated, then took it with fingers that trembled.

"Yes, my lord," she said, and left very fast.

Severin floated in the corridor shaking with rage and badly wanting to hit something, but he knew that if he punched the wall in this weightless state he'd just start ricocheting around the corridor. It wasn't Jaye Nkomo's fault that she was eighteen and had been in the service for less than a year. It wasn't her fault that an officer had given her an order, an order fraught with all the weight of authority and the regulations and the awesome power of the Praxis, that told her to give massive doses of narcotics to the dying women she'd until less than an hour ago been laughing with and serving with and sleeping alongside, and that if she killed any of them by accident that was all right. Nothing in Jaye Nkomo's training had ever prepared her for this.

Nothing in Severin's training had prepared him for giving such an order, either, and the knowledge made him furious. He went back to the pharmacy, found another med injector, loaded it, and went to the male crew quarters.

The smell of it was unforgettable. It wasn't quite the smell of burning and wasn't quite the smell of roasting. It was the smell of ten men dying, and it came with moans and cries. The ones who weren't crying were listless with the apathy that was a symptom of a heavy dose of radiation. Severin went from one rack to the next and administered the doses of endorphin-analog, and by the time he'd finished his anger had passed. He only had the energy left for emotions that might be useful. The emotions that would track down the enemy, whoever they were, and somehow—somehow, given that he was in a crippled, unarmed ship with only seven crew—somehow destroy them.

He went to the warrant officers' cabins, then to that of Lord Barry Montcrief, and then he returned to the control room.

In the control room the emergency lights were on. More than half the displays were glowing softly. Bhagwati sat at the comm board with the lid of the board raised. She was replacing fuses. Chamcha was bent over the sensor board, a puzzled expression on his face. Both were trying to ignore Lord Go, who was curled into a fetal ball and crying.

Severin floated to the captain and placed the injector against his neck and touched the trigger. Lord Go gave a long, ragged sigh, and his clenched body relaxed.

Severin went to the command cage, took the picture of the captain's family, the children and wife and parents and stuffed Torminel, and he returned to the captain and put the picture in Lord Go's hand where he would see it if he ever woke.

"Report, please," Severin said.

"Replaced breakers in Main Busses One and Two," Bhagwati said, "but the engine isn't lit, so we can't get power from anything but the emergency batteries. Battery power should be enough to send a message, though, so I'm trying to get the comm station up."

"I'm looking at the spectra from just before we got fried," Chamcha said. He turned to Severin, his wiry hair floating around his moon face. "There was nothing, and then *wham!*—x-rays."

"*X-rays?*" Severin said. A missile wouldn't produce x-rays. He kicked off and floated gently toward the sensor station.

"They came in pulses." Chamcha's voice was puzzled. "Eight pulses in the first three-quarters of a second, and then the fuses blew and it stopped recording." He looked at Severin anxiously. "Could someone have hit us with an x-ray laser?"

"Pulses," Severin repeated, and his heart sank.

This wasn't an enemy he could fight with a crippled ship and seven crew. Nor was it an enemy he could hope to vanquish were he a Senior Fleet Commander, with a dozen squadrons of warships under his command.

This was an enemy that could wipe out entire civilizations without even noticing them.

"Chamcha," he said, "what exists in nature that sends out twelve massive bursts of x-rays in one second?"

Chamcha's eyes narrowed as he searched his memory. Then the eyes widened, and the color drained from his face.

"Oh, shit," he said.

———

After replacing a fuse in the navigation station, Severin located the enemy within half an hour. One of the seven, or possibly eight, stars in the large system of which Chee's star was an element had been catalogued, over eight hundred years ago, as a brown dwarf, a large gaseous body that wasn't quite large enough to have properly ignited as a star.

That categorization was now demonstrably incorrect, and so was the estimate of the number of stars in the system as a whole. There were not seven, or possibly eight, but rather eight, or possibly nine.

The alleged brown dwarf wasn't a brown dwarf, but a degenerate star. It had once been much larger, and had a companion star that was larger still, forming between them a binary pair that rotated about each other as they moved in even more complex orbits around the other six, or possibly seven, stars of the greater Chee system.

The companion star, nearing the end of its life, had exploded as a supernova, hurling vast clouds of its outer shell into space. Much of this material had been absorbed by its neighbor, making it larger still. The companion, dying, collapsed into a neutron star, and began a deadly dance with gravity, spiraling closer to its neighbor with every orbit. Eventually the neutron star had fallen close enough to begin stripping the outer layers of hydrogen gas off its attendant, drawing the infalling matter into a disk. As the material drew closer, the enormous magnetic fields of the neutron star drew the material inward, compressing and heating it, eventually transforming the infalling matter into powerful beams of x-rays that shot from the magnetic poles.

The neutron star spiraled in, closer and closer, until its orbit was nearly within its companion's outer envelope. The period of its orbit was less than three hours. It had so consumed its companion star that the companion was now indistinguishable from a brown dwarf, especially if the star was being observed from far away, hundreds of years ago, by surveyors who were far more interested in habitable planets.

"Right," Severin said. "Now the question is, what *else* is the pulsar going to hit?"

He and Chamcha sat side-by-side in the sensor cage. Severin called other displays onto his own, piloting and astrography displays, and an estimate of the angle of the x-ray beam when *Surveyor* had been hit, which would provide a figure for the tilt of the pulsar's magnetic pole and a judgment of what other objects the beam might intersect.

The computer simulation of the multi-sun system, with the pulsar now added, ran briefly, then stopped. A tone sounded.

Chee.

"Well, of course," Severin said. He was surprised by his lack of surprise.

Chee and the eight, or possibly nine, suns of its system weren't all in the same plane. The pulsar's course was to galactic north of Chee, and the beam fired from its southern magnetic pole would intersect the planet for all of three seconds, long enough to kill any unshielded animal life-form either in orbit or on the planet's surface.

Severin compiled the information into as terse a message as he could. "Send to Chee Station Command," he said, "with copies to Lord Inspector Martinez and Astronomer Shon-dan at the Imperial Observatory."

"Very good, my lord," said Nkomo. She had returned to the control room without speaking a word, and had taken her place at the comm board. She looked down at the board. "Comm laser three powering up and—we've lost it, my lord."

Severin turned to stare at her. "*Lost* it? Lost *what*?"

Nkomo looked uncertain. "Lost the laser, my lord. It's . . . malfunctioned somehow."

"Use another laser."

The second laser also failed. Severin thought that perhaps the x-ray flux had turned the metal on the ship brittle as glass, and that the metallic semiconductors used to generate the lasers were blowing apart under the strain of excitation.

When a third laser died, Severin decided that his theory was confirmed.

"Try a VHF antenna," Severin said. "Use the emergency channel."

They were going to get their message to Chee, Severin thought, one way or another, if he had to build an antenna himself.

When Martinez returned to his lodgings at the Mayor's Palace, the Lady Mayor herself bustled toward him as he got out of the car.

"I wondered where you had been today, my lord," she said. She looked in surprise at his muddy boots and informal clothing. "There are a stack of invitations that have come in for you."

"Rigger Ahmet was showing me the sights," Martinez said. He turned to Ahmet and winked. "Right, Ahmet?"

Ahmet grinned broadly. "Absolutely, my lord."

The Lady Mayor hesitated. Martinez smiled at her, and then his sleeve comm chimed.

"Pardon me, my lady." He answered.

The chameleon weave on his sleeve shimmered to an image of Lord Ehl. The feathery dark hairs on the sides of his head were standing oddly, as if he'd just suffered an electric shock.

"My lord," Ehl said. "We've just received a transmission from *Surveyor*, and—well—I'd be obliged if you could get back to the station as fast as you can."

As the coleopter began its descent into Port Vipsania, Martinez looked at Shon-dan in the crystal-clear image of his sleeve display and said, "Do you mean to tell me that despite your entire crew of overpaid astronomers at Chee Station, you failed to detect two beams of deadly energy each *over a light-year long*?"

Shon-dan gazed at Martinez with wide golden eyes. "My lord," she said, "we're *cosmologists*. We haven't looked at *anything* within a hundred light-years of this place."

Martinez looked balefully at the image of Shon-dan, and then realized he was grinding his teeth. He unclenched and spoke.

"Tell me what's going to happen, and how long we've got."

"We've got nine and a half days, my lord. Then Chee will move into the path of that beam, and—" Shon-dan clacked her peg teeth nervously. "Anyone without proper shielding will, ah, be very much in jeopardy."

"The atmosphere won't be shield enough?"

"Not for beams of this intensity." Shon-dan tried to look hopeful. "We've worked out the orbital mechanics, by the way, and this should happen to Chee only once every forty-nine thousand years."

Which, Martinez thought, explained the relatively primitive life-forms on the surface of the planet as compared with the superabundant life in the sea. Every forty-nine thousand years any complex species on land was wiped out.

Those fern forests were a clue, if anyone had bothered to read it.

"So," he said, "we'll have nearly fifty thousand good years if we manage to survive the next ten days."

The avian's tone was apologetic. "Ah—there will be problems after the ten days, my lord. Electronics may be destroyed. Food crops may not survive. Metals may turn brittle. And—well, I don't know what will happen to the station and the elevator. I'll have to think of that."

"You do that. I need an estimate of how much shielding people are going to need to hide under."

"Ah—yes, my lord."

Martinez ended the transmission. The coleopter was making its final approach to its landing pad. Martinez thought of people rising from shelters to find the world above destroyed—crops burned in the fields, no communication, buildings with metal frames unsafe, transport liable to fall apart, those beautiful bridges on the railroad collapsed because the support cables could no longer carry them.

And possibly Chee Station destroyed. There was plenty of radiation shielding on the station, but it was all on the outer rims of the habitation wheels and in other parts calculated to protect personnel against a solar flare. The x-ray beam would be coming in at an angle, from galactic north, and very little of the station would be protected.

The wheel and other large structures were made of a tough

resinous material, and thus wouldn't be subject to metal fatigue, but even so enough critical components were made of metal that the structure might be in jeopardy. If it came apart under stress the elevator cable would drop into the atmosphere, where it would burn up, but if the cable dragged enough of the station with it, Chee could be subjected to a dangerous bombardment of large objects burning their way through the atmosphere to strike the surface.

And crashing with the station would be Chee Company stock, to the ruination of his father and family.

Helpless anger burned in his thoughts as the coleopter settled to a landing.

Terza waited by the landing pad with a big Fleet car and a driver. She was wearing her brown Ministry uniform. Martinez walked across the pad and kissed her. Her lips were soft, her eyes hard.

"You've heard?" he asked. He had to speak over the sound of the coleopter's turbines.

"Marcella told me."

He took her arm and walked with her to the car. "We'll get you on the first ship out."

"I can stay," Terza said. "I'm an administrator, remember, and I'm sure they'll find an adequate shelter for us."

They paused by the car. Martinez put a large hand over Terza's abdomen. "I don't want x-rays getting anywhere near the next generation of Clan Chen."

Terza made a face. "I was so looking forward to seeing you in action," she said. "But I suppose caution may be indicated, since the doctor confirmed just this morning there *is* a next generation on the way."

Despite the oppressive weight of his thoughts a flame of joy kindled in Martinez's heart, and he kissed her. "What happens next?" he asked. "I'm not quite sure how this pregnancy business works, since I wasn't around the first time."

Terza took him by the hand and drew him into the automobile. "It's going to be very difficult and taxing, I'm afraid." Her tone was businesslike. "I shall require first-class pampering from you for, oh, several years at least."

"Starting now?" he said hopefully.

Terza gave a sigh. "I'm afraid not. You've got a meeting."

"We've got power in most of the ship," Severin said. "Communication between engine control and main control have been restored. Enough of the computers have been brought online so that we can do what we need to. The injured are being made as comfortable as possible for the deceleration, and we're fighting dehydration with intravenous drips. Since we're uncertain how the ship will respond to a resumption of gee force, we'll start with a tenth of a gravity, then gradually increase power to one gravity."

Severin paused for a reply, and when none came went on.

"When I tried to turn the ship with the maneuvering thrusters, the thruster heads blew out—metal fatigue in the joints won't let them hold pressure. That means we're going to have to maneuver with the main engine, which is of course designed to resist hard radiation, so if you feel some unusual accelerations at first, that's what they'll be."

He paused again, then licked his dry lips. "May I have permission to begin deceleration, my lord?"

There was a long pause before a single word came from the captain's lips, so soft it was almost a sigh.

"Proceed."

"Very good, my lord." Severin checked the captain's intravenous drip, then spun in the air with a flip of his hands and kicked off for the door.

He didn't know how much of his report the captain had understood, but Severin felt better for having delivered it. Lord Go was a good captain and deserved to know what was happening on his ship, and perhaps Lord Go himself felt better for knowing.

The captain had been returned to his bed prior to the commencement of acceleration. Dehydration was a serious problem with radiation burns and Severin and the other six uninjured crewmen had spent the last few hours giving the surviving victims intravenous drips, an arduous process because they had to learn the technique first, practicing on each other by following the steps in a manual.

Severin had debated with himself over whether the step should be taken at all. Prolonging the lives of the victims was only to extend their suffering without a chance of altering the outcome.

But Severin wanted to be able to look at himself in a mirror. He wanted to be able to tell the families of the victims that he'd done everything he could for them. He didn't want to have to say, "I let them die without trying to help them."

He made his way to the control room and worked his way into the command cage, then pulled the display down in front of him and locked it there. Bhagwati, Nkomo, and Chamcha were all strapped into their acceleration couches.

"Engines," he told Bhagwati, "sound the acceleration warning."

"Yes, my lord." The warning clattered through the ship.

"Engines," Severin said, "prepare to maneuver with the main engine."

"Yes, my lord." Bhagwati looked at her board. "Gimbal test successful, my lord. Engine on standby."

"Course one-five-seven by one-five-seven relative."

"Course laid into the computer, my lord."

"Begin maneuvering."

The thrust was gentle, and Severin heard the engine fire only as a distant rumble that seemed to come up his spine. His couch swung lightly in its cage, and a faint whisper of gravity reached Severin's inner ear. The engine faded, then fired again. Severin's cage rattled. His stomach gave a little lurch.

"Come *on,*" Bhagwati urged. The main engine really wasn't intended for this kind of maneuvering.

The engine fired again, a more sustained burst. Severin found himself waiting for the sound of something falling.

Nothing fell. The engine fired thrice more, each minor adjustments. There was triumph in Bhagwati's voice when she announced, "One-five-seven by one-five-seven relative."

"Commence acceleration at point one gravities."

The engine lit, a sustained distant rumble, and Severin's cage swung again. A gentle hand pressed him into his couch.

"Systems check," Severin ordered, just to make certain nothing had broken.

Nothing had. Severin had no worries for the hull, which was tough resin stiffened with polycarbon beams, but there was still enough metal in the ship to cause him concern. There were metal shelves, metal hinges, metal fittings, and the sick crew lay on mattresses placed on metal racks. Pipes and conduits were secured by metal strips. Valves with metal parts pierced the hull to bring in water or electricity from stations, or to discharge waste.

All Severin needed right now was a hull breach.

Severin added gravity a tenth of a gee at a time until the ship was decelerating at one full gravity. Only once did he hear a crash, when a shelf gave way in the captain's pantry.

"Systems check," Severin said.

Nothing was destroyed, nothing breached. Severin began to feel proud of *Surveyor*. It was a tougher craft than he'd expected.

He would get *Surveyor* to Laredo, where there would have to be a complete refit. *Surveyor* was twenty-eight days out from Laredo, so it would take twenty-eight days to reverse the momentum that had built, plus another twenty-eight days to return to port.

By that time all the afflicted crew would be dead. Severin would be conducting funerals every day for many days to come, and in addition *Surveyor* would have a front-row seat for what promised to be a planetary catastrophe.

Severin unlocked his display and pushed it up over his head, out of the way. He unwebbed and stepped out of the cage.

"Bhagwati, you have the ship," he said. "Nkomo, Chamcha, it's time to make the rounds of the sick and make sure they're coping under gravity."

Severin would report to Lord Go that *Surveyor* had done well under acceleration.

He hoped the captain would be pleased.

"Life is brief, but the Praxis is eternal," Severin read from the burial service. "Let us all take comfort and security in the wisdom that all that is important is known." He looked up at Engineer Mojtahed.

"Proceed," he said.

Mojtahed pressed the override button that blew from the cargo airlock Captain Lord Go Shikimori, Lieutenant Lord Barry Montcrief, and four other crew. Since *Surveyor's* engine was blazing a huge radioactive tail during the deceleration, and since the bodies, once out of the airlock, were no longer decelerating, the captain and his crew would be cremated within seconds.

Severin and the four others—two remained on watch—remained at rigid attention until the airlock display stopped blinking. Mojtahed looked through the window on the inner airlock.

"Airlock's clear, my lord."

"Close the outer door and repressurize." Severin said. He turned to the others. "Detail dismissed." He began to walk away, then stopped. "Mojtahed, Chamcha, please join me for dinner."

Though Severin was now the acting captain, he hadn't moved into the captain's quarters, and didn't intend to. He brought Mojtahed and Chamcha to the wardroom, where he sat them at the table normally reserved for lieutenants.

The pulsar had killed all of *Surveyor's* cooks and the meals had become haphazard, mostly stews of things emptied into the pot from cans, and all cooked by microwave because the metal burners on the galley stove were so brittle they failed if anyone turned them on. Severin and his guests were served by today's cook, an apprentice from Mojtahed's engine room department, who fled before any of them had a chance to taste his handiwork. Severin opened a bottle of wine from the wardroom stores. Till now he had tasted the wine only occasionally, because he'd been unable to afford the sort of private stores the other lieutenants were used to, and he didn't want Lord Barry and Lady Maxine to think he was a leech, drinking from the bottles that would have cost him half a month's pay apiece.

But now Lord Barry and Lady Maxine were radioactive dust floating in the general direction of Wormhole Two, and Severin had conducted his second mass funeral in two days and wanted a drink.

He had two goblets of wine while the others sipped theirs and ate a few dutiful bites of stew. Then he spoke.

"We've done a good job of saving the ship," he said. "Now I'd like to try to save Chee."

There was silence at the wardroom table, and then Mojtahed wiped a bit of gravy off her chin and said, "Beg pardon, my lord?"

"I want to save Chee," Severin said. "And to do that we have to turn off the pulsar, and I think I know how that can be done."

There was another moment of silence. Mojtahed and Chamcha exchanged glances.

Mojtahed, the senior surviving petty officer. Chamcha, who was a highly trained sensor operator trained to detect wormholes, and the closest thing *Surveyor* had to an actual scientist.

"Very good, my lord," Mojtahed said.

"Bear with me," Severin said. He called up the wardroom's wall display, and put up a simulation of an x-ray pulsar he'd got from *Anray's Catalogue of Astronomical Objects*.

"The x-ray pulse is driven by matter infalling from the accretion disk," Severin said. "So if we can turn that mechanism off, the x-rays will turn off as well. Unlike an electromagnetic pulsar, an x-ray pulsar can't work in a vacuum."

"My lord," Chamcha ventured, "we're dealing with something the mass of a *star*. A pulsar is one of the most dense objects in the universe, and about the deadliest—how can you hope to stop it with our resources?"

"The pulsar's mass is colossal, yes," Severin said. "But the accretion disk is nothing but hydrogen gas. So what we do is fire an antimatter missile into the accretion disk, and the antimatter *wipes out* the inner band of hydrogen." He grinned at them. "The pulsar's shut down for a few critical hours, Chee is saved, we all get medals. What do you think?"

Chamcha blinked. Mojtahed's response was more practical. "We don't *have* any antimatter missiles."

"We'll use one of the lifeboats. Pack the crew spaces full of anti-hydrogen if we have to, and sent it out on automatic pilot."

Chamcha hesitantly raised a hand, as if he was in a classroom.

"Yes?" Severin said.

"I see two problems," Chamcha said. "First, I don't think we have nearly enough antimatter . . ."

"So *we'll* jump in the lifeboats and then shoot *Surveyor* at the pulsar," Severin said.

"And the *other* problem," Chamcha said indomitably, "is that when the antihydrogen hits the accretion disk, it doesn't just wipe it from existence, it turns into *radiation*. The radiation directed at the pulsar won't shut it off, it'll *heat the pulsar up,* and the x-ray emissions will *radically increase in power.* And the radiation directed outward, into the accretion disk, will *heat up the accretion disk,* so when *that* falls onto the pulsar, you'll get *another* super-powerful burst of x-rays." Chamcha made a kind of exploding gesture with his hands. "And then Chee gets *really* fried."

Severin felt himself mentally rock back on his heels. When the idea had first occurred to him, shaving in his bath that morning, it had seemed like a brilliant strike of lightning, and subsequent consideration had only made it seem better. He rubbed his chin for a moment as he considered.

Mojtahed, who apparently considered the discussion at an end, took a long, relieved drink of wine.

Severin decided he wasn't done yet. "But *between* the two big bursts," he said, "there's nothing, right? The pulsar will actually turn off."

An stubborn expression came onto Chamcha's moon face. "For a short time, yes," Chamcha said. "But I doubt that it would last more than a few seconds, not even if we threw all *Surveyor* at it. And if we got the timing wrong, Chee gets cooked."

"And we *don't* get medals," Mojtahed pronounced.

"A few seconds is all Chee needs," Severin said. He turned back to the display on the wall, and called up rows of figures and the Structured Mathematics Display. "Before breakfast I sent a message to Astronomer Shon-dan at the Chee Observatory," he said, "requesting all available information on the pulsar—its mass, its accretion disk, the power of its x-ray beam. The reply just arrived, so let's do the math."

The math, when it was done, was discouraging. Even if *Surveyor* were packed with antihydrogen fuel, it would barely produce a blip in the pulsar's x-ray yield.

"Sorry, my lord," Chamcha said. "It was an ingenious idea, but it just didn't work out."

Mojtahed finished her stew and rattled the spoon in her bowl.

"Yes, my lord. Sorry." She had clearly dismissed the idea from her mind.

"*Titan,*" Severin said.

The others looked at him.

"*Titan* is a very large ship and it's packed with antimatter and it's just entered the system," Severin said. "And *Titan*'s on lease to the Exploration Service, and Warrant Officer Junot is in command, and I outrank him. So—" He smiled. "Maybe we'd better do the math again."

There were six hundred people on Chee Station, and eight hundred forty thousand on the planet below. Two cargo ships were docked at the station, and if they discharged all their cargo they could take perhaps four thousand people, assuming the people were packed closely enough and a sufficient number of new toilets were installed.

Which left in excess of eight hundred thirty-six thousand people in danger on the planet's surface, and that meant Martinez attended a *lot* of meetings.

Antiradiation shielding was scavenged from the station, and several of the manufacturing plants on the surface thought they could convert in time and produce some more, but most of the people on the planet were going to have to hide from the pulsar the old-fashioned way, in a deep hole, with a lot of dirt piled on the roof.

There was heavy equipment and construction material to provide enough shelter space for everyone, but the population wasn't unanimous in their cooperation.

"The railroad workers want to take their families up the line and into the tunnels," Allodorm told Martinez. "They think they'll be safer with a mountain on top of them."

Martinez glared from the window of his office on the station down at the blue-and-green planet below. His own reflection, heavy-browed and scowling, glowered back at him. Chee rotated slowly in the window frame as the station wheeled on its axis.

"They'll be safer," Martinez said, "until they try to *leave*." He felt his voice rising in frustration. "How are they going to get their families down from the mountain over bridges that are brittle as icicles? On vehicles floating on electromagnets that may explode the second a cur-

rent runs through them?" He looked at Allodorm and spoke with final-
ity. "The railroad workers go into the bunkers like everyone else."

"Yes, lord inspector." Allodorm's beautiful voice showed no sign
of agitation at any point in the crisis. Martinez had to give him credit
for that.

And even if he was a thief, Allodorm was working as hard as anyone to shelter Chee's inhabitants. Martinez had to give him credit for
that, too.

"I've heard from the Lady Mayor of Port Gareth," Marcella said
from around the cigarette she held fiercely between her teeth. "She has
a plan to save the shuttles."

The shuttles were designed to ferry cargo from low orbit to the
surface, and were unable to achieve escape velocity and get far enough
from Chee to avoid the pulsar. They would remain on the ground, with
most of the other heavy equipment, and be subjected to x-ray bombardment and probably ruined.

Martinez hoped the Chee Company had good insurance.

He left the window and dropped heavily into the chair behind his
desk. Pneumatics gave an outraged hiss.

"Is the Lady Mayor any kind of aeronautical engineer?" Martinez
asked. "Has she actually consulted with the shuttle pilots?"

Marcella smiled. "The answer to the first question is no, and as for
the second, I doubt it. She wants to put the shuttles in geosynchronous
orbit on the side of Chee away from the pulsar."

"That won't work," Martinez said. "The pulsar beam isn't coming
in along the plane of the ecliptic, it'll come at an angle from galactic
north. Anything in geosynchronous orbit will be fried. In order to get
the planet between the shuttles and the beam, they'd have to go into a
polar orbit and get the timing exactly right . . ." He paused for a
moment. "Wait a minute, that's a *good* idea. Tell the shuttle pilots that
they can proceed with the polar orbit, but they're forbidden to take passengers. It's too dangerous."

As the provisional governor had declared a state of emergency,
Martinez as the senior Fleet representative had become the absolute
ruler of the Chee system. It was as if all the power of the Shaa con-
querors had become invested in his person.

If the situation hadn't been so desperate, he would be really enjoying himself.

"By the way," Marcella added, "can you make use of the *Kayenta*? I'm happy to offer it, though it won't hold very many refugees."

"Thank you," Martinez said. "Let me think about it."

At another meeting, with Lord Ehl and the captains of the two merchant vessels, there was a discussion of who was going on the ships and who wasn't.

"We should bring off the representatives of our company," one of the captains said. "And then paying passengers, of course."

"You will bring off gravid females," Martinez said, "and children under the age of fifteen, each of whom will be accompanied by one parent. If there's any room left, we can discuss allowing slightly older children aboard."

There probably *would* be extra room: there weren't many children on Chee, as the workers had been recruited chiefly from the young and unattached, and settler families hadn't really started arriving yet.

"My owners will protest!" the captain said.

"That will be their privilege, after this is over." Martinez turned to Lord Ehl. "You will place members of the Military Constabulary on the ships' airlock doors and hatches," he said. "I don't want unauthorized people sneaking on board."

"Yes, my lord." Martinez thought he heard satisfaction in Ehl's voice.

"No Fleet personnel will leave Chee till this is over," Martinez said to Ehl later, after the captains had left. "It's our job to stand between the citizens and danger, and if that means sucking up x-rays, so be it."

"Er—yes, my lord." Martinez thought he detected rather less satisfaction in Ehl's tone than had been there a few moments before.

"I'm going to be the last person off Chee Station," Martinez said. "You'll be the next-to-last, so we'll share an elevator."

"Yes, my lord." A question glowed in Ehl's golden eyes. "We're not staying in Station Command? It's shielded."

"There might be a structural failure of the station. If there isn't, we'll be able to get from the ground back to the station easily enough."

Then Martinez recalled Marcella's offer of *Kayenta*. "No, wait," he said. "*You'll* take the last elevator with the control room crew. I'll see you off, then depart in *Kayenta*. That way I'll be able to return to the station once the pulsar's passed and make certain everything's in order before you bring a crew back up the elevator."

The plan pleased him. Last off the station, and first on again. It was a role that was not only proper for the senior officer in a crisis, but would reflect well on him.

It wasn't as if he minded looking good.

It wasn't until he left his office for the walk to the grandeur of the Senior Officers' Quarters that he found out about another problem. A Terran with a wispy blond mustache and a jacket with a gray stripe came up to Martinez as he walked, and introduced himself as Hedgepath, a stockbroker.

"There are brokers on Chee?" Martinez asked.

"Yes," Hedgepath said, "though most of what I do is invest workers' pay elsewhere in the empire. But Port Vipsania has its own little stock market, for locally raised issues. We even have a futures market."

"Congratulations," Martinez said.

"Perhaps congratulations aren't precisely in order." Hedgepath touched his slight mustache. "There has been an, ah, problem with the market. The futures market in particular. In the hours before the announcement of the threat from the pulsar, there was a lot of selling. Agricultural futures in particular, though there was some selling in industrial and fishery futures as well."

Martinez found himself nodding. "After word about the pulsar came out, the futures turned worthless."

"You might understand that my clients have been complaining. And since you now seem to represent the civil authority as well as the military, I thought I'd pass the complaints to you." He touched his mustache again. "I couldn't seem to make an appointment, by the way. I'm sorry I had to stop you on the street."

Martinez considered this. Hedgepath's lack of an appointment wasn't necessarily an element of a deep conspiracy—a *lot* of people were trying to set meetings with him, and the Lai-own secretary that Lord Ehl had assigned him might well have assigned Hedgepath a low priority.

"I'll look into that," Martinez said. "In the meantime, I'd like to give you some names. Ledo Allodorm. Lord Pa Maq-fan. Lady Marcella Zykov."

Hedgepath seemed surprised only by Marcella's name "I can assure your lordship that Lady Marcella hasn't done any selling that I know of," Hedgepath said. "But there were sell orders from other Cree Company officials—Her-ryng and Remusat, for two."

Martinez couldn't put any faces to the names, though he'd very possibly met them at one or another of the banquets in his honor.

"I'd like you to retain all information of the trades," Martinez said. "Things are urgent right now, and I won't be able to deal with this till after the pulsar's passed. Make sure the data is in hard as well as electronic form."

"Yes, my lord."

"Can you give me contact information?"

Hedgepath sent his information to Martinez from his sleeve display, and Martinez told him that he would be in touch.

"By the way," he said. "How's Chee Company stock doing?"

"It's worth about a third of what it was worth two days ago."

Martinez told Terza this over supper. "I'd been starting to think well of Allodorm and Lord Pa," Terza said. "They've been so responsive in the crisis."

"And all the more responsive for knowing their money's safe. And of course they're working to save their own skins, and their company's assets."

There was a low chime from Martinez's sleeve display. He gave a snarl; he'd forgotten to turn it off at dinner.

"Apologies," he said to Terza, and answered.

The orange eyes of his Lai-own secretary gazed back at him from the display. "I beg your pardon, my lord. A communication has arrived from Lieutenant Severin, logged as personal, confidential, urgent, and immediate."

Martinez exchanged glances with Terza. Severin wouldn't use such a bundle of impressive adjectives without reason.

"Send it," Martinez said.

When Martinez's display indicated that the message had been

downloaded, he broke the connection to his secretary and played the message.

"This is going to be complex," Severin said, "and I'd be obliged if somewhere along the line you could check my math."

Severin had considered not telling anyone of his plan to use *Titan* to shut off the pulsar. He was afraid that someone, frightened of the super-powerful bursts of x-rays that would both precede and follow the pulsar's brief time of quiet, would refuse him permission to act.

He certainly knew better than to ask his own superiors on Laredo. The Exploration Service was an organization that had been starved of funding for ages: every time the government was reminded that the Service existed, it had only inspired them to trim the budget still further. The entire institutional culture of the Service was based on not calling attention to themselves, and the culture hadn't changed even though the budget had grown. Throwing away a whole ship full of anti-hydrogen was calling for attention, and with a vengeance: if Severin approached them with his scheme, their first instinct would refuse to do *anything*.

Yet it would be hard to carry out the operation secretly. *Titan* wasn't exactly inconspicuous, and when its crew took to the lifeboats while the giant ship itself burned for the pulsar at an acceleration that would have killed anyone aboard, someone might well take notice.

So Severin had decided to contact Martinez personally, trusting that the relationship that had developed in the war would continue to work. In the meantime he had told *Titan*'s crew to prepare to abandon the ship and to place it under remote control, and also ordered them to keep their orders secret for the present and not to transmit anything but routine messages to Chee or to anywhere else.

Severin didn't want *Titan* asking their superiors for advice, either.

He was sleeping in his cabin when Martinez's reply arrived. Severin was dreaming of warships that were also, secretly, submarines, submarines that fought a lonely covert war in the chill seas of watery planets like Hy-Oso, and he slowly became aware that the insistent chiming he heard wasn't the sound of sonar, but his sleeve display.

The comm unit in his cabin was still nonfunctional, which was why the sleeve display had to be used. Severin called for lights, then remembered that fuse hadn't been replaced either, and groped through the dark cabin for the uniform jacket that had been hung over the back of a chair. He triggered the display, heard from Chamcha that Lord Inspector Martinez had send him a message logged personal, urgent, and confidential, and told Chamcha to send it.

"Permission is tentatively granted to proceed with your project," Martinez said. His face appeared upside-down in the display, and Severin craned his neck to get a better view.

"I'm ordering complete secrecy on this matter," Martinez said. "You will censor all communication off *Surveyor* and order censorship on *Titan* as well. Absolutely nothing must get out. I'm going to explain *Titan*'s movements as a maneuver ordered by the Exploration Service high command."

Severin could only stare at the inverted image.

Martinez's eyes took on a more confiding glance. "Let's hope you're right about all this. I'll check the math, and enjoy talking with you when it's all over."

The orange End Transmission symbol flashed into place on Severin's sleeve. Thoughtfully he felt his way across the cabin and turned on the lights manually.

Total secrecy, he thought. Now *that* was interesting.

Clearly he wasn't the only one here with a scheme up his sleeve.

"Total secrecy," Martinez told Shon-dan. "I want this to be strictly between the two of us."

"Yes, my lord." The astronomer clacked her peg teeth in thought, then spoke hesitantly. "May I ask the reason for the secrecy?"

"People might be less than committed to the evacuations and the shelter-building program if they thought the shelters weren't going to be needed. Even if the math checks there's still too much that can go wrong with this scheme, and if the plan blows up, those shelters will be necessary."

Shon-dan hesitated again. "Very good, my lord."

"I want you to check these figures," Martinez said, "and I'll check them as well. And *no one else is to know.* Understand?"

"Yes, my lord."

"Because if anyone else finds out, I'll know who blabbed, and I'll throw you into that x-ray beam with my own hands."

After hearing a series of heartfelt assurances from Shon-dan, Martinez ended the conversation. His dinner lay cold on the table before him. Terza lowered the cup of coffee from her lips and said, "I hope this means I'm not going to have to take that refugee ship."

Martinez considered this. "No," he decided, "you're going aboard."

Her mouth tightened. "Why?" she asked.

"Because you're the Chen heir and mother of the *next* Chen heir," Martinez said. "And so you will go on board the refugee ship and be gracious and accepting and thoughtful and considerate of the other passengers, because that's what people expect of the next Lady Chen."

Terza looked cross. "Damn," she said.

"Just as I'll be last off this station," Martinez said, "and first on, because it's what people expect of a war hero."

Reluctant amusement tugged at Terza's lips. "I haven't noticed that you find being a hero much of a hardship."

Martinez sipped his cold coffee. "Well," he said, "not *yet*. But when I'm old and mumbling in my rocking chair by the fire, and multitudes of citizens come to me begging to be rescued from some cosmic menace or other, I'm probably going to find it all *very inconvenient*."

"No doubt," Terza said.

Martinez signaled to Alikhan to fill his coffee cup.

"You'll have to excuse me for the next few hours," he told Terza. "I have to confirm all of Severin's calculations."

Terza rose from her chair. "I'll start the job of being gracious and accepting, then, and leave you to your task."

Martinez's calculations supported those of Severin, and more importantly Shon-dan's supported them both. Martinez called Ring Command to tell them that *Titan* and *Surveyor* would be engaged in a series of maneuvers, and that the sensor operations should be told to disregard them. "Put a memo on the sensor display," Martinez said. "I don't want to get a call from Command whenever a new sensor operator goes on watch."

Then it was back to the endless series of planning meetings. Shelters were being dug with furious efficiency, roofed, and then covered with dirt. The accommodations were primitive, but few conveniences were required by a population that would be in the shelters for less than an hour.

The first of the two refugee ships was sent off, with four thousand aboard, mostly children. The ship would boost far enough away to be safe from the pulsar, and could then return to Chee or continue on to Laredo, depending on whether Chee Station survived or not.

The second ship left two days later. Martinez kissed Terza goodbye at the airlock door, and watched her drift aboard in an elegant swirl of grace and gallantry. Martinez paused for a moment of admiration, and then turned to go past the long lines of refugees patiently waiting to board, each tethered to a safety line as they floated weightless in the great docking space.

Some unused to weightlessness looked green and ill. Martinez sped past them before the inevitable consequences began to manifest themselves.

He made his way to Command, and encountered Lord Ehl leaving. Ehl braced in salute as he drifted past, then recovered in time to snag a handhold on the wall. He made a nervous gesture with his free hand, then stuffed a sheet of paper in a pocket.

"Is something wrong?" Martinez said.

"No," Ehl began. "Well, yes. There have been some arrests, people who got onto the refugee ship that weren't supposed to be there. Officials of the shipping company, apparently." He lifted the paper from his pocket, then returned it. "I have their names, but they'll have to be checked."

"Do you need my help?"

"No, my lord, I thank you."

"Very well. Once you find out for certain who they are, ship them down the skyhook and put them in the deepest dungeon on Chee."

There were no dungeons on Chee, so far as Martinez knew, but perhaps they'd build one.

From Command Martinez followed the saga of the stowaways, who were marched off the ship by the military constabulary. The refugee ship was given permission to depart, and the enormous vessel gently backed from the station until it reached a safe enough distance to light its torch.

Martinez said another silent farewell to Terza as the displays showed her ship building speed, then took a covert look at *Titan*. *Titan* itself was boosting at nearly twenty gravities toward its rendezvous with the pulsar, a speed that would have killed any crew on board. The icon representing *Titan* on the sensor displays had a large text box attached to it, saying the ship was engaged in maneuvers. The two lifeboats containing its crew were on their way to their rendezvous with *Surveyor*, and had been given the cover of a mission to resupply the crippled craft.

If anyone in Command ever bothered to check the ship's heading and acceleration, they would have had a surprise. But the staff had an emergency on its hands, and much to occupy them; their sensor displays were tuned to the awesome might of the x-ray beam spinning ever closer, and a distant ship that did not call attention to itself was something that floated only on the margins of their attention, like a lily floating in the distant reaches of a pond.

No queries regarding *Titan* came to Martinez's attention. One shelter after another was certified, and the population put to rehearsing their evacuation schemes. At the last moment the Lady Mayor of Port Gareth came up with another plan: she wanted to put much of the population of her town into several of the large containers that had brought goods from orbit, and sink them below the surface of the bay for the duration of the emergency. Martinez, torn between irritation and hilarity, told her that it was too late to change the plans, and she should complete all conventional shelters in her town.

Lord Pa and Allodorm were on the ground, coordinating last-minute emergency and evacuation work. Personnel on Chee Station were sent to the surface, leaving a skeleton crew behind. The two huge rotating wheels were braked to a stop, and the antimatter reactor powered down. Even the emergency lighting was turned off in most of the station to keep surges from following power lines. *Kayenta* was readied at the airlock, with Marcella and select Meridian Company personnel aboard, a team that would return to the station with Martinez for a survey before anyone else was allowed to return to the station. One by one the displays and work spaces at Ring Command were shut down, leaving live only the boards that would be needed to begin the restart.

Martinez, Lord Ehl, and the other crew left the darkened, eerily silent Command room and floated along guide cables to the entrance to the great elevator car. Martinez accepted their salute, wished Ehl luck, and watched them file aboard. The car began its descent, diving smoothly along the cable to its vanishing point in the green land mass below, and then Martinez turned for *Kayenta*'s berth.

When *Kayenta* departed from the station, it would go into a polar orbit calculated to place the mass of the planet between itself and the pulsar for the critical few seconds, just as the shuttles were doing. Martinez would be able to return to the station after less than an hour's absence.

With all the ventilators shut down the air was perfumed by the scent of decaying polymers. Empty and without lights the docks were a monumental, indistinct darkness, vast as space itself. The beam of Martinez's hand flash vanished in the blackness. At a great distance Martinez saw the glow that marked *Kayenta*'s docking port, lit not by station power but by the yacht's own power supply. Martinez placed his feet carefully against a wall and kicked off, and was pleased to find that he was straight on course for the airlock.

Two figures bulked large by the door, their feet tucked into handles on the wall, their arms reaching for Martinez. As he drifted closer, he saw they were both Torminel. They wore only shorts and vests over their thick gray and black fur, and their huge eyes, adapted for hunting at night, glittered as they tracked Martinez.

Two of Marcella's survey team, apparently.

Martinez flew into their arms, and they caught him and absorbed his momentum with ease. A furry hand closed on each of his, and placed his hands on handholds by the airlock.

"Thank you," Martinez said. He tried to shift his left hand, but the Torminel on his left kept it pinned.

The other Torminel, he saw, had a med injector in his free hand.

He barely had time to register alarm before he felt the cool touch of the injector against his neck.

And then he had all the time in the world.

———

There was silence in the control room, broken only by the sound of his breath, by the pulse that beat a quick march in his chest.

Severin watched from his acceleration cage as *Titan* flew toward its objective, its engines firing a last series of powerful burns that would inject it into the pulsar's accretion disk at exactly the right angle.

The colossal gravity of the pulsar would tear the ship to atoms, hurling its cargo of antihydrogen into the spinning disk. A great swath of the disk's hydrogen would be annihilated in a ferocious burst of gamma rays, energetic neutrons, and pi-mesons. A percentage of these particles would fall into the neutron star and pump up its x-ray emissions. Another percentage would fly outward into the accretion disk, heating the hydrogen there to blazing temperatures so that when it fell into the pulsar another fierce megaburst of x-rays would blaze forth.

But in between the two ferocious blasts would come eighteen minutes of silence. The mechanism that produced the life-destroying double lance of the pulsar would be shut down.

Or at least it would if Severin's calculations were correct.

"Fifteen seconds," Chamcha reported unnecessarily. The seconds were ticking down in a corner of Severin's display.

Titan was standing on a vast, blazing tail of annihilated matter. Severin was using the cargo ship as a giant torpedo, aimed straight for a deadly enemy.

"Ten seconds," Chamcha said.

"Oh, shut up," Severin murmured. Chamcha must have had more acute ears than Severin thought, because the sensor tech maintained a resolute silence right up till *Titan* vanished into the larger blip that was the pulsar and its brown companion.

Severin's attention immediately turned to the pulsar's rotating x-ray beam, which his display had colored a lurid green. The reaction was immediate: the beam, rotating twelve times per second, blazed into an emerald fury. If the beam hit Chee now, it would strip the planet down to its mantle.

Severin could only hope that the pulsar would switch off when it was supposed to.

And suddenly he thought: *the statue!*

That's how he'd work it. Frenella, the gamine, would send Eggfont the little statue of Lord Mince, and that would tip Eggfont to Mince's relationship with Lady Belledrawers.

He felt a little shiver of delight as he contemplated the perfection of the device. And, as he waited to see whether his plan for *Titan* would work, he thought about what Eggfont would do next.

There was a faint gray mist that swirled through the air, an insistent electric humming in his ears. His fingers and toes tingled as if he'd rubbed them with sandpaper. A furry animal seemed to have got lodged partway down his throat.

With a convulsive heave of his chest he tried to expel the object in his throat. He made several attempts before he realized that the animal was in fact his tongue. His mouth was absolutely dry and his tongue scraped painfully against the roof of his mouth.

He closed his mouth and tried to summon saliva. He worked his jaw and throat muscles for several long moments before he managed to produce a little moisture.

Having relieved some of his discomfort he then he tried to work out where he was. The grey mist had darkened, and the humming sound had largely faded. He could feel nothing, not even air moving against his skin. It was as if he'd been packed in cotton up to his neck.

He touched himself just to assure himself that he was still there. He felt the familiar uniform tunic, the medal of the Golden Orb at his neck, and he bent—knelt?—to feel his legs in their trousers, with the shoes still on his feet. There was something that bobbed and interfered with his right hand, and he took hold of it and realized it was his hand flash, attached to his wrist with an elastic lanyard.

At this point he came to the realization that he was in free fall. He was in darkness and in free fall and probably he had never left Chee Station: he was floating somewhere in one of its huge overdesigned open spaces.

A jolt of adrenaline hit Martinez then, a sudden hot burning along his nerves as he remembered the pulsar. If he'd never left the station, then he was still vulnerable to the burning x-rays.

He raised his left forearm before his face and whispered, past his painfully dry tongue and through dry lips.

"Display: show time."

Yellow numerals flashed onto Martinez's sleeve, pulsing in time to the speeding of the seconds. Through the gray fog Martinez tried to fit to the numbers to the chronology of the last days, and with a chill of horror he realized that the pulsar's beam should have struck nearly five minutes before.

Without willing it he began patting himself again, as if in search of a wound. Partway through the action he realized its absurdity, but he couldn't make himself stop until he had assured himself, again, that his parts were all where they were supposed to be.

He didn't feel as if he'd been blasted through with x-rays. He felt strange, with the grey fog drifting past his eyes and the deep electric hum a distant presence in his ears, but he didn't feel ill.

He tried to remember what might have happened to put him in this situation. He recalled leaving Command with Lord Ehl and the last of the station crew. He couldn't remember anything that happened after that.

Then, with a song of relief that chorused in his bones, he remembered Severin. Severin must have succeeded in his effort to switch off the pulsar.

Good old Severin! he thought wildly. Severin had come through! It made Martinez want to sing the "Congratulations" round from *Lord Fizz Takes a Holiday.*

Instead he wiped his mouth and tried to summon saliva into his mouth. The yellow seconds ticked by in his sleeve display. He still couldn't remember how he got here.

He wondered if there had been an accident, but he thought not. An accident would have resulted in more damage, not least to him.

Martinez remembered the hand flash hanging off his wrist, and he reached for it and switched it on, pointing it above his head. The beam vanished into the darkness without encountering anything. He panned the beam down, and at a downward angle the beam found a wall painted a dark gray. Martinez tracked the beam along the wall until he encountered a large sliding cargo door, on which were painted in white the numerals 7-03. Which meant Warehouse Three, Docking Bay Seven.

Bay Seven was where *Kayenta* had been docked. Apparently he'd got as far as *Kayenta*'s berth before . . . before what?

Perhaps the yacht had left early and stranded him on the station. But in that case, it seemed odd that Martinez had no memory of it.

The cargo door, Martinez saw, had handholds by it. There wasn't a lot of point in hanging in midair and waiting for something to happen. Perhaps he ought to get to somewhere where he could *make* something happen.

He swam awkwardly in midair until he had his back to the cargo door, then he took off his shoe and hurled it as hard as he could in the opposite direction.

Equal and opposite reaction, though unfortunately the masses were unequal. Martinez began drifting very slowly toward the cargo door while pitching backwards in long, slow circles.

Several seconds later, he heard a clang as the shoe hit something on the other side of the cargo bay.

The act of throwing his shoe left him panting and out of breath. Something was clearly wrong with him physically. It was going to take him a while to reach the cargo door, and while he slowly drifted and tumbled he thought about how he had got here, and why he couldn't remember.

He had been drugged, he thought. He had been drugged and only the fact of his veins being full of narcotics had prevented him from realizing it earlier.

He probably hadn't been shot with an amnesia drug: some drugs could cause amnesia as a side effect. It was one of those odd reactions that couldn't be predicted.

As he tumbled, his hair flying in front of his eyes, he felt a sudden chill as he realized what had happened.

He'd been drugged and left to be killed by the pulsar, but the person who had left him to die hadn't known that *Titan* was going to shut off the pulsar, and Martinez had survived.

Which meant that as soon as the person who had left him to die worked out that the x-ray beam hadn't hit the station, he was going to have to come back and finish the job.

Martinez almost wrenched his neck as his head darted around, staring into the darkness for his attacker. Who could be lurking on the station, and loading his gun or his med injector even now.

The wall rotated closer and Martinez reached out to grab one of the handholds by door 7-03. The drug almost made him miss, but he touched it with his fingertips and that slowed his rotation slightly, so that when he hit the wall and bounced he was able to make another grab for a different handhold and brought himself to a stop.

It occurred to him that his hand flash was very possibly making a target of him, so he turned it off and tried to think where he needed to go next.

The person who had tried to kill him could have hidden easily on the nearly deserted station, and then from hiding to strike as Martinez moved from the elevator to *Kayenta*. Wherever the assassin had hidden, though, there was only place the assassin would be *now,* and that was in shielded Ring Command, where he'd be safe from the pulsar. Martinez should definitely avoid Ring Command.

The problem was that Ring Command had all he'd need to establish contact with the outside world: control of all communications systems, the antennae, and the power supply to start everything up.

Martinez tried to think where else he might find communication gear, and then sudden light dazzled his eyes.

Across the docking bay, the floodlights at one of the ports had just lit. A ship had docked, and was powering up the airlock through its electrical connection.

Kayenta! Martinez felt his heart give a leap. *Kayenta* had come to rescue him!

He gathered his legs under him, feet pressed against the wall, ready to spring to the airlock and greet his rescuers the second they came through the door.

And then he hesitated. There was something about the sight of the distant airlock, surrounded by its glowing lights, that caused him unease.

Why? Why was someone trying to kill him?

He hadn't stopped to think about that before.

He had found out that the Meridian Company had been committing massive fraud. That might be worth killing over, he supposed, though assassination seemed an immoderate response.

It was so uncivilized. They might at least have tried to bribe him first.

Kayenta, in any case, wasn't a Meridian Company ship; it belonged to the Chee Company, owned principally by the Martinez family. Lady Marcella Zykov, a Chee company executive and a near relation of the Martinez clan, was on board and in charge.

But there were Meridian Company personnel on board, to inspect and help restart the station. Some of them might have been given orders concerning Martinez and his health.

Perhaps, Martinez thought, he shouldn't jump straight to *Kayenta.* Perhaps he should first hide, and then see who left the airlock, and if they had large firearms.

He glanced around the huge space and found no place to hide. To his left was a corridor, rather distant, that led to Ring Command—and he didn't want to go that way, in case an assassin was heading in the other direction. To the right was a huge bulkhead door that led to another cargo bay, but that had been closed and it would require station power to open it.

That left one or another of the warehouse spaces. 7-03 was as good as any.

The cargo door would require a power assist, but each warehouse space also had a personnel hatch, and the hatches were extremely well balanced so that weightless people could use them. Martinez pushed toward it and snagged a handhold. The hatch opened in complete silence. Martinez slipped in feet-first, then drew the hatch partly shut, so that he still had a view of *Kayenta's* airlock.

The air in the warehouse was close and had an aromatic scent, something like cardamom. Martinez looked over the interior with his hand flash and saw it was packed with standardized shipping containers, all in bright primary colors, stacked atop one another and strapped down to keep them from drifting. Because the weightless conditions permitted it, the containers were strapped to all six surfaces, including those he might arbitrarily designate as walls and ceiling. There was very little open space in the room, only a straight square tunnel that stretched to the back and would permit containers to be maneuvered in and out.

No real place to hide, he realized. He should have chosen another storage room.

Martinez was considering a jump to the next warehouse when he heard the airlock doors open and knew it was too late. He peered over the sill of the hatch and strained to see past the glare of the floodlights. There were at least three figures in the airlock, and from their barrel torsos and squat, powerful legs, Martinez knew the first two for Torminel.

An alarm rang in Martinez's mind. He didn't like the sight of those Torminel, and even though he couldn't remember why, he knew very well that he didn't want to show himself now.

"Lord Inspector?" one of the Torminel called, lisping the words past her fangs. "Lord Inspector, are you there?"

The sound echoed and died away in the vast empty dockyard.

The Torminel turned on bright flashlights and began shining them across the big room. Martinez remembered how well their huge eyes could see in the darkness and shrank from the hatch sill.

"Look!" the other Torminel called. "It's his shoe!"

While the Torminel were inspecting the mystery of the shoe that was floating by itself in the vast room, Martinez drew the hatch shut and locked it down. Unfortunately the manual lock mechanism could be worked from the outside, but at least when it began to move it would provide a bit of warning.

What Martinez really needed was a weapon.

He panned along the wall with his hand flash and saw a small locker on the wall. He drifted toward it and opened it.

In the locker were spare light globes, a pad of stick-on labels for shipping containers, a pair of fire extinguishers, pairs of work gloves, large reels of strapping for holding down crates and containers, and tough plastic clamps for tying down the strapping. But what chiefly attracted Martinez's attention were the two shiny aluminum pry bars, each as long as his leg, that were used to wedge the containers into their proper places. They were octagonal in shape until the business end, where they narrowed into flat, slightly curved blades.

Martinez reached for one and drew it from the clips that held it in place. It was lighter than it looked. He held the bar under his arm and drew out a reel of strapping, thinking that perhaps he could use it to tie down the hatch mechanism and keep anyone from opening the door.

He closed the locker and drifted back to the hatch. He studied the closing mechanism and then the reel of tape.

Martinez did his best, tangling the mechanism in a web of tape. The work left him out of breath, and he panted for air while he gripped one of the handholds next to the door. Once he'd caught his breath he moved to one end of the door, so that he wouldn't be caught like a fly in a bottle once the door opened. He tucked his feet into the handgrips at the top of the door—the metal chilled his stockinged foot—and he took a few experimental swipes with the pry bar. It cut the air with a particularly nasty hiss. With his feet planted firmly he could be confident in doing a heartening amount of damage if he needed to.

And then he turned off his hand flash and waited in the darkness.

Time passed, over twenty minutes according to the flashing yellow numerals on his sleeve display. From time to time he took a swipe with the bar to keep his muscles warm and supple. He was feeling better and thought that the drug had almost worn off.

Martinez had begun to believe that the Torminel had gone elsewhere when he heard a thump on the far side of the wall on which he was standing, followed by a metallic clang on the door. His heart gave a leap and he felt the sizzle of adrenaline along his nerves. He made sure his feet were firmly in the handholds and cocked the pry bar over his right shoulder.

There were another pair of thuds against the door or the warehouse wall. Martinez felt the vibration against his feet. He heard speech but couldn't make out the words. Then the latching mechanism began to creak open.

And jammed. The tangle of strapping was working.

He heard voices from the other side, more urgent this time, and then there was a kind of slamming noise from the mechanism, and the hatch popped open.

Martinez blinked in the light pouring in from one of the big hand lights. He was suddenly aware of sweat patches all damp under his raised arms, and the fact that his mouth was painfully dry again. He couldn't understand why there was so much moisture under his arms when there was none in his mouth.

"It's him," one of the Torminel said in an urgent whisper. "He did that, with the tape. He's in there."

"My lord?" the other called. "Lord Inspector? You can come out. Everything is safe."

There was a moment in which the Torminel waited for an answer, and then he told his partner, "Hold my legs while I go in."

Martinez felt cramps in his feet where they were braced in the handholds. He shifted the pry bar slightly.

The Torminel appeared in the hatch. His back was to Martinez, and he was peering dead ahead, into the long tunnel surrounded on all sides by shipping containers. He had a flash in one hand and a stun baton in the other. A light on the stun baton winked amber.

The blade of the pry bar caught the Torminel in the side of the head and hurled him violently into the hatch coaming. The flash flew from his limp fingers and tumbled, casting wild strobing lights across the expanse of the warehouse. The stun baton tumbled in another direction. A line of irregular crimson blobs flew from the Torminel's head and resolved themselves as they flew into perfect spherical droplets of blood.

Someone pulled the Torminel out of the hatchway, and then there was a sudden *squalling* noise that froze Martinez's blood, and the second Torminel appeared. Her hair stood on end in her rage and her head looked like a giant puffball with huge angry dark eyes and ferocious white fangs. She knew where Martinez was and one hand clutched the sill of the hatch while the other stabbed at Martinez with a stun baton.

Martinez snatched his shod foot out of the hand grip to keep the baton from hitting his leg. He swung the pry bar, but the Torminel managed to cushion the impact with one arm. She flew against the hatch coaming anyway, but bounced back with the stun baton thrust out like a sword blade. Martinez swung again, awkward with only one foot to anchor him.

This time he connected with the Torminel's head, but the impact jerked his stockinged foot out of the hand grip and sent him spinning slowly toward a side wall. The Torminel drifted limp in the hatchway. Her fur had relaxed and become smooth again.

Martinez hit a bright orange shipping container and bounced. Before he got clear he managed to push wildly with one foot and get himself on a trajectory more or less for the hatchway. His breath rasped in his throat. The pry bar felt slippery in his hands.

Somebody pulled the unconscious Torminel out of the hatchway. Martinez's heart sank at the knowledge that there was at least one more assassin.

One of the stun batons floated toward him and he snatched at it with one hand, careful to take it by the safe end. He looked at the readouts and saw that the baton was charged and set at maximum.

He looked at the hatch again and he saw that he was going to miss it, drifting past without getting close enough to seize one of the hand grips. For a few seconds Martinez was going to be in plain sight of whoever was on the other side, and then he would have to wait till he hit the far wall and push off again.

His fists clenched around his two weapons. His eyes were fixed on the hatchway as it came closer, at the erratic bouncing light that danced through the opening.

He drifted slowly past and narrowed his eyes against the light. On the other side, Lady Marcella Zykov wrestled with the limp form of one of the Torminel, trying to lash him down to a hand grip with his own belt

Marcella looked at Martinez and with an expression of great annoyance on her face reached into a pocket and came up with a pistol. The pistol was small and made of plastic and red in color.

Martinez threw the stun baton at her. The reaction sent him tumbling slowly backwards. The pistol made a vast noise and Martinez felt the heat of the bullet flying past his chin.

Martinez craned his neck frantically to keep track of what was happening. The recoil of the pistol had pitched Marcella backwards, rotating at much greater speed than Martinez, and as her legs flew up to replace her head the stun baton struck her on the back of the thigh.

There was a crackle and a sudden electric snap of ozone. Marcella gave a cry and spasmed into a foetal ball as her stronger flexors won the battle over her extensors.

Martinez lost track of her as he flew past the hatch. He hit a shipping container and jumped off for the hatch. When he arrived at the hatch he checked his motion, lined up on the distant form of Marcella tumbling end over end, and launched himself for her, the pry bar poised over his head like a battle-axe.

A battle-axe wasn't needed. He caught Marcella easily enough and found that she was frozen into her ball and barely conscious. With some effort he levered the pistol out of her clenched fist.

Once he had the pistol he was reasonably certain that he was in possession of the only firearm on Chee Station.

He intended to take full advantage of this position.

"It was panic," Martinez said. "Marcella saw the message and panicked."

"That would be the message addressed to me, from my friend Bernardo in the Ministry," Terza said. The scent of her breakfast coffee floated agreeably on the air. "The message informing me of the principal owners of the Meridian Company, and that in the emergency we had rather forgotten about. Lord Ehl got a look at the contents as it got routed through the communication center at Meridian Command, and he intercepted it." She lifted the corner of a napkin tucked around a pastry in a silver wire basket, and offered it. "This is the last. Would you like it?"

"Thank you," said Severin. He took the pastry and waved away a pair of large purple bees that were hovering over the jam. He spread jam and turned to Martinez.

"But why did Lord Ehl intercept the message?"

"Because his name was on it. He owns something like four percent of the company, and his Tir-bal clan owns more. They're clients of Lord Pa's Maq-fan clan, which is heavily invested as well."

Terza sipped her coffee. "Every time Lord Ehl approved an overrun on Chee Station, his net worth grew that much larger."

Severin chewed his pastry as he gazed through the oak alley at the distant Rio Hondo. The rising sun had outlined each leaf in silver. The shadows beneath the oaks were very dark. Tart and sweet flavors exploded on his tongue.

"I suppose Marcella's name was on the list, too," he said. "That's why she panicked."

"Marcella had two percent," Martinez said.

"Two percent hardly seems worth killing someone over," Terza said.

Martinez looked at her. "Marcella's very focused on outcomes," he said. "Processes don't matter as much, they're just a means to an end. If there's a reward, she grabs it; if there's an obstacle, she removes it. We should have taken note of the efficient way she cleaned Lord Mukerji of his money.

"And once she was caught," he added, "once I got her gun and had her tied up with strapping, she began working toward a new outcome, which was a lessening of her sentence. She confessed to everything and blamed it all on Pa and Lord Ehl. So that once I'd restarted the station, and had Lord Ehl and a company of military constables come up from the surface, I was able to put Lord Ehl under arrest as soon as he stepped out of the elevator doors."

"So far," Severin said, "our players have four percent and two percent. Who really owns the Meridian Company?

"Allodorm had ten percent," Terza said. "He got it when the Meridian Company bought out his engineering company. But the largest owner was Cassilda's father, Lord Zykov, followed by other members of the Zykov clan."

Surprise murmured through Severin's veins. "Must be interesting to be robbed by your in-laws," he said.

"Not just robbed," Terza said. "Lord Zykov's plan was to bankrupt the Chee Company, then buy the remnants with its own money."

Severin turned his head at the sound of footsteps coming out of the house. Lord Roland Martinez strolled toward them, a wry smile on his lips. He was dressed casually, in a blousy white cotton shirt and faded red baggy drawstring trousers.

"How's Cassilda?" Terza asked.

"The doctor says she won't deliver for a few hours yet."

Cassilda had gone into labor the previous evening.

Roland leaned over his brother's shoulder to peer into the silver wire breakfast. "Didn't you leave me any breakfast?"

"We didn't know you'd be coming," Terza said. "You can call the kitchen."

"I don't have a comm unit on me," Roland said. "Gare, could you call the kitchens and get me some pastry and a pair of shirred duck eggs?" He sat heavily in one of the whitewashed metal chairs.

Martinez, looking resigned, made the call on his sleeve comm. Severin finished his pastry and freshened his coffee from the silver pot. He looked at Roland.

"Yes?" Roland said.

"Beg pardon?"

"You had a question on your face."

"I—" Severin started, and then decided to take a more tactful approach. "It must be hard for you, with Lady Cassilda about to give birth and her father sitting on a pile of money he's stolen from you."

Roland grinned. "No. That makes it easier, actually." He poured himself a cup of coffee, then looked at Severin.

"It's very simple," he said. "I don't know if Lord Zykov gives a damn about Marcella or not, but if he ever wants to see his daughter again, or see his grandchild ever, he'll do exactly what we tell him."

Severin felt his mouth hanging open, and closed it. "I see," he said.

"You understand," Roland said, "Allodorm and Lord Pa got too greedy—they didn't just cheat *us,* they cheated the *Fleet.* And that's not civil or corporate law, that's a violation of the Praxis, and the penalties are torture and death. Cassilda had some stock in the Meridian Company, and we can make a case against her."

Can you do *that?* Severin wondered.

Apparently he could.

"Any case is amazingly easy," Roland went on. "There's scads of information—we had inspectors on the ground, and other informers as well, but they all reported to Marcella, and she sat on the information and told the others that adjustments were being made."

"Plus of course the conspirators are all informing on one another," Martinez said.

"So in return for not laying the information before the Legion of Diligence," Roland said, "we're asking for half of Lord Zykov's interest in the company, plus all of Lord Pa's, and Allodorm's, and Marcella's. Lord Pa will pay us a large fine, enough to knock him flat for some time. Marcella and Allodorm will be locked up until we're reasonably certain we've wrung out of them every zenith they possess."

"And the *first* thing I did," Martinez said, "was procure Lord Ehl's resignation from the Fleet."

Roland shrugged, as if this was of no concern. "We'll have his shares, too, of course." He adopted a contemplative look. "I'm thinking of having Lord Zykov pass over his elder daughter and make Cassilda his heir. So everything comes to us in the end."

Martinez looked at his brother with dissatisfaction showing in his narrowed eyes. "Speaking as the one who got shot at," he said, "I'm not sure I'm happy that everyone gets off with just fines and spankings. I wonder what you'd have done if Marcella had actually succeeded in killing me."

Again Severin felt a line of tension between the two brothers, and thought again that the two might not like each other very much.

Roland very coolly raised his coffee to his lips. "I suppose that after Marcella was good and bankrupt," he said, "she might have had an accident."

Martinez looked at Roland for a moment, then shrugged. Terza reached over and patted his hand.

"Thanks to Commander Severin," she said, "we're not concerned with that outcome."

"Not so much me," Severin said, "as—" Then, "Commander?"

A tight little smile played across Roland's lips. "You will not find us ungrateful, my lord. We've spoken to the higher echelon of the Exploration Service here, and explained in some detail our considerable admiration for you, and my understanding is that you'll be promoted and given *Surveyor* once it's out of dock."

Severin goggled at him. *You can* do *that?* he wondered.

"In addition," Martinez said, "my father is granting you several sections of prime Chee real estate. You should have a very rich estate to retire to when you leave the Service."

"And I believe there will be a substantial cash reward from the Chee Company," Roland said. "Though I understand we'll have to get your superiors' permission."

Severin's mind whirled. "But," he said, "I didn't really do that much."

"Other than save the Chee Company's entire investment?" Roland smiled.

"I shut off the pulsar, yes, but the reason that Captain Martinez hasn't joined the Great Masters is that he insisted that what I did with *Titan* remain secret. I didn't have anything to do with that."

Martinez grinned. "I had to protect my investments," he said.

Severin looked at him. "My lord?"

"I took the money I won from Lord Mukerji and bought every futures contract on Chee from the poor fools Allodorm and Pa sold them to," Martinez said. "Some will be worthless, no doubt, but I believe I'm now a rich man." He leaned back in his chair and smiled out at the world. "I've never actually had money of my own before," he said. "It's all come from Terza or my father. I wonder what I'll do with it?"

"The possibilities are staggering," Terza murmured.

Martinez looked at his brother. "And of course some of the fines from the conspirators will go to reimburse the investors who were cheated."

Roland was annoyed. "They were gambling, really. It's not as if they can complain. It was the *futures* market, for all's sake."

"Roland." The voice was firm.

Roland flapped his hands. "Very well. If you insist. But if you go on this way, you're going to make me wish Marcella were a better shot."

Martinez smiled. "I seek only perfect justice for the entire universe."

"Ah!" Roland said happily. "My shirred eggs!"

A smiling white-haired servant brought Roland his breakfast and another basket of pastry. Terza looked at Severin from over the rim of her coffee cup.

"Will you be seeing Lady Liao while *Surveyor*'s in dock?" she asked.

Severin darted a glance to the opal ring on his finger. *Does everyone know?* he wondered.

"I've sent her a message," he said. "But I imagine a lot will depend on her schedule." *And her husband's.*

"Any plans for the meantime?" Terza asked.

"Well," Severin said, "I'm thinking of building a puppet theater."

There was a moment of silence broken only by the calls of morning birds.

"That's original," Martinez murmured.

"Do you think so?" Severin asked. "Let me tell you about it."

And, as the long morning stretched before them, he did.

—With thanks for technical assistance to Michael Rupen, Kristy Dyer, and Bob Norton